GOD AIN'T BLIND

GOD AIN'T BLIND

MARY
MONROE

KENSINGTON BOOKS
http://www.kensingtonbooks.com

DAFINA BOOKS are published by

Kensington Publishing Corp.
119 West 40th Street
New York, NY 10018

All Kensington titles, imprints, and distributed lines are available at special quantity discounts for bulk purchases for sales promotion, premiums, fund-raising, educational or institutional use.

Special book excerpts or customized printings can also be created to fit specific needs. For details, write or phone the office of the Kensington Special Sales Manager: Attn. Special Sales Department. Kensington Publishing Corp., 119 West 40th Street, New York, NY 10018. Phone: 1-800-221-2647.

Library of Congress Card Catalogue Number: 2009928070
ISBN-13: 978-0-7582-1221-4
ISBN-10: 0-7582-1221-6

First Printing: September 2009
10 9 8 7 6 5 4 3 2 1

Printed in the United States of America

This book is dedicated in loving memory of Ocie Mae Bonner, my mother. She was the first person to tell me that "God don't like ugly." But she didn't stop there. She also told me that "God *still* don't like ugly, God don't play, God ain't blind, God ain't through yet, God don't make no mistakes, God ain't no fool, God ain't crazy," and so on. When it came to my writing, she told me, "Girl, if you gonna be a bear, be a grizzly." That was her way of telling me to reach for the stars. My mother had to drop out of school in the fifth grade and go to work in the fields of rural Alabama. Before she crossed over, she read as much of *God Don't Like Ugly* as she could understand. That was when she told me that God was still working on her through me.

ACKNOWLEDGMENTS

Andrew Stuart is one of the best literary agents in the business. I am truly blessed to be one of his clients.

I am also blessed to be a member of the Kensington Books family. Thanks to Selena James, my wonderful editor and mentor. Thanks to Maureen Cuddy, Laurie Parkin, Jessica McLean, and especially the wonderful crew in the sales department for going all the extra miles for me. To everyone else at Kensington, you guys make me feel like royalty!

From the bottom of my heart I thank Ella Powers (Las Vegas), Lizel and Wyrita (Baltimore), Louise Cooks (Richmond, California), the Komatsu Yakamoto family (Japantown, San Francisco) and every single one of my other readers for supporting my work. And to each of the hundreds of fans who claim to be my "number one fan," you are all number one to me.

Thanks to Lauretta Pierce for maintaining my Web site and promoting my books with so much vigor.

A lot of my readers sent ideas and plot suggestions from around the world to me for this book. A few called me up to put in their two cents during my live telephone interviews while I was on my book tour! Well, I listened. Are you all happy now? And, yes there will be more books in my God Don't Like Ugly series.

Please continue to send your e-mails to me at *Authorauthor5409@aol.com* and visit my Web site at *www.Marymonroe.org* as many times as possible. I love the attention!

All the best,

Mary Monroe
September 2009

CHAPTER 1

"If you don't get yourself out of this vehicle and into that motel room and screw that man, I'll go up in there and do it myself!"

I never expected my best friend to encourage me to have an affair. I always thought that she'd be the main person who would try and talk me out of it. Especially since she and my husband had been like brother and sister for most of their lives. But that was exactly what she was trying to do now. I knew this sister like I knew the back of my hand, so I knew she was not going to stop until I had stepped out of my panties, stretched out on my back, and opened my legs for a man who was not my husband. One of the reasons was that my girl was having an affair herself. I knew that if I got involved in one, she wouldn't feel so guilty.

I was still strapped in by my seat belt, and I was in no hurry to unfasten it. "I don't know if I'm ready to cheat on my husband," I admitted. Despite the words of protest that tumbled out of my mouth and my reluctance, I was not going to reject Rhoda's orders. I just didn't want her to know how eager I really was to jump into bed with another man. I liked to mess with her from time to time, just enough to provoke her. It kept our crazy relationship exciting. "I really don't know if I can do this," I mumbled for the third time in the last two minutes. I sounded so weak and unconvincing that even I didn't believe what I was saying. "So stop trying to rush me!"

"Rush *you*? Woman, we've been sittin' here for ten minutes—tick-tock, tick-tock. And you rushed *me* to drive *your* horny black ass over here." Rhoda gave me a disgusted look before she unfastened my seat belt like I was a stubborn two-year-old.

"I know that. I just need to think," I whimpered.

"You need to think about what?" she demanded, slapping the side of the steering wheel with the palm of her hand.

"I need to think about what I'm doing and why," I replied, wringing my sweaty hands.

Now that the moment had arrived, I was sitting here acting like a frightened virgin, and it made no damn sense. This had been in the works for weeks. And me—with my weak self—I was just as eager to fuck the man who was awaiting my arrival in the motel room as he was to fuck me. He had made his intentions known the moment he stuck his fingers inside my panties in a restaurant booth the first time I spent time with him in public. I'd wanted to throw him down on that restaurant table and fuck his brains out then. And that was exactly what I planned to do as soon as I got up enough nerve to take my ass into that motel room.

"Honey, I can tell you why you're doin' this. You need it. Your fuckin', uh, *fuck* quota is bankrupt." Rhoda laughed.

"That's not funny, and I wish you'd stop making jokes about my personal life," I snapped.

"I'm sorry, girlfriend," she said, stroking my hair. "All I want is for you to be happy. I'm gettin' sick of your long, frustrated face, and of the jealous looks I always get from you when I get mine. It's time for you to get yours, and I am not goin' to let up until you do. Do you hear me?"

"I sure do hear you, Miss Pimp," I said, my voice dripping with sarcasm.

"Excuse me?"

"Rhoda, if I didn't know any better, I'd swear you were getting paid for this. And for the record, I am not jealous of you. You can get that notion out of that head of yours right now. You don't have a damn thing I'd want."

"Except a man who knows and wants to take care of my needs.

Now you move it. Go on now." Rhoda clapped her hands together twice like a drill sergeant, bumped her knee against mine, and motioned with her head toward the door on my side. "You go into that room so you can get laid like you're supposed to be. Shoo!" This time she tapped the side of my leg with the toe of her black leather boot.

I still didn't move. I couldn't stop myself from glancing toward the motel entrance from the motel's parking lot, where we had parked. And I couldn't stop myself from hoping that the "good loving" that the man in the motel room had promised me was going to be worth my while. Rhoda was right. My fuck quota was bankrupt. I had not had any good loving in a while. As a matter of fact, I hadn't had any loving period in a while now. I was so hot and horny, I was about ready to explode like a firecracker.

The Do Drop Inn was the kind of motel that people snuck in and out of, in disguise if they were smart. It was a cheap, one-story place in an industrial area off the freeway, with a sign that advertised rates by the hour, cable TV, XXX-rated movies, a heated pool, and vibrating beds.

Last month, during Memorial Day weekend, when a sister from my church was checking into this notorious love nest with her white lover, her husband was checking out with his lover at the same time. All hell broke loose that night. The husband, an avowed racist, seemed more pissed off about his wife having a white lover than he was about her having an affair. Not only did the cops have to be called, but an ambulance, too. The two sisters ended up in the hospital; the husband went to jail. And the only reason that the white man escaped injury was because he had fled the scene before the husband could get his hands on him. It was the kind of scandal that the people in Richland, Ohio, sunk their teeth into. Especially when it involved somebody in the church.

As a member of the Second Baptist Church—even though I attended services only about once a month now—I knew that if I got caught entering or leaving a motel with a man other than the one I was married to, my goose would be cooked alive. My dull husband would die. Not because I'd kill him in self-defense, but because he'd be so shocked and disappointed, he'd probably drop dead. And knowing my mother, she'd probably come after me with a switch. Given all these facts, why the hell was I doing this? If I had an answer to that question, it was hiding somewhere behind my brain.

I shaded my eyes and scanned the parking lot, sliding down into the passenger seat of my girl Rhoda's SUV each time I thought I saw somebody we knew. "Is that Claudette who owns the beauty shop coming out of the liquor store across the street?" I said, with a gasp.

"Shit! Where?" Rhoda asked, jerking her head around like a puppet. We slid down into our seats at the same time and stayed there for about a minute. Rhoda eased up first, peeping out the side of her window like a burglar. "No, that's not her. Claudette never looked that hopeless from behind. Whoever that sister is, her ass is draggin' on the ground like a tail."

I exhaled and sat back up in my seat. "I just wish Louis had picked some other motel. One with a little more class and one where we didn't have to worry about running into somebody we know," I complained, speaking more to myself than to Rhoda.

"What's wrong with you? This is the only one of the few motels in this hick town that employs people we don't know. You go to the Moose Motel out on State Street, and I assure you that Sister Nettie Jones, who works her mouth more than she works that vacuum cleaner when she cleans the rooms, will blab so fast, everybody we know will know about your visit before you even check out." Rhoda let out an exasperated breath, rubbed her nose, and shook her head. I looked away from her. "Lord knows, this is one straight-up, low-level place, though. I wouldn't bring a dog that I didn't like here. If Louis was a real man, he'd take you to his place."

My breath caught in my throat as I whirled around to face Rhoda again.

She leaned to the side and gave me a puzzled look. "What's wrong now?"

"I'd rather get a whupping than get loose in Louis's apartment," I declared.

"Well, other than it bein' located in a low-rent neighborhood, two doors from the soup kitchen, what's wrong with Louis's apartment? Why don't you do him there?"

"I can't do that. I'm not the kind of woman who hangs out in a strange man's apartment," I answered. When I realized how ridiculous that statement was, we both laughed, but only for a few seconds. I cleared my throat and got serious. "Please don't mention Louis's apartment to me again after today unless you have to. I want to keep this thing casual."

"Well! All I can say is, this man better have somethin' good between his legs," Rhoda retorted through clenched teeth. "If he doesn't, I'll help you slice it off with a dull knife and feed it to a goat I don't like. But I still feel that he ought to be ashamed of himself for plannin' a romantic evenin' in a dead zone like this," Rhoda said, looking around the area.

I didn't like the look on her face, and she didn't have to say what was on her mind, because I already knew. On one hand, she approved of me committing adultery, but she had a problem with me doing it with a broke-ass man like Louis Baines. But since she'd introduced me to him and did business with his struggling catering service herself, she usually didn't harp on his financial status that much.

"You know that he is putting most of his money into his business. You are the main one who keeps talking about how you want to see a black business succeed in this town," I said in Louis's defense. "I don't expect him to take me to the Hilton . . . yet."

"I know, I know," Rhoda replied gently, giving me a smile and an apologetic look. "I just wish that he could afford to take you to one of those nice hotels near the airport, like *my* gentleman friend does for me. Did I ever tell you about that?"

"You've told me everything there is to know about you and your lover, Rhoda," I said, my eyes rolling around in my head like marbles. "Year after year after year . . ."

"Oh. Well, a real nice hotel makes it seem, uh, less illicit, I guess. I like to be with my sweetie in my house only when I have no choice. Believe it or not, I still have some respect for my husband. It's the least I can do. He's a beast, and his dick gets about as hard as a slice of raw bacon these days. But as long as he keeps his nose out of my business and hangs on to that six-figure-amount-a-year job, the only thing I'd leave him for is to go to heaven. Shit." Rhoda sniffed loudly and tapped my shoulder. "Well, what's it goin' to be?" She glanced at the clock on the dashboard. "I've got other things to do, you know."

I couldn't figure out why, but for some reason, I had to stall a little more. Even though I *knew* that I was going to go through with my first indiscretion since I got married ten years ago. "I have to think about this some more, Rhoda. I shouldn't have come here yet. Maybe I should get to know Louis a little better."

"Better than what?"

"Better than I know him now. Other than the fact that he's the best caterer I've ever dealt with, I really don't know everything that I'd like to know about the man."

"What do you think sex is for, girl? What better way is there to get to know a man? Look, you know him well enough to do business with him. He wants you. You want him. What else do you need to know? How big his dick is? How long he can keep it hard? Well, there's only one way for you to find that out."

CHAPTER 2

Rhoda's words amused me. I shook my head and let out a gentle laugh. "I know you are not going to stop until I do what you want me to do. But I shouldn't have let you talk me into doing this. I shouldn't have even told you about this man. I should not have let him get close enough to me for him to think that I'd . . . What's wrong with me? I'm a happily married woman." I put a lot of emphasis on my words. I was now at a point where I couldn't tell if I was trying to convince myself that I shouldn't be having an affair, or Rhoda.

"Happily married, my ass." She guffawed. "You show me a happily married woman, and I will show you a woman who has at least one spare. And I don't mean a spare tire."

"I'm glad most people don't think that," I shot back. "That's one of the most ridiculous things I've ever heard you say. You ought to be ashamed of yourself."

"If you are so happily married, why are we sittin' in this motel parkin' lot, havin' this conversation? Why did you ask me to lie to your husband about where you were goin' tonight? Is that what you call bein' happily married?"

"You know what I mean. Having an affair could ruin my life."

"I'm married, too! I've been havin' an affair with my husband's best friend for almost twenty years. Do I look ruined? And for the record, I am about as happily married as a woman can be."

"I should go back home before it's too late."

"Look, Annette, if you've come this far, it's already too late. Now stop actin' like this is your first day of kindergarten. Get a grip. You've got four hours to play with. And from the looks of that young stud, you're goin' to need every last minute of those four hours to satisfy him. Shit!" Rhoda laughed as she looked in the rearview mirror to check her makeup and hair, something she'd do even on her way to her execution. "I hope you douched with some vanilla extract, like I told you. I noticed his tongue, and it's long enough to make a woman very happy. He sure seems like the type who likes to do a little *grazin' in the grass.* And he should. As a matter of fact, I haven't seen a tongue that length since I saw *Godzilla.*" Rhoda laughed some more.

I didn't like the fact that she was getting such a kick out of this. Now I really was sorry that I had ever told her about Louis and the fact that he'd been trying to get into my panties for weeks, tongue and all.

"You're making me nervous, Rhoda."

"You're not nervous. We're both way too old to be gettin' nervous about fuckin'. You're just confused." Not looking away from the mirror, she fished a Kleenex tissue from the beaded purse in her lap and blotted her plum-colored lipstick. "This is just, uh, jitters. But you'll get used to that. I did." She paused and gave me a thoughtful look, then a quick but weak smile. "I am so happy for you. You're finally goin' to get what you need after sufferin' for so long."

"I am not suffering," I protested.

"Whatever you say," she said with a sigh, balling the tissue and tossing it into a litter bag hanging from the dashboard. "I don't know how you've managed to last this long without mountin' the pizza delivery guy and humpin' the hell out of him. Almost a whole damn year without some dick is not normal!"

"It is for some people," I insisted. "And what's so bad about going without sex for a year, anyway? Some women go their whole lives without it."

Rhoda nodded. "They are called nuns, invalids, and freaks. Of which you are neither. Or we wouldn't be sittin' here." Rhoda glanced at her watch, then gave me an exasperated look. "I'm too through. Are you goin' into that motel room or what?" She started her motor and adjusted her rearview mirror.

"I'm going," I said quickly, opening the door on my side.

"I'll pick you up around eleven fifteen. I want to be home in time to watch at least part of *Jay Leno*!"

The woman who had been my best friend for most of my life gave me a hearty push with her hand. I practically slid out of the front passenger seat of her SUV and onto the ground, landing on my feet like a panther. She sped off before I could even catch my breath.

Despite all the shit that Rhoda had said, I couldn't determine what she *really* thought. And I couldn't understand how she could pressure me into having an affair and still grin in my husband's face. This was one of the few times that I wished they were not friends. But no matter what she thought or said, this was my call. I wanted to have an affair with Louis Baines. It was nothing for me to be proud of, but I had to pat myself on the back for attracting such a young, handsome brother in the first place. And he was the one who had come on like gangbusters, not me. That was something that had rarely happened to me, even when I was young.

My marriage had become a stale joke. My husband had already put me out to pasture, like I was a Guernsey cow that he had milked bone dry. Louis had come to my rescue just in time. His actions had done wonders for my ego. At least that was what I kept telling myself. But before Louis entered my life, I had almost convinced myself that my sex life was over at the age of forty-six.

I looked around the parking lot some more. Summer was just around the corner, so the weather was nice. But the wind was howling in a way that made me even more nervous. This was a rough neighborhood, so nosy acquaintances were not the only people I had to be concerned about. A couple of months ago somebody had attacked a man from behind and robbed him in the same parking lot that I was in now. A few weeks before that, somebody had dragged a woman between two cars parked behind the motel, sexually assaulted her, and taken off with her purse and jewelry.

I coughed and tightened my grip on my purse. One thing I had learned from growing up around rough people was that it was stupid to look too prosperous. The woman who had been raped and robbed had had the nerve to come to this neighborhood in a fur jacket, wearing diamonds on everything but her toes. She had to be either stone crazy or suicidal, because that was like waving a piece of raw meat in front of a wolf. I was sorry about what had happened to that woman. But like everybody else, I felt that she should have known better. I had some very expensive clothes and jewelry, which I never wore to this part of town. I rarely carried much money or more than two or three credit cards in my purse in this neighborhood, or anywhere else. I had a large can of Mace in my purse, which I prayed I would never have to use. The air was foul. It reeked of gasoline and oil, dust, and despair. I sucked in some of that air, anyway. Then I looked around and checked my surroundings one more time.

At night when the Do Drop Inn sign was turned on, some of its letters blinked on and off; some didn't light up at all. And if that wasn't tacky enough, the molelike Pakistani man who owned this motel had had it painted pink last year and had propped up some plastic flamingos in front of the entrance. There was a truck stop a block away. Tired hookers brought their tired truck driver tricks to this motel.

A huge buckeye tree loomed over the building like a gigantic umbrella. In the fall, the buckeye nuts fell off the tree and covered the motel roof like brown rocks. I knew about the buckeyes because my mother used to clean the rooms in this dump thirty years ago, and I used to help her.

Louis had told me that he'd be in room 108 and had warned me that he'd already be naked. "I just hope you can handle this dragon in my pants, baby," he'd also said. "I've got something that has made some women weep from joy and others weep from pain." You would have thought that he had a footlong brick between his legs, the way he was talking. But I knew better.

"I hope I can handle it, too," I'd replied, rolling my eyes. I didn't know why Louis, or any other man for that matter, felt the need to brag about the size of his dick. As a former prostitute, I was pretty sure that I'd seen it all when it came to sex. For one thing, there was probably nothing left that could surprise or scare me. I didn't think that there was anything that could top the trick that had a two-headed dick, which I'd encountered one rainy night. But Louis didn't need to know all that, though. As a matter of fact, he already knew more about me than I wanted him to know.

The way I was dragging my feet, you would have thought that I was on my way to a job I despised. I was glad that the room was on the other side of the motel, so I'd have a few more minutes to compose myself. However, before I could do that, a pay phone on the corner in front of the motel caught my attention. Before I knew it, I was rooting through my purse for some loose change so I could make a call.

"Hello," my husband answered on the tenth ring. Even though one of the four telephones in our house was never more than a few feet out of his reach, he always took his time answering one when it rang. This was just one of the things he did that had irritated me for years.

"Hi, baby," I began.

"Who is this?"

I gasped so hard, I almost dropped my purse. I couldn't respond right away.

"Hello? Who is this callin'?" Pee Wee asked, sounding truly annoyed.

"I want you to tell me how many women call you up and address you as baby, fool," I demanded, anger rumbling inside me like gas. I didn't know what the hell I was going to do with that husband of mine! No wonder I was about to have an affair.

CHAPTER 3

"After all the years that we've known each other, don't you know your own wife's voice by now?" I snarled. This was not the first time that my husband had not recognized my voice on the opposite end of a telephone in the last few years. I usually gave him the benefit of the doubt, because I wasn't as sharp as I used to be, either. But this time it angered me. In a strange way I was glad. It made it that much easier for me to justify the reason I had come to the Do Drop Inn.

"Oh, it's *you*. Hi, baby. Where you at?"

"Uh, I'm with Rhoda on our way to the bowling alley. I joined her bowling team, and I'll be bowling with them every Thursday night, starting tonight. Don't you remember? We've discussed it several times. Even this morning."

"We did? Hmm."

"We did, Pee Wee." The more I talked to this man, the more his credibility plummeted.

"Oh! If you say so, we must have. I sure enough don't remember nothin' about givin' you permission to join no bowlin' team."

Permission? Oh, he must have been entertaining a death wish. Had he said something like that to my face, I wouldn't have been responsible for my actions.

"Look, goddammit, I don't need permission from you or anybody else to do a damn thing," I hollered. "My damn daddy lives across town, and I don't even ask his permission to do what I want to do."

"Hold your horses now, baby. You know I'm just talkin' off the top of my head. I didn't mean no harm. You don't have to be gettin' all loud and ghetto on me. Did you take your pill today?"

"What damn pill?"

"Them change-of-life pills I heard you and Rhoda talkin' about the other day."

"I think we need to end this conversation immediately, if not sooner," I suggested.

"That's a good idea. I can see that you ain't in no good mood."

"All right. Like I just said, I am going bowling with Rhoda and her bowling team tonight. I will see you around eleven or eleven thirty. Understand?"

"What's there to understand? I ain't no dummy. You goin' bowlin' with your girls. I understand that."

"I'll see you when I get home, Pee Wee," I huffed.

"Listen, if you ain't too mad or too tired when you finish bowlin', would you stop by Al's Rib Shack on Patterson Street on your way home and bring me some ribs and coleslaw? And tell them stingy Negroes not to be so scarce with that slaw."

"Is that all you've got to say?"

"Have Al throw in a few pieces of chicken, too. All wings. I keep tellin' you and him that I do not like nothin' on a chicken but the wings."

"That's not what I meant," I complained.

"Huh? Then what did you mean?"

"Nothing," I said in a tired voice. I took a deep breath and continued. This time my voice was full of vigor. "I might go with the girls to have a few drinks after bowling. And I'm not asking for your permission. I'm just letting you know in case you need me to come straight home for something else."

"As long as you drop off my order from Al's first, you can do whatever the hell you want to do."

"Don't worry about that. I will make sure you get everything you got coming," I quipped. The sarcasm was lost on my husband. Just like so many other things lately.

"And another thing, get me some *mild* sauce. As long as we been together, you ought to know better by now. I only like mild sauce. Last week, when you came steppin' up in here with that hot-ass sauce, it danced through my bowels like James Brown. And every time I peed, my dick felt like I'd struck a match to it. I was useless for days."

Useless was right. As far as I was concerned, my husband's dick was the most useless appendage on his body these days. No matter what I did, he didn't want to do it with me. I ate and slept alone most of the time. And even when we were in the house at the same time, it seemed like I was alone. It saddened me to know that after ten years of an almost perfect marriage, it had come to this: my husband was no longer attracted to me. Well, he didn't have to be now! There was a handsome young man waiting on me in room 108, with a dick that had my name on it.

"I'll see you when I get home," I said in a weak voice, knowing now what I had to do if I wanted to hold on to my sanity.

"You've been lookin' and actin' mighty gloomy these days. So you need to go knock yourself out, baby. You need to go have some fun. Y'all go drinkin' after you leave that bowlin' alley and have at least one on me."

"Oh, you can count on that," I said with a smirk. I hung up so hard and fast that the coins I had dropped into the slot dropped into the hamper. I sniffed as I scooped them out and dropped them back into my coin purse. Then I marched back across the motel parking lot, itching to get my hands on the hard, young body reserved for me in room 108.

Louis must have been peeping out of the window, because he opened the door just as I was about to knock. "Hey, baby. It's so good to see you. Girl, every time I look at you, I get an instant hard-on."

I was taken aback by his comments, but I tried not to show it. I was so cool and calm, you would have thought that handsome men said things like that to me every day. The truth of the matter was, Louis was the *first* man to be this bold and frisky with me. "Thank you," I managed. "I needed to hear something like that, Louis."

"Let me tell you one thing, sweetheart. Now that I've got you where I want you, you will be hearing everything you ever thought you might want to hear from a man," he vowed.

He took me by the hand and pulled me into the semi-darkened room, with its dull furniture. He kicked the door shut with his bare foot and wrapped his arms around my waist. Then he cupped my face in his hands and stared into my eyes. I couldn't figure out how he was able to look at me for several moments without blinking. I was blinking like a railroad signal.

"I am so happy," he said, swooning.

I tried to speak, but nothing came out. I just blinked again.

Louis was as naked as the day he was born. I could feel something rock hard between his legs, pressing against my hip bone. It didn't feel like anything that was big enough to scare me, but it felt big enough to put a big smile on my face. I finally got up enough nerve to reach down. I was impressed with what I felt. When I did look down, I was impressed with what I saw. I was too shy to look down long enough to give his goods a thorough inspection. But I had seen and felt enough to know that he wasn't as well endowed as my husband. I knew that I couldn't have everything, and besides, I didn't want it to be *so* good that I would forget about my husband altogether. I wasn't that kind of woman.

It was so refreshing to see a nice firm body again. Despite the fact that my husband's body had turned into something that resembled Silly Putty, and he now had more hair on his legs than he had on his head, he was still attractive to me. That didn't matter, though. He no longer felt the same way about me, and I looked much better now than I had when we got married ten years ago! Louis had already told me several times how much he appreciated the way I looked. And I never got tired of hearing it.

He must have read my mind. "Annette, I swear to God, you look so damn good to me," he said.

"You should have seen me last year," I mumbled as I stumbled behind him across the floor. I didn't know what made me say something that stupid. It didn't mean anything to Louis, anyway. I could tell that from the puzzled look he gave me. The truth of the matter was, had he known the husky, muumuu-wearing plain Jane that I was last year, we probably would not have been in this motel room right now, preparing to fuck each other's brains out. Well, he might have still been in the room, but not with me.

Losing four dress sizes and getting a complete makeover, from my thin, thorny hair down to my flat feet, had given me a lot of confidence. For the first time in my forty-six years, I didn't consider the mirror my worst enemy. A lot of men had begun to notice me. A few had been so aggressive that I'd had to cuss them out and threaten to beat them off with a stick.

Unfortunately, the only man who didn't seem to be the least bit fazed by my improved appearance, or even to notice it, was my husband. And he was the main person that I'd hoped to impress by going through my long-overdue metamorphosis!

"Annette, you don't know how long I've been waiting for this moment," Louis whispered in my ear. Then he licked it like he was licking a stamp. He kissed me gently on the lips and started to unbutton my white silk blouse and tug at the side of my leather skirt. "The first time I saw you, I said to myself, 'If that was my woman, I'd treat her like a Nubian queen.' From that day on, I dreamed about you, with your sweet self, day and night. I never thought such a dream would become a reality." This time I kissed him. "Now tell me what you want me to do for you. This is all about you. How much time do we have?"

"We don't have to worry about the time. We've got plenty of it," I assured him, my hand massaging the prize between his legs.

"Is that right? Well, what about . . . uh . . . the dude?"

"What dude?" I asked, my voice sounding so husky that I almost didn't recognize it.

"Your *husband,*" he said, giving me an incredulous look. "The last thing I want is for the brother to come busting through that door to reclaim his . . . uh . . . stuff."

I tilted my head back, patted the micro braids wrapped around my head, and let out a loud sigh. "My husband wouldn't bust through an eggshell to reclaim any stuff from me." I pulled Louis to the bed, and for the next four hours, it was all about me.

CHAPTER 4

I was already dressed and standing outside the motel room when Rhoda rolled up into the parking lot at ten minutes after eleven. Not because I was anxious to leave, but because I didn't want her to blow her horn and attract attention, or knock on the door and strike up a conversation with Louis. For some reason, I wanted Rhoda to be as far removed from this situation as possible. She knew all the rest of my deepest, darkest secrets, but this one was special. And I wanted to keep most of it to myself for as long as possible.

"How was it?" That was the first thing she said as I climbed back into her SUV. My legs were so sore, they almost buckled. I wasn't sure if it was because of my age or the thorough workout I'd just received. The blinking light in front of the motel made her vehicle look white, but it was silver. And she kept it in such pristine condition, it still looked and smelled new, even though it was almost two years old. She already had thick pads on the seats, but I noticed a sheet of plastic on the passenger seat, which had not been there before she dropped me off. I got offended right away, thinking that she had put it there so I wouldn't drip or spread anything nasty on the seat after my tryst. I wanted to say something about it immediately, but I didn't. Because had it been my car, I might have covered my seat with some plastic before I sat down, too. Even though

I had taken a quick shower with Louis, I still felt a little unclean, to say the least.

Now that I'd seen the extra protection that Rhoda had put on her seat, I was more determined to keep her as far out of the loop as possible. I was sorry that I had agreed to let her drive me to and from the motel, but she had insisted. The more I thought about that damn shit she'd put on the seat, the more it bothered me, so I knew I had to say something right away.

"Rhoda, you know I'm a clean woman," I clucked, adjusting the seat belt.

"Say what?"

"I'm a clean woman. You didn't have to put this plastic shit on your seat." I pouted, my head bowed submissively.

"What is your problem? I put that plastic on the seat because I didn't want you to drip barbecue sauce on it again, like you did the other night, when we picked up ribs for Pee Wee after we left the movies. And if you look down, you will see that I also put some plastic on the floor so you wouldn't drip sauce on it, either."

"Oh," I mumbled, looking down and straightening the plastic on the floor with my shoe.

"Look, if you're goin' to be this fuckin' paranoid, I advise you to stop this shit before it gets too deep. Or leave me out of it. I am your friend—your best friend—and I would never do somethin' that damn tacky to you or anybody else that I invite into my SUV. What made you think that I put plastic on my seat on account of what you did with your body?"

"I don't know," I said, with a mighty shrug. "I've never done this before."

"I know that. I know your black ass better than you know yourself." Rhoda gave me an affectionate pat on my thigh. "Now answer my question and tell me. How was it?"

"Okay, I guess," I told her, shifting myself into a more comfortable position. I was glad that I had mentioned the plastic on Rhoda's seat. She was the kind of person who liked to deal with negativity right away, and I admired her for that.

I felt better now, but the insides of my thighs were so sore, I had to sit with my legs spread a few inches apart. Other intimate parts of my body were also sore. My breasts felt like I'd been nursing a very hungry baby, and in a way, that was exactly what I had done. My butt felt like it was on fire. I couldn't wait to get home so I could take a long, hot bath with some Epsom salts and a very thorough douche. I had douched before I left the house, per Rhoda's instructions, and Louis had used a condom. But douching with hot water helped ease the soreness after having prolonged and rough sex. I had learned this during my brief stint as a prostitute in my youth. "How was bowling? Did we win or lose? I need to know in case my husband asks me. Or did anything happen that I need to know about?"

"Is that all you've got to say?"

"What?" I asked dumbly.

Rhoda snorted and turned off her motor. She nodded toward the motel. Since Louis had paid for the room, he had decided to spend the night there, and I couldn't blame him. As tacky as that room was, with its ugly brown plaid furniture and plastic curtains, it was still a step up from his apartment. I smiled just thinking about him roaming around in that room, still naked. There was no doubt in my mind that if I had stayed the night with him, we would have made love all night.

"Well, he still had a hard-on when I left." I paused and chuckled. "He's a little countrified, though. A Southern homeboy to the bone."

"Aren't we all? Last time I checked, you were still from the South, too. And I know you worked on gettin' rid of your Southern drawl when you moved north, but I worked on keepin' mine. I want the world to know that I'm from what the Yankees call Bigfoot country. Besides, I get compliments all the time about how cute and quaint my accent is. . . ."

I shrugged. "He's from Greensboro, North Carolina, but you can hardly hear a trace of an accent. I guess he's not as dedicated to that Southern twang as you are. And, frankly, I don't give a damn, Miss Scarlett."

Rhoda gave me an amused look and rolled her eyes. That was what she always did when I compared her to the incomparable Scarlett O'Hara from *Gone With the Wind*. "Then how is he countrified? Does he eat with his fingers, wear high-water pants and suspenders, or does he pick his teeth with a straw from a broom?"

"All of the above, and then some. He says 'gwine' for *going* and 'rightcheer' for *right here.*" I laughed. "But I thought I'd die when he referred to the cover on the motel bed as a kivver. My mama and daddy don't even use that word anymore."

Rhoda guffawed. "I haven't heard a cover called a kivver since I was a young'un growin' up in Alabama. But gwine is my favorite. Now tell me, was he worth it?"

I nodded. "He was. He's got a good head on him, if you know what I mean."

Rhoda gave me a look of envy. "He sounds like my kind of man," she squealed. "Are you, uh, gwine to see him again?"

I shrugged and giggled for a few seconds. "I don't know what I'm gwine to do," I replied. "It depends on a few things."

"Annette, if you don't want to talk about this, just say so."

I shuddered and let out a loud sigh. "Rhoda, he made me feel like a teenager again. He made me feel like a beauty queen. He . . . he was like dope. And I couldn't get enough. . . ." I turned to Rhoda, with a concerned look on my face. "This scares the hell out of me," I admitted. "How have you managed to do your thing with Bully for all these years and not lose your mind?"

"Let me put it this way. Had I not started my affair with Bully, I would have lost my mind a long time ago." Rhoda started the motor again and eased out into the street, looking straight ahead. "And by the way, we won the tournament tonight."

"Excuse me?"

"Girl, you joined my bowlin' team so you could have a cloak to cover this thing you started with Louis. Now if you don't get your shit together, you will never be able to pull this off. I am your alibi for tonight, and any other night or day that you want to hook up with your baby boy."

I cringed. The reference she'd made to Louis was true but disturbing. It was a painful reminder that there was a very wide gap between our ages. "Don't call him that," I pleaded. "That makes me feel like one of those aging celebrities known for fooling around with youngsters."

"Well, he is a little on the youthful side, Cher," Rhoda teased.

"I can see that, so you don't have to remind me," I snarled. "His age was the one thing that made me hold off this long. I had to tell him to stop saying 'Yes, ma'am' to me, because it made me feel my age." I gave Rhoda a guarded look. From the blank expression on her face, I got the feeling that she didn't know what to say next. I decided to steer the conversation in a less painful direction. "Now, going back to that countrified thing, he says 'nome' for *no, ma'am.*"

"Nome? Now you are goin' real far up into the backwoods, Andy Griffith–Beverly Hillbillies country with that one," Rhoda howled.

"He dozed off for a few minutes and snored so loud, the manager called from the office and said that the people in the rooms on both sides of us had called to complain." We both laughed, cackling like hens.

"That's hysterical, but let's get back to his age. He's at least as young as twenty-five, if he's a day."

"He's thirty," I said, nodding. "Had you and I not aborted my first child, he or she would be thirty. The truth is, I'm old enough . . . I . . . I'm old enough to be Louis's mother."

"Uh-huh. That's a fact. But if it doesn't bother him, it shouldn't bother you. And I meant what I just said. If you don't want to talk about him, I understand."

"No, maybe we should talk about him. If I had known I was going to live this long, I would have prepared myself better for, uh, certain things. Like losing my appeal to my husband. I was beginning to think that the fun part of my life was over. But I'm not ready for a rocking chair," I declared.

"If you think that forty-six is old, the fun part of your life is over. I'm a few months older than you, and I sure as hell don't think my fun is over. My kids are grown, my house is paid for, I've got my husband and my lover under control, and I look damn good for a woman my age. Girl, these are the best years of our lives. You'd better enjoy them while you still can. Life is shorter than you think. Do you want to stop off at that rib place and pick up a plate for Pee Wee before I drop you off? You usually do."

"Yeah. That man would choke my tongue out if I came home without a rib dinner for him," I said with a forced chuckle.

"Husbands! Bah! After a while they are as hard to keep in shape as a pair of cheap panty hose. My husband has become so fuckin' irritatin' that whenever I get constipated, all I have to do is look at him for a few minutes. He's the best laxative in the world. My bowels never had it so good."

"Rhoda, that's one of the most disgusting things I have ever heard you say! Otis is your husband. If he's that bad, why are you still with him?"

"For the same reason I keep those old house shoes I've had since I gave birth to my last child. He's comfortable, familiar, and convenient—and he used to be good and sexy. Just like that old shoe you married." I didn't like the smug look on Rhoda's face, but it was one I was used to seeing. "Here we go," Rhoda said, sucking on her teeth as we stopped in front of Al's rib joint. "I think I could go for some hot links myself."

CHAPTER 5

My husband, Jerry, whom we all called Pee Wee, was in the same position in his shabby blue La-Z-Boy recliner in our living room that he was in when I left the house more than four hours earlier.

"I'm home," I said, coughing at the same time to clear my throat.

I used to look forward to coming home. But that was back in the day when my husband greeted me with my housecoat and slippers, a cold drink, and a mind-boggling French kiss. And when I got home before he did, I would greet him the same way. Things had changed, and not for the better. Coming home nowadays was like visiting a relative I didn't like. Every time I heard that old song by the Supremes called "Where Did Our Love Go?" it reminded me of my marriage. There had once been so much affection in my home that I thought it would never fizzle out. Well, it did. I didn't know how to resurrect it, either. I was thankful that I now had another man to focus on. Like a lot of women my age, I still had a lot of love to give, and I still needed a lot of love myself.

"You bring them ribs?" Pee Wee asked. At the same time, he released a silent fart. Even though I didn't hear it, the stench was so unholy, it made my eyes water and the insides of my nostrils burn. "Excuse me. I had chili for lunch, and I've been payin' my gas bill ever since," he drawled. He didn't even turn around to face me as I stood in the doorway.

I held my breath and fanned my face with my hand, but it didn't do much good. The closer I got to him, the more my eyes watered from his gas.

I was disgusted, to say the least, and glad that I had not brought company home with me. Without a word, I set the Styrofoam container, which contained a large order of ribs, three chicken wings, two slices of wheat bread, some coleslaw, and baked beans, on the coffee table in front of him. And, without a word, he flipped open the container and started eating, gnawing on one of the wings like a beaver.

Pee Wee spent more time with that old chair of his than he did with me. He looked like an old man stretched out in it, with his graying hair and his bony, reptilian-like bare feet. His belly was so bloated and low, it looked like he was about to give birth. Had I known that the "worse" of the "for better or worse" part of our vows was going to be this bad, I would have deleted or rewritten that outdated, unrealistic shit myself. It was a damn shame that my once near-perfect marriage had become so unbearably dull. I was now the wife of a caricature.

I sat down gently on the arm of the sofa, facing him, and cleared my throat to get his attention. That didn't work. "Did you make Charlotte take a bath before she went to bed?" I asked, looking around my spacious living room, admiring the new beige shag carpet and the gold velvet sofa and love seat that I had purchased two months ago. I was glad to see that he had not made too much of a mess. The only things I could see worth complaining about were the four empty beer bottles on top of my red oak coffee table; a limp switch in his lap, which he must have used on Charlotte to make her behave; and some toenail clippings on the floor in front of him. I made a mental note to scold him about all that later. As tired as I was, the last thing I felt like doing was arguing with him. "Pee Wee, I am talking to you."

He grunted and gave me a surprised look, like he had just noticed me sitting in front of him, with my suede purse still in my hands and the yellow cashmere sweater he'd given me last Christmas still draped around my shoulders. "Did you say something?"

he asked, with his mouth full of food. When I didn't respond right away, he gave me an annoyed look, and then he dismissed me with a wave of his hand.

I didn't know what I had done to make my husband treat me like a nuisance. This behavior had been going on for several weeks now, and it was beginning to get on my last nerve. I didn't like to brag, but if anybody had asked me, I would have told them that I was a wife and a half. I was attractive, I kept a clean house, I brought home half of the mighty big piece of the bacon that it took to make us comfortable, and I was a good mother to our only child. No man in his right mind could ignore that. Apparently, that was no longer enough for my husband. But that was his problem. If he didn't appreciate me, I'd find somebody who did. And tonight was a good start.

"I asked you if you made Charlotte take a bath before she went to bed."

"Uh-huh," he replied, chewing so hard, his ears wiggled. I was beginning to feel like I was trying to pull his teeth. That was how hard it had become for me to make him talk. Barbecue sauce had saturated his goatee. But instead of using one of the napkins that had come with his order, he kept right on chewing. It disgusted me, but that didn't seem to bother him a bit. Then he started to smack so loudly, it made me want to help him eat. You would have thought that he was gobbling from a platter at the Last Supper.

"You had to whup her?" I asked, nodding toward the switch in his lap. I had received more than my share of whuppings during my childhood, but I didn't approve of hitting kids. However, every now and then, it took a few whacks across Charlotte's butt to get her attention.

"She had it comin'," he managed.

"Well, don't do it again unless I'm here," I said. "You men get too heavy-handed when it comes to whupping a child."

He rolled his eyes, broke the switch in two with one hand, and dropped the pieces to the floor, next to his toenail clippings.

"Did anybody call for me?" I asked, with an exasperated sigh, rising from my seat. I dropped my purse and sweater onto the sofa, and then I slid out of my shoes and kicked them to the side.

"Naw." He chewed and smacked some more. Then he swallowed

so hard, he had to tilt his head back and lift his butt a few inches off his seat. "Damn," he complained, with his face contorted. My husband had become one of those people who made eating look like a sporting event. He punched himself in the chest with his fist, and then he expelled a grunt and a mild belch. "This grub is so screamin' good, I want to put my whole face in it. You didn't get yourself nothin' from Al's?"

"We had pizza and beer at the bowling alley," I replied. "Uh, I really enjoyed bowling tonight. I'm glad I joined Rhoda's bowling team so I can do this *every* Thursday night. . . ." I paused and held my breath, anxious to hear what he had to say.

"That's nice. I hope you do. You need to get out of this house more, anyway. If you don't do somethin' for yourself, ain't no tellin' how soon you'll get old before your time."

His last comment made my ears ring.

"Pee Wee, I wish you would tell me what is wrong. We can't go on like this." I held my breath again as I awaited his response.

He stopped chewing and smacking for a moment and gave me a surprised look. There was a large wad of food in the left side of his mouth. He didn't even bother to swallow it before he spoke again. "What the hell are you talkin' about, woman? Who said somethin' was wrong?" he replied, with a shrug. He swallowed the food, and now his face had a slack-jawed appearance.

"Something is definitely wrong," I insisted.

"Not with me!" he yelled, looking even more surprised. "I'm not the one goin' through the change." His words felt like a stab.

"This has nothing to do with menopause! Whether you will admit it or not, you are the one with the problem!" I hollered.

"Well, if you are so smart, why don't you tell me what my problem is?"

"That's what I'm trying to figure out. That's what I was hoping you'd tell me. You . . . you're not the man you used to be," I wailed.

The food on his plate was good, but it couldn't have been that good. He blinked and stuffed another wad of coleslaw into his jaw. I was glad he swallowed it before he responded to my last comment.

"Well, since you brought it up, you ain't the woman you used to be, neither," he told me, with a pinched look on his face. "But like old blue-eyed Mr. Frank Sinatra sung in one of his songs, *that's life.* Don't nothin' stay the same forever. What's your point?"

He finally lifted one of the napkins and wiped his mouth, releasing another mild belch. Now he looked so calm, it was frightening. I had not seen him look this satisfied since the last time we made love, last year. He yawned and stretched his arms high above his head, letting me know that he was about to end his participation in this tense conversation.

"I know that nothing stays the same forever, but you've changed so much I hardly know you anymore." I walked over to the large front window and continued to talk, with my back to him. "We used to talk about so many different things. We used to do so many things together. We were so busy, we needed a pie chart to keep up with all our activities. And . . . and now our bedroom seems more like a morgue. We had one of the best marriages in town. If you don't love me anymore and want to . . . want to move on, just tell me, and I won't stand in your way." A few moments passed before I spoke again. "Did you hear what I just said, Pee Wee?"

He responded with a resonating snore.

CHAPTER 6

I didn't treat my battered body to the long, hot bath that I had planned to take during my ride home from the motel. I settled for another brief shower instead, like the one I'd taken in the motel with Louis.

After I had dried myself off, I stood in front of the full-length mirror behind the bathroom door and admired my naked body. Even as agitated as I was because of my conversation with Pee Wee, I couldn't stop myself from smiling. I liked what I saw in that mirror. I never thought that I would live to see the day that I'd have a waistline that was where it was supposed to be. I was nowhere near Janet Jackson territory in the body department—even when she was going through one of her plump periods—but I no longer had to turn sideways to tell where my back ended and my butt began. I still had some cellulite on my thighs, but according to the tabloids I read every week, so did Goldie Hawn, and she was still one of the most glamorous human beings on the planet. Most of the dimples, lumps, fleshy flaps, and bumps that had once decorated more than 50 percent of my body had disappeared. I could even see my navel now, because all the flab that used to encircle my middle like a tutu was completely gone. I was going to do whatever it took to make sure it never returned.

Pee Wee didn't know what a good thing he was losing, but his loss was another man's gain. That belief was probably the only thing that kept me going.

Louis was a man who was good not only with his dick and his hands; he had a way with words, too. He always seemed to know just what to say to make me feel good. "I can't keep my hands off you," he had told me just before I left the motel. "I just don't know what I'm gwine to do with myself for the rest of the night."

"You can spend the rest of the night thinking about me," I'd told him. "And I will be thinking about you." I was thinking about Louis right now. I was thinking about him so hard that I knew I couldn't get to sleep until I heard his voice again.

I could hear Pee Wee snoring in the living room all the way from our upstairs bedroom at the end of the hall. When he fell asleep in that damn chair, I usually left him there for the night. I had stopped trying to drag his deadweight black ass upstairs ever since that night a few months ago when I pulled a muscle trying to do so. It didn't matter to me where he slept anymore. Because when he was in bed with me, I was just as alone as when he was not there at all. But tonight was different.

I didn't go straight to bed after my shower. I slid into one of my sleaziest Frederick's of Hollywood negligees. A sad smile crossed my face when I recalled how Pee Wee had referred to this short, see-through red night wear as a "naked-la-gee" when it arrived in the mail on the morning of his last birthday. I picked up the telephone on the nightstand next to my side of the bed and had the operator connect me to the Do Drop Inn motel, room 108.

"Hello," Louis answered on the first ring. I could hear loud, angry voices in the background, which meant the hookers and the truck drivers had locked horns.

"Hi. It's Annette," I said, trembling like a schoolgirl.

"Hold on, baby. Let me close this window. Those fools outside in the parking lot are getting on my nerves." He was gone so long, I thought he'd joined the melee in the parking lot. "I'm back," he told me, huffing and puffing. "Damn, this place is a dump. I had to wrestle with the window to open it and to close it."

"I hope I didn't wake you up."

"Oh no, baby. I am so glad you called. My dick is buzzing like a killer bee and throbbing like a lawn mower," he told me.

"That must be a sight to behold." I laughed. "I wish I could see that."

"I wish you could see it, too."

"You were still heavy on my mind, so I just thought I'd call. I hope I didn't disturb you."

"You could never disturb me. I was just lying here in this bed, roasting up under the kivver, listening to that jazz station you told me about. That damn air conditioner is about as useless as a third leg."

"It would probably help if you got out from under the kivver," I suggested.

"Then these flies would be lighting all up and down my body."

"Then you should have left the window open. I don't mind the noise."

"Well, I do. And another thing. My dick is as hard as Chinese arithmetic."

"That must be a sight to behold, too." I laughed again. It felt so good to be amused.

"Is everything all right?"

"Everything is fine. I just wanted to say that I really enjoyed your company tonight."

Louis took his time responding. Whenever a person got hesitant during a conversation with me, it made me nervous. The first thing that came to my mind was that they were trying to come up with whatever they thought I wanted to hear. I was usually right. No matter who it was, they usually said exactly what I wanted to hear at the time. This time was no different. He said, "Well, if you enjoyed my company half as much as I enjoyed yours, I'm in good shape." He should have stopped while he was ahead, but he didn't. "I never know how these things are gwine to go. All kinds of things can come up, with you being married and all. Lord knows, I don't need any more complications in my life. I've been in the storm too long as it is."

"Now what in the world does that mean?"

"I know what kind of mess I could get myself into by dipping my bucket in another man's well. There are way too many other fish. . . ."

That was something I *hadn't* expected to hear or wanted to hear. "Bucket? Fuck it!" The last thing I wanted to be was just another link in some man's chain of fools. "You don't have to worry about me," I assured him.

"What's *that* supposed to mean?" he asked, with a gulp.

"We had a good time tonight, but if there is something else you want to do, or some other fish you'd like to catch, please don't let me stand in your way. I was doing fine before I met you—"

Louis wasted no time cutting me off. "Now, you just hold on! You hold on there right now. Where is that gobbledygook coming from?"

"I don't know. But since you brought it up, you ought to know. So why don't you tell me? The last thing I want to do is complicate things for somebody else. I do enough of that to myself."

"Annette, I've been looking for a woman like you all my life. You're beautiful. You're funny and smart. And they ought to stuff that body of yours and put it on display when you die." He laughed. I laughed at the thought of that. "I want to see you again, and I hope you want to see me. What happened tonight was just the beginning of a wonderful relationship. Don't you think so? Wasn't tonight wonderful for you?"

"It was," I admitted, looking toward the door. My husband had stopped snoring. I held my breath as I heard him shuffling up the steps, dragging his feet like a zombie with a clubfoot. "Oh shit! I have to go!" I announced. I hung up before Louis could say another word. I was kind of glad to end the call. We'd both said a couple of stupid things. The last thing I wanted was for one of us to say something that was stupid enough for us to end our relationship before it grew legs.

By the time Pee Wee entered the room, I was facing the wall, with the covers up to my neck. I was wrapped so snugly in my red silk sheets, I felt like I was in a body bag. When he slid under the covers and started patting and rubbing me on the butt, I got excited. For years that gesture had usually meant only one thing: he wanted to make love. It didn't matter that the last thing I needed right now was more sex. I sat bolt upright and turned to face him so fast, I almost rolled to the floor. Despite the fact that I had made love for hours with another man, I would have jumped through hoops to share some passion with my husband tonight.

"Yes, baby," I cooed, trying to sound as seductive as a forty-six-year-old, size-sixteen sister could.

I was disappointed to see that there was no look of love or lust on his face like I had known back in the day. He just looked uncomfortable, like he was constipated. "I know you just got your nails silk wrapped again this afternoon, but can you scratch my back for a few minutes?" he asked. "I'm itchin' like a hound."

"You want me to scratch your back?" I wailed, disappointed. "Is that all you want?"

"Why else would I be pesterin' you this time of night?" he replied, with a mighty belch. "And why you layin' up in this room this time of night, half-naked? You ain't in no doctor's office."

I just looked at him and blinked. Then I gripped his shoulders and spun him around so I could scratch his back.

CHAPTER 7

I was glad that it was June. For one thing, school was out, so I didn't have to worry about getting up an hour earlier to get my ten-year-old daughter, Charlotte, ready for school before I left for work. But I had gotten up early this particular morning, anyway. As a matter of fact, I had rolled out of bed two hours earlier than I normally would have. I hadn't slept but three or four hours, anyway. I couldn't stop thinking about the fact that I'd done the one thing that I'd promised my husband and God I'd never do: I'd committed adultery.

The mild guilt that I had felt before and after I left the motel the night before was gone. And I do mean completely gone. Pee Wee's behavior had helped me get over that. As a matter of fact, I had the nerve to walk around with a smile on my face this morning. His request for me to scratch his back so he could get to sleep last night was the straw that had broken the camel's back in two. There I'd been, lying next to him in a see-through gown, ready, willing, and able to do anything he wanted me to do, and all he'd wanted from me was a back scratch!

It was all good, though. It had made him happy. Even though that back-scratching episode had caused me to break two of my nails. But if that was all it took, I was way ahead of the game. As long as I kept him somewhat happy, I didn't have to worry about him checking up on my outside activities. I wondered if Louis would ever ask me to do something as mundane as scratch his back. The thought made me laugh out loud.

"What you guffawin' about so early in the mornin'?" Pee Wee asked, walking into the kitchen.

I sat at the table, nursing my second cup of coffee. I had already dressed for work and read the morning paper. "Huh? Oh, nothing," I muttered, fanning my face.

There was nothing wrong with our air conditioner, but it still didn't do the job. I was sweating like a seal. I had on a navy blue skirt and a white sleeveless blouse. I'd left the two top buttons on my blouse undone so that I could enjoy the mild June breeze, and show a little bit of cleavage. Since my bosom was so attractive now, I couldn't help showing it off a little from time to time—as long as I did it tastefully. Had I not had to go to work, I would have been walking around the house, naked, trying to keep cool. I often did that when I was home alone.

"Nothin'?" Pee Wee gave me a dumbfounded look. "Most people don't go around cheesin' like a hyena about nothin'." He stopped and stood in front of me, with his hands on his hips. Even though he had lost his shape and most of his looks, he still looked good to me in his crisp white barber's smock. The creases in his black slacks were razor sharp.

"I was just thinking about something funny that one of the girls on the bowling team said last night. You remember Lizel Hunter?"

"Who don't? She's one of them sisters that helps Rhoda look after them kids at her child-care whatnot. What about Lizel? I bet she's pregnant again."

I shook my head. "She's looking for a new husband," I reported.

"What happened to the husband she had? Wasn't he her fifth or sixth? How many more she need to be satisfied? She must have one hell of a meat grinder between her thighs."

"She's had only four husbands. She's still with husband number four, but she's always looking for a better one."

Pee Wee groaned and shook his head in disgust. "You women need to find better things to do with your time than look for a better husband," he retorted. "I hope her bad habits don't rub off on you. Lord knows, you got enough bad habits of your own already."

"Thanks, Pee Wee. I needed to hear that," I scoffed, giving him a look that would have killed him if looks could kill.

"Aw, woman, you know what I mean. I know you know that I know you got better sense than to be out there looking for a better husband. I don't mean to brag, but you can't do no better than me."

"Do you want me to find out?" I offered. One of the things I liked about having a lover, especially one as young, handsome, and aggressive as Louis, was that it brought out courage in me that I didn't know I had.

Pee Wee removed his hands from his hips and folded his arms. "Woman, do I have to remind you that there wasn't nobody, not even a cat, standing in line behind me when I went up to you and asked you to get married? You ain't Halle Berry."

I shook my head and rolled my eyes. "Don't you have to get to the shop and open up?"

"I'll be home late tonight," he told me, looking away as soon as I met his gaze.

"So will I," I told him. "I'm going out for drinks with Rhoda." I wiped the slight smile off of my face because I didn't want him to see it.

"What about Charlotte?" he asked, with one eyebrow raised.

"She's spending the night with the Peterson twins down the street."

"Oh. Well, I hope you and Rhoda have a good time gettin' drunk tonight." He turned and walked out the back door, slamming the screen door so hard, a pot holder fell from its hook on the wall to the floor.

"I hope you have a good time tonight, too. Doing whatever it is you do these days," I said, knowing he couldn't hear me.

It saddened me to know that it had come to this. We were more like indifferent roommates than we were husband and wife. It had been almost a year since we'd had sex—with each other. I didn't know about his sex life, and the way I was feeling this morning, I didn't want to know. At that moment, I knew what I had to do. Especially since I had ended my dry spell last night.

As soon as I heard Pee Wee start the motor in the candy-apple red Firebird in our driveway, which he'd bought three months ago, I stumbled over to the telephone on the wall next to the refrigerator. I waited until I heard him drive away before I dialed the motel again.

"Louis, did I wake you? I'm sorry I had to get off the phone so quick last night. My husband came into the room," I said, without pausing to take a breath.

"That's all right, baby. I understand. Where are you?"

"I'm still at my house. I'll be leaving for work in a few minutes," I replied, looking at my watch. "I just have to check on my daughter before I go."

"I can't wait to meet her. I am looking forward to it," he told me. That was good to know. That meant he planned on being around for a while. "And I know she's as much of a fox as you are."

"Uh, she's only ten, so we'd have to be careful around her. We'd have to watch everything we said and did," I warned. "She's at that age where she blabs everything she sees and hears. Intentionally and unintentionally."

"Baby, we are gwine to take things real slow. Maybe by the time I meet your daughter, we won't have to be sneaking around. The way you say your old man has been neglecting you, it sounds like he's got a little something on the side himself."

"I don't want to talk about that right now," I said, with a heavy sigh. Pee Wee's lack of interest in me was one thing, and that was bad enough. That was all I could handle. But if the reason was another woman, I'd find out soon enough, and I'd deal with that then.

"When can I see you again?"

That question brought a broad grin to my face.

"Uh, let's talk about that later tonight. I'll be at the Red Rose, having a few drinks with a friend. You can meet us there around six if you can make it."

"You'll be with a friend?" I could tell he was nervous by the way he was whispering. "Is she cool? She know about us?"

"Louis, she knows everything. She's the one who, uh, encouraged me to get to know you better. She drove me to the motel and picked me up last night."

"Bless her heart. When you see her, hug her for me."

"She's the only person on this planet that I would trust with my life."

There were a few moments of silence before he spoke again. "I'm gwine to knock off work around five thirty. I've been working till eight almost every night this week. Last night I realized I've got something much better to do with my time in the evenings now."

His last sentence made me grin even more.

"Does that mean you're coming to the Red Rose tonight? Friday night is buy one drink, get one drink free. And all the free buffalo wings you can eat. And they are the best—no offense." I immediately wanted to bite my tongue. I should have known better than to brag about another cook's abilities to a struggling caterer.

"None taken." He laughed. "I know I can hook up a mean meal. I'll be at the Red Rose tonight. There and any other place you want me to be."

I was smiling so hard when I got off the phone, my cheeks hurt. I was still smiling when my daughter pranced into the kitchen, already dressed in jeans and a white T-shirt with a black Barbie's face on the front. She was spoiled, materialistic, self-centered, and manipulative. But she was also smart, generous, loving, and cute. Even though she had the same habits and mannerisms, and the nice, slim build and soft, gentle features, that her daddy *used* to have, she was my most treasured creation.

"What are you smiling about, Mama? You look like that cat in *Alice in Wonderland,*" she said, with a smirk.

I cleared my throat and stopped smiling. "Nothing," I managed.

CHAPTER 8

I was probably the only person at the company I worked for who didn't look forward to Friday. I didn't know what to do with myself on the weekends anymore. My personal life had become so humdrum that I preferred being at work to being in my own house.

I loved my husband. He was the most important man in my life and probably always would be. I loved him more than my own flesh-and-blood daddy. I still loved my daddy, and I always would, but he had not fulfilled my needs as thoroughly as Pee Wee. And even though I had forgiven my daddy for deserting me and my mama for another woman when we had needed him the most, some of the pain that that betrayal had caused would remain with me to my grave.

When Pee Wee was home, he spent most of his time slumped in that damn La-Z-Boy, watching TV, or outside, tinkering around under the hood of his car. His parents were deceased, and most of his family lived in Erie, Pennsylvania. The only time he left the house was to go to work at the barbershop that he owned and managed, fishing with some of his buddies, or out for a few drinks at one of the local bars. He hadn't been to church in over a year, and the only time he visited my parents' house a few blocks away was when I dragged him along with me. We had not been to a party, picnic, or any other social event together in months.

I loved my daughter, too, but when she was in the house, she wasn't much company, either. I knew she loved me, but she took me for granted, almost as much as her daddy. In her case, it didn't bother me so much. She was a typical child. As long as I fed her and took care of all her other needs, she was satisfied. And like most of the kids her age, she didn't want to hang out with her mama. She had a lot of friends in the neighborhood that she liked to visit and hang out with at the malls and playgrounds. When she wasn't with her friends or my parents, she liked to lock herself in her room and read. She had inherited her passion for reading from me, and I encouraged her to do it as much as possible. I just had to monitor what she read. Even though she was just ten, I didn't have a problem with her reading material meant for teenagers. However, I did have a problem with her reading "adult" books, such as those by mega-writers Danielle Steel and Jackie Collins—even though I enjoyed and admired both writers myself.

To this day I believed that if Rhoda had not allowed her daughter, Jade, to read books by those two writers, and others like them, when she was Charlotte's age, the girl might not have turned out the way she did. She was the daughter from hell, and that was the nicest way I could describe her. I cringed when I recalled the times I'd caught Jade reading *The Joy of Sex* and *The Happy Hooker* when she was just twelve. I would always believe that books like that had contributed to her two abortions, her torrid lesbian relationship with another teenage girl, her arrogant personality, and only God knew what else. Lately, I'd been thinking about writing a book myself after all the shit I'd been through. It would give me more to do with all the time I had on my hands.

Had it not been for my job as a manager at Mizelle's Collection Agency, I didn't know what I would have done with myself. I usually took my breaks in my office. Since I had a large corner office all to myself, which I had decorated with a red oak desk and matching cabinets, I had privacy and all the comforts of home. I had a portable black-and-white TV on a small oak credenza next to my desk, which I could watch during my breaks or lunch. I kept a mini-refrigerator in a corner by the window, which was always stocked with bottled water, juice, and even a few beers. There was even a low sofa against the wall by the door, which I could stretch out on when I wanted to.

I had worked most of my adult life, but Rhoda had lived a life of leisure for most of hers and still did, in my opinion. During our teens, while I had worked in the bean fields to earn some of my spending money, she'd lounged around the huge house that her daddy owned, trying to decide what to buy next with all the money she had access to. Her daddy had been the only black funeral director in Richland, Ohio, at the time. One thing about black folks back then was that they could always be counted on to keep a funeral director in business. Sadly, that was still true today, even more so. We had an increasing problem with gangs and drugs to thank for that. The current black funeral director was the wealthiest black man in town.

Rhoda called my office around ten that morning. "Are we still on for drinks this evenin'?" she asked, yawning into the phone like she didn't have a care in the world.

"I hope so," I said, my voice dry. "I can't leave until five, though."

"You are the boss. You can leave whenever you want to," Rhoda replied. "I do."

"You don't have a real job, Rhoda. You can afford to do whatever you want to do," I reminded her.

"You might not think what I do is real work, but it is," she replied and pouted.

Rhoda operated a licensed child-care center. She took care of several children in her home, all under five, five days a week, while their parents worked. She had Lizel and another woman from the church working for her. They did most of the work, while Rhoda kicked back with her lover or went shopping with me on my lunch break. I was used to Rhoda protesting and pouting when I accused her of not having a real job.

"Uh, I hope you don't mind if Louis joins us. I really want you to get to know him better," I blurted.

"I already know him. I'm the one who hooked you up with him in the first place, remember?"

"I know that. I just want you to get to know him as well as I do now."

"Look, girl. My agin' pussy gets enough action already," Rhoda said and chuckled. "You sharin' your barbecued ribs or chicken with me is one thing, but Louis is one piece of meat you can keep all to yourself."

"Be serious," I scolded. "He . . . he's already changed my life in a big way. I can't stand not being around him."

"Now you just hold on there a minute, Glenn Close, as in that old movie *Fatal Attraction.* I do not want to be part of any crazy stalking shit, if that's what this is. I hope you tell me that this little ditty is nothin' more than a fling." I could hear Rhoda grinding her teeth.

"I would never get that crazy over a man," I snapped.

"I sure as hell hope not. I don't want you to get so caught up in this affair that you leave Pee Wee. I can't hurt him after all these years that he and I have been so close."

"Rhoda, I'm the one sleeping with Louis. Not you," I reminded her.

"Didn't I just remind you that I'm the one who hooked you up with the man? Had I not, we would not be havin' a conversation about you leavin' Pee Wee. He's been my boy since we were eight, and you know that."

"Woman, I wish you'd make up your mind. You didn't let the fact that Pee Wee was 'your boy' stop you from encouraging me to have an affair. There is a possibility that I would have done it on my own, anyway, but it probably wouldn't be with Louis if you hadn't pushed me."

"Oh no, you didn't! No, you didn't just say what I think you just said! You are a grown-ass woman, and you've got a mind of your own. You got involved with Louis because you wanted to, not because I wanted you to. And for the record, had it not been him, like you said, it would have been some other man. Don't you dare try to lay this shit on my doorstep. I'm not goin' to take the blame for your marriage goin' kaput."

"Is that what you think? You think my marriage has gone kaput?"

"You tell me."

"I love my husband as much as you love yours."

Rhoda clucked like a wet hen before she started to laugh like a hyena. "That's not sayin' much."

I gasped. "Are you telling me that you no longer love Otis?"

"Oh, I still love him to death. He was my first love, and he will be my last. I'm better off with him than I'd be without him. He's a good man . . . I guess."

"You *guess*? That doesn't sound very romantic," I pointed out.

"I learned from my mama and the other women in my family that at some point a husband's functions have to change. So what if the sex is over? As long as the man does the other important things that he's supposed to do, it's still all good. It's unrealistic to expect one man to fulfill all a woman's needs in this day and age."

"Mine used to," I said in Pee Wee's defense.

"*Used to* is right. And I am sure that every single one of the Kennedy wives can say that, too. The bottom line is, I love my husband. He's a good man, and I want to hang on to him."

"I'm glad to hear you say that. My husband is a good man. But Louis is . . . He's a good man, too. He's what I need right now, and as long as he's keeping me happy, I will be with him . . . unless we get caught."

Silence hung in the air for a few seconds like a bad odor. "I'm scared of you," Rhoda gasped. "This sounds like more than just a fly-by-night fling. Is this thing with Louis really goin' to go somewhere?"

I wasn't exactly sure how to respond to Rhoda's question. I took my time answering.

"Hello? Are you still with me?" she hollered.

"I'm still with you," I mumbled, still trying to come up with an answer to her question.

"Did you hear what I just asked?"

"I did. I don't know if this is going to go anywhere or not. From what Louis has said so far, it sounds like he wants it to."

"Do you want it to go somewhere?"

"I don't know. . . ."

CHAPTER 9

"You don't know?"

"That's what I said," I whimpered.

"I know damn well what you just said. What I want to know is, what the hell do you mean by that? What do you not know? And don't start talkin' that shit about you bein' a happily married woman again. It's borin' as hell, and I don't believe in that shit. Life is too short for you, me, or any other woman to be sittin' around claimin' to be so happily married, nothin' else matters. Fuck that shit, and fuck whoever said it in the first place."

"Rhoda, you know me better than anybody, including my own husband and my mama. You know I don't jump into anything too fast or too deep," I said, pausing to catch my breath. I was about to continue, but Rhoda cut me off.

"There is a first time for everything, Annette. For one thing, you need to get with the program before it's too late. You need to start goin' with the flow like the rest of us, while you still can."

"I am . . . I mean, I will. I have been frustrated a lot lately, and I'm getting damn sick of it."

"That's why you are doin' somethin' about it," Rhoda told me. "And Louis is the perfect specimen for you to experiment with for your first affair."

I couldn't believe my ears! Rhoda was my best friend, and she was as smart as a whip, but she sure knew how to tune up her mouth to say some of the stupidest shit I'd ever heard. "My *first* affair?"

"You know, in case Louis doesn't get the job done right. You might have to try on another one."

"Girl, I know damn well you don't think I'd make a habit out of having affairs. If it doesn't work out with Louis, that's it for me. But do you know what, Rhoda? I like Louis. I like him a lot. And that scares the hell out of me. If he wants to take this to another level, I will. I mean, how long could it last, anyway?"

"Speak for yourself. Bully and I have been goin' at it for more than a generation, and we haven't slowed down a bit. As a matter of fact, that dick he whips me with is sweeter than ever," she said and snickered.

"I know, Rhoda," I said, rolling my eyes. "You've told me that fifty or sixty times." I sniffed and looked toward my door. Before I could speak again, my other line rang. "Rhoda, hold on. Somebody's calling on line two." It was Louis.

"Hello, Lou," I cooed. There was something about this man that made me feel downright dainty. That was something that neither my husband nor any other man had been able to do so far. That made Louis all the more special to me. "I hope you don't mind me calling you Lou."

"Baby, you can call me Quasimodo if you want to. Just as long as you call me."

My entire body got so hot, I had to spread my legs so I could fan my crotch with the *New York Times,* one of several newspapers I read each day. Then I smiled so demurely, I could hardly stand myself.

"Is there any way you can get away for a few hours later tonight?" he asked.

I stopped fanning myself and dropped the newspaper back onto my desk. "Tonight?" I asked stupidly. "Uh, I think so. What do you have in mind?" I rubbed my thumping heart as I listened.

"Girl, I'm gwine to roll you like your back don't have no bone," he vowed.

"Hmm. That sounds like fun. And I'm gwine to let you roll me like my back don't have no bone."

I was not trying to be funny, and I was not intentionally making fun of his semi-countrified diction. He had such a nice deep voice that I would have enjoyed listening to him even if he spoke to me in Gaelic. Even that would have sounded poetic to me coming from him. I didn't want to share something this silly with Rhoda, because I didn't want her to tease me about it or think that I had gone off the deep end. I had to shake my head to clear my thoughts. I was beginning to think, act, and feel like a lovesick old fool

"Well, after drinks with your friend, I thought I'd bring you to my place so I can treat you to one of my gourmet meals. Nobody, and I do mean nobody, can whup up a Yankee pot roast as good as I can. I just want to warn you that I don't live in a penthouse or a nice house, like I know you must live in. But I am proud of my little home, anyway."

"Louis, if you lived in a shoe, that would be your business. I appreciate you wanting me to see it." What I wanted to say to Louis was, "If you will let me come to your residence, that's proof that I don't have to worry about another woman." Even though he had told me that he was not involved with somebody else, that didn't mean that it was true. It was always in the back of my mind. But that thought was on its way out of my mind now. "I'd love to see your place."

"And just to show you that I mean business, I will give you a key to my place. That way you can drop in anytime you want to," he told me, his voice full of emotion. If this was not a declaration of sincerity, I didn't know what was. No man in his right mind would give a woman, especially a married woman, the key to his residence unless he meant business. "If I give you my address, will you meet me at my place? Or would you like to ride with me? My building doesn't have a garage, and I don't want you to worry about parking on the street or in our parking lot and somebody you know seeing your car."

"I can park a block from your building," I offered. I had a valid reason for wanting to drive myself to meet Louis. As long as I had my own transportation, I would have better control over my departure. The last thing I wanted to happen was for me to get bored with him and want to leave early and not be able to. Or for something unexpected to happen that would require me to leave in a hurry.

"Then you will come?"

"I think I can do that." After I hung up with Louis, I clicked back to Rhoda. "I'm sorry I took so long with that call."

"That's all right. I had to take one myself."

"That was him," I said, swooning.

"Him who?"

"Louis. He wants to cook dinner for me tonight after we leave the Red Rose."

"I see. Do you want to reschedule our date? That way you can spend the whole evenin' with him."

"Now, you know I'm not the kind of woman who cancels plans with my female friends so I can be with a man, so you stop that!" I scolded.

Rhoda laughed before she spoke again. "But I am," she told me. "Bully, the only lover I'll ever need, just called me from the gym, with a major hard-on, and I'm feelin' right frisky myself. I need to take care of some business with him this evenin', so to speak. We haven't had a chance to do it since he got back from London yesterday."

"Just say it, Rhoda. You need to get laid."

"I need to get laid," she told me, speaking loud and clear.

"All right. I'll talk to you tomorrow."

I called my husband at his work to let him know that I'd be home even later. Bobby Jones, one of the young barbers who worked for him, answered the telephone.

"Hi, Bobby. Is Pee Wee available?"

"Um, no. He had a doctor's appointment."

"A doctor's appointment? Are you sure?" My husband was the kind of man who'd use every home remedy in the book before he'd go to a doctor.

"I'm sure. He's been going every other Friday for almost a year now. Well, now it's every Friday since last month. If you want to come by, me and Lester got everything under control until he gets back."

"He told you he's been seeing a doctor?"

"Yes, ma'am. You didn't know that?"

"Oh, that's right. I forgot. Yes, he did tell me. Look, don't tell him I called, Bobby. If you do, don't tell him you told me about his doctor visits. He told me not to worry about him, and I promised him that I wouldn't bring it up unless he did. Bobby, please promise me you won't tell him I called."

"I won't tell him. Do you want me to have him call you when he gets back, Miss . . . ?" Bobby paused for a brief moment. "Uh, who is this, anyway?"

I breathed a sigh of relief. Bobby was a little on the slow side, so he did not recognize my voice. I was glad that I had not identified myself. "Oh . . . this is Sister Holmes." I was sure that there was a woman or two in Richland by that name, but this Sister Holmes was a figment of my imagination. My husband had so many regular customers that he wouldn't have been able to keep up with all their names, anyway. "Pee Wee is the only barber that my little grandson will let cut his hair, and I was hoping that he'd be able to squeeze him in today. You know how two-year-olds can be."

"I heard that. My baby mama got my son so spoiled, he won't let nobody but me cut them naps on his big head." Bobby laughed. "I'm sure enough sorry, lady, but I need to get off this phone. We got heads lined up neck to neck for the next two hours. You want me to have Pee Wee call you back, Sister Holmes?"

"No. You don't have to tell him I called. I'll call again tomorrow."

"Yes ma'am."

I hung up and sat there, trying to digest what I had just heard, and I couldn't do it on my own. I immediately dialed Rhoda's number. This was one time that I couldn't wait for her to call me. I was glad when she picked up the phone on the first ring.

"Girl, you are not going to believe what I just found out!" I didn't give her a chance to respond to my outburst. "Pee Wee is having an affair!" I yelled.

CHAPTER 10

"Excuse me, sir?"

My breath caught in my throat. I had to cough a few times before I could find my voice again. "I said . . . Uh, is this Rhoda I'm speaking with?" I was already angry, so it didn't really bother me that much when I realized it was Rhoda's nineteen-year-old daughter, Jade, who had answered the phone. This girl hated my guts because I was one of the few people who saw through her. I was able to do that because the girl was soulless.

It was so hard to believe that this was the same girl that I used to hug and kiss and treat like a princess, up until last year. That was when she tried to drive me crazy and take my husband. She was such a bad seed that it would be a big surprise to me if her children didn't come into the world with hooves, fangs, and scales.

Jade took her good ole time responding, which was just another way she liked to annoy me when she answered my calls to Rhoda's house. She never wanted me to forget how much of a peon she considered me to be. "No, this is not Rhoda you're speaking with," she replied in a voice that was so nasty, I could almost smell it. "Is that you, Reverend Upshaw? Are you all right? You sound like you've got a frog in your throat. . . ."

This girl didn't know when to quit. I sounded nothing like Reverend Upshaw, or any other man. The sad thing about people like Jade was that they were too stupid to see how stupid they really were.

I cleared my throat. "No, this is not Reverend Upshaw. This is Annette." I was proud to identify myself in this case. One thing I wanted Jade to know was that I was not going to run for cover from her ever again. I avoided her as much as I could, but when I couldn't, I dealt with her head-on.

"Oh. I should have known this was *you*! You always did call this house at a bad time!" she roared.

"Yes, it's me, Jade. Now if your mother is there, would you please put her on the phone?"

Instead of a response, there was complete silence, then a dial tone. I spat out a few choice words and dialed Rhoda's number again.

"Hello," Jade said.

"May . . . I . . . speak . . . to . . . Rhoda?" I asked through clenched teeth. I didn't even try to hide the anger in my voice, even though I knew that it didn't faze her.

Jade did not respond. About ten seconds later, I heard muffled voices in the background on Rhoda's end. I was just about to hang up when Rhoda came on the line.

"Annette, I'm sorry. That heifer is so fuckin' rude and crude, it's a shame. I will deal with her later."

"That's all right. This sounds like a bad time. But can you call me back at my office when you get a chance? I'd like to talk to you before I go home today, if possible."

"We can talk now."

"No, that's all right. Later would be fine. It sounds like you've got enough to deal with right now."

"This is my house, and I am the one in control," Rhoda assured me. "But since you mentioned it, this is a bad time. Bully just walked in the door and can't keep his hands off me. I'm havin' a hard time holdin' him off until we can get out of the house and into a hotel room. As if that isn't bad enough, that nosy-ass, big-mouthed Wyrita walked into the kitchen with two of the children and saw me in Bully's arms earlier today. She's good helpin' me with the children, but she's also a mild pain in the booty."

"Oh. Well, Rhoda, you should stop getting too friendly with Bully in your house. You know how Lizel and Wyrita like to spread gossip, and it doesn't matter to them that they work for you. Not to mention Jade. She's the last person who needs to know about you and Bully."

"I'm more worried about the children seein' me with Bully than I am Lizel, Wyrita, or Jade. I don't think Wyrita is goin' to shoot off her mouth about this. Not as long as I'm the one signin' her paycheck. Now, what's up with you? I guess I can spare a minute or two."

I let out a deep, loud breath before I told her. "Pee Wee's having an affair." Just saying the words again gave me a bad taste in my mouth. This was not something that I would have ever in my lifetime shared with Jade, but I had just done so by mistaking her for Rhoda when she answered the phone. There was just no telling what was going through that girl's sick mind about me and my husband now. But this was one time that I didn't give a damn.

"What did you say?"

"Pee Wee is having an affair," I said for the third time, my voice firm and cold. I silently prayed that she'd heard me this time, because this was one thing that I didn't want to hear myself say again on the same day.

"What makes you think that?" Rhoda paused, and I heard her slam a door. That made me feel somewhat better. It sounded like she was in her bedroom. Lizel and Wyrita usually stayed in the back room with the eight preschool children that Rhoda was in charge of, but their ears and mouths were almost as big as Jade's. I knew that if those two magpies overheard Rhoda talking to me about Pee Wee's suspected infidelity, they'd be in gossip heaven, despite the fact that Rhoda signed their paychecks. And with everything else that was going on in my marriage at the moment, I didn't want this piece of information being discussed all over town. "I thought you said he had lost his sex drive."

"He did lose his sex drive, but just with me! How could I have been so stupid! How could I not have realized that he was involved with another woman? No wonder Pee Wee has been playing a game with me since last year. That devil! Well, I've got news for him. I can play the same game, and I can beat him at it, too. I should have known that another woman was what he was up to. And all this time he had me walking around thinking that I had lost my sex appeal. Oh! I can't wait to get my hands on Louis tonight!"

"Pee Wee's havin' an affair? Shit, girl! I didn't know he had it in him! Do you know who she is?"

"Huh? Oh! No, I don't know who the bitch is yet. And to tell you the truth, I am not going to waste my time trying to find out. I will be damned if I go through some shit like that again, like I did last year."

"But last year was a witch hunt. Pee Wee was not fuckin' another woman," Rhoda reminded me.

"Bah! That was then. This is now!" I hollered.

"What makes you so sure he's doin' it this time? Did somebody see him? What's the smokin' gun?"

"He's having an affair, Rhoda. I feel it in my bones. It all makes sense now," I insisted, speaking so fast, the words shot out of my mouth like cannonballs.

"Annette, please calm down and speak more slowly. You sound like you are about ready to explode."

"I am about to explode!" I told her, my lips trembling and my teeth grinding so hard, I almost bit my tongue. "That man had no reason to go outside his marriage."

"Annette, if that's the case, you didn't, either," Rhoda said calmly. "Even if Pee Wee is involved with another woman, I don't understand why you are takin' it so hard. You've still got Louis to fall back on."

"This is not about me. Pee Wee was up to no good long before I met Louis."

"All right then. Just tell me what makes you so sure this time. How did you find out Pee Wee was foolin' around?"

"Well, the fact that he hasn't touched me in all these months was my first clue. It never occurred to me that he'd be doing his dirt during the day, when he's supposed to be at work! According to Bobby, he's been going to visit a doctor every Friday! Doctor, my ass! When was the last time he went to a doctor?"

"Shit, I don't even remember," Rhoda told me. "Every Friday, huh? He's been spendin' some time with 'somebody' every Friday?"

"Since last year! That and the fact that he no longer makes love to me confirm it. Maybe not to you, but they do in my book."

"Hmm. Well, he is a man, and men do have affairs. Especially around his age, when that thing between his legs realizes how close it is to retirement. Nature plays the cruelest jokes. A man reaches his prime before he's twenty-one. Us, we don't reach ours until we're almost ready for the boneyard. And that's a damn shame."

"Rhoda, do you mind if we stay on the subject?"

"We are still on the subject. I just wanted to remind you of the cruel facts of life."

"So you agree with me now?"

"I didn't say that, but I won't say that I don't agree with you, either. I will go so far as to say that he *probably* is sleepin' with another woman. A young heifer at that. We are looong in the tooth, honey. We don't have a chance in hell anymore with all the young pussy out there up for grabs, and every middle-aged man and his brother standin' in line, waitin' to stick his dipstick in it. They want something that will remind them of their long-gone youth, not douche bags and Maalox. We don't have to worry about tryin' to fight the war, because we don't have the right weapons to arm ourselves with anymore. If an affair is the case, let me give you the universal sister-girl advice. What's good for the goose is good for the gander. Praise the Lord that there's still *somebody* out there who can still appreciate a well-used but grateful piece of pussy. Pee Wee's got his thing on the side. Now you've got yours. Enjoy it while you can."

"I will!" I snapped.

CHAPTER 11

I kept my office door closed and locked for the rest of the day. This was what I usually did when I had to make phone calls to people whose bills had been submitted to us for collection.

There were enough deadbeats among the forty-five thousand individuals in Richland to keep a small army busy. The folder in the in-box on my desk was so thick with files that I could have easily spent the next four hours on the phone, using one ruse after another, trying to get delinquent debtors to take my calls. Along with funeral directors, lawyers, the IRS, and the police, bill collectors never had to worry about running out of work. There were some people who did everything that they could think of not to talk to me or one of the collection agents I supervised. When a particular file landed on my desk, it was because the case had reached the critical level. I'd been cussed out and threatened so many times, it had become entertaining. And I had heard every excuse in the book. After almost four years, I was used to it. But that didn't make my job any easier.

However, I had something a little more important to me on my mind this particular afternoon. Well, actually two things. I decided to address first the one that was bothering me the most. I called my husband's barbershop again. When one of the apprentices answered, I hung up. I waited a few minutes and called again, this time disguising my voice. I was glad Pee Wee answered, because I didn't want to keep hanging up and calling back until I got him.

"Hi, baby," he said. He sounded tired and distracted. If he had been doing what I suspected, it was no wonder he sounded that way. I was tired and distracted, too. I had worked hard to make my marriage work, but apparently, I had not worked hard enough. I didn't like the fact that my husband was probably having an affair, but I wasn't going to let it drive me crazy, especially now that I was having one, too.

"How's work?" I asked in a casual manner.

He hesitated for several seconds before he responded. "The same as it was yesterday. The same as it'll be tomorrow," he replied.

"Are you feeling all right? Is something going on with you?" I asked, trying not to sound confrontational.

"I'm feelin' fine. Why are you askin' me somethin' like that?"

"You looked a little peaked before you left the house this morning, and you sound kind of weak now." If his story about visiting a doctor every Friday was true, this was the perfect time for him to tell me.

"Woman, I am fine," he said sharply. I hated to be referred to as "woman" by him, and he knew it. "Now, is somethin' the matter with you? You ain't pestered me at work in months." *Pestered* was another word he knew I hated when it was used in reference to me. He sounded impatient on top of everything else. This conversation was almost in the toilet, and I couldn't wait to flush it.

"Nothing is wrong with me. I just called to check in with you. I had thought about coming over there earlier, on my lunch hour."

"Why?" he asked with a gulp.

Why?

"We haven't had lunch together in a while, and I thought . . . I thought it would be something nice for us to do. We used to do it all the time," I snapped. "That's why."

"Well, I'm glad you didn't come over here. I've been busy all day. I ain't even had time to take a lunch break or no other kind of break."

"Oh." I glanced at my watch. "It's three thirty. You haven't taken any breaks at all today?"

"Naw."

"You didn't even go out for lunch or coffee, or to get some fresh air, or anything else?"

"Naw. Woman, ain't you listenin' to me? Didn't you just hear me say I ain't been out this door since I got here this morning?"

"Oh, I heard you all right. I just wanted to be sure I was hearing right," I said, my jaw twitching.

"You heard right. Annette, if you want to lollygag on the telephone, you goin' to have to call up somebody else. I am really busy."

"I know that, Pee Wee. You've already told me. But since I am your wife, I thought that no matter how busy you were, you'd always have a few minutes for me. I don't call you at work that often. And as a bill collector, I know how annoying unwanted phone calls can be. If you don't want me to annoy you at work at all, just tell me and I won't." I let out an involuntary hiccup, and that prompted his next question.

"Annette, have you been drinkin'?"

"No, but I wish I had a nice strong one in my hand right now. I will be drinking later, though."

"Oh, that's right. You still goin' with Rhoda for drinks after work?"

"Yeah," I said, making a note that I'd have to call Rhoda again so I could make sure our stories matched. "Do you want me to pick you up another rib dinner on my way home tonight?"

"Naw, don't worry about that. I'm goin' to wrap things up here in a little while. Then I'm goin' to stop at that new restaurant that you do so much business with to get me a plate. I've heard from a lot of people that the brother—Louis, or whatever his name is—who runs it cooks a mean meat loaf. It's no wonder. Most fags can cook up a storm."

Fags?

"You . . . you think that brother is gay?" I asked, my voice quivering.

"Oh, there is no doubt about it! The dude is as gay as an Easter basket!"

If Louis Baines was gay, he was also a damn good actor. In my opinion, he had more machismo in his baby finger than the average man had in his whole body. I chose not to address that touchy subject with Pee Wee. He was a fairly intelligent man, but his mind was as nimble as a slab of concrete when it came to his opinions.

He was one of the many black people I knew—even though they had no evidence—who continually insisted that some government officials had gotten together in some remote lab somewhere and created AIDS. Then they'd used it to try to wipe out black folks, gays, Hispanics, and other "undesirables."

"Do you mean Off the Hook?" I asked, my heart skipping a beat. As much as I wanted Louis's business to succeed, I didn't want my husband to get too close to it.

"And what the hell kind of name is Off the Hook for a restaurant? Sounds more like the title of a Rick James song."

I thought that the name was *cute,* but I knew if I said that, it would only add more credence to Pee Wee's gay notion. "The meat loaf at my mama's restaurant is pretty good and closer to you," I pointed out.

"Yeah, but your mama done turned into a real shylock over the years. I don't feel like givin' up a pound of my flesh for somethin' I can get for a lot less. Her prices would break me. Besides, your mama's place ain't hurtin' for business. I'm just tryin' to help that young brother get a toehold so another black business in this town can prosper. Ain't that what you've been preachin' for years?"

"Uh-huh." I was really ready to conclude this phone call now or change the subject. "I guess I'll let you go now. I know how busy you are."

Pee Wee was busy. However, he still had time to keep talking about Louis. "I heard that that young brother who runs that new place thinks he's cute, with his long, fuzzy hair and sweet voice. I know for a fact that he thinks his hair is too good for him to get it cut in black barbershops. Dwayne, the only other black barber in town besides me, told me that hisself. He seen that sissy struttin' out of that white barbershop on Baxter Avenue, with that shit on his head slicked back like Al Pacino in one of his gangster roles. Me, I'd rather cut a dog's butt hair than that limp shit that dude got on his head." Pee Wee grunted like some creature, and then he let out a harsh chuckle. "I bet he'll dye it blond or get it styled like Shirley Temple or Farrah Fawcett eventually."

"I still hope his business succeeds," I said firmly.

"And it will. The women in this town will see to that. Y'all like to eat out. Women are so dumb when it comes to pretty boys. Oh well. At least you ain't as dumb as women like Rhoda and Scary Mary. But like I said, most fags can cook up a storm. You women get off on shit like cookin' on account of it's one of y'all's best natural roles. That sissy could cater a woman a cake with a booger *and* a roach on top of it, and she wouldn't complain. She'd just pluck them off, with a smile. But the brother must be doin' *somethin'* right if *you* do so much business with him. What's his name again?"

"His name is Louis," I said flatly. "And I doubt very seriously if he's gay," I added with conviction. "People used to accuse you of being gay when we were kids, remember?"

"Well, if anybody knows that ain't true and never was, it's you." Pee Wee laughed and muttered a few obscenities under his breath. "I'll tell your favorite caterer you said hello, anyway. Oh! Do you want me to get a plate for you, too? He got anything you want?"

"No," I said quickly and stiffly.

"That's a damn shame. On account of you doin' business with him, I bet he'd give me a plate for you half price if I told him I was married to you."

"No, don't do that. I want to keep my relationship with Louis on a professional level. I don't like to get too personal with my business associates."

Pee Wee let out a loud breath. "If you're on a first-name basis with *Louis* already, it sounds like your relationship with him done already got personal to me. I got clients that I've been dealin' with for twenty years, and they still call me Mr. Davis. I want to keep it that way."

"Uh, it was his idea. He wants to be addressed by his first name. He's from down South."

"I see. That figures. It's a Southern thing. I don't want to touch that one with a stick, with my Pennsylvania-born self. The South is another planet, if you ask me. No wonder we Northerners call it Bigfoot country." He laughed again. "Now I got to get off this phone and get back to work."

CHAPTER 12

I didn't waste any time addressing the second issue on my mind. I called Louis at his work. I was on hold for five minutes before he came on the line.

"Louis, are you still going to see me this evening?" I asked, wrapping the telephone cord around my finger.

"I hope so. Unless you can't make it."

"I just talked to my husband. He's going to pick up one of your meat-loaf dinners on his way home from work this evening," I stated, forcing the difficult words out of my mouth like an extracted tooth.

"Oh?"

"Yes, and it sounds like he's going to become a regular customer," I said in a nervous voice. "Like everybody else, he likes good cooking."

"Good. I'll fix his plate today with my own two hands. If there's anybody I want to keep happy, it's him. As long as he's happy, we'll be happy. You sure he doesn't suspect anything? I am sure that if he was smart enough to get a woman like you, he's not so stupid that he won't get suspicious if you give him a reason."

"My husband has no reason in the world to think that I'm up to no good. I haven't done a damn thing to make him suspicious, which is more than I can say about him."

A long silence followed. I didn't want to be the one to break it, because I didn't know what else to say on the subject. But I was willing to respond to his comments and concerns.

"Annette, I don't think it's my place to get nosy about what goes on in your personal life, but if you want to talk to me about something, please feel free to do so."

"I'm glad to hear you say that."

"I mean it. I want you to know now that I am here for you, day or night. If you are willing to talk to me about your problems or concerns, even if it's a problem with your husband, I am willing to listen."

"Louis, let's confine our relationship to just you and me for now. If we don't have to bring my husband into our conversations, we won't."

"But if your husband is going to be a problem for us, I need to know."

"My husband is not going to be a problem. My marriage is not a problem."

"Well, there's a problem somewhere, baby. There must be! I can hear it in your voice. The man sleeps in the same bed with a juicy-butt woman like you and has not made love to you in almost a year. You told me that yourself. If that's not a problem, I don't know what is."

"I'll call you just before I leave work, and don't worry about anything I just said. It's nothing that I can't handle by myself," I assured Louis. But it was. As soon as I hung up with him, I called Rhoda back.

"He lied like a rug," I said as soon as she answered.

"Who?" she asked with a snort.

"Pee Wee. I called him up and gave him every chance in the world to tell me he's been seeing a doctor."

"Maybe he doesn't want you to know. Maybe he's goin' for somethin' that's too embarrassin' for him to discuss with you. Like excessive gas."

"Rhoda, if my husband was farting all over the place, I'd know about it," I snapped.

"It could be somethin' else then. Like one of those things that men don't like to talk about because they think it's too embarrassin'."

"I'm his wife!" I hollered. "If he can't share something embarrassing with me, who can he share it with?"

"He must not think that if he told his apprentice he's seein' a doctor, but he didn't tell you. It could be somethin' a man will discuss only with another man. What's that new drug they got now for men to use when they need a little help in the bedroom? Viagra, I think they call it, right?"

"If my husband is seeing a doctor, it's certainly not for Viagra. I could, and do, parade around in front of him naked. All he does is tell me to put on some clothes before I catch a cold or to move from in front of the TV."

Rhoda laughed.

"You think this is funny?"

"Hell yeah," she said and snickered.

"I'm not laughing, Rhoda."

"I'm sorry," she managed, snickering some more.

"Pee Wee is not going to a doctor to get Viagra. If he is, he's wasting his money and time, because it's not working for him. There's more action going on in a hospital bed than in ours."

"Annette, maybe I shouldn't say this, but . . . maybe it's not for you," Rhoda said gently.

"What do you mean by that? Like I just said, I am his wife!"

"And this is the real world. His old ass went out and bought a Firebird, and a red one at that. That's one of the most popular chick magnets in the geriatric community. For males. We women have to use a lot more props to attract attention. But I don't want to go into that right now."

As soon as Rhoda paused, I jumped in. "I don't want to go into this shit right now, either."

"Just let me finish. If Pee Wee's with some other woman, I can assure you she's not some douche bag our age that he can satisfy by playin' with her titties and a few half-ass thrusts—"

I cut her off in midsentence. "Rhoda, speak for yourself. It takes more than a few thrusts and playing with my titties for a man to satisfy me!"

"You're missin' the point—"

I cut her off again. "I'm his age. You're his age. What does that say about us?"

"Annette, you know as well as I do that men our age rarely cheat on us with women our age. To them, there's no more sugar left in a woman's bowl by the time she reaches middle age."

"Louis is only thirty, and I can assure you that he doesn't think my bowl has run out of sugar."

"Now that's a horse of a different color. Men his age don't know any better. To them, tail is tail."

"What's that supposed to mean, Dr. Rhoda?"

"When a man Louis's age wants a woman your age, it's for a different reason than a man our age."

"I'm not following you at all," I complained. "And to tell you the truth, we can end this conversation right now, because wherever it's going, I don't want to go."

"I told you to let me finish. Anyway, men our age eventually stop seeing women our age as sexual options. We've become too convenient, too familiar to them. And in some cases, too flabby and worn out. It's sad but true. But they still like us enough to keep us around. Like beer or their favorite tool or somethin'. I bet if somebody offered Pee Wee a brand-new easy chair to lounge around in like a lizard, he'd grab it so fast, it would make your head spin. But, he still wouldn't dispose of that damn old, faithful La-Z-Boy of his, which annoys you so much."

"Then explain to me why Louis finds me so sexy and irresistible?"

"I just told you, men his age don't know any better. Maybe his mama weaned him too soon, and now he's got a mama complex."

"Rhoda, if I were you, I'd stop while I was ahead. This conversation is wreaking havoc on my ego. If I keep listening to your theories, you'll have me convinced that my life is no longer worth living."

"I'm only tryin' to help," Rhoda said sharply.

"Well, you're helping me all right. Helping me lose what little dignity I have left. Because of what you've said so far, I'm already tempted to go throw my old, used-up ass off that bridge over the Mahoning River." As grim as this conversation was, I still had to cover my mouth to keep from laughing. But I got serious again right away. "What about you and Bully? You're forty-six, and he's almost fifty," I reminded her.

"Well, Bully and I are exceptions to the rule. We've been together almost as long as I've been with my husband. You know that."

"Rhoda, do you think that Pee Wee is seeing a doctor, and do you think that he's spending time with some woman every Friday, like I thought in the first place?"

"Both. But if I had to choose one, I'd pick the woman. It makes the most sense. He's at that age when men start foolin' around. And like we both know, your husband would rather get a whuppin' than go to a doctor."

"That's what I think."

"Are you goin' to confront him?"

"Why should I? All he'll do is lie about it. Remember last year, when I thought he was having an affair with—"

"Yes, I do. And you thought it was with my daughter."

"I didn't suspect it was your daughter when I first got suspicious."

I didn't like the silence that followed.

"Anyway, he denied he was having an affair with anybody then, too," I said.

"He was tellin' the truth."

"How do we know that for sure? The only thing that we know for sure now is that he was telling the truth about not being involved with the women I accused him of seeing. He could have been fucking five other women, for all we know."

"So what if he was? Annette, you've already fucked another man and lied to your husband. You don't need to justify it now. And certainly not to me. This is the real world, and you can't change it to suit you, so you may as well go with the flow like the rest of us, like I've already advised you to. If Pee Wee is screwin' somebody else, you can't stop him."

"I know that, Rhoda. And I'm not going to try and stop him," I snapped.

I didn't bother to mention to Rhoda the time that she had violently ended an affair her husband had drifted into years ago. When she had found out the woman's name and address, she'd paid her a visit and attacked her. But fighting over a man was one thing that I felt women our age were above. However, I could only speak for myself.

"I'm glad to hear you say that. You've done your job, and if he can't appreciate it, that's his problem. In my opinion, you'd be a fool to get in his face about another woman—unless you want to give him up altogether. Besides, Louis is in the picture now."

"I don't want a divorce," I whined. "And I don't want to grow old by myself. I like Louis, but I don't know if I could live with him. Besides, he's still a young man. He'll want children someday."

"Who the hell said anything about divorce? If Pee Wee drops dead tomorrow, you'll be alone, anyway. And as far as you movin' in with Louis and havin' his babies, I don't think you have anything to worry about in that area."

"What's that supposed to mean?" I asked. Feelings of insecurities that I thought I'd laid to rest crept up on me like armed muggers.

"Girl, Louis is not stupid or naive. That man can see that you are not anybody's spring chicken. I am sure he knows that Mother Nature has put your baby-related equipment in the attic and left you nothin' but a playpen. All he wants is to join you in that playpen for a while. And as fine as he is, he could pick and choose. So if you don't want him, he won't have any trouble findin' a woman who does."

"Pee Wee and I have been through so much together. He's as much a part of my past as you are. I can't dismiss any of that."

"Who said you had to? Look, this is your life now. Enjoy it while you can. Let me get off this phone. I need to go make myself beautiful for my man, and my husband. You should be doin' the same thing for yours."

"I will," I replied. I was already reaching for my compact and lipstick.

"And stop thinkin' about the past!" Rhoda ordered. "You can't do a damn thing to change it."

CHAPTER 13

The Wizard of Oz couldn't change my past, so I knew I couldn't. Hell, I didn't even like to think about it. And I was glad that I had forgotten a lot of it, anyway. But there were some things from my past that entered my mind almost every day. Things that most people experienced only in bad dreams or bad movies.

One was the fact that I'd been sexually abused by one of my mother's oldest and dearest men friends throughout my childhood. He was the man who had fathered the child that Rhoda had helped me abort when I was sixteen.

I could hardly remember a lot of the details of my abuse. But I could never forget how Rhoda had ended my nightmare. She had smothered my elderly abuser to death with a pillow as he slept in the bed in the room he'd rented in the house I now owned.

That low-down, funky, child-raping, horny-ass old Mr. Boatwright's murder had become a blur in my mind, and Rhoda hadn't mentioned it in years. Nor had she mentioned the four others she'd committed that I knew about. I could barely remember the other people she'd killed—and never been held accountable for—but I could remember that they'd all got what they deserved. Those traumatic events still haunted me, but not nearly as much as the one that I'd endured last year.

For several months, I had been viciously harassed by an anonymous enemy. Not only had I received hate mail and a visit from a male prostitute at my home, but I'd received vile packages at my office. I had also received threatening phone calls at home and at work, and once even at my mother's house. My perpetrator had wanted me out of the way so she could be with my husband.

That was why I'd suspected Pee Wee was having an affair back then. That brazen bitch had known things only a woman as close to him as I was could have known. She'd even mailed me a pair of his shorts that were still funky with his body odor. One of the packages that had been sent by FedEx to my office had contained a pile of horseshit.

Throughout that ominous episode, the only thing that kept me from going completely to pieces was the support of Rhoda and her teenage look-alike daughter, Jade.

"Annette, you know I have always had your back, and I always will," Rhoda had told me. Knowing what I knew about my best friend, like how she'd had no problem killing the man who had taken my innocence, I knew that if anybody could "protect" me, it was Rhoda.

"And I'm right behind her, Auntie," Jade had said. The girl had always been a little too grown, vain, sneaky, self-centered, and big for her britches. But so had most of her friends, so none of those character flaws seemed out of the ordinary. I had loved her despite her many flaws, and she'd had me convinced that she loved me, too. Every time she saw me, she bombarded me with so many hugs and kisses, it often annoyed me. But I never complained.

I had been Jade's play auntie, and I had trusted her so much, she had a key to my house. She'd come and gone as she pleased. I'd stood by like a damn fool and let that little hussy walk all over me like I was a doormat. I hadn't realized that she was making a fool out of me at the time, because I was getting what I needed from her and Rhoda. And that was the emotional support I felt I couldn't get from anybody else. I hadn't had the nerve to tell my elderly parents or husband about everything that was going on. But Rhoda and Jade had known every little detail. They had read most of the vicious letters and notes and had seen the contents of most of the disgusting packages.

Not only had Rhoda and Jade been particularly anxious to comfort me after I had received an exceptionally vicious call or letter, they had even offered to help me apprehend and chastise my tormentor. "Auntie, my mama and I can take care of this bitch if you want us to. *Real good,*" Jade had told me. I certainly hadn't wanted Rhoda to kill another person on my account. And once she'd assured me that she wouldn't let it go that far, I agreed to let her and Jade "straighten out" the culprit as soon as we identified her.

We'd zeroed in on Betty Jean Spool, one of my husband's exes. But when she died in a drug-related incident and the threats continued and got even more vicious, I knew I'd accused the wrong person.

I'd been so close to a nervous breakdown, my flesh crawled when I thought about it now. But it had got worse. A threat had arrived in the mail that was directed toward my daughter. It was a picture of her that had been cut and trimmed into the shape of a coffin. My only child meant the world to me. I would have gone up against Satan himself to protect her, and in a way I did.

The perpetrator, the person who wanted me completely out of the picture, even if it meant my death, had turned out to be the last person on earth that I would have suspected: Rhoda's daughter, Jade. I had treated and loved that child like she was my own, but she had convinced her foolish self that my husband was in love with her and the only thing standing in the way was me.

Jade's elaborate stunt had almost destroyed me and my relationship with Rhoda and my husband. And even after that little heifer came clean and "apologized," things were never the same again.

I had never felt so betrayed in my life. That girl had caused me more grief than Mr. Boatwright, and he had raped me for ten years. But I had got over that. I had eventually touched base with others who had experienced sexual abuse on some level. To my horror, I'd realized that that taboo was common and as old as time. But to this day, I didn't know of anybody else who had gone through something like what I'd gone through with Jade.

Somehow, Rhoda and I managed to work through the mess that Jade had created, and things between Pee Wee and me returned to normal. Those things didn't stay normal long. About a month after Jade's confession, Pee Wee started to withdraw. It was a gradual change, but by the end of that month, he had stopped making love to me. When I tried to initiate intimacy, he responded like a cold fish. Not long after that, he was more like a dead fish. I got the message, so I stopped trying. I had a lot of other things going on in my life that I could focus on, and that was just what I did.

One of the things I got more involved in was work. I had a job that a lot of people wouldn't have wanted if it had been handed to them on a silver platter, but there were still some people who were jealous of me because of my job.

Gloria Watson was one of my bill collectors. She had been with the company longer than I had. She had kissed more upper-management butts than a politician, and it had done her no good. I had been promoted from a low-level position as a caller to the coveted manager's position.

Managing thirteen people was not easy. Most of them had chips on both of their shoulders and attitudes that the Devil must have been proud of. During my first two weeks as manager, two of my people threatened me with lawsuits for "harassing" them after I docked their pay because they'd come to work two hours late. I compromised by letting them make up the time on a weekend. I had more trouble with the women than the men. The sisters did so much eyeball rolling and neck rotating in my presence that eventually I started doing it. Those were things that I had specifically avoided doing all my years as a black woman because I didn't want people to stereotype me. The sisters on the daytime talk shows were already doing enough damage to our image.

I had to be very careful about what I said and how I disciplined my female employees. Not just the black women, since the white, Asian, and Hispanic women were just as aloof and mildly hostile toward me. One white woman threatened to go to some affirmative action watchdogs and file a complaint against me, claiming that I was a racist because I had asked her to remove the Confederate flag that she had hanging from a coat hook in her cubicle. I let that go when it was brought to my attention that one of my black male employees had a menacing poster of Huey Newton displayed on a wall in his cubicle. Aside from all that, I enjoyed my work.

"You should try to make that place more sociable," Rhoda told me one day, when she met me for lunch. "I felt like I'd stepped into a walk-in freezer when I walked in today."

"I think it's too late for that. These folks barely speak to me, so what could I possibly do to make the place more sociable?" I asked. I was glad that Rhoda and I had decided to have lunch in my office that day. She had picked up some french fries and salads at Off the Hook, the new restaurant that had just opened up a few blocks away.

"Well, bein' the boss, you can do certain things that might help. Like I did."

"Rhoda, you run a child-care center in your house. The two women who work for you do most of the work. How many times do I have to remind you of that?" I said, rolling my eyes and rotating my neck. I cleared my throat and took a drink from the tall cup of iced tea that Rhoda had bought, and then I laughed.

"And not only do my people adore and respect me, but they never complain." She was right. Lizel Hunter and her cousin Wyrita Hayes, both in their late twenties, adored Rhoda. They had quit their backbreaking jobs at the steel mill where Rhoda's husband worked on the same day to come work for her.

"Well, you must be paying those sisters well, or they are bigger fools than I thought."

"I do pay them more than they were makin' at that damn mill. But I do more than that. Me, I believe in the incentive factor. If there is incentive, there is process improvement and job satisfaction. You know how most folks hate Mondays? Well, every Monday I treat Lizel and Wyrita and myself to a nice catered lunch. And I always let them pick out what they want the week before. Neither one has missed a Monday in weeks."

I looked at Rhoda and blinked.

"They are so motivated and eager to please that I'm more of a figurehead than I am their boss. I love takin' care of children, but I rarely have to lift a finger. Food is the answer to all of life's problems." Rhoda nodded toward the french fries left on her plate. "A good meal is the American dream and the only thing that could give sex a run for its money. And food could give money itself a hearty run, too, for that matter."

"I'm sure a lot of people would argue with you about that. But I won't go there myself right now. Yes, food is a great pacifier. To some of us, it's too much of a pacifier." I paused when Rhoda gave me an amused look. "But I don't think that a catered lunch is what

I need in my life right now. You, of all people, know about the war I've been fighting with the scale most of my life. I've made some real progress, but I'm still trying to lose a little more weight," I told her, sucking in my stomach.

The one good thing that had come out of that fiasco with Jade was the fact that the stress of it had altered my appetite. I had been wrestling with my weight since I was a toddler. I had tried every diet in the book. Once, I'd even fasted on nothing but water for four days straight and had *gained* five more pounds. Nothing had ever worked for me, until Jade's betrayal.

"So?"

"So, I don't want a lot of temptations around me anymore if I can help it."

"Then don't participate. This is for your workers. But since you've been so disciplined lately, I don't see any reason why you can't participate in moderation. Shit. Just because there's a slab of ribs starin' you in the face, that doesn't mean you have to eat the whole damn thing."

"I'll think about it," I said, giving Rhoda a thoughtful look.

CHAPTER 14

The more I thought about Rhoda's suggestion about the catered lunches, the more I liked it. But I still had some concerns about my relationship with food. I could never forget that it had once been my best friend and my worst enemy at the same time. However, my eating habits had changed dramatically since last year. It was the only thing that I had Rhoda's daughter to thank for, even though her antics had almost cost me my sanity.

I hadn't run into the arms of Reverend Upshaw and fellow church members to get comfort and guidance from them when Jade was on my case. I certainly could have used their support during that living nightmare.

One reason I hadn't run to the church was that I was too ashamed to let the world know how naive and stupid I'd been to let a teenager pull so much wool over my eyes. Another reason was that I knew every member of the congregation would have tried to convince me that I needed to "forget and forgive" what had happened.

Even though Rhoda was my best friend, I knew in my heart that I could never forget and forgive what her daughter had done to me. There had been a few hellish events in my life that I had been able to forget and forgive, but not this one. It was unspeakable.

As far as I was concerned, Jade's "apology" after she'd been exposed, had done no good. Her remorse had been so weak and insincere, a blind man could have seen through it. She had fooled her mother, but she had not fooled me.

I had not even opened the ninety-nine-cent Christmas card that she had had the nerve to send to me last year. It had been postmarked a week after Christmas and had postage due, and she'd misspelled my name in the address. As far as I was concerned, it was a subtle way for her to let me know that she could still torment me.

I wanted to keep that shit fresh and at the front of my mind as a reminder and a warning so that I could remain alert. I knew that even that wouldn't be enough for me to avoid another betrayal. But if and when it happened again, at least I'd be better prepared.

In addition to my always being on high alert now, I could no longer even eat some of the food items that Jade used to supply me with. The sight of them made me sick now. Like the Big Macs she used to deliver to me at home and at my office—three at a time—and the whole slabs of ribs that she used to bring to me, because it amused her to watch me eat them. Then there were the banana splits that she used to make, which were so huge, she had to put them on a platter. As much as I had enjoyed stuffing myself with all that crap, I was glad that those days were over. Looking back on all that now, I realized Jade had tried to kill me with food by making me eat myself to death.

I never would have guessed that it would take something that extreme and bizarre for me to get down to a more healthy weight. I was still a full-figured woman, but a size sixteen was a lot more attractive on me than the size twenty-four that I'd become so accustomed to.

For the first time in my life, I felt good about my body. But I didn't give all the credit to Jade. The fact that my husband had changed so much had also affected my eating habits. I couldn't remember the last time I'd crawled into bed with a family-size pizza and eaten it all by myself. Since the scale had been my enemy for so many years, I rarely weighed myself. But when I went shopping now, the clerks led me away from the muumuus, the shapeless blouses, and the elastic-waist pants with legs so wide you couldn't tell where one ended and the other began.

Last week I entered a clothing store that I had not been near since high school. For one thing, it was for petite women. They didn't have any large women working there and didn't even want them on the premises! The last time I'd entered Little Bits with Rhoda, during our senior year in high school, a rude clerk had promptly informed me that they didn't carry my size, but that there was a Tiger's Den across the street, a run-down warehouse of a store, with an elephant in a tutu on its logo, that catered to the "big-boned" women. I had never felt so humiliated in my life. I went home and ate a whole baked chicken that day. My life was so different now, and I wanted to keep it that way. With the exception of my shaky marriage, I was a happy woman.

Rhoda and I had almost finished our lunch. I was glad, because I was ready for her to leave. I didn't like all the thoughtful looks she kept giving me and some of the things she was saying.

"You are at a fairly acceptable size now, Annette. But you've lost a lot of weight in a short period of time, and that can't be too good for a woman your age. But you can still eat most of the things you like as long as you know when to push your plate away. It can't be that hard." Rhoda speared a slice of cucumber from her salad. More than half of her french fry order was still sitting in front of her, getting cold. Leaving that much food uneaten was something that I rarely did. Even now. But the difference now was, I didn't overload my plate. Therefore, when I did leave half of my food uneaten, it wasn't that much. "I know how you feel." Rhoda had on a Bob Marley T-shirt and a pair of jeans that I probably couldn't have squeezed one of my legs into.

"You are a goddamn liar. You can sit here, with your size three–wearing self, and talk all that shit and still not know how I feel. You've never had to walk in my shoes." I stabbed a sliver of carrot with my fork, then started to nibble on it like a rabbit. "It is not easy to resist good food. Sometimes it's still a struggle for me to eat only when I'm hungry."

Rhoda gave me a dismissive wave and shook her head. "Well, it must be comforting to know that most men love women with more meat on their bones."

"And that's another thing. That's one of the worst clichés in the

English language. That's something fat women say to make themselves feel better. No man has ever told me that."

Rhoda gave me an exasperated look before she popped a bouquet of french fries into her mouth. That gesture evoked a memory that brought tears to my eyes. The first conversation that I'd had the nerve to initiate with Rhoda, in the school cafeteria in eighth grade, was about me eating the leftover french fries on her tray. We'd been best friends ever since. Despite the fact that Jade used to shower me with french fries, too, it was the one thing that she had not ruined my taste for.

"That catered lunch really sounds like a good deal. But I don't know if my budget will allow me to treat my employees to a weekly feast," I said. "I'll call up my boss before I leave work today and run it by him."

I knew that Mr. Mizelle, one of the nicest bosses in town, would probably let me do just about anything I wanted to do. It was no secret that he was basically our boss in name only. I had been running the show single-handedly for years. And, as a matter of fact, he had also encouraged me to be more sociable with the people I supervised. He hosted regular potlucks and a few catered affairs at the main office downtown, where he occupied a huge office on the top floor of one of Richland's biggest office buildings.

Rhoda must have been reading my mind. "That old goat you work for loves you and would make a budget for treats if you asked him to. If you work out a contract or an informal agreement, if you're more comfortable with that, Louis Baines will give you a really good deal. Off the Hook is the kind of place that has potential. It could be a huge success. But we have to help make that happen."

"You have a contract with this Louis Baines?"

Rhoda nodded. "No offense to your mama and all the good old down-home treats she offers at the Buttercup, but newcomers like Louis need our support more."

I had cruised by the new restaurant in question a few times and had been meaning to check it out. I guessed I had no choice but to do so now.

"My mother would have a fit if she found out I was using somebody else's catering services instead of hers," I groaned.

"That's true. But what your mama doesn't know won't hurt her," Rhoda responded. "Please do yourself a favor and give Louis a chance."

"I'll think about it. But if I do and he disappoints me, your name will be mud in my book."

CHAPTER 15

Thanks to my generous late stepfather, my mother had inherited the restaurant that he'd opened and had worked it into a huge success. The Buttercup, which would eventually be mine, was the most exclusive black-owned restaurant in town. Even though Richland was an hour away from Cleveland, and just a fraction of its size, people came from as far away as Cleveland to feast at the Buttercup.

"Your mother doesn't have to know," said Rhoda. "And besides, that woman can't handle all the jobs she gets now! Have you forgotten how my bowlin' team had to get on a waitin' list last month, when we tried to use your mama's caterin' services to celebrate our anniversary?"

"Yeah. But my mother had to turn down a lot of jobs last month because of that strawberry farmers' convention," I said. "She got paid big-time to feed them."

"Just think about it," Rhoda suggested, rising. The jeans she wore looked like they belonged on a doll. Her long jet-black hair was in a single braid, which touched the middle of her back. It seemed like the older she got, the more beautiful she got. And her dark brown skin was as smooth as a baby's behind. Her eyes were as large, clear, and green, as they'd been the first time I laid eyes on her, at thirteen. But now there was often an unbearable look of sadness in those beautiful eyes.

When it came to looks, Rhoda and I were an odd couple—in high school we were referred to as Beauty and the Beast—but like me, she had had her share of traumas. Not only had she lost a brother and a son, she'd lost part of herself. Cancer had robbed her of her breasts, and a mild stroke had disrupted her life and temporarily disabled her about ten years ago. I was glad that even though she had endured so much pain, she still had an optimistic outlook on life. As my best friend, she had enriched my life in so many ways.

"By the way, I am glad to see you wearin' makeup on a regular basis now," Rhoda said, smiling. Her eyes rolled up to the top of my head. "And keep the braids," she advised, with a wink.

I wobbled up from my seat and walked her out of my office. As soon as we reached the main floor, everybody stopped talking and tried to act like they didn't see me. That was what they always did when I approached their work area, and I didn't like it one bit. It made me feel like an outsider.

I let out a loud sigh. "You see what I mean," I said in a low voice as Rhoda and I headed to the nearest exit. I was glad that our company was on the ground floor of the midsize gray building, which we shared with several other businesses.

"The first time you cater an event with Louis Baines, you get a ten percent discount," Rhoda mentioned. "And free beverages."

We stopped as soon as we got outside.

"You sure are trying hard to get me to work with this guy. If I didn't know any better, I'd swear that there was something in it for you," I teased.

"There is. I get an event catered for free each time I send him a new client."

I gave Rhoda a pensive look. "Let me think about it. But before I do anything, I'd like to sample what this dude has to offer. Maybe you and I can have lunch there one day soon so I can check him out," I suggested. "Personally, I am always interested in sampling somebody else's down-home cooking. But you do know that I don't have just black folks and whites working for me. I don't know if my Hispanic and Asian employees like greens and fried chicken."

"That's another thing," Rhoda chirped, waving a finger in my face. "Even though Off the Hook is a black-owned restaurant, they offer a variety of cuisines. Tacos, spaghetti, and fried rice to die for, just to name a few." Rhoda pursed her lips and shook her head. I shook my head, too, because this conversation was bringing back too many memories. The items she had just mentioned used to be music to my ears. "Just tryin' to help, girl."

"And I appreciate that. I'll call you," I said, giving Rhoda a hug before I turned to go back inside.

Before I went back to my office, I strolled over to Gloria Watson's cubicle, which was located across the hall from the ladies' room. I cleared my throat to get her attention.

"What's wrong now?" she asked as soon as she looked up from her cluttered desk and saw me standing in her doorway. There was a scowl on her face, which was normal for a pit bull like Gloria. She was one of the most confrontational women I knew. For reasons she kept to herself, she was mad at the world. My predecessor had abruptly resigned because of all the stress Gloria had caused her. Even our boss, Mr. Mizelle, was terrified of this sister. For the sake of my nerves, I addressed her only when I had to.

"Do you have a few minutes?" I asked. Even though I had approached her in a nonthreatening manner and with a smile, her body stiffened. Within seconds her perpetual scowl intensified.

From the way she reared back in her chair, I could tell that her neck was ready to roll. I diffused that with an even wider smile. She still asked me in a guarded tone of voice, "What did I do now?"

"Nothing's wrong, Gloria. I was just wondering if you could do me a favor."

She hesitated and eyed me with suspicion and exasperation. "That depends on what it is." Her voice was already on the husky side, but when she was not in a good mood, she sounded downright masculine. Like now. It sounded like I was listening to Darth Vader.

Even though Gloria and I were close in age, she looked like somebody's grandmother. Most of her frizzy hair was white at the roots. She had permanent frown lines around her mouth and on her forehead. Now she was the one wearing muumuus to work three or four times a week. Last year I had occupied that role, and she used to offer comments of pity on my attire from time to time. Had she been nicer to me, I would have donated some of my fat clothes to her, instead of to Goodwill and the Salvation Army.

Gloria didn't even attempt to hide her impatience. She moved a Snickers Bar wrapper and a half-eaten scone on a napkin around on her desk until she located a pen. "What is it?" she asked, tapping the tip of the pen on her desk.

I took a very deep breath before I opened my mouth again. "Gloria, I . . . Girl, that's a lovely blouse you have on today," I told her, clapping my hands together like a seal. "Is it new? Red looks so good on you. But then you look so nice every day. . . ."

Gloria was the kind of person that you had to use a lot of butter on if you wanted to bring her up to an acceptable level of civility. I didn't like to be insincere or phony, but I had come to believe that you had to do what you had to do when it came to people like Gloria. As soon as I stopped talking, she seemed to soften right before my eyes. The generous helping of butter that I'd just offered her melted in her mouth. A wide grin immediately replaced her trademark scowl.

"Oh? You like my blouse?" she replied, twisting around in her seat so I could see the blouse better. It really was a lovely blouse, but it didn't do much for her. For one thing, it was so small that the thread around each button had already started to unravel. I guess I didn't respond fast enough with another compliment, because Gloria wobbled to her feet, brushing off the sleeve of her blouse, still grinning. "I got it at the Tiger's Den the other day. I go there all the time. I've seen you in there before, too, so I know *you* know how hard it is for big oxen like us to find something cute." She smiled. I was disappointed to hear that she still thought of me as a big ox.

"Yes, I do know," I said. I felt so abruptly defeated that my shoulders slumped, and I shifted my weight from one foot to the other. Her assessment of my appearance was a veiled insult. Apparently, I had not used enough butter on her.

Her next comment caught me completely off guard. "But you are blessed because you don't have to go to the fat women's store no more since you lost all that weight. And I've been meaning to tell you how sharp you look these days," Gloria said, with a nod. I was pleased at the way she looked at my outfit with admiration and envy.

"Thank you, Gloria." I stood up straighter and cleared my throat. "Now what favor did you want?"

"I know you are busy, but could you please check around and see who all is available for lunch next Monday?" I said. "And let them know it's on me."

Gloria's jaw dropped, revealing a mouth full of cavities, even though we offered all our employees an insurance plan that covered 90 percent of their dental needs. "Lunch? Are you taking us to lunch?"

I nodded. "Yes and no. I'm going to have lunch brought in and served in the break room. You all deserve it, and, I've been meaning to do it for a while now." I didn't like telling that lie, but it was such a small one, it didn't bother me that much.

"All right," Gloria said, picking up a notepad. "I know I'll be available for lunch next Monday. What kind of food are we talking about? Please don't include fried chicken wings. Black folks done worshipped chicken wings so much, it's a wonder we ain't all sprouted feathers and wings ourselves."

"We won't be having any chicken wings," I said, with a chuckle. "But when and if we ever do have chicken, you don't have to eat any of it. I will make sure you have a lot of other things to choose from."

"But I do love me some chicken breasts and thighs, so don't cross chicken off your list yet," Gloria said, holding up her hand like she was trying to defend herself.

"I am going to check out Off the Hook, that new place I keep hearing about."

I could tell from the look on Gloria's plain, round face that my choice pleased her. Her eyes got wide, and she smiled even more. I was tempted to tell her that she should smile more often. Despite her cavities, she still had a fairly nice smile. When she smiled, she looked a lot more attractive and younger. But I didn't want to move too fast. This sister was the kind that you had to approach with extreme caution.

"What you say!" she shouted, with a look of pure ecstasy on her face. This time she was the one clapping her hands like a seal. "That's some good stuff, girl. My godchild Gootie had Off the Hook cater her wedding last week. I will get you a list of names for lunch right away."

Gloria was so excited, she almost knocked me down while trying to get out of her cubicle so fast. She wore a black, floor-length skirt that fluttered and flapped like a bedsheet on a clothesline with each step she took. The tail of it swept the floor like a whisk broom. From her body language and reaction, I knew that I had hit on something good. Now all I had to worry about was this Louis Baines and me hitting it off.

CHAPTER 16

I knew that Gloria liked to eat. That was obvious. And it was no secret that I had not missed too many meals. At least half of my other employees were carrying around more meat on their bones than they should have, too. Food was obviously the drug of choice in my workplace. Therefore, I was convinced that the lunch proposal was a brilliant idea. Work would be a lot more pleasant if my employees were more cheerful and more cordial to me. And the way things were in my personal life, I needed something to boost my morale.

I felt so good the rest of that day that I didn't even think about the fact that my husband was giving me the cold shoulder on a regular basis, with no explanation.

When I got home that evening around six, Pee Wee was already slumped in his La-Z-Boy, snoring like a moose. The TV was on, and there was a ball game on that he had taped a few months ago. My daughter, Charlotte, had taped a note to the front of the microwave oven to let me know that she was across the street, having hot dogs and baked beans for dinner with one of her little friends. It was a Wednesday sleepover. She had school tomorrow, but she had taken a change of clothes with her, so I didn't have to worry about that. There was some leftover baked chicken in the refrigerator, which I had planned to serve for dinner.

Charlotte was growing up and anxious to spend even more time with her friends and their families. Since I'd led such a sheltered life and had so few friends, I was pretty lenient with her in that area. But I thoroughly checked out each family that she associated with. The only friend I didn't allow her to sleep over with was a girl named Lonna Trapp. Lonna had an alcoholic stepfather and three teenage brothers, who had already fathered a few babies. I knew that I wasn't God and that I could not protect my child from everything, but I did everything I could possibly do to keep her from being victimized by some predator. I didn't want her to repeat my history.

I didn't even bother to remove my black leather jacket. I looked at my watch and turned back around and went outside. I didn't realize I was walking on my tiptoes until I had stepped off the porch. There was no reason for me to be so quiet and cautious. Armageddon would not have disturbed Pee Wee, with the state of unconsciousness that he was in. But I didn't want to take that chance. I didn't want him to wake up, because I was not in the mood for another brush-off. Before I knew it, I was driving toward Louis Baines's restaurant.

I was greeted at the door by a fairly young brother, with a body that immediately made my mouth water and my crotch itch. "I'm Louis Baines, your host and head cook," he told me.

I didn't see any reason to tell him my name yet, so I didn't. But I told him that it was nice to meet him. He was balancing a large silver platter in the palm of one hand as he smiled at me. The whole scene seemed symbolic. Here was a gorgeous man coming in my direction, about to serve himself to me on a silver platter. He was not that much taller than me, but he was built like a linebacker. He had smooth light brown skin and long, thick black hair, which he wore combed back like a duck. He reminded me of Ron O'Neal, the man who had starred in that gangster movie from the seventies called *Super Fly*. His eyes were so black, they sparkled when the light hit them. He had nice full lips and a nice smile, even though his teeth were a little dingy and crooked. But he was so fine, he could have had fangs like Dracula's hanging out of his mouth and it wouldn't have mattered.

"Sister, will you be eating here, or would you like to order to go?" he asked, handing me a menu with his free hand.

The platter that he was balancing contained a meat loaf in the shape of a heart. I couldn't tell if that was gravy or sauce flowing from the top of it like lava. But whatever it was, it belonged in heaven. I had planned to get a plate to take home, but I felt so comfortable, I decided to stay.

"Uh, I will be eating here. May I have a booth?" I asked, giving him one of my biggest smiles.

"Follow me," he ordered.

I trailed behind him like a puppy. He stopped abruptly and turned to face me, still balancing that platter in one hand. Without a word of warning, he draped his arm around my shoulder and led me to a booth in the back of the small main room. He gently helped me sit down, guiding me as if I was an old woman. But he wasn't looking at me as if I was an old woman.

It was a small restaurant and nothing to write home about. Plastic curtains covered the windows, and the floor looked like it had not been waxed in weeks. There were six dull brown vinyl booths along the wall and several tables in the center of the room. Despite the fact that the tablecloths looked cheap and outdated and the place mats were made out of paper, the restaurant had a nice, homey feel to it. My host must have been reading my mind.

"I hope to have this place looking like a showroom in a few months. But I was warned that it would be a struggle to get a new business off the ground. If we survive the first few months and make a decent profit, I will be happy."

"Well, I hope that you will," I told him.

He sucked in a deep breath and pursed his lips, looking at me like I was a piece of meat on a silver platter myself. The thought of that almost made me laugh. "If you don't mind me saying, you sure do look nice today," he said. "Those braids make you look so regal." He must have been having a damn good day—or I was hotter than I gave myself credit for!—because he was beaming.

"Thank you," I replied in a low voice, patting the side of my head, glad now that I'd let my hairdresser talk me into wearing braids again. I shifted my butt to a more comfortable position. I tried not to look at my charming host, but it couldn't be avoided. He was looking me straight in the eyes.

"Now, if you will excuse me, I have to get back to that newlywed couple over there," he said, with a grin, nodding toward the heart-shaped meat loaf on the platter and then toward the other side of the room. I was not interested in the newlyweds, so I didn't even bother to look in their direction. "Your waitress will be with you in a few moments. I wouldn't want to keep a sister like you waiting long." He winked at me. I didn't know if he was just being nice or if he was flirting. I was relieved when he disappeared from my view.

He returned so fast that I didn't have much time to inspect his place more. But I didn't need to. I was already impressed with everything I'd seen so far. When a young waitress approached my booth, with her pad and pencil ready to take my order, he politely waved her away.

"Did you decide yet?" he asked me, that beaming look still on his face.

I hadn't even looked at the menu. "No. But why don't you tell me what I'd probably like?" I suggested. I swallowed hard, and I wanted to pinch myself for saying something that sounded so suggestive. The last thing I wanted this man to think was that I was on the prowl and looking for some action, because that was not the case. Despite the fact that I was neglected and ignored at home, I had no desire to start something with another man.

"I'll take good care of you," he told me, giving me a mysterious smile.

If he was trying to provoke me, he was doing a damn good job. But like I said, I was not looking for any action. I had had it, and if that was all the action I was going to get, I had to live with that. However, I liked knowing other men still found me attractive.

No matter how innocent the encounter was, and despite our mutual innuendos, I should have gotten my meal and run the hell out of that place. But I didn't, and I would live to regret that decision for the rest of my life.

CHAPTER 17

I was glad that I had ordered just a half order of the deep-fried shrimp. But even that was too much. The order included fries and a roll, but I had requested that those two items be left off my plate. After just a few bites, I started to burp like a baby. And even though I covered my mouth with my hand each time, a man in the booth in front of me turned around and gave me a dirty look.

After finishing just half of my half order and half a glass of iced tea, I felt so stuffed, I knew that it would be to my advantage to stop eating. My stomach felt the way it used to feel during my all-you-can-eat days, like I was about to explode. It was a feeling that I could no longer tolerate, and I avoided it as often as I could. I had read somewhere that when a woman lost a lot of weight, her stomach shrank. I didn't know if that was true or not, but I couldn't eat nearly as much as I used to eat.

I didn't know how long my body would continue to reinvent itself, so I planned to enjoy it for as long as I could. I loved having a real waistline. I recalled how Aretha Franklin had lost a tremendous amount of weight back in the seventies. Then she'd flaunted her new body in a pair of hot pants! But her weight had returned with a vengeance. The last time I saw her on TV, she looked like Moby Dick, the same way I used to look. I didn't want the world to ever see me like that again.

I was looking downright cute today, and I knew it. I had on my moderately tight black leather skirt with a modest split up the side. It was one of my favorite pieces of clothing. I had liked it so much when I tried it on in the boutique on Jersey Street where a former Miss Richland shopped that I had purchased two more just like it at the same time. Under the matching jacket, I had on a white blouse that was cut just low enough to tease. I still had most of my ample bosom, and it was a lot firmer than it used to be. My sporadic trips to the gym had paid off. I had noticed how Louis's eyes had lingered on my bosom when he seated me.

I had paid the cashier and was on my way back to my booth to leave a tip on the table when Louis came back out of a room I assumed was the kitchen. I'd seen a couple of waiters and the same waitress who had attempted to wait on me coming out with trays of food and tall drinks.

"Sister, I hope you enjoyed your meal," Louis said, his eyes traveling from my face to my bosom. He stood dangerously close to me in front of the booth.

"I did," I assured him as I dropped a 30 percent tip on the table. "Uh, can I take a menu with me to look over? I understand you do catering."

I already had the goods on this man and his business. Before I'd left my office, I'd called Rhoda up again. She had told me what was on his menu and all the catering details. And he was such a nice dude that I liked him already.

"Yes, I do offer catering services." His eyes sparkled even more. "You can take a menu and anything else out of here that you want. Including me," he offered, with a wink.

I was glad that I was too dark for him to see me blushing. My face felt like it was in front of a campfire. I gave him a slightly exasperated look and shook my head. "Thank you, but a menu will be enough," I said, winking back at him.

"Just kidding. I hope I didn't offend you." I could see clean through the apologetic look that he offered with a sheepish grin. Had I been naked, this man could not have shown more interest in me.

"You didn't," I told him. "It takes a lot to offend me."

He sniffed and smiled, and then he shifted his weight from one foot to the other. "When I get too close to the speed limit, would you let me know?"

I shrugged. "I don't know what the speed limit is in this state," I said, and I was telling the truth.

"I don't either, but something tells me I might be getting close to it. I know I'm gwine a little too fast. . . ."

I smiled at him and blinked. "But you can keep going. You might catch me, and you might not." I had *never* behaved in such a brazen and flirtatious manner before in my life. Even during my days as a prostitute. "Are you this friendly with all your female customers?" I asked boldly, folding my arms. It seemed like everything I did drew attention to my bosom. At least in his case. He looked at my bosom again, this time so long that I shifted the strap on my purse so that it was in front of me, as opposed to hanging off the side of my shoulder.

"Just the beautiful ones." He pursed his lips and shifted his eyes like he was processing some information in his head. "And that's not too often. This is the kind of place that attracts mostly water buffalo. Last night a herd coming from a bingo game stampeded this place." He laughed. I didn't.

"Oh," I said, with my lips stiff and my eyes narrowed.

"Not that I'm making fun of women in that category!" He held up his hands and shook his head. "I'm just trying to make you smile, because you look so cute when you do. You seem like the kind of lady who can appreciate a good joke."

"I am. You got one?"

He gave me a dry look; then he laughed. "I'm sorry. I wasn't raised to make fun of people, especially my sisters. Now what was that you were saying about us doing business?"

"I'd like to consider your restaurant for some catering for my office," I said nervously. I knew that if I was going to do business with this man, I had to respond to him in a businesslike manner. No matter how frivolous he was behaving.

"And we'll do it with a smile," he announced, grinning. "How did you hear about me?"

"Rhoda O'Toole is one of your regular clients. And she's anxious to get that free meal for referring me."

"Bless her heart. I didn't catch your name," he said, dipping his head so that he had to buck his eyes to look at me. He was drop-dead gorgeous, and that little gesture made him look downright cute, too.

I sniffed and tilted my head. I was finally at a place where it gave me a great deal of pride to identify myself. "I'm Annette Davis. I am a manager at Mizelle's Collection Agency. Earlier today I made my employees an offer they couldn't refuse."

"Oh? I hope it includes my services on a regular basis," Louis said, with a hopeful look on his face. He turned his head to the side and cupped his ear. He had small hands and small ears, not a good sign. According to Rhoda that meant a small dick. I couldn't believe what I was thinking! Just because this man had paid me some attention and flirted with me so blatantly, I had the nerve to be fantasizing about his dick. I forced myself not to look at his feet to see if they were small, too.

"It could." I grinned. "Uh, I don't know about setting up a contract yet, though. I thought I'd have a couple of events, and if my people like your food, we'll go from there. There are a couple of other places I'd like to consider, too," I lied. I had already made up my mind. I wanted to work with Louis, but I didn't want him to know that yet. I wanted to get as good a deal as I could.

"Let me do this for you. How many folks are we talking about?"

"Well, including myself, I have a staff of fourteen full-time employees. There are two boys who work in the mail room, but they only work a couple of hours in the morning and a couple in the afternoon. My boss drops in from time to time."

"So roughly speaking, we're talking about a nice-size party," Louis said. He glanced around and paused. "Would you be more comfortable discussing this in my office?"

I was glad that he was looking and acting more businesslike now, but I was still leery of him. There was no telling how he would behave if he got me in his office. I was not the smartest woman in the world, but I could tell that this man wanted more from me than a catering agreement.

CHAPTER 18

"I don't think that discussing this in your office is necessary." I paused and exhaled. "But thanks for the offer."

Had I been just a little more disgusted with my husband, I would have followed Louis to his office with bells on. His attention had intrigued me, and that had caused me to let my defenses down. But the fact of the matter was that I needed some attention. And, without even trying, I had caught the eye of a young, smart man with the looks of a movie star.

"Are you afraid I might bite?" He leered at me.

"I think you're getting close to that speed limit," I warned.

"Guilty as charged!" he said, his hands in the air as if he was a guest on *COPS*.

"I have to get home soon. Do you have a business card? I can call you up and arrange an appointment in the next few days."

"I don't have my business cards yet, but you can call me at the number on the menu," he said, nodding toward the menu that he had placed in my hand. "What is the best day for you and your employees?"

"Huh? Oh. First of all, I have to let you know that everything depends on the budget I can get my boss to approve."

"Hmm." His face dropped like a lead balloon. "So this is not a sure thing?"

"I'm not sure yet. Like I just said, everything depends on the budget that I can get approved."

I had worked out a tentative agreement with Mr. Mizelle and my employees just before I'd left work. We would use the funds for our Christmas cash bonus to each employee, which was taxable, our holiday celebrations—in addition to the regular major national holidays, we had office parties to celebrate everything from St. Patrick's Day to Flag Day—and our annual company picnic to cover the cost of a weekly feast, to be catered by Louis Baines—or some other caterer, should his services not satisfy our needs and palates. This was also information that I felt I didn't need to reveal to Louis yet. I was convinced that if I did, it would weaken my leverage.

"Is there anything I can do to help you make up your mind?"

I shook my head. "I don't know your prices yet. I don't know anything about your dependability and service. And, I hate to say this, I don't know the quality of your selections. Now the prawns were good, but that's not all we would be ordering. The bottom line is, I can't commit to anything, or approach my boss, until I compare you with some of the other caterers that I'm considering." Because of Rhoda's glowing recommendation, I had not approached any other caterers before Louis. And now I knew I wouldn't. I was dead meat as soon as I'd tasted those fried shrimp.

However, I had to admit that Louis's good looks and aggressive approach had a lot to do with my decision, too. I didn't want to reveal that information to him. He didn't need to know what a pushover I was. I couldn't tell if he already had a big head; most men who looked like him did. His good looks and business ownership were more than enough to give him a head the size of a watermelon. I didn't want to contribute to it.

The cost of the weekly catering service didn't matter. I had already turned over that stone. My boss, Mr. Mizelle, had agreed to pay the difference, if it was necessary. "This is a splendid incentive, Annette! I support you wholeheartedly. All for the sake of productivity. If this gets our folks to improve their attendance and not resign after a few bad experiences with some of our debtors, we'll meet our goals more frequently," he had told me through his birdlike lips.

Louis coughed to get my attention back. "I can assure you, I will offer you an arrangement that will be within your budget." The fact that he seemed somewhat desperate concerned me, too. I didn't want to do business with him out of pity. I did not make it to a manager's position by working with people because I felt sorry for them.

"We'll see. Anyway, I was thinking about setting up something on a regular basis, like lunch every other Monday, to begin with. Then, if things work out, maybe we'll do it every Monday. Or if you make me an offer I can't refuse, we can start out by doing it every Monday for a few months on a trial basis. If things go well, we'll do something more permanent, like my friend Rhoda does. She told me that she's committed for a whole year."

"That's right. And she won't regret it. Let's focus on you and your needs now. How about this coming Monday? Just tell me what you want and what time you want it delivered. I already know your work address. Uh . . . several of my irresponsible friends have received a few lovely calls from your collection agency." This seemed to embarrass him. He gave me an uncomfortable look. "I want you to know right now that I don't condone people running out on their financial obligations. That's why I don't offer credit or take checks or credit cards from my friends."

"I know exactly what you mean. I have friends like that, too," I admitted. We both laughed. "Now, if you don't mind, can we get back to what you can do for me this Monday?"

"Oh? You'll go for it on a trial basis?"

I nodded. "On a trial basis," I agreed.

"We also set up everything and do all the serving. That part is optional, and there's no charge for it."

"Like I told you, I can't commit to anything definite just yet. I need to . . . to, uh, think about this a little more. Let me sleep on it, and I'll call you tomorrow. How is that?"

"That's fine if that's what you want. But this Monday will be a complimentary meal. . . ."

I let out a mild gasp. "A complimentary meal for my whole staff? What a nice surprise!" This man was after my own heart, and at the rate he was going, he'd have me in his hip pocket in no time.

He nodded. "And we'll include enough for the two boys in the mail room, and your boss, in case he shows up. As a matter of fact, I will make sure that there are plenty leftovers for you and your staff to enjoy later."

"That's very nice of you. Do you do this for all your new customers?"

Louis looked at me for a long time before he responded. "Just the special ones," he said. "The only thing is, I choose the meal."

"Oh, I see." I expected him to tell me that he would slap together a few trays with some cheese, crackers, salami, and bologna, or something along those lines. He surprised me again.

"I do a really nice Yankee pot roast, with smashed potatoes, green beans, and Hawaiian dinner rolls, and pecan pie for dessert."

I had to look down for a moment to compose myself. "My stepdaddy called them smashed potatoes, too," I said, getting misty-eyed. I had to blink hard to keep from shedding a tear or two. I had adored my stepdaddy.

"I'll include enough for your stepdaddy, too."

I looked down again. This time my gaze landed right on his feet. They were fairly large. I cleared my throat and quickly returned my attention to his face. "He passed some years ago," I croaked.

"I'm so sorry to hear that. And I hope I didn't upset you. Would you like a glass of water?"

"I'd rather have a glass of wine, if you serve it here," I admitted, looking around for a bar.

"I don't have a liquor license yet, but I'm working on it. If you'd really like a drink, there's a cute little Irish place across the street—"

"Oh no," I protested, holding my hand up. "I really do have to get home. But thanks, anyway." I started to back toward the exit.

"What time do you want us to deliver on Monday?"

My jaw dropped. "Oh. Were you really serious about that complimentary meal for my whole staff?"

"Miss Davis, I don't say things I don't mean."

I don't know why I didn't tell him then that I was a Mrs., not a Miss. It was obvious that he was attracted to me, and as much as I hated myself for it, I was attracted to him, too. "You can call me Annette," I said stiffly.

"How about eleven thirty? We can set up and have everything ready by noon."

"That's fine," I said, leaning against the door. His gaze lingered on my face until I opened the door and stumbled back out onto the sidewalk, breathing through my mouth.

He stood in the doorway and watched until I got in my car and drove off.

CHAPTER 19

Pee Wee was *still* laid out in his La-Z-Boy like a corpse about to be embalmed when I got home, and I had been gone for a couple of hours. I stood in the living-room doorway for a few minutes, just watching him. All I could do was shake my head and wonder what I had done to deserve this mess of a husband that I now had on my hands.

But he was my mess, and I had to make the best of the situation. After all, I did still love him.

For some reason, Pee Wee was not snoring. That concerned me right away. I kicked off my shoes and padded across the floor to make sure he was still alive. I was satisfied to see that his chest was moving and that he had a pulse.

There was a test pattern on the TV screen, so I had no idea what he had been watching. A blanket covered him up to his neck, which meant that in his chair was where he planned to spend the night. And that was all right with me.

I took a quick shower and got into bed, but before I turned out the lights, I called Rhoda.

"How come you didn't tell me how cute that caterer was?" I demanded, my head propped up on three pillows.

"I didn't think it was important. So you did go by there?"

"Yes, I did. The food was wonderful. Your boy Louis, he sure knows how to cut a deal. He made me an incredible offer."

"Oh? And what offer is that?"

"He's preparing a complimentary meal for me and my entire staff for Monday. Yankee pot roast with all the trimmings. I'll wait until next week to tell him, but I'm going to work out a weekly deal with him. On a trial basis for a couple of weeks, though. I don't want to commit to something I might regret."

"Oh, he's good. The man really knows how to work on a woman, all right. That pot roast screams. That's one dish that he really puts his foot in! It's one of his best meals. That's how he wooed me into that twelve-month contract. But it's a hell of a contract. If I default, I still have to pay him for the remainin' months. Not that I plan on lettin' him go—with his sexy self."

"And that's another thing." I paused and looked toward the door. "He is a very sexy man, and I almost made a complete fool out of myself, skinning and grinning in his face like a schoolgirl." I laughed, but then I got real serious. "He's kind of young, though."

"Why do you care how young he is?"

"Nothing. I just thought I'd mention it. And he seemed a little . . . countrified. He called mashed potatoes, *smashed* potatoes. That makes a person sound so dumb."

"He's the kind of man that a woman who already has everything needs. Young, dumb, and full of cum."

"Why are you telling me this?"

"Just thought I'd mention it."

"I'm going to call him up tomorrow. The only thing is, I don't want to commit to a yearlong contract, like you did. I'll try him out for a few weeks, and if it works out, maybe I'll agree to something more permanent."

I slept like a baby that night. Pee Wee was gone by the time I made it downstairs the next morning. Just as I was about to leave the house, wearing a yellow silk scarf around my neck, which my daughter had given to me for Mother's Day, and a pair of navy blue slacks with a yellow blouse, Rhoda called. She rarely called me this early in the morning, and when she did, something was usually wrong. I braced myself.

"I just received a disturbin' phone call from New Orleans," she reported, her voice weak and edgy.

"Oh. I hope it's nothing too serious," I replied hoarsely. The last thing I needed to hear was bad news about somebody I cared about.

Rhoda's mother was a major hypochondriac. If you believed that woman, she'd been afflicted with almost every ailment in the book, and with a few that were not in the book. When I used to visit Rhoda when we were kids, her mother was always in a nightgown. Every single day she swallowed pills like candy and ran from one doctor to another, and she had already planned her own funeral. Rhoda's parents had moved to New Orleans years ago so her mother could be closer to her family and "better doctors." Since New Orleans was an hour behind Ohio, a call from somebody back there so early in the morning had to be bad news.

"Is it your mother?" I asked. I couldn't think of anything left for her mother to claim she had. "Is she . . . gone?"

"No, my mother's fine. It's nothin' like that."

It was obvious that Rhoda was stalling. I didn't want to pressure her or sound impatient, so I just remained silent.

"It's Jade," she said finally. It sounded like the life was slowly leaving her voice.

I knew that if it had anything to do with Jade, it had to be bad. Either she had finally killed somebody—like mother, like daughter—or somebody had finally killed her. Despite my feelings toward that child, I hoped that it was neither. I had come to the conclusion that Jade was beyond redemption, but as long as I didn't have to deal with her, I could live with that assessment. It was painful for me to have such feelings toward someone that I had once adored, but that was what it had come to.

"Oh. What did she do this time?" As soon as I said that, I cringed. For one thing, it sounded unreasonably harsh, and the last thing Rhoda needed when it came to that girl was more aggravation. "I didn't mean that the way it sounded, Rhoda," I said quickly.

"Yes, you did. And you know I don't blame you," she said in a distant voice.

"Is Jade in trouble?"

"She *is* trouble, Annette," Rhoda announced. It almost felt like she was talking about somebody we'd seen featured on *America's Most Wanted.* "If anybody knows that, it's you." Rhoda paused and let out something that sounded like a cross between a sniff and a snort. "I just wanted you to know that she's coming home. She hates New Orleans. Daddy called me up to break the news this mornin'."

"Is she coming to visit?" I asked hopefully.

"I wish I could say that that was the case, but I can't. She's comin' to stay. She's even shipped some of her things back already. I found that out when the UPS truck stopped here yesterday evenin', while we were havin' dinner. But I didn't know what she was up to until I got the call from Daddy this mornin'. I don't know what I'm goin' to do with that girl. She flunked out of college and spends most of her time partyin' and drivin' my parents crazy. They can't handle her anymore."

"Well, she is your child, Rhoda. You need to be there for her no matter what she does. I respect that. I'm glad you told me in advance. When is she coming?" My insides had already begun to tighten into a knot. The last person I ever wanted to see again was Jade.

"I'm not sure. Last week she ran off to Mexico to be with some bullfighter that she'd hooked up with during spring break in Cancún. My daddy went down there to try and talk some sense into her hard head. It didn't do a damn bit of good, though. That poor little Mexican boy won't know what bullfightin' is until he locks horns with my wild child. And it's goin' to happen sooner or later."

"What is she going to do back here? Richland, Ohio, is pretty dull compared to New Orleans and Cancún, Mexico." The knot that had formed in my stomach now felt like it was the size of a basketball.

"That's a good question. I called up her big brother down in Mobile. He offered to take control and suggested I ship her to him. But Julian's in a new relationship, and I don't want to burden him with something this big. You remember my daddy's white relatives? Rednecks to the bone, but they are good people. Aunt Lola and Uncle Johnny told me to send her to them so they could whip her into shape. Lord knows, if anybody can do that, it's them."

"She should go live with them," I advised.

"I love my white relatives, but they have white friends and white relatives that still think the old way. The Klan way. If I sent her to Alabama and somethin' happened to her, I'd never forgive myself. Besides, they live in a trailer park, with nothin' but dim-witted, snaggletoothed peckerwoods in the vicinity. Jade wouldn't last a day in a situation like that."

"Rhoda, you've got to do what you've got to do."

"I love my daughter more than I love life itself, but I know how she is now. I will *never* forget what she did to you. And no matter what, I won't let her come between us. I promise you that."

Rhoda's words were a comfort, but I knew that Jade's return was going to cause all kinds of new problems in our relationship. "Thanks. I appreciate hearing that. I guess I'd better get up out of here and be on my way," I said, trying to sound cheerful. "Just do one thing for me."

"What's that?"

"When you find out for sure when she's coming, would you please let me know as soon as possible? I'd like to be prepared." Now it sounded like the life was leaving my voice, too.

"I will," Rhoda assured me, with a groan.

She hung up first. I slammed my telephone back into its cradle on the wall so hard, a cup on the counter below it fell over.

CHAPTER 20

I sat in my car, with the window rolled down, so I could get some fresh air for ten minutes before I started the motor. Thanks to the unpleasant news that Rhoda had called to report a few minutes ago, my day was off to a bad start. And there was nothing I could do about it. Taking the day off from work was not an option. I knew that if I stayed home, all I would do was mope around the house and try to figure out how I was going to deal with Jade this time around.

Knowing Jade as well as I did now, I knew that she was going to torment me in some way. She was already doing that again. She was the only person I knew of who didn't even have to be in the same state with me to aggravate me. Just hearing her name was enough!

"I will not have anything to do with that girl," I said out loud, socking the side of my steering wheel with my fist. I had to stop myself before I got too worked up. Had I reached a point where I was overacting? I asked myself. After all, even when Jade returned, I didn't have to see or talk to her. However, I knew that as long as I associated with Rhoda, her daughter would be in the picture on some level. And as small as Richland was, it would be hard to avoid her.

I let out a mighty sigh, checked my makeup and hair in my

rearview mirror, and said the Lord's Prayer in my mind. *Well,* I told myself, *Jade's presence will dominate my mind, so I won't dwell on my problems with Pee Wee as much.* I didn't know if that was a good thing or a bad thing, because as far as I was concerned, both problems were equally upsetting.

Once I pulled out into traffic, I drove like I was in a funeral procession. Then I meandered down side streets on the other side of town, trying to give myself a little more time to organize my thoughts. Disturbing images were swirling around in my head like oil swirling around in hot water. A couple of times I had to slap the side of my head to minimize my thoughts, but that backfired, because then I had to deal with a headache, too. Other motorists, who didn't honk at me to increase my speed, passed me like salmon swimming upstream.

As soon as I got to work, I locked myself in my office. I called Louis's number and left a message. After a half-hour staff meeting at nine, I returned to my office and locked myself in again. For ten minutes, I read Scripture from the Bible that I kept in my desk drawer. Despite the fact that I hadn't been to church in weeks, I still tried to address my spiritual needs. That helped me relax a lot. After I had read some of my favorite passages, I started to flip through the Bible, looking for something that would really shake me up. I started to read a Psalm of David and had just got to the part that said, "The Lord is my shepherd," when a gentle knock on my door startled me. I took the interruption as God's way of trying to get my attention back. He wanted me to know that it was time to get my butt back to church. I wondered if it would help if I brought Pee Wee with me.

"Yes? What is it?" I asked, glaring at the door. I snapped my Bible shut and returned it to the drawer.

The door opened slowly, and a moon face peered into my office. It was Gloria Watson. "Annette, Toni baked some coffee cake last night. Would you like a piece?" This woman had treated me like shit for years, but now you would have thought that she was my best friend. Had I known that a proposed free catered lunch every Monday was going to be this effective, I would have done it a lot sooner.

"Yes, I would," I said, rising as Gloria maneuvered her large frame around the door and stepped inside. She wore a yellow muumuu. It hurt my eyes to look at it. A sharp pain shot through my stomach because it brought back a painful memory. I used to own a muumuu just like it. Jade used to tell me that I looked like a school bus every single time she saw me in it.

"It's so good," Gloria told me, handing me a saucer with a sliver of coffee cake that looked like somebody had been playing with it. "You want some coffee to go with it?"

"No, this is fine," I said, giving her a smile. She smiled back. "Thank you, Gloria. Your hair looks nice in braids. And that yellow muumuu is . . . you."

"Girl, that's what everybody keeps telling me. But I'm telling you, y'all won't be seeing me in these muumuus too much longer. I'm tired of looking like I got on a colored bedsheet. I won't need them."

"Oh? Are you on a diet?" I asked.

"Hell no! Diets don't work for me. I'm going to start making my own clothes, and the last thing I'm going to bother with is more of these damn muumuus," she said sharply, slapping the side of her voluminous dress. "I'll be making me some of them sharp skirts and blouses like you wear now. Girl, my wardrobe is just screaming for a makeover! And since the Tiger's Den don't sell no cute outfits, I decided to start making my own."

It seemed like Gloria was becoming me. The woman I used to be, not the woman I had become. This was the first time I'd seen her in braids and a loud yellow muumuu at the same time. And the style of her braids was almost identical to mine. I agreed with whoever it was who said, "Imitation is the sincerest form of flattery. . . ." But when a woman like Gloria Watson started to imitate me, I knew I had to keep my eyes and ears open. I knew I had to get back to church. If Gloria was up to something, too, it was going to take some serious spiritual devotion to keep me afloat.

"Annette, are you all right?"

"Huh? Oh yeah, I'm fine, Gloria. I just lost my train of thought for a few moments, that's all," I mouthed, my tongue almost tripping over my words. I had almost forgotten that Gloria Watson was still in the same room with me.

"I was just wondering. I was getting concerned at the way you started staring at me with that strange look on your face," Gloria said, with a strange look on her face.

"Oh, it's nothing," I assured her, with a casual wave. "I was just thinking about something crazy that my daughter said last night." I cleared my throat and sniffed. "Gloria, would you do me a favor and let everybody know that we are having Yankee pot roast for lunch on Monday?"

Gloria's face lit up like a neon sign. "All right," she said breathlessly. Then she made such a sudden and sharp turn that she almost fell while trying to get out of my office so fast. Just knowing that my relationship with my subordinates was looking brighter made me feel somewhat better. That and the fact that when I heard back from Louis, I was going to set up a lunch date for today if possible. He seemed like the perfect distraction I needed to divert my attention away from Pee Wee and Jade.

CHAPTER 21

After I'd eaten the coffee cake and got settled in, I called Pee Wee at the barbershop and told him what Rhoda had called me up to tell me before I left the house.

"Shit! Jade's comin' back to Ohio? Fuck me!" he hissed. "I thought that wench was gone for good. Well, I'm tellin' you now, I don't want her in our house or around us or our daughter. I love Rhoda and Otis to death, but I am not ready to deal with that girl again after that stunt she pulled on you last year."

"I am glad to hear you say that because I feel the same way," I assured him. "I don't know if I will ever feel comfortable around her again or trust her."

"Well, I *know* I won't ever feel comfortable around her or trust her again, and I'll tell her so to her face. The girl is bad news and always was." Pee Wee paused and mumbled a string of cuss words under his breath. "Exactly when is she goin' to be back here?"

"I'm not sure. Rhoda said she'd let me know as soon as she could. It must be soon, because she's already shipped some of her things back."

"Maybe we should move over to Erie. Uncle Arlester has been beggin' me for years to move back over there and help him run his barbershop. He wants me to take it over when he retires in a couple of years."

"Like hell!" I hollered. "Nobody is going to run me away from my own home. If that's what you want to do, you do it. But Charlotte and I are staying right here."

"I'll talk to you more about this when I get home this evenin'. I got customers comin' in."

"We won't need to talk about this when you get home. I have nothing else to say about this. What do you want for dinner?"

"Don't worry about me. I'll stop off somewhere and get me somethin' to eat. I don't like bein' around you when you're like this."

I huffed and hung up. While I was tapping my fingers on the top of my desk, Louis returned my call. It was such a relief to hear from somebody who had nothing to say that would upset me.

"Annette, did I call at a bad time? You sound real bothered about something."

"I am. As a matter of fact, I just might go back home and get back in my bed and pull the covers up over my head," I admitted. I was immediately sorry for being so blunt with him. "I'm sorry. I don't want to burden you with my problems."

"I'll let you go. We can talk at another time."

"Wait! Don't hang up. I was going to call you again, anyway. Is the complimentary lunch still on for Monday?" It felt so good to talk to him that I didn't want him to get off the phone. "I hope it is, because my folks got real excited about it when I told them in our staff meeting this morning."

"It sure is. Say, how about lunch today? You and me. I can tell you about some more of my selections that are not on the menu I gave to you, and we can get to know each other a little better."

"I don't know," I muttered. "I have to check my calendar." I was glad that he was so forceful. Even though I had planned to invite him to have lunch with me today, I was glad that he was the one who had taken the initiative.

"I'm sorry. I didn't mean to be that forward. But . . . I like you, Annette. I liked you the minute I laid eyes on you. I don't know what you think about me, but I'd really like to get to know you better, whether we do business or not."

"I'm married, Louis."

"Oh. I should have known. Your husband is the luckiest man in this town."

"Thank you, Louis. I needed that."

"Do you think he'd mind if I take you to lunch today? Strictly business."

"Lunch? No, I don't think he would mind that at all. I have lunch with a lot of the people I do business with, and it's never bothered him. Where would you like to go?" Shit! This was turning out better than I had expected.

"You like Italian? My favorite restaurant, other than my own, is Antonosanti's. It's very secluded, so we can enjoy a nice meal, a bottle of Chianti, and discuss a possible working relationship."

"That sounds really nice, Louis. I'd like that, because it's one of my favorite places, too."

"I'll make a reservation, and I'll pick you up from your office at noon."

"Uh, if you don't mind, I'd rather meet you at Antonosanti's, in the lobby," I told him. "Your picking me up here might be a little awkward."

Louis took a while to respond. "I thought you said you do lunch with a lot of the people you do business with."

"Yes, but . . . they don't look like you. Louis, you know how women like to make something out of nothing when a handsome young man is in the picture. And some of the worst ones work for me. All my other business associates look like various versions of Santa Claus. Even the black ones." I laughed; he didn't.

"I see," he said, sounding disappointed. "Then I'll meet you in the lobby around noon. And, Annette, I'll *try* to behave myself, but if you look as good as you did when I first saw you, I won't be responsible for my actions."

"Now you stop that!" I scolded. Louis got so quiet, I thought that I had scared him off. But when he laughed, I felt better. "All right. I will see you at noon in the lobby at Antonosanti's," I told him.

"Most definitely," he replied. I almost dropped the telephone when he made a kissing noise. For the second time, I felt apprehensive about Louis Baines, but I didn't listen to my instincts this time, either. I was already convinced that he was what I needed to help me keep my mind off all the other things breathing down my neck.

I had so many thoughts dancing around in my head that I could barely think straight. But one thing was for sure: this man was cooking up something other than a Yankee pot roast for me. And as long as it wasn't my goose, it was all good.

CHAPTER 22

With the wide variety of pasta, seafood, and meat dishes on the lunch menu at Antonosanti's restaurant, I had the nerve to order a Caesar salad. And that was so out of character for me.

Carlo, one of the cute young Italian waiters, who knew me by my first name, stared at me, with his mouth hanging open. "Is everything okay, Annette?" he asked, looking more than a little concerned. And it was no wonder. This man had been taking my orders for years. He was used to me ordering a steak and some pasta every time I dropped in. Even after my weight loss, I still enjoyed a good steak and some pasta, but in moderation. "No steak and pasta for you today?"

"Not today, Carlo. Thank you for asking." I gave him a wink. I didn't know why I did that, because it didn't mean anything. Well, it didn't mean anything to me, but it did to Carlo, with his meddlesome self.

He glanced from me to Louis. Then he looked back at me and winked. I was a little embarrassed to know that a waiter suspected that I was up to no good. I wasn't so sure that he was wrong. Especially since I didn't protest when Louis grabbed my hand and squeezed and kissed it right in front of Carlo.

"A salad will be fine," I told him.

"Just a salad?" Louis asked, with a raised eyebrow. "Are you sure?"

"Yes, I am sure," I responded, beginning to get annoyed. I didn't like to be badgered about anything, especially when it came to food.

The way Carlo and Louis were looking at each other and then me, you would have thought that they were in cahoots. I couldn't figure out what it was about men that made them want to stuff women with food. A salad was all I wanted, and that was all I ordered. For one thing, I was not hungry. It had not been that long since I'd eaten the coffee cake that Gloria had given to me. Nowadays when I got nervous, I lost my appetite. Besides, I wanted to leave a lot of room in my gradually shrinking stomach for all the wine I planned to consume as soon as Carlo set it on our table.

Another reason I couldn't eat much was that I was somewhat nervous about being out in public with a man other than my husband. For years, the only men other than my husband that I had been seen alone with in public were my daddy and Reverend Upshaw.

Carlo was not going to give up on me. "Let me tell you about our specials today—"

Louis startled the waiter by cutting him off in midsentence. "Hey, Pisan! If the lady says all she wants is a salad, that's all she wants. Now will you please do your job?" Louis smiled as he addressed Carlo, but Carlo got the message. He gave Louis a dirty look before he left our table in a flash. Then Louis turned to me. "Are you sure that a Caesar salad is all you want to eat?" he asked again, looking at me with his brows furrowed.

I nodded and let out an impatient sigh. "I'm sure." I thought he got the message when I concluded with a sharp roll of my eyes.

We occupied a booth facing the bar, but I didn't have to worry about anybody I knew seeing me. For one thing, most of the people I knew didn't want to pay the high prices that Antonosanti's charged, and that kept them away. Secondly, my mother's restaurant, the Buttercup, was one of Antonosanti's biggest competitors. The black folks in Richland felt obligated to support her. But she didn't attract just the black folks with her sweet potato pies, neckbone casseroles, barbecued gizzards, and chicken dipped in buttermilk and flour and then deep-fried in butter. More than half of the people who patronized the Buttercup were white. As a matter of fact, the entire Antonosanti family often dined at the Buttercup. And that tickled my mother to death.

The service was always good at Antonosanti's. Even on a busy day like today, I expected our orders to arrive within fifteen minutes. It was a long fifteen minutes, and I didn't know what to talk about with Louis. I encouraged him to do most of the talking, which he seemed to enjoy doing. He revealed some interesting details about his background.

"I came up here in March from Greensboro, North Carolina, where I was born and raised, to visit my last living uncle. I hadn't seen him since I was twenty-six, and I wanted to check out the new restaurant he'd just opened."

"And you liked Richland so much you decided to stay?"

"Something like that." Louis blinked hard a few times and took a deep breath. "Three days after I got here, my uncle had a stroke. It was pretty bad. He couldn't talk much, and there was some paralysis on both sides. His right arm became completely useless."

"I'm sorry. I didn't know. If you don't want to talk about it, that's fine."

"I want to talk about it. This is the first time I've done so, and I do need to get it out of my system. Anyway, I decided to stay so I could help him out. He didn't have any kids, and his wife died four years ago. He had a lady friend, but as soon as he had the stroke and needed to wear diapers, she took off. He was a veteran, and he'd always had tons of insurance. Thanks to that, I had no problem hiring a full-time nurse to help me look after him. There was no way I could leave him. Besides, I'd been laid off from my job back home, so there was nothing for me to rush home to."

"You didn't have any females waiting for you back in North Carolina?" I asked.

"Other than my grandma and the three aunties who helped raise me after my mama and daddy died in a boating accident, no."

I looked at Louis in disbelief. "That's so hard to believe. You're very handsome," I told him, with a demure chuckle.

"Oh, I wasn't completely derelict in that department. I'm sorry I made it sound that way." He paused and stared into my eyes for a few seconds. I had no idea why, so I motioned with my hand for him to continue talking. He cleared this throat and blinked. "I had a lady friend or three back there, but nothing serious enough for me to go back to."

I was glad to hear that. "How is your uncle doing now, Louis?"

He bowed his head for a moment before he looked back at me. "He never recovered. He died a month after his stroke."

"I am so sorry," I said, patting his hand. "So is that why you took over his restaurant?"

Louis nodded. "It was a hard decision to make, but I couldn't turn down my uncle's deathbed request." His voice cracked. I patted his hand some more. "I kept his employees and took a brief business course at night school. Now, if I am lucky, I'll turn Off the Hook into the success my uncle wanted and deserved. He worked hard, and he was a good man. It didn't seem fair for him to end up like he did."

I realized from the tears in Louis's eyes that his late uncle was a hard subject for him to discuss. I decided to steer the conversation in a more positive direction. "I will do all I can to help you succeed."

"So you can squeeze us into your budget?" Louis seemed as eager as a little boy on Christmas morning now. He sniffed and looked at me with renewed interest.

"We'll have to see," I said. The last thing I wanted to do was lock myself into a commitment that was so firm, I'd have trouble getting out of it, if I needed to.

"You won't regret it," Louis vowed. "I promise you that."

CHAPTER 23

I was thoroughly enjoying myself. Louis was good company and one of the most interesting individuals I'd ever met. He told me how he had learned his cooking skills from his grandmother. She had cooked for some fussy old millionaire for three years. After that, she'd cooked for one of the wealthiest white families in the state for ten years. He had no siblings and had received a lot of attention growing up with nothing but females. He didn't seem to be spoiled, but I could tell that he liked to have his way. When the waiter brought the wrong wine and insisted that we try it, Louis firmly ordered him to bring us the selection that we had requested.

"I can't believe the way some waiters behave!" he hollered, looking at me with his face screwed up like a can opener. "He wouldn't last a day if he worked for me. I'd fire his ass so fast, his head would spin. It was bad enough when he gave you a hard time about ordering just a salad."

"You did, too," I reminded him in a gentle voice, punching the side of his arm.

Louis looked embarrassed, then amused. "That was different. I'm not a waiter." He sniffed. "Then the dude brings us wine we didn't order! Oooh, there's a two-cent tip coming his way."

I gave Louis one of my most thoughtful looks. "Can I share something with you?" I asked.

"Please do," he said with a shrug. There was an apprehensive look on his face.

I cleared my throat and assumed an authoritative demeanor, hoping it didn't make me seem too matronly. "Louis, I'm a, uh, little older than you. Therefore, I've seen and experienced more, so I don't want you to take this the wrong way or think that I'm preaching."

"Annette, where is this conversation going?" he asked, with a puzzled look on his face that made him look five years younger.

"I'm getting there," I told him, my hand in the air. "My mama cooked for a lot of people when I was growing up. Some of them were not nice to her. But because she did all the cooking, she had ways of getting back at the people who mistreated her." I paused and gave Louis a knowing look.

"So she spit in their food," he said, with another shrug. "So what? That's very common in restaurants."

I gasped. "No. My mother would never do anything like that." I paused again and considered my words carefully. "I know we are about to eat, so I will say this as delicately as I can. Are you familiar with something called juju juice?"

"Isn't that some kind of potion that the witch doctors and voodoo folks use to get revenge on their enemies?"

"It probably is, but it's also the name of this stuff that the old slave masters had their slaves cook up to use as a laxative for the mules and horses."

Louis blinked. "Oh shit," he mouthed, squirming in his seat like he had ants in his pants.

"Shit is right. Big-time. You couldn't taste or smell the juice, and it was so potent, it took effect within an hour after it was injected."

"Injected?"

"That's how they got it into the horses' or mules' systems. During a job in Miami, my mama's boss slapped her because she'd made his coffee too weak one morning. When he made her make another pot, she stirred in enough juju juice to teach him a lesson he'd never forget." Louis looked like he wanted to faint, but I kept talking. "Without going into too much detail, that old man was sitting in the back of his limo when the laxative started to work on him—in his designer underwear and designer suit. His driver rushed him back home and literally carried him into the house, straight to the bathroom, with him dripping all the way."

Louis gave me an incredulous look and shook his head before he laughed long and hard. "Did my man ever find out what your mama did?"

I shook my head. "But he told her that she and I had to wash his underwear and detail the back of that limo. Mama told that old goat that she was quitting that damn job," I reported, my tone bitter. "That whole family had always treated us like crap. They had a house with three bedrooms that nobody used, but they made my mother and me sleep on pallets in their basement." A wicked smile crossed my face.

I continued. "Before we left that house the next day, my mother fixed breakfast for the family and she stirred juju into their grits. Enough to completely empty the bowels of every horse and mule in the county. The two girls, who had always called me Cheetah, after that monkey in the Tarzan movies, they had to go to their fancy private school right after breakfast. And that bitch of a wife, she was going to have tea with the mayor's wife later that morning. The old man had a meeting scheduled with his lawyer. The whole family was going to be in the back of one of their other limos right after breakfast." I stopped because judging from the look on Louis's face, he'd heard enough.

"Whew. Thanks for sharing that. But what was the point?"

"The point is, you don't want to make the people who prepare your food mad."

"Damn good point," Louis agreed with a vigorous nod.

I was glad when our orders arrived. I began to sip my wine right away. We ate in silence for a couple of minutes, but I was glad when Louis spoke again.

"Annette, I'd feel so much better if you'd at least add a bowl of soup to go with that salad," he insisted.

"I usually don't eat that much for lunch. I get lazy and sleepy if I overdo it. Dinner is my biggest meal."

"I hope I get to know you well enough to have dinner with you, too."

Our booth was large enough for six people. But if Louis had sat any closer to me, he would have been in my lap.

"How's your lasagna?" I asked, taking a mighty sip from my wineglass. I already had a mild buzz, and it was so smooth, my head was swimming, but the rest of my body felt like it was floating on a magic carpet.

"Not as good as mine," he quipped.

"You're not shy when it comes to promoting yourself or standing up for yourself. I never could have stood up to Carlo the way you did. I like that. You're a very confident man."

Louis stopped eating for a few moments and held his fork in midair. "Annette, is your husband good to you?"

I wondered where that question had come from, but I didn't ask. I just nodded and took another sip of my wine.

"So there is no chance that you and I could ever be anything more than business acquaintances, huh?"

"We can be friends, Louis."

"I've got more friends than I need now. I need a woman in my life. A beautiful, strong sister like yourself."

"Louis, we just met. I barely know you, and you barely know me," I said, with a chuckle and a dumbfounded look. "You might not even like me after you get to know what I'm really like," I advised him, scooting a few inches away.

"I know all I need to know. Now answer my question. Can we ever be more than business acquaintances and friends?"

"I've never cheated on my husband, if that's what you mean," I told him, trying to sound firm. "And we've been married for ten years."

"What you mean is he's never given you a reason to cheat. He must put some serious loving on you if you and . . . what's wrong? You suddenly look like you want to cry."

It took me a full minute to respond. All during that minute, Louis was patting my shoulder with one hand and squeezing my hand with the other. "My husband no longer makes love to me. My marriage is a sham," I whimpered.

"Oh." He had such a strange look on his face, I couldn't figure out if my news made him angry or happy. "That's his loss," he said gruffly. "Do you want to talk about it?"

I didn't really want to discuss my marital problems with him yet, but I did. I needed all the sympathy I could get. "I've known him since we were thirteen, and I always knew that eventually he'd lose interest in me. I just never thought it would happen this soon. By the way, I'm forty-six." I held my breath and looked at Louis out of the corner of my eye, hoping his reaction wouldn't disappoint me.

"You could have fooled me. You don't look a day over thirty-five."

"Thank you."

What he did next was such a profound surprise, I almost rolled to the floor. I didn't even see it coming. He removed my glass from my hand and hauled off and kissed me. His lips were the softest and sweetest that had ever touched mine. When he parted my lips with his tongue and then stuck it into my mouth, I almost swallowed him whole.

"Don't fight it, Annette. Let nature take its course," he said as soon as he pulled away. "Your eyes give you away. You want me as much as I want you, don't you?"

"Do I?" I said, my lips tingling. I started to blink my eyes like a puppet. I held my breath, hoping that it would delay the burps threatening to pop out of my mouth.

"You do! Say it, and say it right now."

I gasped and reared back in my seat. His arm went around my shoulder and pulled me closer to him. His face was so close to mine, his hot breath almost melted my mascara.

"I . . . do," I admitted. "But—"

"Don't say it. I don't want to hear about you being married, because I don't care. That sucker! He doesn't deserve you."

By now I was panting like a wolf. "I should get back to work, Louis."

I was horrified by what he said next. "You are not gwine anywhere until I lick that pussy and then give you a tune-up with my dick. I dreamed about it all last night." He let out a moan, checked his watch, and then turned to me, licking his lips. "We can either go to my place or get a room. What is it gwine to be?"

I gasped so hard, I burped, anyway. "Look, I am flattered that you want to take me to a room and do all kinds of interesting things to me, Louis. I am sure that it would be a lot of fun," I admitted, fumbling around in my purse for some breath mints. As soon as I located my Certs, I tossed four into my mouth. The last thing I wanted my employees to know was that I'd been drinking during business hours. I had strongly advised them not to do it, but here I was, drinking like a sailor.

"I just told you what I want to do, goddammit," he said, his jaw twitching.

"I can't let you do that," I bleated. I had to cough to keep from choking on the breath mints. "Now if you don't mind, I really do need to get back to work." My butt was so numb, I knew that I was no longer responsible for what it did. I reached for a napkin and wiped off the trail of sweat sliding down the side of my face.

"Do you know where the Do Drop Inn motel is located?"

I nodded. When I attempted to stand, he grabbed my wrist and pulled me back to my seat.

"Meet me there tonight," he ordered.

"What?" I gulped. "I can't do that," I said, removing his hand from my wrist. "Not . . . uh . . . tonight," I added, unable to face him.

"Then when?"

"I don't know. Look, I can't even think straight right now. Why don't we worry about business first? Did you bring a list of the other menu items you want me to consider?"

"Fuck a menu. What I want to eat is not on my menu, or any other menu," he said with a growl.

"Shh! You want these people in here to hear you talking all this nasty trash?"

It was impossible not to be flattered and turned on. Especially when his hand went up under my skirt. Good God! Before I could stop him, he stuck two of his fingers inside me, strumming my most intimate body part better than Jimi Hendrix ever strummed his guitar. I gasped as a mind-blowing orgasm caught me off guard. All four of the mints that I had been sucking on flew out of my mouth. They landed on my salad plate, click-clacking like tiny hailstones.

CHAPTER 24

I was still trembling and panting five minutes after I'd been finger fucked. The ecstasy that I'd just experienced had been just that potent. I had no idea whatsoever why Louis was laughing, so I asked. "Why . . . why do you think this is so funny?" I stammered.

"You should have seen the look on your face," he teased. He looked like a cat that had just swallowed a canary. He laughed again.

"You . . . you shouldn't have done that," I stuttered as he gently wiped sweat off my face with his cloth napkin. "That was so . . . *nasty*." There was so much love juice between my legs, I felt like I had peed on myself. "You ought to be ashamed of yourself," I half-heartedly scolded, slapping the same hand that he'd used to "violate" me. I was horrified when he licked his fingers.

"Aw, come on. I know that your husband, or one of your boyfriends along the way, has done the finger deed to you before."

"Not in public!" I snapped. I had never felt such a pleasant sensation on that level before in my life. Not even close. My husband and all the other men, more than I cared to think about, had never satisfied me with their fingers.

"Let's get out of here," Louis ordered. He dropped some bills on the table and led me by the hand out into the parking lot.

I was so stunned, I couldn't speak, and when I tried to unlock my car door, I dropped my keys. He had to open the door for me.

"I will see you for lunch on Monday. Have a nice day," he said. Then, just like that, he was gone. I watched him climb into a dusty, battered white van a few cars over from my freshly waxed Mazda.

As soon as I got back to my office, I put my DO NOT DISTURB sign on my door. There were a couple of folks who ignored that sign from time to time and just walked into my office like they were walking into a room in their own home. I locked my door this time.

I spent the next hour stretched out on the sofa facing my desk. I could not believe what had occurred during lunch. I could not believe that I had allowed it to happen, and I could not believe how fast Louis was moving. What was even harder to believe was the fact that I was letting him take me along for the ride.

I had hoped and prayed for something to happen that would keep me from fretting over Jade's return and dwelling on issues related to my faltering marriage. Now I was concerned that I'd need something to divert my attention away from Louis! I sat bolt upright on the sofa and looked around my office. Then, all of a sudden, I shuddered. I had just tried to imagine a full-blown sexual relationship with Louis. What he had done to me with his fingers in the restaurant had sent me into orbit. What could he do to me with his dick? I wondered. The thought made me so wet, I had to remove my panties. As dazed as I was, I was still lucid enough to hide them in an interoffice envelope before I stuffed them into my purse. The first thing I planned to do when I got home was to put them in the dirty clothes hamper. All I needed was for Pee Wee, or my daughter, to root through my purse, looking for loose change, and wonder why my nasty panties were in my purse. What a fine mess my life had become!

Louis was a man of his word. He showed up the following Monday right when he said he would with three of his employees to help him set up and serve me and my staff Yankee pot roast with all the trimmings. Not once did he make even a remote pass at me. As a matter of fact, he was so businesslike and aloof, I thought he'd lost interest in having anything to do with me, other than feeding me and my staff.

He called me later that afternoon, about two hours after we'd finished our lunch.

"Well?" he asked.

"Well what?"

"Are we going to do business or not?"

"We will. My employees can't stop raving about your food and your service. But only if we can do this on a trial basis. Say for three months. If things work out, then we can talk about a formal contract."

"You've already told me that," he said sternly. "Repeatedly."

"I know. I just want to make sure we keep that information in the forefront."

"That sounds reasonable enough to me. Now what about that other thing?"

I swallowed hard. "What other thing? What are you talking about?" I whispered, even though I was in my office, with the door closed.

"You know damn well what I'm talking about."

"Oh, *that.* I'll have to get back to you on that." The telephone suddenly felt so hot in my hand, I could barely hold it. Even after I hung up right away, I could still feel its heat. I didn't know if it was just my imagination, or if I was truly losing my mind.

I made a few calls to clients and got cussed out royally. Then I called Rhoda.

"I'm so glad you called," she stated. "Jade just called me collect from Mexico. She's flying in this evenin'—with that bullfighter. Her daddy is about to have a heart attack."

"Where is this bullfighter going to stay?"

"In the spare room, with Bully, when he returns from London."

"I didn't know Bully had gone back to London," I said, trying to avoid talking about Jade as long as I could.

"I put his horny black ass on the plane last night. Like always, he'll be back in a few days. Before he packed last night, I washed a few of his clothes. While I was in the laundry room, he snuck up on me, bent me over the top of the dryer, and fucked me from behind like a hound dog. Otis almost caught us again."

Rhoda had been carrying on with Ian "Bully" Bullard, her husband's best friend, right up under his nose for so long, he had to know. But if he did, he didn't care. And no matter what I said, she always dismissed my comments and opinions about her extended affair. It had become such a worn-out subject that we discussed it only when she brought it up.

"Is Bully going back to his wife again?"'

"Oh, hell no. She's livin' with *his* best friend in a flat in Paris, fuckin' his brains out. Bully's just goin' home to check on his property. I tried to talk his dumb ass out of buyin' those two apartment complexes, and now he wishes he'd listened to me. They've been nothin' but trouble. That's what he gets for rentin' to illegal immigrants! He's spendin' a fortune goin' back and forth from here to London a couple of times a month."

"Well, it is his money and his property. And you are not his wife, so you really don't have a right to tell him what to do, Rhoda."

"I know, I know. He just seemed so much happier when he was just managin' that luxury hotel. Anyway, it's a good thing he's goin' to be out of the way for a little while. With Jade comin' home and all, I'm goin' to be busy as hell keepin' her in line."

Rhoda's last sentence saddened me even more. "I guess I won't see much of you for a while, huh?"

"Why do you say that?" she asked, sounding alarmed.

"You just said you're going to be busy with your daughter," I replied in a meek voice.

"Horsefeathers! Nonsense! You'll see just as much of me when Jade gets home as you do now. I've already told you that I am not lettin' her come between us again. And I meant that from the bottom of my heart."

"I'm glad to hear you say that. I was worried about it," I confessed.

"Well, don't worry about it, because you don't have to. Jade's my problem. Now, tell me somethin' good."

It took me a few moments to decide what was "good" enough for me to share with Rhoda. "Is this a good time for me to tell you about that caterer?"

"Louis? What about him?"

"He's a . . . really sweet guy."

"I told you. And isn't he sexy?"

"He is. We . . . he wants to . . . you know, get to know me better."

"You mean he wants to fuck you?"

"You could say that," I answered, without hesitation.

Rhoda started to breathe so loud and hard, for a moment I thought she wanted to fuck me, too. "Do you want him to? And don't lie to me."

"I like him, Rhoda. I like him a lot. As a matter of fact, I'm going to call him up and see if he wants to meet me for a drink after work."

"You'd better enjoy it while you can. Life is shorter than you think," she said. The last part of her comment had an ominous undertone, but I chose to ignore it. "Look, I'd like to continue this conversation, but I've got to get ready to drive to that damn airport. I know I said Jade's return won't interfere with us, but I might not be able to call or see you for a couple of days. I need to get her settled in first. I hope you understand."

"I understand."

As soon as I hung up, I immediately called Louis and asked him to meet me at Antonosanti's again after work. He didn't ask why, but I told him, anyway. I simply said, "I need to talk to you about something important."

He was there when I arrived, waiting for me in the same booth where he had worked me over with his fingers. "You said you wanted to talk to me about something important," he stated, pouring me a glass of wine. "Is it about your husband?"

I shook my head. "It's a lot worse than that," I said. He listened with bated breath as I told him everything there was to tell about my horrific experiences with Jade. When I stopped talking, half an hour later, he gave me a profound look of pity and shook his head.

"She tried to drive you crazy and take your husband. What a bitch!"

"Thank you for listening to me, Louis. I don't really like to discuss this too much with my husband anymore."

"Well, you can discuss it with me anytime you feel like it." He gave me a hungry little kiss on my cheek. "I am here for you, Annette. Day or night, seven days a week."

"Uh, you remember that motel you mentioned?" I said, blinking hard. "The Do Drop Inn?"

He nodded.

"Maybe we can go there to relax or something, *real soon.*"

He nodded again.

"My best friend belongs to a bowling team, and they go bowling every Thursday night. I can use that as my alibi when I need to get out of the house. I'll have her pick me up and drop me off wherever you are so it'll look real convincing—in case my husband gets nosy. Besides, a lot of people know my car, and I wouldn't want them to see it parked somewhere it shouldn't be." I paused to catch my breath. "And . . ." I wasn't sure how I wanted to finish my last sentence, so I decided to stall.

He took the cue and ran with it. "This Thursday night would be a good time for us to get together at that motel, right?"

This time I hauled off and kissed him. "Right," I said.

That following Thursday, we made the first of many visits to the Do Drop Inn.

CHAPTER 25

It was a little after four on Sunday afternoon, two weeks after my first motel rendezvous with Louis. I had not spent last Thursday with him, even though we had made plans to. But Mother Nature had pulled a prank on me and made my period start a day early, which happened to be last Thursday. I had actually gone bowling with Rhoda and her team that time, like I was supposed to, and had been bored to tears.

Pee Wee had gone fishing, or so he claimed, somewhere near Akron. Charlotte was at my mother's house, where she had spent the weekend. My mother had called my house and left three messages on my voice mail, all within the last hour. I had ignored them all until now.

Her messages were always the same. All she ever said was, "Call me back." It didn't matter what the reason was. Last month when I returned a call to her, it was because she wanted to know if I could remember the name of the first blonde who had replaced Suzanne Somers on *Three's Company.* The "call me back" message that she'd left the very next day had to do with the death of a girl I went to school with.

She answered on the first ring when I finally called her back. Before she could start one of her rambling conversations, I immediately told her about my joining Rhoda's bowling team and how I was going to bowl with them every Thursday night.

"Every Thursday night? You are gwine to be bowlin' with Rhoda and her bowlin' team *every* Thursday night?"

"Yes, Muh'Dear. You've been telling me for months that I need to have more activities outside of work and my home."

"Well, one of them outside activities needs to be you spendin' more time in church. I didn't see you at the service this past Sunday or any other Sunday this month. Pastor and half of the congregation ask me about you all the time. They don't want you to be lost."

"I'm not lost, Muh'Dear," I protested.

"Well, you must be! You get lost when you stray away from the Word and get too caught up in the world. Me, I know, because I used to be in the world in a big way. You been weak these last few months and backslidin' like you was travelin' on a sled."

"Muh'Dear, please don't be so negative," I said. Her comments usually exasperated me, but this was one time that I was not going to let her rain on my parade.

I had called Louis again Saturday morning and told him again how much I had enjoyed our time together in the motel. We had also met for drinks at the Red Rose that Friday after work. That had been wonderful, too. But the bartender and some of the other patrons there knew me. Therefore, we'd kept our encounter businesslike. Not once had his hand slid up under my skirt.

We'd spent a couple of hours discussing, over drinks, his menus and other items that he wanted to experiment with. Then he'd walked me to my Mazda, which I had purposely parked two blocks from the bar, in an alley behind a Burger King. Leaning against the door on the driver side, and pressing against me like a Siamese twin, Louis had kissed me so long and hard that I had to push him away before I could breathe again. That was when he had proposed—no, he'd *demanded*—to see me on a regular basis and any other time I could get away.

"Is Pee Wee gwine to bowl, too?" Muh'Dear asked.

I had been so deep in thought that I had almost forgotten that my mother was still on the telephone. "Huh?"

"You didn't hear what I said?"

"Yes, I did. No, Pee Wee is not going to bowl with me. This is a women's bowling team. He's not interested in bowling, anyway," I said in a dry voice. I was no more interested in bowling than Pee Wee was. But it was the best that I could come up with to explain going out at night on a regular basis. Rhoda had convinced me that this would be the perfect alibi for me to use when I wanted to be with Louis. And after I had heard about my husband's mysterious "doctor visits" every Friday, it had been easy for me to make up my mind. "No husbands, period."

"I don't know what's wrong with you," my mother said as soon as I paused.

I continued talking, as if I had not heard her comment. "And when they have their tournaments in Cleveland, I will have to go for the whole weekend."

I hated lying to my own mother, but it was necessary and prudent for me to add this "tournaments in Cleveland" clause to my declaration. And it was all because Louis had already hinted about us embarking on a romantic weekend getaway every now and then. I had already told Pee Wee all the stuff that I was now telling Muh'Dear. He had not even remotely protested or challenged me in any way. As a matter of fact, he had responded with extreme indifference, which consisted of a nod, a shrug, and a blank expression on his face.

"When is all this gwine to start up?" Muh'Dear asked, speaking in such a gruff and loud voice, it sounded like she was in the same room with me. "You ain't never been into no bowlin' in all these years. Why now?"

"I just started bowling a couple of weeks ago, but I had been thinking about doing it for a long time. And, like I just told you, you've been after me to get involved in more outside activities. I promise I will be in church next Sunday, sitting on that pew, right next to you and daddy."

My mother grunted before she replied. "Well, you might be in church next Sunday, but you won't be sittin' on no pew with me and Frank. We won't be there," she informed me.

"Oh? And why not?"

"Me and Frank is gwine to spend the rest of the summer in the Bahamas."

"Excuse me?"

"On top of everything else, you need to get your ears checked or cleaned. You didn't hear what I just said?"

"It sounded like you said you and Daddy are going to spend the rest of this summer in the Bahamas. Did I hear you right?"

"Yeah, you heard me right. That's what I called to tell you when I left those messages."

"Well, will you at least tell me how this came about all of a sudden?"

"It's a long story," she began. Just as I suspected, Muh'Dear was going to answer my question in a roundabout way.

"I've got time," I insisted, rubbing my forehead with the balls of my fingers.

"You remember old Miss Jacobs, whom I used to work for when we lived in Florida? That white woman with them real hairy legs, remember?"

"I remember the Jacobs woman," I said, groaning. My mother was reopening one of the many wounds from our past. "How could I not remember that old battle-ax? She hit you with her cane that time for not cleaning something right, and I bit her on her hairy leg."

"And you shouldn't have done that to that white woman. It could have got us lynched. White folks was straight-up bloodthirsty back then."

"She used to fart in front of her company, and you used to claim it was you," I reminded her.

"That was part of a servant's job. No decent white woman in America would *ever* own up to somethin' as gruesome and unladylike as a public fart. I can't even begin to imagine dainty white ladies like Sophia Loren or Princess Diana pootin'. They like to keep a dog or a servant around so they can blame it on the dog or the servant, if they have to."

"Muh'Dear, where is this conversation going? Are we going to sit here and discuss white women's gas problems?"

"You the one that brought it up!" Muh'Dear got silent and stayed that way for a long time.

I was getting more and more frustrated and sorry that I had returned her call without having a few drinks first to make it less painful.

"I thought you were going to tell me how this trip to the Bahamas came about," I said, hoping that she could tell from the curt tone of my voice that I was impatient and tired. I always tried to hurry my mother along, but it never did any good. She did and said everything at her own pace.

"Well, old lady Jacobs passed away a few weeks ago, and her son Ezra got a detective to hunt me down. She's the Jew lady that used to play with your ears so much when you was a young'un. Remember her?"

"I just told you that I remember the Jacobs woman," I stated flatly.

"Her boy wants to sell the beach house that Miss Jacobs bought in the Bahamas after her husband died so she'd have somewhere to go in the wintertime. At least that was what she told her boy." At this point, my mother lowered her voice and said what she had to say next in a whisper. "Your daddy said she probably bought that place down there so she could take advantage of them black island men." Muh'Dear paused long enough to suck her teeth in disgust.

She continued, speaking in a loud voice again. "Anyway, her son has to be in Spokane, where he lives, for a long murder trial. He's a prosecutor. Miss Jacobs had fired every single one of her servants a few days before she died. To make a long story short, the boy wants me and Frank to go down there and look after the place until he can get down there to sell it and do whatever else he needs to do."

My ears were almost numb, and I was so exhausted, I didn't even care what the rest of the story was. But I knew that my mother was not going to release me until I'd heard it all. "I'm glad to hear that, Muh'Dear. I know how much you love the Bahamas," I managed, rolling my eyes up toward the ceiling.

"Well, this time when I go, it'll be free, and I won't be in no economy hotel, like all them other times we went down there. Old lady Jacobs always bought the best that money could buy, so I know her place will suit me just fine. Jenny Rooks, my day manager, will run the business while me and Frank is away. All I need for you to do is check on the house from time to time."

"When are you leaving? When do you want me to pick up Charlotte?"

"That's the other reason I called. I don't want Charlotte to miss out on all the things you missed out on when you was her age, so she's gwine with us. This will be a good experience for her. How soon can you get all her summer clothes packed up?"

My breath caught in my throat, and I was stunned speechless.

"Annette, you still there?"

"I was a little taken aback by what you just said," I told her. "I don't know if I want my child to be out of the country for that long."

What I meant was I didn't feel comfortable with my only child gallivanting around in a foreign country with two senior citizens who sometimes didn't know if they were coming or going. My mother was still in reasonably good physical and mental condition. I knew that I could trust her to take good care of Charlotte. But since Daddy was in the mix, I had a few concerns. He had occasional memory lapses and lost things left and right. One day last year, he had come to my house, wearing two different shoes, couldn't remember where he'd parked his truck, and couldn't remember where he'd just come from. I didn't know that he'd left my mother stranded at the beauty parlor until she came to my house with a police escort.

"Muh'Dear, I have to think about this. I have to discuss this with Pee Wee," I said, one hand on my hip.

"He already said it was all right with him."

"Oh? When did you talk to him about this?"

"This mornin', before he left to go fishin'. Didn't he tell you?"

CHAPTER 26

"No, Pee Wee didn't tell me," I said, grinding my teeth. "He has not said anything to me about you, Daddy, and Charlotte planning to spend the summer in the Bahamas."

"Humph! Gal, I don't know what's wrong with your marriage, but whatever it is, you better fix it, and you better fix it quick. Time ain't on your side. You can't afford to lose that good man, which the good Lord done blessed you with. I know you think that since you lost all that weight, you're cute, and that's true. But your booty still stinks when you don't wash it, just like everybody else's. It's true that Pee Wee ain't no Prince Charmin'. But at your age, who else would want you but Pee Wee, with your ashy self? I hope you been usin' that lotion on your neck that I got for you at that candle shop when I went to Cincinnati last month!"

Who else would want me, with my ashy self? Louis's handsome face and long, thick dick flashed through my mind. I had to bite my lip to keep from responding to my mother's last insensitive comment. I knew it would have blown her mind if I had told her who else wanted me, with my ashy self. I swooned to myself when I recalled how Louis had made love to me in that sleazy motel room, and how he had made me feel about myself—and my ashy body parts. Yes, I still used the lotion that Muh'Dear had supplied me with, but I couldn't see any difference. She was the only person who thought that my skin was ashy in the first place, so it didn't matter if I used that lotion or not, unless I was in her presence. And it had a foul taste to it. I found that out when Louis licked my neck and complained about how bitter it tasted.

"Yes, I'm still using the lotion you gave me," I told her with a smirk.

"Good! I gave you enough to get you through the summer, so you don't have to worry about that until I get back. You just worry about that mess of a marriage you got on your hands."

"Muh'Dear, I'd appreciate it if you'd let me worry about my marriage. I don't need your advice."

"Don't you sass me, girl. I'm your mama, and I will be your mama till the day I die. If a mama ain't got no right to give her own young'un some advice, who does?"

I wanted to conclude this conversation as soon as possible. "I'm sure Pee Wee just forgot to tell me that you talked to him about Charlotte going with you," I stated, trying to sound nonchalant.

"And Charlotte can't wait to go! She's been runnin' around the house, singin' "Day-O" better than Harry Belafonte ever sung it." My mother laughed.

Right after she finished laughing, I heard my daughter and my daddy in the background, singing off-key the line from that old Belafonte song, which the whole world seemed to associate with *any* part of the Caribbean. "Daylight come and me wanna go home. . . ."

I heard some muffled voices next, and then Charlotte was on the telephone. "Hi, Mom! I'm going to the islands with Granny and Grandpa."

"I don't know about that, Charlotte," I said gently.

"What! I . . . you . . . Ayee!" What do you mean you don't know about that? Granny said I could go!" my daughter wailed.

"I am your mother, girl," I reminded her firmly.

"Dang! You spoil everything! You always act crazy when I want to do something, Mama!"

"I advise you to shut up while you still can, young lady. If you don't watch your step, you won't be going to the Bahamas, or anywhere else this summer but this house. Do you hear me, Charlotte?"

"Yes, ma'am," she mumbled, sounding like she had a mouth full of food.

"That's better."

"Mama, can I please go to the islands?" Charlotte sounded so cute and humble and contrite now, I wanted to take her to the Bahamas myself on my back.

"I'll have to think about it," I insisted.

"What? When? We have to leave tomorrow morning!" she whined. "I already got a new bathing suit!"

"You went to the Bahamas last summer," I reminded her.

"That was just for one week! I got that rash from that eel I caught on the second day and had to spend the rest of the week in the room, wearing that smelly salve on my legs and arms! Please, Mama! I have already told all my friends that I was going. I even made a list of things they want me to bring them back. Mama, I can't let my friends down. I have to go!"

"And the year before, you went to Jamaica with Rhoda and Jade."

"But, Mama, that was just for two weeks!"

"Annette, what's wrong with you, girl?" Speaking now was my father. His deep voice was loud, not because he was hard of hearing, but because he got loud whenever he got angry or upset. "You done upset your mama and now your baby. With a disposition like you got, Lord knows what you puttin' your poor husband through."

I didn't even respond to my daddy's last comment. I had no idea where it had come from. Other than Rhoda, and now Louis, nobody knew how dismal my marriage had become. I certainly had not said anything to my parents about it. When they came around, Pee Wee and I acted no differently than we'd ever acted in their presence.

I closed my eyes and rubbed them with the ball of my thumb. When I opened them, things were blurred for a few seconds, just like my life had become.

"How many times will your daughter get to spend a summer in the Bahamas, in a beachfront house, for free?"

"All right, Daddy," I said with a heavy sigh. "I'll go pack her things right away."

"Good! We'll slide through there either this evenin' or around eight tomorrow mornin' to pick up her luggage, so be there."

"What about a ride to the airport? Do I need to get you all there?" I asked.

"Don't worry about how we gettin' to the airport. You need to be worryin' about yourself and your husband. We'll just swing by there, grab this child's stuff, hug y'all, and be on our way. Now let me get off this phone. My bladder is about to let me down." Daddy wasted no time hanging up.

I sat in the kitchen, looking out the window, for ten minutes before I went to pack Charlotte's things. I needed to talk to somebody. I figured that Rhoda was probably still at church with Jade, which was a story within itself. Jade was the biggest devil I knew, but she spent more time in church than the Pope. And Rhoda had told me that everywhere Jade went, she took along that Mexican that she had dragged home with her from Cancún. Even to the nail shop!

I had not seen or heard from Jade since her return, and that was fine with me. I had not met her young Mexican yet, but according to Rhoda, he seemed like a nice enough guy. However, Rhoda had also told me in no uncertain terms that the poor man had seemed thoroughly confused and uncomfortable since he'd entered her house. And only God knew what that man saw in a whippersnapper like Jade. I couldn't see a Chihuahua following her home from Mexico, let alone a man.

I had a few other friends that I could have called, but I was not close enough to them to discuss the things that were on my mind now. I even thought about calling up Louis, but I dismissed that idea right away. I had already burdened him with a lot of my problems. If he dumped me, I didn't want it to be because he got sick of hearing my tales of woe.

Shopping! As soon as the word popped into my mind, I leaped up from my chair. "I'll spend a few hours at the mall," I said aloud, blinking as I looked around my neat, sweet-smelling kitchen. There was nothing I needed for the house. Charlotte and Pee Wee had everything they needed, so I could focus on myself. Since I no longer had to buy so many generic muumuus and girdles, shopping had become one of my most enjoyable adventures.

I packed Charlotte's three Barbie suitcases and left them sitting in the living room, on the floor by the front door, in case my parents came by while I was at the mall. And then I made a beeline to the Melden Village Mall, armed with three credit cards and several hundred dollars in cash.

I wandered into a few stores and meandered up and down the aisles for about half an hour, but I didn't see anything I wanted. But as soon as I approached the front entrance to my favorite boutique, I got the shock of my life. Strutting out like a vain ostrich, with a "when God made me, he was showing off" look on her face, was the bride of Satan herself: Jade.

CHAPTER 27

That Jade. She was the kind of offspring that would make most mothers wish that birth control was retroactive. Before she even opened her mouth, she looked at me like I had just vomited on her shiny black satin shoes. I looked over her shoulder and behind her, hoping to see Rhoda so that she could help diffuse the situation. No such luck.

I had known that I would eventually run into Jade again. With her being Rhoda's daughter, there was no way it could be avoided. And even though I had prepared myself for an inevitable encounter with her, I was as unprepared as I could be now. The girl was such a pig in a poke, I had no idea how she'd react when she saw me again. But one thing in my favor was the fact that she no longer intimidated me.

I had hardly noticed the tall, young Hispanic man standing next to Jade. He wore skintight jeans and a T-shirt that said in bold black letters across his chest IF BO DEREK IS A 10, MY WOMAN IS A 40! Jade and her companion had large shopping bags in each hand; the man also had a smaller bag underneath his arm. With the exception of the smaller bag, every bag was from a women's store.

"Hello, Annette," Jade said, with that same smug look on her face that I had come to hate over the years. She was as dazzling as Rhoda. Nature was so unfair. It made no sense to reward two women in the same family with so much beauty. They both looked like Naomi Campbell, the ultimate black supermodel.

Jade's long jet-black hair was parted down the middle. It hung past her shoulders like a silk shawl. She wore more makeup than she needed. She had on a bloodred dress that was so short and tight, it looked like it had been spray painted on. She had obviously had her breasts surgically enlarged. Those puppies were rising over the top of her dress like two full moons. The black stilettos on her narrow, tiny feet made her almost as tall as her companion. They made a striking couple. He had firm, sharp Spanish features. His skin was just a few shades lighter than mine and Jade's. His thick black hair resembled a stallion's mane. He was good-looking, yet he was not classically handsome, like I had expected. But he could definitely give Antonio Banderas a run for his money. Despite all that the man had going for him, there was a blank expression on his face.

"Hello, Jade," I said, sucking in my breath. It tasted pretty foul because of the sudden bad taste in my mouth.

"Honey, this is Annette. She's that great, big, fat woman in the pictures with Mama in the photo album I showed you the other day," she said to the Mexican. They both snickered. "Annette, tell me something good." She looked at me with contempt.

"What would you like to hear?" I asked in a casual tone of voice. It was taking every ounce of strength I had to keep myself from slapping her face. I knew what she was up to, and I braced myself for the insults that I knew she was about to hurl my way.

She ignored my question. Instead, she set some of her bags down, leaned toward me, and sniffed like a dog. "That's an *interesting* fragrance you're wearing. You're still picking up your smell goods from places like the drugstores and discount stores, huh? And knockoffs at that . . ." She leaned back and gave me a shark's grin.

"Your mama gave me this one," I told her. "It's the same one she sent to you last Christmas."

"Oh. I thought I recognized that stench. I called up my mama and told her she knew better than to send a girl like me something that tacky and ghetto. You can have the rest of mine if you want it."

"That's mighty generous of you. But I'll pass," I said with a stiff upper lip.

Jade put her hand on my shoulder before she continued. "My goodness. Let's forget about that, and let's talk about you! I am tickled to death to run into you at *this* mall, with all these expensive stores."

"Jade, this is the same place where I've always shopped. I used to bring you here, remember?"

"Oh. I forgot." She sniffed and cleared her throat. "By the way, you look hella good for a woman your age. And I had heard that you'd lost a lot of weight." She removed her hand from my shoulder, snapped her fingers a few times, and looked me up and down again.

"It took me long enough," I said with a chuckle. "As you know, I have been trying to lose weight off and on for most of my life. I tried almost every diet in the book, and none of them worked for me."

"Well, *something* finally worked." Jade paused and gave me a look of pity. "Was it because of some disease or something? I bet it was some kind of cancer, huh?"

She got that right.

According to Reverend Upshaw, cancer came in many forms. And Jade was the disease that had almost destroyed me. But her plan had backfired. I was stronger, confident, and more attractive than ever. And I was brave. There was no way in the world that I was ever going to let a little fool like Jade, or any other fool, walk all over me.

"Something like that," I said. I could tell from the way her face froze that she was wondering why I flashed a smile right after I finished my sentence. "But I'm fine now," I added, still smiling.

"Fat is so gruesome and unhealthy," Jade said with a sour look on her face. "No offense."

"None taken," I quipped. "I agree with you."

"Thank God you had the good sense to do something about yours." Jade's face looked so tight when she smiled, I was surprised it didn't crack open.

We stared at each other for a few excruciating moments.

"I hope you are still on that diet, or whatever it was, because you're still a little husky."

"I'm comfortable with this size."

"Oh?" she asked with a frown. "And if you don't mind my asking, what size is that?"

"I'm a size sixteen now," I revealed with a proud sniff.

You would have thought that I had just swung a dead skunk at Jade, the way she reacted.

"A size sixteen! Good God!" she roared. Then, as if she was imitating Scarlett O'Hara in *Gone With the Wind,* she turned to her boyfriend and fell dramatically against him, almost knocking him to the ground. She set the rest of her bags down to fish a handkerchief out of her purse and to wipe her face. "Marcelo, if I ever get that humongous, would you please cut my head off with a dull sword?" Jade whimpered like a puppy for a few seconds. Then she stuffed her handkerchief back into her purse.

"Sí!" Marcelo hollered with a vigorous nod.

She let out a long, deep breath before she picked up her shopping bags. I ignored the horrified look she gave me. "A size sixteen. Hummph, hummph, hummph!"

It seemed like she was shooting her words at me from a Gatling gun, because each one hit me like a bullet. But I did not waver. I stood strong and proud, and I knew she didn't like that. She shook her head and then mumbled something to her boyfriend in Spanish. He mumbled something back. They looked at me at the same time and guffawed like hyenas.

"I'm sorry. I didn't mean to laugh. This is not anything to laugh about," Jade said, then sucked on her teeth.

"I agree with you, Jade. That's why I am not laughing," I snarled. This was one conversation that was shitty enough to be in a toilet, and that was where it seemed to be going.

Despite what Jade had just said, she snickered some more. This time so hard, tears filled her eyes. "Oh my God! Annette, I *know* I didn't hear you right, did I?" she asked, shaking her head like she had water in her ear.

"You heard right. I am a size sixteen," I said proudly. I reared back on my still slightly thick legs like a proud stallion. And, I didn't even suck in my stomach, which I still did around certain people. "I am a size sixteen," I said again, this time with more emphasis on my words. "Any questions?"

Now that I knew what an evil person Jade was, nothing she said surprised me. She had already hurt me emotionally as much as she possibly could, so there was no more room for that. Now she just annoyed me. Like the horsefly that had buzzed around my head in my kitchen earlier that morning until I swatted its ass.

At the rate Jade was going, she was going to destroy herself. She didn't need my help or anybody else's to get to that point. That made me sad. I had once had feelings for this girl, and I still had feelings for the rest of her family. The pain that she habitually caused them affected me to some degree.

"Well, since you asked, what were you before, Annette?" Jade had not called me by my name since she was in elementary school. Until I'd trapped her in her own spider's web of deceit last year, she had affectionately addressed me as Auntie.

"Uh, I was a pretty big woman," I admitted, rolling my eyes.

"Absolutely!" she agreed with a vigorous nod and a grimace. "I hope you don't mind me saying this, but were you like a size twenty or a size thirty?" The smug look had returned to her face. She was the embodiment of evil. The smug looks that she liked to plaster on her face only made her look even more sinister.

"I was a size twenty-four when I was at my heaviest," I confessed. Then I sniffed and tilted my head, looking from her companion to her. "By the way, I heard you flunked out of Louisiana State," I said with a sneer. "That's a damn shame."

That cheap shot hit Jade right below the belt.

Her smug look disappeared so fast, you would have thought that she'd just slapped on a mask.

CHAPTER 28

It took Jade a few moments to recover from the smack-down I'd just delivered. She let out a little gasp and blinked a couple of times.

"That was a bunk college! A pooh-butt, Mickey Mouse college that didn't allow me to use all my talents! Those professors hated me!" she shrieked. My comment had upset her tremendously. She was so mad that her bottom lip was poked out so far, it looked like the tip of a penis.

"Now that's a damn shame," I quipped, shaking my head.

"I can do so much better! You know I can!"

"I'm sure you can. But, Jade, I hope you don't mind me saying this, but I was surprised that you got into any college at all. Your grades were not that good. . . ." Under normal circumstances, I wouldn't have wasted my time bickering with somebody young enough to be my daughter. However, there was nothing normal about this situation. It felt good to fight fire with fire.

Her voice changed in the twinkling of an eye. She sounded so gruff and disembodied, it seemed like I was watching *The Exorcist*. "I know I can get into Morehouse next if I want to!"

"Well, when you do, you be sure and let me know, because you'll be making history," I replied.

She released a major gasp. "What do you mean by that?"

"Last time I checked, Morehouse was a men's college."

"I knew that! I meant Spelman or Yale!"

I nodded. "Well, maybe you'll do better at Spelman or Yale," I said, turning to leave.

"How is your husband? Is he still with you?" Jade asked, speaking louder than was necessary. She had always enjoyed having an audience. Out of the corner of my eye, I could see two of the boutique clerks watching and listening.

"My husband is doing just fine, and, yes, we are still together," I reported.

"Well, whoop-de-do for you," Jade said. Then she wrapped her arm around her companion's waist and finally introduced him. "Have you met Marcelo, my fiancé?"

As soon as she said the word *fiancé,* the man with her gulped and turned his head so fast to look at her, his hair slapped the side of his face.

"Hello, Marcelo," I said, extending my hand. He had a nice, firm handshake. But something told me that he was not as strong as he looked. Jade was in charge. He nodded and gave me a shy smile.

"Marcelo and I were going to grab a bite to eat. Would you like to join us?" Jade said, looking down at my feet. Then she looked back up at my face, with her trademark fake smile.

I'd rather break bread with Idi Amin, I thought. But I said, "No thanks. I've got a few more stops to make." I was glad that another customer approached the entrance to the boutique, so we had to move out of the way. But there was one more thing I had to ask Jade before she got away, because I didn't know when I'd see her again. "Are you really back in Richland for good?" I sucked in so much air and held it that my chest felt like it was going to explode. I was forced to exhale before Jade responded.

"I'm home for good," she told me with her chin tilted in the air. "And I'm sure I'll be seeing you around. Now you do have a blessed day, and don't do anything I wouldn't do," she added, wagging a finger in my direction. Her nails were almost as long as her tongue.

"That's highly unlikely," I said under my breath.

"What did you say?" she asked, looking at me with her eyes narrowed into slits.

"I said for you to have a blessed day, too."

Why she felt it was necessary to blow me a kiss before she departed was beyond me. She motioned with her head for the boyfriend to follow her, then they strolled into the record store next door. I suddenly lost my desire to shop. Now all I wanted to do was go back home. But I dismissed that idea right away. If Jade was on the loose at the mall, that meant Rhoda was probably available. I called her from a pay phone a few feet away. I was disappointed when I got the answering machine.

Without giving it much thought, I called Louis up next.

"Annette, ooh, baby, I am so glad you called. I've been thinking about you all day. Can you get away for a couple of hours tonight?"

"What time?"

"Things are kind of busy here right now. We always get huge church groups every Sunday. Say around seven or eight?"

"I think so. Where do you want me to meet you?"

"Let's start with a few drinks at Antonosanti's. Then we'll play it by ear."

"I'll meet you in the lobby at seven thirty," I said. My heart was racing. I was suddenly so giddy and happy that I started humming an old Luther Vandross ballad right after I hung up.

I continued walking through the mall, with renewed strength. Before I talked with Louis, I'd prayed that I wouldn't run into Jade again. Now I didn't care. I went back to the boutique where I had seen her, and this time I went in. Five minutes after I entered the store, while I was going through the items on the clearance rack, I heard somebody call my name. I whirled around. It was Lizel Hunter, and with her was her cousin Wyrita Hayes. These were the two women who helped Rhoda operate her child-care center. Like almost every other woman I knew, these two were nosy and meddlesome, and they loved a good piece of gossip.

"Annette, you seen that Jade yet?" Wyrita asked, looking at me from the corner of her eye.

Wyrita and Lizel were both petite and attractive, with nut brown skin, thick black hair that reached their shoulders, and the same soft, delicate features. They didn't even need makeup to enhance their looks, but they never left home without a generous coat of powder, rouge, and lip gloss. Like Rhoda, they would check their makeup on the way to their autopsies if they could.

Lizel had been married four times and couldn't wait to marry husband number five. She referred to her long-suffering fourth husband, Clarence, as "that thing I married." I didn't know the man that well. But he couldn't have been that bad, because every time he left her, she tracked him down and brought him back home. According to Rhoda, Lizel was just too picky when it came to men. If she made it to husband number ten, she'd find something wrong with him, too.

Wyrita had the opposite problem. She had never been married, and that was her main goal in life. She had tried everything to find a husband, from enlisting a notorious dating service to visiting lonely men in halfway houses. She was currently not involved with anybody, but she was so confident that she'd eventually get a man to the altar that she had already purchased her wedding dress and compiled a guest list. She also had blank wedding invitations ready, the church picked out, the date set (Christmas Day in a year to be determined), and the wedding reception feast decided. She had everything to indicate that she had a fiancé, except a fiancé.

"Yes, I've seen Jade. Just a little while ago," I said, rolling my eyes. "She and I had a lovely reunion."

"I bet y'all did. I love Rhoda to death, and helping her care for them children is a dream job, but if Jade keeps coming up to me, telling me how to do my job, both of us are going to quit," Lizel told me, looking at her cousin for confirmation.

"Sure enough," Wyrita promptly agreed.

"I don't blame either one of you," I said, looking at my watch. "Well, I don't want to hold you two sisters up. I know you must have more shopping to do."

"You seen that Mexican hottie that Jade got?" Wyrita asked, with a gleam in her eye. "I got an itching to run for that border lickety-split and pluck me one of them hombres off a beach when my vacation comes up."

"You ain't got to go all the way to Mexico to get you no husband. You can have that thing I married," Lizel grumbled, looking at her cousin like she wanted to slap her.

"If you don't want Clarence, what makes you think I want him?" Wyrita snapped.

"Uh, ladies, I really do have to go!" I said, walking toward the boutique entrance. I could still hear Lizel and Wyrita fussing at each other when I reached the door in the mall that led to the parking lot.

Talking to Louis had brightened my day tremendously. I started humming my favorite Anita Baker tune, "Caught Up In the Rapture." And that was exactly what I was feeling like. I was still caught up in the Rapture when I got to my car at the end of the parking lot. As hard as it was to believe, Jade had parked her mother's SUV two cars over from mine. She was loading packages into the backseat and didn't see me this time. But seeing her again didn't seem to bother me now. I had convinced myself that since I had Louis to fall back on now, it would be a lot easier for me to endure all the negativity that I had to deal with.

CHAPTER 29

Pee Wee and I arrived home at the same time, which was around five thirty. He parked in our driveway; I parked on the street in front of our house.

"I see you didn't catch anything," I said, following him onto our front porch. I was no longer humming Anita Baker. But I was still in a fairly good mood because of my conversation with Louis and our upcoming date in a couple of hours.

"The fish wasn't bitin' worth a damn. I guess them night crawlers I used to bait my hook with was too old," he told me, sliding Charlotte's dusty bicycle to the side with his foot. "Where you comin' from?"

"Uh, I went shopping at the mall," I muttered.

He looked at my empty hands as he fumbled with his keys to unlock our front door. He was moving like an old man, slow and uncertain. I didn't know if he was doing it on purpose just to antagonize me, or if he had really gotten to that point. But as far as I was concerned, age was just a number. I felt that way because he and I were the same age, and I certainly didn't feel or act old. Once we got inside, he took his time clicking on the living-room light.

The house was so quiet, it was eerie. It was always quiet when Charlotte was absent. My daughter was popular, so when she was home, the phone rang off the hook until I chased her to bed. And if her friends weren't calling her on the phone, they were knocking on the front door and the back door. I was not looking forward to the day she moved out and into a place of her own. It was times like this that I regretted having only one child. The thought of spending the rest of my days alone in the same house with Pee Wee gave me a headache—but only because of the way he was acting toward me now.

"What happened? Did all the stores close up before you got there?" I didn't like the suspicious look he gave me, so I gave him one, too.

"What's that supposed to mean?"

"I see you didn't buy nothin'," he said, looking at my empty hands again. "You don't never come home empty-handed after you been shoppin'."

"I guess that makes us even," I told him as we moved slowly into the living room. He didn't even respond to that. He put his fishing pole back into the kitchen closet, then stumbled back into the living room and plopped down in his chair.

"I packed Charlotte's things for her trip to the Bahamas. Daddy said they'd pick up everything in the morning on the way to the airport," I said, not taking my eyes off his face. Even if I had drunk a couple of glasses of rum and Coke, which made me very mellow, my jaws would have still been tight. I managed to display enough disgust in my face for him to see it.

"Why you lookin' all hot and bothered?" he asked, speaking as casually as he did when he asked me about dinner.

"I just told you that I packed Charlotte's things for her to go to the Bahamas tomorrow."

"Yeah. So what? Somebody had to do it," he responded with a shrug. I plopped down hard on the sofa, facing him with scorn. "I hope you packed some of that salve in case she has another incident with another eel or somethin' worse."

"I packed everything she'll need." I paused and cleared my throat. "I guess you forgot to tell me that you already knew about this Bahamas trip this morning. My mama told me they had already talked to you about it. She was just as surprised as I was that you hadn't mentioned it to me." I tried to keep the anger out of my voice, but he knew me well enough to know when I was pissed off at him.

"I forgot," he replied, his lips barely moving. "I got a lot of things on my mind these days."

I am sure you do, motherfucker! I wanted to scream. I had *never* known him to go fishing and return empty-handed. I figured that the weekly "doctor's visit" excuse was not enough now. His fishing trips were just another ruse for him to spend time with whomever he was spending time with, doing whatever philanderers did. I had to freeze the thoughts running through my tortured mind. Despite my own guilt, and maybe because of it, I was determined to beat him at his own game. The only thing that kept me from going completely off on him was the fact that I had my own agenda now.

I groaned when I noticed how hard Pee Wee was looking at the TV remote control on the coffee table. He looked like he wanted to eat that damn thing. I leaned over and picked it up and dropped it on the end table next to me, guarding it like a mad dog.

"I wish we could go to the Bahamas, too. I sure need a vacation, and you probably need one, too, huh?" I offered.

He gave me a blank look before he responded. "You can go if you want to go. For a couple of weeks at least. I am sure that collection agency won't fold if you take off for a little while."

"What about you? As grumpy as you've been lately, a vacation would probably do you a world of good."

"Grumpy? You think I'm grumpy?" he asked. His mouth remained wide open, like a small commode.

"Never mind," I said with a heavy sigh.

"I can't go nowhere as busy as things are at the shop." He gave me a rare smile. "But it's all right with me if you go. . . ."

My lips tightened; my jaw twitched. I couldn't stop the man from having an affair, but I damn sure was not going to make it easier for him by making myself scarce!

"I'm not going anywhere," I said firmly. "I've got just as much going on at work as you got."

"I'm sure you do. You always was a busy woman. You and Rhoda spend so much time patrolling them malls, y'all ought to be put on the payroll out there." He laughed.

"I'm going out for dinner tonight," I said, rising. "Either you can heat up that neck-bone casserole and those greens in the refrigerator, or I can pick something up for you on my way home."

"Yeah, you can do that. Pick me up a plate. That ain't a bad idea. That sissified caterin' dude cooks a mean meat loaf. Bring me a plate from there. I went by there for lunch today."

Just the mention of Louis made me shiver. "Oh? You like the food at Off the Hook that much?"

He nodded.

"Oh, that's nice," I said in a low, hollow voice. I left the room so slowly and quietly, you would have thought I was a burglar.

"You know me. I'm like you and Rhoda. I'm tryin' to support black businesses more," he hollered. "Them sissies need just as much support as the rest of us."

I stopped in my tracks and whirled back around. "Sissies? I wish you wouldn't use that word," I snapped.

"What's it to you? You ain't one."

"How do you know that the man is gay?"

"How do I know? Who don't know? That brother got more sugar in his tank than RuPaul, Michael Jackson, Boy George, and Little Richard put together."

"How many times do I have to remind you that a lot of people thought you were gay when we were kids? And I was one of them!"

I was immediately sorry for making that last comment. Pee Wee's face looked like it wanted to melt and slide down his body like lava.

"And how many times do I have to tell you that if anybody knows I ain't no fag, it's you?"

I forced myself to laugh.

"Oh, so this is funny now?"

"No, it's not funny, and we need to change the subject before one of us says something they will regret," I replied.

"I think we've both already crossed that line. But to tell you the truth, I ain't got nothin' else to say on the subject."

"Neither have I," I declared. "Uh, I'm going to take a quick shower before I go out."

"That's nice, baby. Hand me the TV remote," he said. "And tell that fag not to be so stingy with the gravy on my meat loaf, like he was the last time. I straightened him out real good that time, and he bowed down like I knew a sissy would. He gave me a side order of gravy on the house! But if he get ghetto mean with you on account of you bein' a woman, you tell him who your husband is."

"I'll do just that, Pee Wee," I said with a gloomy sigh. I handed him the remote control on my way out of the room.

CHAPTER 30

The evidence that my husband was having an affair was purely circumstantial, and I knew that in my heart. I also knew in my heart that even if he was having an affair, that didn't justify me having one. But none of that mattered to me. I was having too much fun.

I felt like I was on a string and that Louis was the one controlling that string, like a yo-yo. When he wanted me, all he had to do was roll me up. Nobody could have talked any sense into my head or made me think seriously about what I was doing. And as far as me feeling any real guilt or weighing the consequences for my actions if I got caught, I forced myself to think about all of that as little as possible. I was a woman who believed that if you ignored something long enough, it would go away.

Nobody could have talked me into giving up Louis as long as I wasn't getting what I needed from my husband. But there was something that stood out in my mind even more than that. I couldn't ignore the fact that Louis had pursued me with so much vigor. No man, including my husband, had ever made me feel as special as Louis did. It was because of him that I felt young *and* beautiful for the first time in my life. I wanted to enjoy it while I could.

Instead of a quick shower, I filled the tub with hot water and rose-scented bubble bath. My body felt as tense as a gangster's hatband, and I couldn't think of a better thing than a long, hot bubble bath to remedy that. I didn't know if my evening with Louis would include any serious physical contact. But in case it did, I wanted to be more relaxed, and I wanted to smell and taste good to him. As special as he made me feel, that was the least I could do.

I had been marinating in that hot water up to my neck for about ten minutes when I heard a commotion downstairs. I held my breath and listened.

"Shit," I said, splashing water all over the floor as I flopped around in the tub like a fish in a bucket. "Not tonight," I groaned. Muh'Dear, Daddy, and Charlotte were yip-yapping at the same time. I snatched a towel off the rack and dried myself off as fast as I could. I didn't even take the time to put on any underwear. Cursing under my breath, I threw on my housecoat, slid into my house shoes, and trotted downstairs as fast as I could.

"We want to get an early start tomorrow mornin', so we came to get Charlotte's stuff," Daddy told me, picking his teeth with a straw from one of Muh'Dear's whisk brooms. He looked like a field hand, standing in the middle of my living-room floor in his dingy bibbed overalls and wide-brimmed straw hat. For a man in his late seventies, my daddy was still a sight to behold. It was hard to tell that he'd once been a handsome man, with rich, healthy-looking dark brown skin and exotic features. Now he was just a mess. He had lost most of his hair, teeth, and vision. He was fussy and cantankerous most of the time. Some days all he did was complain and sleep. Then he'd wake up and complain some more. He removed his horn-rimmed glasses and stared at me with dark eyes that looked like they'd seen all the troubles of the world. "Don't forget to go by the house and water them plants and check the windows, like you done that last time we took off out of town."

"I won't forget," I mouthed. Charlotte rushed up to me and gave me a big hug. I rubbed her back and patted the side of her head. "You better behave yourself down there," I warned.

"I know, I know," she replied, rolling her eyes. As soon as I released her, she ran to the suitcases I had packed for her.

"Y'all ain't got to rush off," Pee Wee said. He stood next to my mother as she bent over my coffee table, running her fingers across the top. She seemed disappointed not to find any dust. "Frank, you want a beer? Muh'Dear, you want a beer?"

"Don't mind if I do, Pee Wee," Daddy said, flopping down on the sofa with a piercing groan.

"I guess I'll have one, too," Muh'Dear said, now standing by my front window, inspecting the gold brocade curtains that I had purchased last week. "Even though I know I shouldn't be drinkin' on no empty stomach."

"Oh, we got plenty of food. Why don't y'all get comfortable while I heat up some of them greens and that neck-bone casserole left over from yesterday," Pee Wee said, looking at me. "Baby, do you mind whuppin' up some hush puppies?"

"Uh, I guess not," I said. I sounded flat and distracted, and I knew it. There was no way I could look and sound like I was happy to be making some hush puppies! I had left my watch on the counter in the bathroom, so I glanced at the clock on the wall by the door. "I guess I have time to make some hush puppies before I go."

"Where you gwine this time of night?" Muh'Dear asked. She was talking to me but looking at my husband.

"I was going to meet a friend for dinner," I said quickly.

"Well, don't let us stop you," Muh'Dear said with a pitiful look that made her face look twice as long as it really was. "If you don't want to visit with us, that's fine." She sucked on her teeth and blinked. "Even though we won't see you until the end of August after tonight . . ."

I couldn't remember the last time I'd felt so trapped.

"I told my friend that she could count on dinner with me tonight. I sure hate to stand people up," I said. "I'd hate for somebody to disappoint me that way." I glanced around the room, but I saw no sympathy for my predicament. All I did see was mild contempt, and I knew why. Unless it was a matter of extreme importance, nothing was more important to my parents than family.

"Why don't you call your friend and have her come over here? We got plenty of food. And, like your mama just said, after tonight you won't see them, or your daughter, until the end of August," Pee Wee said. It was just like him to join forces with my folks. "I know you don't like to disappoint people, but when it comes to family, you need to make some exceptions." That sucker looked from Muh'Dear to Daddy and received their sheepish looks and nods of approval.

I heard Charlotte whimper and then mutter something unintelligible under her breath. "I wanna go now," she insisted, stomping her foot. She stood next to the suitcases I had packed for her, toying with the handle on one. "I thought we was just going to come over here to get my stuff, then go get some hot dogs at the Weenie Dog House." This was the first time I didn't mind my daughter pouting like a toddler.

"Shaddup, young'un," Muh'Dear ordered. "We ain't gwine no place until we get them greens and hush puppies."

Muh'Dear slipped off her pink sweater and kicked off her fuzzy pink house shoes. A shower cap covered her thick hair, which was almost all white now. She had earned her share of lines and wrinkles on her light brown face, but she was convinced that she was as foxy as she was fifty years ago.

Suddenly, all eyes were on me, and I knew what I had to do to keep the peace intact and the questions and suspicions at a minimum: I had to cancel my date with Louis.

"I'll go upstairs and put on some clothes," I managed, stumbling back toward the steps that led to my bedroom. "And I'll call, uh, Gloria Watson and tell her that I have to cancel our plans for tonight."

"Gloria Watson?" Pee Wee gasped, and then he gave me a dumbfounded look. "Ain't she that jealous, blockheaded woman you work with that's been a thorn in your side ever since you got that manager job?"

I nodded.

"Since when did you and Gloria become so chummy?" Pee Wee looked from Muh'Dear to Daddy again. "Gloria is a evil ghetto woman that Annette works with that gives her such a bad time." Then he looked at me with both eyebrows raised. "You and that woman have been at each other's throats for years."

"Well, things are different now. I've become more tolerant, and Gloria's a changed woman . . . since she started going back to church," I replied.

"See there! If church can turn that Gloria woman around, just think what it could do for you!" Muh'Dear yelled.

I ignored my mother's outburst. "And I've learned to be a little more patient with Gloria," I explained. I cleared my throat and excused myself.

As soon as I got to the top of the stairs, I held my breath and shot down the hall like a missile toward my bedroom. I called Louis immediately, but he had already left work for the night. I tried to reach him at home but had no luck. I whirled around and looked at the clock on the nightstand by the side of my bed. It wasn't quite six yet, and I was supposed to meet him at seven thirty. There was still a chance that I could meet him on time.

But when I got downstairs and saw that Pee Wee had popped a video into the VCR with the last six episodes of *The Cosby Show* that he'd recorded, I knew I was in for the night. I let out a sigh of defeat as I headed for the kitchen to make the hush puppies.

Charlotte fell asleep on the sofa, with her head in my lap, right after the third episode of *Cosby*. Muh'Dear, who was on the sofa with me, had started yawning right after she finished her second plate of collard greens. Daddy had fallen asleep on the floor, with his head propped up on four pillows, a few minutes before I announced that those damn hush puppies were done.

I didn't know if Pee Wee was really asleep in his La-Z-Boy or just playing possum, because every time I tried to get up and go use the telephone to try and reach Louis, he stirred and moaned.

As soon as I turned off the VCR and the television, everybody came back to life.

"What time is it?" Daddy asked, with a gaping yawn. He sat bolt upright, looking like a deer caught in somebody's headlights. He rolled up the sleeve of his plaid flannel shirt and wobbled up from the floor. "We better get home so we can get up in time to get to that airport in the mornin', y'all." He grabbed Muh'Dear by the arm and pulled her up from the sofa.

Charlotte sprang up like a jack-in-the-box on her own, rubbing her eyes and mumbling under her breath. "We still going for hot dogs?" she asked with a pleading look.

"You should have et when we did," Muh'Dear scolded.

"I didn't want no greens and neck bones!" Charlotte wailed. "I wanted some normal American food for a change."

"If you don't stop sassin' grown folks, you ain't goin' to the Bahamas or nowhere else," Pee Wee threatened. "Now do you want them greens or not, girl? You missed out on them neck bones and hush puppies. I gobbled up the last of them bad boys myself."

"No! Collard greens is for old folks and rednecks!" Charlotte declared.

"Charlotte, don't you never let me hear you use that word in this house again!" Pee Wee yelled, shaking his finger at Charlotte.

"Which word, Daddy? Greens or rednecks?" she asked, looking confused and innocent at the same time.

"*Redneck* is a bad word. That's the white folk's version of *nigger,*" Muh'Dear explained.

The explanation didn't help, or make Charlotte feel any better. She still looked confused. And now a major pout was on her face, too.

"Well, y'all, we best get to steppin'," Daddy said, stretching and yawning again. "We don't want to wear out our welcome."

After several group hugs, they finally left.

I had already turned to head upstairs when Pee Wee stopped me in my tracks.

"Uh, I'm takin' the day off tomorrow. I'm goin' to ride over to the Blue Creek. They tell me them carps is bitin' like mosquitoes," he informed me. "Maybe you can call up that friend you had to stand up tonight, and y'all can go eat tomorrow evenin'," he said.

I nodded. "Maybe I will," I replied. "Maybe I will."

He slept in the bed with me that night. Had he not been snoring like a chain saw, breathing on my neck, and blasting farts in his sleep like a skunk, I would have sworn that he was dead.

CHAPTER 31

It was a difficult night for me. I tossed and turned so much, I developed a cramp in my neck. I got up around midnight to take some Advil, but that didn't help. Even though it got rid of the cramp in my neck, it didn't stop me from continuing to toss and turn like a washing machine. I grabbed the remote off the nightstand and turned on the portable TV on the dresser facing the bed. There was nothing on worth watching. I tried to listen to the radio at the head of the bed, but what was on it was just as boring as what was on the TV.

I got up again around two and read an article in a two-month-old edition of *Ebony* magazine. Then I read the latest edition of *Jet* magazine, from cover to cover. It didn't take long for me to realize that the magazine articles were so intriguing that I didn't want to go to sleep now. But I knew I had to if I wanted to be able to perform like a normal person at work in the morning.

After I put the magazines away, I padded downstairs to the kitchen and heated some milk. Before I could drink it, I remembered that somebody had told me a glass of merlot was good for insomnia. I didn't hesitate to try that. I snatched open the refrigerator, popped open a fresh bottle, poured a glassful, and drank it as fast as I could. I knew right away that I would have no trouble getting to sleep now—if I could make it back upstairs to bed. I got such a mellow buzz so fast that it felt like was I walking on a cloud. I was so dizzy, I couldn't even find the light switch in a kitchen that I'd been familiar with for more than thirty years. I left the light on and staggered out of the room. I literally crawled back upstairs. As soon as my head hit the pillow, I was out like a light.

When I opened my eyes the next morning, Pee Wee was already up. I could hear him stumbling around and bumping into things downstairs. That man was so clumsy. It sounded like he was tearing down the house.

I groaned and rubbed the back of my head. Even though the merlot had helped me get to sleep, I promised myself that I would never drink as much as fast as I'd done the night before, because now I had a mild hangover. Then I took a shower, because the wine had made me sweat, so I felt unclean and sticky. I had no idea how my day was going to go, so I was a bit apprehensive. I was even tempted to play hooky from work and go shopping again, since my recent shopping expedition had been interrupted by Jade.

Just as I entered the kitchen, already dressed for work, Pee Wee dropped a glass. It was just a small glass, but it sounded like a chandelier when it hit the linoleum floor. He squatted down and started to scoop up the pieces, cursing under his breath.

"I'll take care of that. You'll be late for your fishing trip," I said. I was glad to see that he had made a pot of coffee. I poured myself a cup immediately.

"I got it," he insisted. A second after he said that, he howled like a wolf. "I cut my damn finger!" He rose from the floor, cursing under his breath and shaking his hand.

I put the coffeepot down and got a Band-Aid from the drawer by the stove where we kept a variety of notions. Without a word, I grabbed his hand and wiped the spot of blood off his middle finger with the tip of my finger.

"You'll need to change this Band-Aid in a few hours," I informed him. "You'd better take a few with you to that creek." I looked in his eyes, and for a moment, I saw the man that I used to know. He looked away first as I took my time wrapping his finger. "I saw Jade yesterday," I said.

"Humph! I seen her, too. That heifer! She was struttin' down Main Street yesterday like she was Diana Ross's cat. Had some foreigner with her, holding on to his arm like he was her pocketbook that somebody was tryin' to snatch." There was a grimace on Pee Wee's face as he spoke. "She seen me, but you would have thought I was a rank stranger by the way she looked clean through me. I spoke to her, but that little ninny didn't even speak back!"

"I had my run-in with her at the mall," I groaned and shook my head. "I feel sorry for her family and everybody else who enters her orbit. She's going to cause them so much misery."

"She done already caused half of Richland enough misery to last 'em a lifetime. And us, too."

"I don't want her in this house unless I'm here. It's too dangerous for you to be alone with her," I announced. I checked the Band-Aid and tapped it. "Try not to get this wet."

"You ain't got to worry about me. I wouldn't let Jade in this house if I had a SWAT team standin' by." Pee Wee shook his hand again and looked at me. "Annette, by the way, you are still a real good wife," he told me.

Still a good wife? I appreciated that comment, but it also confused me. I asked myself if there was a time when I wasn't a good wife.

"I'm glad you still think that. I'd like to think that I've always been a good wife," I squeaked.

"And you didn't have to lose all that weight for me. I was happy with you bein' a real big woman. Your weight was never no problem to me. You were the first extra-large woman I ever got serious about, and I never regretted it. I loved the fact that you was so soft and mushy and cuddly and shit. That was a unique experience for me." Pee Wee leaned to the side and checked out the snug linen dress I had on. "One of the best kept secrets in America is that big women give the best sex. . . ."

My husband was not a stupid man, but he sure knew how to come up with some dumb shit. I was reluctant to respond to his off-the-wall comments. I gave him a disgusted look and rolled my eyes, and he got the message. "You're giving me more information than I need," I said in a deliberately dry voice.

"Don't you want to hear the truth?" He had a contrite look on his face, so I could not understand why he was still on the same subject.

"You just told me all I need to know," I insisted. "Can we put this puppy to bed?"

"Oh. Well, now you know what I think."

"And for the record, I know what I looked like before I lost the weight, and I know what I look like now. I don't need you or anybody else to remind me." A sharp pain shot through my chest, because at that same moment, I recalled some of the hurtful things that Jade had said at the mall in reference to my weight.

It was obvious that Pee Wee wasn't going to get off this subject until he was good and ready. I was clearly annoyed, but that didn't seem to bother him. If he was trying to get my goat, he had already done that.

"Do you have anything else to say about my weight?" I asked with a sneer.

He gave me a thoughtful look. "Now that you mentioned it, I just want to say that I don't see why you get so sensitive about your weight now." He shook his finger at me. "You done made your point by losin' so much of it, and I want you to know that I am real proud of you. You done good."

"I didn't lose all that weight for you," I told him. "I did it because I needed to. And besides, it pretty much happened on its own, thanks to Jade." I took a sip of my coffee. "And to think that I treated her like family for all those years. Boy, was I a fool."

"Sure enough," Pee Wee agreed, pouring himself another cup of coffee with his uninjured hand. "They say that the folks closest to you can be your best friend and your worst enemy at the same time." He set his cup down and whirled around, looking at his watch. We stood in the middle of the kitchen floor, looking at each other. "You look real nice today, Annette. If I didn't already have plans, I'd take you somewhere to show you off."

I gave him a hopeful look. It was the closest he had come to propositioning me in months.

"I can take the day off, too," I told him. If this wasn't the perfect opportunity for him to make a choice that would make me happy, I didn't know what was. "We can spend the whole day doing some of the things we used to do." I gave him a pleading look.

"Uh, that's all right," he said abruptly. "Listen, if you don't see me for a couple of days, don't worry about it. If them carps really is bitin' as good as I was told, you might not see me for a while." He grabbed his fishing pole and the rest of his fishing gear off the counter and practically ran out the back door.

I didn't know what I had done for him to lose so much interest in me. But it seemed like every day he did something to push me farther and farther away. And Louis just happened to be moving closer and closer to my bruised heart.

CHAPTER 32

I couldn't wait to dial Louis's number! For one thing, I owed him an apology and an explanation as to why I had missed our date at Antonosanti's last night. And I couldn't wait to hear more of the sweet things that he liked to say to me that made me feel so good about myself.

But it was too early for me to call him. I wanted to chat with Rhoda, but with Jade in the house, that wasn't so easy anymore. It was better for me to wait for Rhoda to call me, and she still did as often as she could.

Even though I was already dressed for work, I decided at the last minute to take the day off. I was already missing my parents and daughter, and they hadn't even left for their summer vacation yet. I thought it would be nice to follow them to the airport in my car to see them off. But when I called, they had already left. With them gone, Pee Wee acting like a part-time husband, and Rhoda now having to devote some of her time to Jade and her boyfriend Marcelo, I knew it was going to be a long, hot, lonely summer for me. Then there was Rhoda's in-house lover, Bully. He took up a lot of her time, too. That man was in and out of the country—and in and out of Rhoda—more than a drug runner. If things didn't work out between me and Louis, I didn't know what I was going to do with myself.

I looked at my watch every few minutes. I knew Louis opened for business at eight in the morning, but I didn't want to call him too soon. Knowing what I knew about the restaurant business, thanks to Muh'Dear making me work with her from time to time at the Buttercup, I was certain that Louis was probably busy getting things ready for the day. He was so dedicated and ambitious. Some woman was going to be very lucky, but not until I turned him loose.

By ten I could no longer stand it. I called him up and didn't mind waiting the ten minutes it took for him to come to the phone after one of his workers answered.

"I'm so sorry about last night," I began. "Something came up that I couldn't get out of."

"I'm glad to hear you're all right. I was worried sick when you didn't show up. And I had to force myself not to drive around in my old jalopy, looking for you," Louis said.

"Oh? Well, I'm glad you didn't," I told him.

"Are you at work? Maybe you can come by for lunch. The daily special is assorted seafood, with catfish stew at the top of my list. When you didn't show up, I came back here and was up half the night mixing up batter so I could offer some hush puppies to go with today's special."

"I am taking today off," I announced, tilting my head and pursing my lips as if I was vamping for *Vogue* magazine. Even though I knew he couldn't see me, I felt good doing it, because when I did it in front of him, he told me how cute it made me look.

"That's nice for you, but what's in it for me?"

"It means my whole day is up for grabs," I teased.

"Ooh, girl," Louis said, swooning. "Oh, that's perfect. I can sacrifice a day, too. That's the best advantage to being the boss. Maybe we can spend today together to make up for last night?"

I had not expected him to propose another date so soon, but I was glad he did. The fact that he had presented it as a question made it easier for me to respond.

"I'd like that very much," I quickly told him. "Just tell me where and what time."

"Let me address a few things here first. I'll call you back as soon as I'm done. Uh, that is, if it's all right for me to call you at home.

I don't want your husband to walk in on you having a phone conversation with a strange man and wonder why."

"You're not a strange man, Louis," I stated firmly. "You . . . we have a valid reason to be talking on the telephone. We do business together. Other vendors call me at home from time to time. You can call me at home when you have to." I wasted no time giving Louis my home telephone number.

"It's all good now. I'll call you back soon, baby. I can't wait to see you."

"I . . . I can't wait to see you, too," I panted. "If you ever want to talk to me and don't want to call here, call my girl Rhoda and have her get in touch with me."

"And that's another thing. I've been meaning to talk to you about one of your friends."

"One of my friends? What about one of my friends?" I panicked. My first thought was that he had had a disturbing encounter with Jade. The last thing I needed was another situation involving that heifer and a man in my life. For one thing, she was the last person on the planet that I wanted to find out I was having an affair. I'd feel better if my husband found out before her! "Who?" I asked in a shaky voice.

"That elderly sister that runs what she calls a hospitality house. That old lady pimp. She said she helped raise you." Louis let out a sharp laugh. I laughed, too, but mine was more like a nervous chuckle.

I breathed a sigh of relief. "I'll tell you all about Scary Mary when I see you." I chuckled again. "She's a real piece of work."

"Rhoda sent her to me, too. She's planning some big shindig for her girls next month. She's gwine to rent the special events room at Antonosanti's and everything. She's real picky and messy, so I know this is gwine to be a real challenge. But I don't mind. Whores got to eat, too."

I planned to tell Louis a G-rated version of my relationship with Scary Mary and her prostitutes. I saw no reason to reveal that I'd been one myself back in the day.

"Call me back when you can," I told him before I got off the telephone.

I went up to my bedroom, humming all the way, stepped out of the snug linen dress, and returned it to my bedroom closest. It gave me a lot of satisfaction to stand there and look at all the new smaller clothes that I had been forced to buy to accommodate my newly streamlined body. But I didn't get too carried away with that thought. To keep from getting too far out of touch with reality, I had retained at least half of my fat clothes. The flowered muumuus, maternity tops, bras with cups that looked like Big Dippers, and dresses that I could have used for bedsheets occupied the far end of the rack. I had no way of knowing whether or not my metamorphosis was permanent or not. Especially since my frame had always been used to hauling around a much larger load. I grabbed a cute sleeveless top off its hanger and a pair of beige running pants from my dresser drawer. After I'd re-dressed, I returned to the kitchen and awaited Louis's call.

He didn't call me back until eleven thirty.

"How much time can you spend with me today?" he asked, speaking in a low voice.

"My husband claimed that he was going on an overnight fishing trip."

"Spending the night with you would be a dream come true. We can have dinner at Antonosanti's since we missed it last night."

"I'm so sorry about that. Let me make it up to you. This time dinner will be on me."

"No, baby. I've never let a woman pay my way, and I am not about to start that shit now. Now, this is what we're going to do. . . ."

When I got off the telephone, I couldn't even feel my feet on the ground. It was like the walk of a dead woman.

CHAPTER 33

"Speak of the she devil!" I had just given Louis some background information on Scary Mary when she hobbled into Antonosanti's, leaning slightly sideways on a cane that was so long, it could have passed as a staff. The way that old crone walked straight to the last booth, in a corner in the back of the elegant restaurant, you would have thought that somebody had told her I was sitting up in there with my lover. I had met Louis an hour ago, at five thirty. I was enjoying every moment of our time together, until I spotted Scary Mary.

Louis had enjoyed hearing about the meddlesome old madam who was still lying about her age, even though she now looked like something straight out of a mummy's tomb. For some reason, she thought her claim to be "just eighty" was something to brag about. Scary Mary was ninety if she was a day. To this day, she had not revealed her full legal name or how many ex-husbands she had racked up.

I had told Louis how the slick old madam had meandered into my life and helped me and Muh'Dear relocate from Florida to Ohio when I was a child. From the looks on his face, he'd found my stories quite entertaining. It felt good to know that somebody other than Rhoda paid attention when I spoke.

"Annette, is that you?" Scary Mary asked when she stopped in front of our booth, shading her eyes to look at me.

"Yes, ma'am," I said, with a sheepish grin.

"Girl, ever since you lost all that blubber, you just don't know what to do with yourself, do you?" she said.

She wore a long black outfit, with a white collar so high, it looked like a priest's frock. Her robe, or whatever it was supposed to be, touched the ground, so I couldn't tell what she had on her feet. She always wore a lot of makeup, even slept with it on. But it didn't hide the wall-to-wall wrinkles, the liver spots, and the long scar—from a fight with some straight razor–toting individual more than seventy years ago—on her face. And she had moles all over the place, even in the corners of her mouth. Since I had never seen any pictures of her as a young woman and she'd been in middle age when I met her, I couldn't verify her claim that she'd once resembled Lena Horne.

She was a tall, big-boned woman who loved sopping up money more than the IRS. And with no relatives she liked enough to leave it to, she'd vowed that she wouldn't die until she spent every last dime she'd stashed away. She was probably the oldest living resident in Richland and could still get around like a teenager. She purchased a brand-new van every year, which she drove herself. She always maintained a stable of five prostitutes, and she had powerful friends and clients in high places who worshipped the ground she walked on. With her connections, she was one sister you didn't want to cross. They didn't call her Scary Mary for nothing.

"How are you this evening, sister?" Louis asked in a voice so polite, I almost didn't recognize it. He rose and gestured for her to sit. "Would you like to join us for a drink?"

Scary Mary declined, with a vigorous wave of her hand. Louis chuckled under his breath, eased back down in his seat, and bumped my knee with his.

"What's wrong with you, boy? I'm here on official business. I ain't got time to be socializin'," she snarled, waving her cane threateningly in Louis's direction. "I came down here to talk to these white folks about me rentin' that dinin' room, but I'm glad I run into you, Lucious." She sucked in some air and offered a broad smile. "My daddy was named Lucious. That's a nice name, ain't it?"

"Yes, it is, ma'am. But my name is Louis."

I had not had a chance to tell Louis that Scary Mary didn't like to be corrected, no matter how wrong she was. But from the look on his face, I had a feeling he had got the message from the look she gave him. She pressed her lips together, glared at him, and then slapped one hand on her hip. She remained that way for about ten seconds. Then she shook her head and gave him another dismissive wave.

"You don't look like no Louis," she said. She tapped her cane on the floor and sucked in even more air. Then her eyes settled on his hair. "You got some good hair, but you need to go home and rake a comb through it. Part it, and then layer it to the side like Duke Ellington. That duck do you wearin' now would do a lot for a all-white cracker like George Clooney. But the only thing it's doin' for you is makin' you look like a fool. I noticed that the other day, when I came to your place, and I been meanin' to mention it to you ever since."

I heard Louis gulp. From what I knew about him, he didn't strike me as the type to argue with an elder. That was good to know, because he would not have a chance with the one standing in front of us. Before she spoke again, Scary Mary gave us something that was either a sinister smile or a facial tick. Her lips curled up at the ends, and she gnashed her teeth.

"Anyway, I checked with my girls about the menu for our little hoedown next month. They want to go with them soul-food entrées."

"That's a great choice!" Louis said, excitement rising in his voice.

"It ain't no great choice in my book! That's a stupefied choice," replied Scary Mary. "I tried to get them hussies to order steaks and twice-cooked taters. Them dummies! They can eat up greens and neck bones at my place every day! It's a damn shame that you can take a ho out of the ho house, but you can't take the ho house out of the ho."

Poor Louis. There was an extremely uncomfortable look on his face. And the way he started to shift around in his seat, you would have thought that he was sitting on a tack. "Uh, we don't get too many requests from black folks for some good old down-home cooking anymore," Louis said in a gentle voice.

Just as I expected, Scary Mary changed her opinion and went in the opposite direction. A scowl crossed her face as she continued her rant. "That's what I been tellin' them dummies that work for me! Them heifers! Except for stiff dicks and long tongues, they don't know what else is good for them! They are just like the rest of these uppity black folks in Richland that's still tryin' to be white. Our peoples should never forget that we will always be just one step from the jungle as far as the white man is concerned. The only thing our peoples is missin' is some spears, loin cloths, and bones in our noses." Scary Mary paused and slowly looked around, like she was looking for somebody else who could offer her more things to complain about. She let out a great sigh and returned her attention to Louis and me. That peculiar smile was back on her face.

I disagreed with everything I had just heard, and from the stunned look on Louis's face, I was convinced that he disagreed, too.

"I hope you ain't heavy handed with salt," she said to Louis.

"If you have any special dietary needs, all you have to do is let me know. I'll do whatever I have to do to make sure you are happy with my service," he replied.

That made her smile even more. "I declare, you ain't as stuck-up as you look, young man. You clean?"

"Ma'am?" There was a horrified look on Louis's face now, and I could understand why. This old woman was more brazen than Charles Manson. Had Louis not been with me, I would have bolted long before now.

"I asked you if you was clean," said Scary Mary. "Do you wash your hands every time after you masturbate or take a dump or pee pee? If I ever find out that you served me somethin' with nasty hands, I'm gwine to report you to the board of health, if I don't coldcock and lay you out first."

I still had a lot of respect for the older people I knew, even if they were as obnoxious as the one in my presence now. How Louis managed to contain himself was a mystery to me. I felt him stiffen, and I heard him gulp again.

"Excuse me. I have to run to the gentlemen's room," he said with a fractured cough. He rolled his exasperated eyes at me before he rushed away, almost tripping over his feet while trying to get away so fast.

"You sure you don't want to join us?" I asked, feeling uncomfortable because of the way Scary Mary was looking at me. I knew this woman well enough to recognize when she was up to something. "Uh, I met Louis here to go over some catering menu details," I volunteered.

"Yeah, right! And I'm here to suck one of them dago waiters' peckers."

I lowered my head. When I looked back up, she was still staring at me. "Louis needs, uh, all the business, uh, he can get if he's going to succeed," I said, fumbling over my words as if my tongue had been tied into a knot.

"Uh-huh," Scary Mary replied, nodding and narrowing her eyes. Then she grunted under her breath like a hog and opened the large beaded purse hanging from her shoulder. She removed a white handkerchief with her initials on the bottom tip. I thought she was going to blow her nose. But she handed the handkerchief to me, winking like she had something caught in her eye.

"What's this for?" I asked, giving her a puzzled look.

"You know damn well what it's for!"

I shook my head.

Scary Mary leaned forward and shook her cane in my face. "When that boy get back from the toilet, you wipe your lipstick off his jaw," she told me.

CHAPTER 34

"I was born at night, but it wasn't last night," Scary Mary informed me. "That boy got more of your lipstick on his jaw than you got on your lips." There was a devilish twinkle in her fishlike eyes. "You and him came here just to go over caterin' menus, my ass." She looked at the table, then back at me. "I don't see nary a menu. What y'all do? Eat 'em?"

"Oh," was all I could say. I looked up at the old woman and just blinked. That was what I usually did when I knew the jig was up. "It's not what you think," I said in a very unconvincing voice.

"Girl, shet up. You ought to know by now that you can't fool a fool," she told me, shaking a gnarled finger in my burning face.

"That was nothing," I continued, handing her the handkerchief back. I lifted myself up in my seat just high enough to look around her. I was glad to see Louis coming back. But when he got close enough to see that the old woman was still present, he stopped in his tracks. There was an exasperated look on his face as he stood there shaking his head.

Scary Mary held her hand up to my face and cackled. "Girl, shet up. You ain't got to waste up no excuses on me. Save that shit for your husband."

"Would you do me a big favor and keep this to yourself?" I asked with a pleading tone of voice. "Can you do that?"

"What's wrong with you, girl? You know me by now. I know how to keep my mouth shut. I ain't never told nobody how you stole business away from me," she said, leaning forward and giving me an accusatory look. I was glad that Louis was still out of earshot.

"I was just a teenager when I did that," I hissed. "A stupid, desperate teenager who would have done anything to make enough money to leave Ohio."

"You got paid big-time for that young pussy, too. Part of that money you made off my tricks behind my back should have come to me. It would have been fair, on account of you wouldn't have never known nothin' about sportin' if y'all hadn't met me." I couldn't think of a sight that was worse than an old woman pouting like a baby. "I could have done a lot with that money that you didn't give me. . . ."

"Will you put this behind us if I pay you what you think I owe you? I'll write you a check right now if it'll make you happy." I glanced over at Louis; he looked confused, but there was no indication that he was in a hurry to return to his seat.

"A check?" Scary Mary croaked. There was such a twisted look on her face that for a moment I thought she had had a mild stroke. "What the hell would I do with a damn check, girl?" She threw her head back and laughed. That made me feel a little less uncomfortable, but her presence was still getting on my last nerve. "Annette, you know I still love you. I don't want your money, and I wouldn't do nothin' to hurt you. Don't you know that by now?"

I nodded. "But if you blab that you saw me out with another man, people might get the wrong idea," I said, my voice getting weaker by the second.

"Wrong impression? Then explain to me why his face is so stiff?"

"Stiff?"

"Yes, stiff! The last time I seen a face that stiff, it was in Orleans, and it was a mask some fool had on during Mardi Gras. You sittin' up in a out-of-the-way place with a man that ain't your husband, and y'all was sittin' closer than Siamese twins when I walked in. What other impression could a person get?"

"It's a long story," I said, holding my hand up defensively. What else could I say? "I'd appreciate your discretion."

"*Discretion?* You stop chunkin' them ten-dollar words at me, girl.

You was just out of diapers when I met you. Ain't I always had your back?"

"Yes, ma'am," I admitted.

"I still got your back," Scary Mary assured me with a nod. "I ain't got a damn thing to gain by broadcastin' your shame. Shit. I'm a businesswoman. If somethin' ain't got nothin' in it for me, it don't interest me." Scary Mary lifted her chin and gave me a dry look. "However, it's always good to be in the know about some of the things I stumble up on. It just might benefit me some day."

Louis threw up his hands in exasperation when I looked at him again. There was no telling how much longer Scary Mary planned to honor us with her presence, and he must have come to that conclusion. He returned to the table, looking like an unruly schoolboy on his way to the principal's office.

"Ma'am, I'll call you tomorrow so we can finalize our catering arrangements," he said, sitting back down with a grunt.

"And that's another thing," she yelled, swiftly turning her head to the side so she could look Louis in the face. "Don't keep callin' me ma'am. I ain't *that* old." She still had the handkerchief that I had returned to her in her leathery hand. Shaking her head and mumbling under her breath, she leaned over and wiped my lipstick off Louis's cheek, and then she left without another word.

"You sure know some *interesting* folks, Annette," Louis said, rubbing his cheek. Scary Mary had rubbed it so hard that now it was a different shade of red from the friction of her heavy hand. "I'll bet you got some stories to share that would curl my hair."

"You don't know the half of it," I told him.

Like with Rhoda, I was confident that I could trust Scary Mary to be discreet. I knew that I didn't have to worry about her exposing my dirty little secret. Other than Rhoda, she was the only person I knew that I could say that about. However, the old woman's intrusion had put a damper on the evening, to say the least.

"I'm not so hungry now," I told Louis a few minutes after our intruder had departed. I finished my wine and rubbed the side of my head, which was now throbbing with a mild headache. "Maybe we should leave."

"But it's still early," he whined, giving me a pleading look. "And after last night didn't happen the way we wanted it to, I was really looking forward to seeing you tonight."

"Let's go someplace else then. What about that same motel where we got together that first time?" I suggested, already rising and looking around to make sure nobody else I knew had entered the premises.

"I've got a better idea. Let's go to my place," he offered. "But I have to warn you about the litter box, which I haven't emptied in two days. And the thin walls . . ."

I nodded. "Any place is fine with me as long as it's a place where we don't have to worry about unexpected company showing up."

"You can count on that."

Louis promptly paid our wine tab, and we left. I followed his van to his apartment, which was about ten blocks away from Antonosanti's.

He lived in a three-story complex near downtown Richland. His building was nothing to write home about, but from the outside, it looked clean and secure.

As soon as we entered his cluttered studio apartment on the first floor, he trotted across the room to a padded jacket hanging on a hook on the wall and removed a set of keys. A plump gray cat waddled from behind his plaid sofa in the middle of the floor and started rubbing its bloated cheek against my leg. The cat looked up at me and let out a loud meow. I noticed that the creature was cross-eyed, a condition I'd never seen in an animal before.

"That's Sadie. She's real friendly," Louis explained. "I rescued her from the shelter. Not too many folks want a cross-eyed cat."

Was there no end to this man's kindness? I quickly decided that if just half of the men in America were as thoughtful and concerned as Louis, we'd all be so much better off. I couldn't believe how lucky I was to be in the position I was in. Louis canceled out all the things that had been bothering me lately. Well, at least he did when I was with him.

The cat didn't bother me, but I shuddered when I saw an albino roach crawling up the wall in front of me.

Louis strolled back over to me, removing a key from the ring. "You take this," he said, handing the key to me. "I want you to know that you can come by here anytime you want to."

I shook my head, but I still accepted the key. "Louis, isn't it kind of soon for you to be giving me a key to your apartment?" Before he could answer my question, a scratching noise made us look toward a slightly opened window by the door we had just come through. Something was trying to crawl under the window sash from outside. We could hear it squealing, and we could see the top of its furry black head.

"What the hell?" Louis mouthed, running toward the creature with a fork that he had grabbed off a small round table sitting at the end of his sofa. But before he reached it, the small bat squeezed under the window sash and flew straight toward me!

What happened next happened very fast. The squealing bat, which was probably more frightened than I was, because I was squealing just as loud, flew straight at my head and got tangled up in my hair. I beat at that creature with one hand and flailed my other like I was trying to flag down a train.

"Louis, do something! Get this damn thing off me!"

I was frantic as I hopped up and down, praying that I wouldn't lose control of my bladder. I could not believe what was happening. Because of the incident in the restaurant with the madam and now this, I could not ignore one of Muh'Dear's most frequent warnings: God don't like ugly. I didn't like it when somebody confronted me like Scary Mary had done, and especially in a public place. And as far as bats were concerned, well, no woman in her right mind would ever want to deal with a bat, whether it was dead or alive. Those creatures shared the number one spot with mice on a woman's shit list.

I had to wonder if God was trying to tell me something by putting roadblocks in front of Louis and me. If He was, I was listening. I just wasn't listening hard enough.

"Baby, hold still! I got everything under control!" After Louis beat that bat out of my hair with the fork, he stomped it to death. I practically ran out of the door.

We ended up back at the Do Drop Inn motel, after all.

CHAPTER 35

I was still shaking when we entered the motel room. The first thing I did was run into the moldy-smelling bathroom and wet a towel to blot my hair. My heart was still beating like a drum, and my skin felt like it wanted to crawl right off my body. The light in the bathroom was so dim, my skin had a green tint when I looked in the mirror. But that still didn't diminish the terror in my eyes.

I closed the door with my foot and sat down on the commode. I wrapped my arms around my stomach, because it felt like somebody was break-dancing on my insides. I could even hear a rumbling noise. That commotion was being caused by my bladder and bowels. They were fighting with each other to see which could embarrass me first by making me lose control of my bodily functions. It was a tie. I remained on the toilet so long, Louis knocked on the door.

"Annette, are you all right in there?" he asked.

He sounded concerned, but I knew he was embarrassed, too, about what had happened in his apartment. I had been too frazzled to drive my car, so we had come to the motel in his van. Throughout the ride, he had apologized profusely about the bat, but even more so about taking me to his shabby apartment. He had gone on and on about how he couldn't afford to live like a king and keep his business afloat at the same time yet, but that he would in a year or two. No matter how many times I told him that I understood, he'd insisted on running that subject into the ground. I'd been glad when we reached the motel. I had waited in his van while he ran into the office to register and pick up the key.

He was all over me within minutes after I emerged from the bathroom, fondling me, kissing my lips and face, and purring in my ear. I responded immediately, doing the same things to him. The way we started clawing at each other's clothes, while still fondling, kissing, and purring, you would have thought that we had both just been released from prison and hadn't fucked in years.

He had removed his shirt and shoes, but I was already completely naked on the bed by the time I clumsily unzipped his pants and slid them down to his ankles. He attempted to finish getting undressed so fast, he stumbled and fell on top of me. We both laughed.

Louis was not a better lover than my husband. He could certainly give him a run for his money, though. But I had to be fair to the man. For one thing, he was not as familiar with my body as my husband, whom I'd been making love with for more than twenty years.

I had just reached my sexual peak when Pee Wee pulled the plug on my action. I had to do something to keep from going stone crazy. Had Louis not come into my life when he did, I didn't know what I would have done with myself. When it came to sex, self-service and sex toys didn't cut it with me. The one time that I'd experimented with a sex toy, which Rhoda had recommended, some banana-shaped thing that had to be plugged into an electrical outlet, it was so clumsy and complicated that the only thing I managed to do was almost electrocute myself.

And if that wasn't bad enough, Pee Wee came home early from a fishing trip and caught me tangled up in that shit. After we'd shared a good laugh, he gave me just enough loving to calm me down. But from that point on, everything went downhill. We went from a guaranteed six-nights-a-week fuckfest to a one-day maybe, and finally to nothing. I felt sorry for Pee Wee, but I was not ready to throw in the towel. Had Louis not rescued me from sexual bankruptcy, it would have been somebody else. That was one thing that I was totally convinced of.

The mattress on the bed had a slight valley in the middle. I couldn't decide if that was because it was just a cheap-ass mattress or because so many heavyset people like me had spent so much time fucking on it. During the first few minutes of our lovemaking, I had glanced in the mirror on the dresser by the side of the bed. Because of the slump in the mattress Louis had resembled a swaybacked mule as he pumped into me. I had snickered.

After our first round, we lay naked in the bed, on our backs, with our eyes on the ceiling. I couldn't tell which one of us was breathing the loudest.

"Why did you laugh a little while ago?" Louis asked. He turned to me with a worried expression on his face. "Am I that bad?"

"Huh? I wasn't laughing at the way you were making love. And you are not bad. You're one of the best lovers I've ever had," I told him. He continued to look at me with the same worried expression on his face. I lifted myself up and nodded toward the mirror. "I laughed because of the way this damn mattress made you look like . . . a swaybacked mule on top of me," I explained. I was glad when he laughed and lay back down.

A few minutes went by before either of us spoke again. "Tell me more about yourself, baby," he said, but then he interrupted my thoughts with a passionate kiss. I could taste myself on his tongue. And I could still feel the aftermath of his tongue between my thighs. My breasts were tender from him playing with them nonstop for the last five minutes.

"There's not a whole lot more to tell," I said with a sigh. I was in his arms, running my fingers through his soft hair. It reminded me of the soft, wispy hair on a newborn baby. I didn't like to even think about the "good hair, bad hair" debate that black folks had been waging for the past few centuries. But compared to Louis's hair, my husband's hair felt like cockleburs. And Pee Wee was so tender-headed, he pushed my hand away every time I tried to rake my fingers through his hair. Louis enjoyed me doing that to him. When I attempted to stop, he ordered me to keep doing it, telling me how good it felt.

"Annette, you told me one time that your mama raised you by herself, but now your daddy is back in the picture. What's up with that?"

I snatched my hand away from his hair. Then I sat up and wrapped my arms around my knees.

"If I'm getting too personal, just say so," Louis said. He propped himself up on his elbow and kissed me some more. And then he caressed my chin and turned me to face him. "I just want to get to know you better, baby. That's all."

"My daddy left us for another woman. We were still in Florida, and it was really bad for black folks back then. Especially interracial couples."

He gasped. "The other woman was a peckerwood?"

"I never thought of her as a peckerwood, or any other white person, for that matter. That's such a crude word. She's the mother of my half siblings, and I love them."

"Oh. I didn't know."

"It was really hard on us for a while. My mother worked her fingers to the bone cleaning and cooking for rich white folks. Some treated her like shit. Some didn't. Like Judge Lawson. He's the one who left us the house I live in now."

"You own your own house? Free and clear?"

I nodded. "Free and clear. All I have to do is pay the property taxes every year. And when my mama passes, the Buttercup restaurant will belong to me, too."

"Don't tell me that Judge Lawson left the restaurant to you and your mama, too."

I shook my head. "My late stepfather left it to my mother in his will."

Louis gave me a look that I could not interpret. It seemed like he was studying me like I was a piece of artwork. "You and your mother have always managed to hook up with people that come through in a big way, huh?"

"That's what happens when you treat people right. One of the old white women that my mother used to clean and cook for more than forty years ago, she owned the house in the Bahamas that my parents and daughter were headed to this morning to spend the rest of the summer, for free. But they have to do all the upkeep and maintenance on the property until the son returns from some out-of-town business in August. After the woman died, her son went out of his way to locate my mama. We've been blessed so much, I know it pays to be good to people. I had it hard when I was young, but I've got more than I will ever need now."

"It's good to see a sister doing so well," Louis said, squeezing my shoulder. "Black women deserve more glory than any other race of women. And I love me some strong, ambitious, successful sisters! The next time you offer to pay for dinner, I'm gwine to let you." Louis laughed.

"Well, since we didn't order dinner at Antonosanti's, I'll treat you this time, like I offered," I declared.

"That's fine, baby."

CHAPTER 36

I paid for the medium-size pepperoni pizza that we had ordered. Then I suggested that Louis trot across the street to the liquor store to get us a bottle of wine. I attempted to hand him the change from the fifty I'd just broken, but he refused to accept it.

"Nuh-uh. The wine is on me," he insisted, rooting through several of his pockets and flipping through his battered wallet until he came up with enough bills to pay for the wine.

After we made love again, Louis told me more about himself. He had such an endearing quality about him that I was not surprised to hear that we had some things in common. Like me, he had been raised in the church and had had no relationship with his father. There had been a lot of love in his home, but the money had been so tight that he had to do odd jobs after school and contribute to the household expenses. He had played with used or hand-me-down toys, and his grandmother had bought his clothes from secondhand stores, including the suit he'd worn to his high school prom.

What I admired about Louis was the fact that he was working so hard to get his catering business off the ground. Richland needed more successful black men like . . . my husband. But Pee Wee had not had to work that hard to succeed. His barbershop, the most successful of the two black-owned barbershops in Richland, had been passed on to him by his late father. By then, my father-in-law had already set the stage and filled it with dozens of loyal customers. All Pee Wee had to do was walk in and take over. However, my husband was a good barber, and he treated his customers well. If he didn't, I was convinced that the business his father had built would have folded by now. Even if my relationship with Louis didn't last that long, I still wanted to see him succeed.

"If my customers paid me on time, I'd feel a whole lot better," he revealed.

"Well, if you ever need any help collecting from some of those slow-paying folks, you can talk to me about that," I offered, speaking in a firm voice. "My collection company goes after debtors like gangbusters."

"I'm glad to hear you say that. Uh, your first invoice from last week is still outstanding. It was supposed to be paid within three days after the event . . . per our agreement."

"What?" My face felt like it was on fire. What could be worse than a collection agency not paying its bills on time? I shook my head and laughed. Louis gently punched me on the arm and laughed, too. "I didn't know! I'm going to have to speak to the girl who pays our invoices. And while I'm at it, I'd better check to see who else hasn't been paid on time. I am so sorry." We both laughed again.

"I didn't want to bother you about it. But if I don't get paid, I can't pay my bills, either. And I sure enough don't want my name to end up on your shit list for collection!"

"From now on, you give your invoices directly to me after one of our events. I will personally see that you get paid on time. As a matter of fact, I will do that for all the rest of our new vendors and clients as well. I'm glad you told me. This is so embarrassing!" I had to laugh again.

Monday was the first day of work that I'd missed in over six months. Louis had requested that I spend Monday night and part of Tuesday with him, but missing two days in a row was something I didn't do unless I really had to. Especially when I had to charge the time to sick leave when I was not really sick. As an office manager, I wanted to set a good example for my employees. With Charlotte on an adventure in the Caribbean and my husband doing his own thing, I had extra time to do pretty much whatever I wanted to do, so it wasn't really necessary for me to play hooky from work too much, anyway.

"Baby, can't you just call in sick again tomorrow? I can do the same thing. It would be nice to spend two days in a row with you," Louis suggested for the third time in the past hour. He pawed my back, even though I had put my clothes back on.

It was almost midnight, and I wasn't that anxious to get back to an empty house. The main reason I wanted to leave the motel was that I was tired and sore from my chin on down from all the wallowing around we'd done in that motel bed. Because of my dramatic weight loss, I needed to exercise so that I could firm up and feel more energetic. Therefore, I visited a gym every now and then on my lunch hour and some weekends. But a woman my age had certain limitations. I couldn't flip and flop around in a bed with a man the way I used to. My arthritis, rheumatism, and sciatica constantly reminded me of that. Louis had ridden me front, back, and sidesaddle like a mule. My body had been out of practice for so long that I needed to get home to recuperate now.

Louis claimed that it didn't bother him to be involved with an older woman, and I believed him. But I didn't want to remind him too often that time was no longer on my side.

"I've told you before, but I will tell you again. One of my dreams is to spend a night with you," Louis said in a hoarse voice. That comment deserved a kiss. I gave him one of the most passionate ones I could manage without swallowing his tongue.

"Lou, I appreciate that, but I really can't spend tonight with you," I told him, my lips still close to his. "Mr. Mizelle is coming by the office tomorrow. We're having a staff meeting in the morning, and I need to be there to facilitate it."

Louis gave me a puzzled look. "If your boss is gwine to be there, can't he facilitate it?"

I shook my head and snickered. "I love Mr. Mizelle to death, but he's a typical boss. He does as little as possible."

"Don't you have somebody to back you up? What happens when you can't make it to work?" The puzzled look was still on Louis's face.

"Uh, I'm there ninety-nine percent of the time. There's never been a need for me to have backup support. When I do take off, my workers keep the place running. Besides, I'd like to find out how the luncheon went."

"What do you mean by that?"

"Well, you were not there to supervise things today. These catered lunches are very important to me."

"My folks know how to take care of business almost as good as I do. If I was in a coma for a year, I am confident that my workers would do as good a job as if I were there."

I nodded. "I'm glad you feel that way. Now I know I don't have to worry about things falling apart during one of the luncheons. This is an important project for me, and I want to make sure it works out for everybody. My boss is going to join us for lunch next Monday. He's so impressed with how productivity and attendance have improved since I started this morale-boosting activity. Because of it, I can't get any of my folks to miss a Monday even if I pay them." I laughed. "A nice free lunch goes a long way with a lot of folks."

"When will we get together again?"

"Well, since I've already set things up for Thursdays, we'll get together again this Thursday, I guess. Unless something comes up."

After a few more kisses, we left the room. Louis attempted to hold my hand as we walked across the parking lot to his van, but I slapped it away. I had to keep reminding myself, and him, that Richland was a small town full of signifying, instigating people with big eyes, big ears, and big mouths. After we glanced around to make sure we didn't see anybody we knew, Louis drove me back to my car, and then I drove home.

I got mildly depressed as soon as I pulled into my driveway. I couldn't remember the last time I'd come home to such a dark, gloomy house. When Pee Wee and I went out at night, we always left at least one light in the house and the one on the front porch on. But since I'd had other things on my mind when I left the house, I hadn't even thought about the lights.

I removed the mail from the mailbox, grabbed the newspaper from my front porch glider, where the paperboy had tossed it, and then I slowly turned the key in the lock. An eerie feeling came over me, so I hesitated before I entered my house. I clicked on the living room light before I shut the door. It was so quiet in the room, it was scary. When the telephone on the end table by the sofa rang, it startled me. But I was glad for the noise, and I was glad that it was Rhoda calling.

"Have you seen today's paper?" she asked.

"Not yet. I just walked in the door," I told her, staring at the newspaper in my hand like it was Pandora's box. "Is there something in it I probably don't want to see?" I asked. The paper suddenly felt hot against the palm of my hand.

"Get it!" she barked.

From the tone of Rhoda's voice, I could tell that whatever was in the newspaper was something she didn't like. I was afraid to ask what that was.

CHAPTER 37

"Something tells me I should have a drink before I read the paper," I said. I was only half-joking.

"That might help. I've got a shot glass full of tequila in my hand right now. Hurry up! I'll wait," Rhoda said, her voice rising.

Something was wrong. From the tone of her voice, I couldn't tell if she was anxious about something or angry. But whatever it was, it had to be serious if she thought we both needed some alcohol.

"Is it something that involves me?"

I heard her slurp her drink and then swallow, with a groan and a single hiccup. "Indirectly, I guess. Now, go get your drink, and you'd better make it a strong one."

I trotted into my darkened kitchen, almost knocking over the chair that I had occupied that morning and left sitting a few feet from the table. I clicked on the light and snatched open the cabinet above the sink, where we hid our best liquor from greedy visitors. Drinking from my own shot glass as I walked, I returned to the living room as fast as I could and resumed my conversation with Rhoda.

"I'm back." I swallowed some more Jack Daniel's and let out a mild burp, and then I picked up the newspaper and scanned the front page. "What's going on, Rhoda?" I asked. "What's in today's paper that's got your panties in such a twist?"

"Turn to the society page!" she yelled. She was definitely angry.

"Hold on." I held the telephone in place with my cheek and shoulder as I flipped through the newspaper. I gasped as soon as I got to the society page. "What in the world? Jade and Marcelo are getting married in two weeks?" I shook my head as I stared at a picture of Jade, grinning like a fool. There were two paragraphs announcing Jade Marie O'Toole's upcoming nuptials to Marcelo Antonio Ricardo Jose Gomez, son of one of the most prominent families in Cancún, Mexico. I blinked at that last part. Rhoda had told me that Marcelo's toothless daddy sold T-shirts and chewing gum on the beach, and his mama cleaned hotel rooms. "Is this for real?"

"Yes!"

"Oh. Well, what's the problem? They were engaged, weren't they?"

"If they were, it's news to me! Who told *you* that?"

"I ran into them at the mall. Jade introduced Marcelo as her fiancé." I folded the newspaper and dropped it onto the coffee table as I eased down on my living-room sofa. "You don't want her to get married?"

"Yes, I do want my daughter to get married."

"But not to Marcelo? He seems like a nice enough guy."

"Jade can marry Dracula, for all I care. As long as she's happy, her daddy and I will be happy. And, as long as the man she marries treats her well."

"Well, I hate to say this, but if she married Dracula, I doubt very seriously if she'd be happy for long."

"Annette, this is no time for comedy. I am mad as hell!" Rhoda howled.

"You're not making much sense, Rhoda. If you want your daughter to get married, and you don't care who she marries, I don't understand why you are so upset. Besides, maybe marriage will tame her down a little," I offered. I sighed and rubbed my chin and crossed my legs to get more comfortable. Whenever Jade was the subject of conversation, my body reacted by getting tense, and it throbbed in some places. However, this was one time that I could not blame Jade for all my aches and pains. Louis had to take most of the blame. Regardless of who or what had caused me some pain, I knew I'd have to swallow some Advil as soon as I got off the phone with Rhoda.

I set my shot glass on the coffee table, leaving half of my drink. I knew enough to know that alcohol and pills didn't go together.

"Maybe marriage will tame her, but maybe it won't. I can deal with that. And Marcelo is a sweetie. I'd be proud to have him for a son-in-law. But it's her timin' that is so fucked up. My mama is too sick to travel anytime soon, and nobody else in my family, or Otis's family, can drop everything else goin' on in their lives and make it to Ohio on such short notice. What kind of weddin' would it be without the rest of my family? Jade is my only daughter."

"Rhoda, you and I both know by now that Jade is going to do what Jade wants to do. We have to live with that."

"I guess you're right." Rhoda sounded so defeated. I was sorry that I was not with her so that I could give her the bear hug she needed. "As long as you'll be there for me to lean on when it happens, I'll be all right, I guess."

"Me? There? You mean at Jade's wedding?" I asked, the words burning in my mouth and ears.

Rhoda hesitated before she spoke again. And when she did, it was in a low, weak voice. "Yes. I hope so." She paused, as if waiting for me to confirm my attendance or decline the invitation. I remained silent, because I honestly didn't know what to say next. "Since I don't have enough time to plan the wedding that I always wanted for her, it'll have to be here. In my house."

"Rhoda, I don't know if I can make it. And under the circumstances, my presence might not be appropriate or welcome, anyway," I protested. "Jade would not hesitate to clown me in front of her guests. Even after all that's happened, she was not that excited about seeing me at the mall recently." A sharp pain shot through my stomach from just thinking about how nastily she had treated me in front of that boutique. I saw no reason to reveal too many details about that encounter to Rhoda. She had enough of a mess on her hands.

"I understand and I respect you for bein' so open about it. But Jade gettin' married is a once-in-a-lifetime thing, I *hope*. And you'd be doin' it for me, not Jade. I need you there."

"Let me think about it," I said. "Does this invitation include my husband?"

"Of course, it does! I am surprised that you would even fix your lips to ask me such a dumb question. Pee Wee is always welcome in my house. In fact, I want him at the weddin' as much as I want you there. He and I have a long, wonderful history, and that's somethin' that I can't ignore. But . . ." Rhoda's sudden pause made my heart skip a beat.

"But what?"

"I'm goin' to ask Louis to cater and serve. If you don't have a problem bein' around your honey and your husband at the same time, I don't."

"Oh. Now I really have to think about that. I played hooky from work today and spent part of it with Louis, and I don't even know where that husband of mine is right now."

"What do you mean you don't know where Pee Wee is? He didn't tell you he was goin' fishin'?"

"Yes, he did. But that doesn't mean that's where he is. We haven't been communicating that well lately. He could be anywhere and with anybody, for all I know."

"Well, I know for a fact that he's with Lizel's husband, Clifford. That hillbilly woman with the orange hair and crooked teeth who runs that bait shop out on Newburg Road told me that Pee Wee and Clifford stopped by there this mornin' to get some bait and other fishin' shit. I ran into her at the market a little while ago."

"Oh. Maybe he really did go fishing this time," I said with a smirk.

"Listen, I have to go, but we can talk tomorrow. I've got so many things to work out if I want this weddin' to be a success. And, I've got to pick up Bully at the airport. He'll be arrivin' back from London in a couple of hours. Then I've got to take him and my husband to the mall to find them suitable suits to wear to the weddin'. If I send them to the mall on their own, they'll come steppin' back here with plaid zoot suits and sombreros."

"Your lover is going to attend the wedding, too?"

"He'd better be there."

"What about your husband, Rhoda?"

"What about him?"

"Won't he be present? He's Jade's daddy."

"Of course, he'll be there, too. I'm in the same boat you're in, remember? Sometimes a husband is not enough to get us through. Know what I mean?"

"Yeah, I guess I do," I responded, my voice dragging and dragging me along with it. "I do know what you mean," I rolled my eyes. And I did know. Having a husband was no longer enough for me. The deeper I got into my relationship with Louis, the more I wondered just how deep I'd allow it to go.

CHAPTER 38

It had rained during the night, and now the air had that damp, gloomy, musty smell to it. The sun was hiding behind dark clouds that looked like big balls of gray cotton. It was the kind of morning that would normally put me in a dark mood, but I was already in a dark mood and had been since my conversation with Rhoda the night before. But this darkness was more profound than usual. I could feel it creeping into everything. Even my soul. I was determined to rise above it, though. And I knew that with Louis's help, I would.

As grumpy as my parents were, I missed them and my daughter already. They had called me up as soon as they'd made it to the Bahamas. I was confident that my mother would take good care of Charlotte. That didn't stop me from worrying, though. But at the same time, I was glad that they were all away for the summer. I had more than enough on my plate to keep me busy.

I didn't want to admit it, but right now, Louis was about the only thing that could put a smile on my face. I knew that when I discussed Jade's upcoming wedding with him and whether or not I would go, I'd feel better about it.

In the old days, meaning my fat days, I used to get up every single morning and fix a breakfast fit for a Bigfoot family. That feast usually included coffee, milk, *and* juice; eggs, toast, *and* biscuits;

bacon, sausage, *and* ham; dollops of jelly; and mounds of butter big enough to choke a mule. I still enjoyed an occasional down-home breakfast. But nowadays a couple of cups of black coffee and one slice of melba toast were enough breakfast for me.

I had eaten only half of my slice of toast and was halfway through my second cup of coffee when Pee Wee returned from his alleged overnight fishing trip. Since pussy and fish smelled so much alike, I wouldn't have been able to tell which one he had spent the night with. It was just a few minutes before I had to leave for work that Tuesday morning. He shuffled in through the kitchen door, with a bucket full of assorted fish, but that didn't mean anything. He could have paid his woman a brief visit and still gone fishing. She could have even gone with him, like I used to. Some women would do anything to be with their man.

He had not shaved the area around his goatee since I'd last seen him. One thing I could say about my husband was that he was one of the few men I knew who looked good with stubble on his face. It brought back some fond memories. I was glad to see him, but that feeling didn't last long. His khaki jacket and matching pants were so filthy and wrinkled, he looked like a mountain man. He smelled like one, too. He dropped his fishing pole and bait bucket onto the counter, next to the microwave oven. Then he dumped the fish, most of them still flipping and flopping, into the sink. I didn't know what kind of fish he had caught, but those critters had my kitchen smelling like a whore's moneymaker after a busy night.

"Hi, baby," he mumbled dryly, barely moving his dried, cracked lips. "Ain't you kind of overdressed for work?"

"This is a skirt and blouse," I told him. I had on a sleeveless white cotton blouse and a denim skirt. It was one of the most conservative ensembles I owned.

Of all the people in my life, my husband was the only one who didn't seem all that impressed with my weight loss. As a matter of fact, it used to amuse him when people mistook me for his mama if I wore one of my outlandish muumuus when I went out with him. He didn't even notice anything different about my appearance until I had lost the first fifty pounds. And even then he thought that I'd only changed my hairdo. I had to tell him that I'd lost a substantial amount of weight.

A thought crossed my mind that I dismissed immediately: maybe Pee Wee had lost interest in me because of my weight loss! I refused to give that possibility too much consideration right now. But if it was true, I knew my marriage was in serious trouble. I had no desire to spend the second part of my life trapped in a mountain of blubber—even if it meant he'd never make love to me again.

Pee Wee washed his hands in the sink and dried them on a paper towel. "Is everything all right, Annette?" He glanced at the black pumps on my feet. I knew he didn't like them, and had it been up to him, I'd still be sliding around in a pair of flat moccasins or flip-flops.

"I guess it is," I muttered, barely looking in his direction. Without giving it much thought, I uncrossed my legs and hid them under the table as much as I could. But then he concentrated on my face and hair.

"And ain't you got on too much makeup just for work? Y'all havin' a staff meetin' at the Red Rose bar today or what?" He stood in front of me, with his arms folded like a prison guard.

"You think I have on too much makeup? All I have on is some lipstick and mascara," I pointed out.

"You look like you got on more makeup than Ronald McDonald to me," he insisted, his eyes landing on my hair. "And what's up with them girly braids? You ain't no teenager. You old enough to be somebody's grandmother."

"Well, I'm not somebody's grandmother," I snarled, patting my braids. They had loosened up since the incident with the bat in Louis's apartment. I had already planned to make an appointment with my hairdresser as soon as I got to work. Not to have her remove my braids, but to have her retighten them. "And in case you haven't noticed, there are a lot of women in Richland who are old enough to be *my* grandmother, and they're still wearing braids!" My husband was losing so many points with me, it was frightening. I was beginning to wonder just how much more of him I could stand before I bounced a skillet off of his head. "And since Charlotte's only ten, I won't be anybody's grandmother anytime soon!"

He threw his hands up and shook his head. "I ain't talkin' about them other old women wearin' braids. They could walk down Main

Street bald headed and naked, for all I care. I just thought that since you are so, uh, sophisticated these days, braids done got too ghetto for you."

"I don't agree with anything you've just said. You're talking crazy," I said firmly, patting the side of my head. I didn't want to remind him that when the world-famous actress Cicely Tyson wore her hair in the same style, he'd raved about it.

"Well, it's your hair," he remarked with a shrug. "You can do what you want to do with it, I guess. I just hope I don't come home one day and see you settin' up in here with no blond dreadlocks hangin' off your head. Not unless it's Halloween."

I ignored his last comment and took another sip from my cup.

The stench coming from the sink was unholy. The fish were splashing around like toddlers in a wading pool. Water was all over the counter and on the floor. Had things been normal, I would have complained, sopped up the water with a mop and a towel, and sprayed some room deodorizer. But this time I just sniffed, sneezed, and rubbed my nose. I did get up and open the window above the sink, though. Since he'd made the mess on the counter and the floor, I'd leave it for him to clean up.

"By the way, we've been invited to attend Jade's wedding in two weeks," I announced, returning to my seat at the table.

Pee Wee was leaning over the sink, but he whirled around so fast to face me, he almost fell to the floor. "Say what?"

"Jade is getting married in a couple of weeks, and Rhoda wants us to be at the wedding. Jade didn't give Rhoda enough time to plan the big, fancy church wedding she always wanted, so it'll be at Rhoda's house. I'll get your blue suit cleaned this weekend."

"Listen to me. You ain't got to worry about gettin' my blue suit cleaned this weekend or no other weekend. I won't need it—unless somebody dies, and I need to attend their funeral."

"So you are not going to go?" I asked dumbly.

Pee Wee gave me an incredulous look. "Look, I wish the girl well, and I know that sometimes I sound a little harsh when we talk about her. But I do not want to be in the same room with that girl after what she did to us, you especially."

"We have to move beyond that, Pee Wee. I'm having a hard time getting completely over what Jade did to me, but I'm trying, and

I've made some progress. Enough to agree to attend her wedding. You have to move forward on this issue, too."

"I have! And that ain't got nothin' to do with me bein' around Jade if I don't have to be. Especially to see her get married."

"I totally understand. But just being in the audience won't be that bad. We don't even have to say anything to her. Other than to wish her well, I won't say anything to her if I don't have to."

"I'm glad to hear that," he replied.

"If that's the way you feel, I'll let Rhoda and Otis know you won't be attending the wedding."

"You ain't got to speak for me, Annette. I intend to call up Rhoda myself as soon as I take a bath and de-funk. I know Rhoda is your girl, but she was my girl first. She deserves to hear how I feel from my lips." Pee Wee let out a mighty breath and turned on the water in the sink. He leaned his head into the sink and drank straight from the faucet, slurping like a dog. I waited until he had finished and stood back up.

"I'm glad you didn't do that in front of your daughter," I scolded. He ignored my comment as he wiped his lips with the back of his hand.

"By the way, what man is fool enough to marry Jade?" he asked with a grimace.

"That Mexican she brought home with her."

Pee Wee shook his head and waved both hands in the air. "I haven't met the dude, but when you see him, tell him he has my sympathy," he said, shaking his head again. From the looks of all the bushy, knotty hair on my husband's head, it was hard to believe that he was the most popular black barber in town.

"Is your decision final? Are you really not going to the wedding?" I asked.

Pee Wee looked at me like I'd asked him to do a ballet dance. "I doubt it very seriously. And after what she done to you, I am surprised that you would even think about goin' yourself."

"I'd be going for Rhoda," I said.

He gave me the most aggressive wave of dismissal he'd ever given me. He did it with both hands. "Woman, if you go to that damn weddin', that's all the proof I need to know you done completely lost your mind," he declared.

CHAPTER 39

Pee Wee's words had left me temporarily speechless. My mama's suggestion that I "fix" whatever was wrong with my marriage echoed in my head like a veiled threat. How could I fix something when I didn't even know what it was that needed to be fixed?

Just being in the room with the man I had vowed to love, honor, and obey until the day I died made me so uncomfortable, I could barely stand it. I was glad when the telephone rang. Had it been a wrong number, a telemarketer, or an obscene caller, I would have prolonged the conversation for as long as I could, just so I wouldn't have to continue talking to Pee Wee. It was not one of those three; it was even better. It was my mother.

Muh'Dear was calling to let me know that they were having a wonderful time and that they had already enjoyed a whole day on somebody's boat. "I had me three of them sweet drinks with them little umbrellas. I got so tipsy, I almost fell off that damn boat." Muh'Dear paused and laughed long and loud. I was so happy that she was happy. Especially given the hard life she'd endured and the fact that she'd raised me alone. "Your daddy is loungin' on the beach, with a drink in each hand. And that Charlotte. That hard-headed scamp is in her room, whinin', because she done already disturbed an eel and contracted the same rash that caused her so much misery on previous trips to the islands."

"Muh'Dear, I'm glad you all made it to the islands safe and sound, and I'm glad you're having such a good time. But let me tell you something real quick. Jade's getting married in a couple of weeks. I just found out," I blurted.

"Aw, shuck it! I hope Rhoda and Otis don't expect us to cut our vacation short to come home for that. You know I don't like that little jezebel no way. I loved her to death when she was a little girl, but she grew up to be a stone-cold heifer," my mother hissed. "Let me go tell Frank what you just told me and see what he wants to do. Shoot!"

"Don't you dare come back home for that!" I ordered. "I don't even know if I am going to that wedding myself."

"Oh? Well, do us a favor and don't tell Rhoda or Otis you even talked to me or Frank. Matter of fact, if they ask about us, tell them we will be out on somebody's boat for the next two weeks. Make that the next three weeks, in case they delay the weddin' on account of us. And if they delay it even more, tell them you can't get in touch with us at all."

I looked at Pee Wee and pointed to the telephone. He promptly shook his head and held up his hand. Muh'Dear made a few more rhetorical comments. Before she hung up, she complained about Jade some more, her arthritis, and about having to clean the fish that my daddy had caught that morning.

"Muh'Dear said to tell you everything is going fine for them down there," I told Pee Wee. "And in case Rhoda or Otis asks you if they can make it to Jade's wedding, tell them that they are on somebody's boat and can't be reached. And make sure you say that they can't be reached *indefinitely*."

He gave me a blank look and shrugged. "Whatever you say." That was the last thing my husband said to me before I left for work.

From all the smiles that greeted me when I got to the office, I decided that the Monday luncheon had gone well. I could see that everybody was busy making calls and dodging some of the colorful assaults that they received from almost every delinquent debtor they called.

"Annette, I hope you are feeling better," Gloria Watson told me as she handed me a stack of folders. "You still look a little peaked, though. Maybe you should have taken today off, too."

"I'm feeling much better, thank you," I said with a cough. "Uh, did I miss anything important yesterday?"

"Girl, you missed a hella good lunch yesterday." Gloria followed me into my office and stood in front of my desk as I plopped down. "We had all kinds of Chinese goodies. Who would have thought that a restaurant run by black folks could offer that much diversity? That Louis Baines sure knows his stuff, don't he?"

I gave Gloria a noncommittal look. "He sure does. Oh, on the same subject, please call Hannah and tell her to send all the invoices from Louis Baines directly to me," I instructed. "From now on."

Gloria hesitated so long, I glanced up at her with a slightly impatient look on my face. "Oh? Did she lose another invoice again?" she asked.

"Uh, not that I am aware of. But since this is a new account, I'd like to give it my personal attention." I cleared my throat and glanced at my nails.

"And it's an important account, too. Them oxtails over fried rice that we had for lunch yesterday were screaming." Gloria swooned and rolled her eyes. "Girl, the only time I eat this good is when I visit my grandma or my ex's mama. I have to put up with all kinds of foolishness from them just so I can get me a good meal. This is . . . this is perfect, Annette. This is way better than us having office picnics and them dull Christmas parties. And Off the Hook is *off the hook*."

"Well, you all deserve it," I proclaimed. "I just wish I had thought about sponsoring the Monday lunches sooner."

"What about the rest of the new accounts?"

"Huh? The other new accounts? What about them?" Gloria's question had startled me. However, it was a reasonable thing for her to ask.

"Yeah. Like the new office supplies vendor you decided to switch to." There was a confused look on Gloria's face.

"Uh, I'll give them my personal attention, too," I said, knowing I didn't need any more work than I already had on my desk. But I was glad that Gloria had mentioned the other new accounts. This way it wasn't so obvious that I was singling out Louis's account.

Gloria nodded and folded her arms. She was so satisfied with herself that I could have knocked her over with a toothpick. I read her like a book, so I knew that she felt like she had a little more power in the office now that she and I were more civil to each other.

"You sounded like you were at death's door when you called in yesterday morning. I hope you are feeling better. I prayed for you last night."

"Thanks, Gloria," I said, with another mild cough, trying not to overdo it.

"I got some cough drops in my desk," she offered.

"Oh, don't worry about me," I told her, holding up my hand. "I'll be just fine."

"Well, like I said, you still look a little peaked to me." Gloria folded her arms and gave me a motherly look. "Now don't you let this job get in the way of you taking care of your health. It'll be here when we are all dead and gone." She glanced around, then back at me, and said in a whisper, "These white folks wouldn't jeopardize their health if we owned this company. We don't need to do it for them." She winked.

I chuckled and winked back. "Gloria, if I don't feel any better by noon, I'll go back home," I said. That seemed to satisfy her, but she gave me another motherly look before she left my office.

There were already four messages on my voice mail. Two delinquent debtors had returned my calls just to tell me in no uncertain terms not to call them again. Rhoda had left an "urgent" message for me to call her ASAP. And Louis had called to say that he missed me and was "itching" to see me again.

I decided to return Rhoda's call first. To my everlasting horror, Jade answered the phone.

"May I speak to your mother, please?" I asked in as nice a voice as I could manage.

"You don't have to be so rude, Annette," Jade retorted.

"I didn't realize I was being rude," I snapped.

"Look, lady, you need to loosen up. I don't know why you just can't get over that little prank I pulled last year. I have."

"I'm sure you have, Jade. And believe it or not, I have, too. Now if you don't mind, please put your mother on the phone, if she's available."

Jade took her time responding. "I heard you want to come to my wedding." I didn't have to be in the same room with her to see the smirk on her face. I knew it was there, and I was certain that it was more severe than it usually was.

"Believe me, I don't want to come. Your mother asked me to be there. But if you don't want me there, I won't come."

Her response was a loud, exasperated groan. Suddenly, I heard a slap and then a whimper. From what I could determine, Rhoda had slapped Jade upside her hard head. That gave me a great deal of satisfaction. The next voice I heard belonged to Rhoda.

"Hey, girl," Rhoda said. Her voice was so calm, I never would have guessed that she'd just slapped her daughter, had I not heard it with my own ears. "I really didn't want to bother you about this, but I need your help. I've got a hundred invitations to send out, a million and one things to attend to before the wedding. Could you, uh, work with your friend Louis on the caterin'? At this point, he could serve peanut butter and jelly sandwiches, for all I care. I just want you to make sure that whatever he serves, it's somethin' good. Work out all the details for me, please."

"I can do that," I said with fake eagerness.

"I spoke to Louis this mornin', and he's very excited about it. And because it's such short notice, he's goin' to get a huge gratuity."

"Will he be there to help serve and supervise?"

"Well, he didn't really commit himself to that. But I have a feelin' his attendance depends on you. And, you know I don't like to beg, but you'd be doin' me a huge favor by bein' there. You *and* Pee Wee."

"You can forget about Pee Wee," I said quickly. "And my folks, too, for that matter. They are off somewhere on a boat and can't be reached," I lied.

"Well, I didn't expect your folks to come back here just for a weddin'. Especially since my own parents can't come, either. But I am sorry to hear that Pee Wee won't be present. He's Jade's godfather, you know."

"How could I forget?" I said dryly.

"What about you? Please tell me you're still goin' to be there for me!"

"I will," I replied, almost biting off the tip of my tongue because I had such a hard time getting the words out. "I promise."

CHAPTER 40

Louis called me up before I left work and invited me to have dinner with him that night. I appreciated his offer, and as much as I wanted to be with him again, I reluctantly declined.

I didn't know how long our romantic relationship was going to last, so I wanted to do everything I could think of to keep it fresh and exciting. I knew from experience that too much of a good thing too soon was not a good thing. Even though he had asked several times to see me more frequently, I didn't want to get bored with him by seeing him too often. And I didn't want him to get sick of seeing me. I decided that once or twice a week was enough for now.

Later in the week, I regretted not taking Louis up on his offer, because I didn't see him the following Thursday, like we had planned. And there was more than one reason for that. Rhoda was too busy planning Jade's wedding, so I had not been able to catch up with her to coordinate our Thursday night bowling ruse.

With all the last-minute preparations and running around she had to deal with, she was too exhausted to go bowling that night she said when she finally did return one of my calls. And since she was my cover, I couldn't use her as my alibi, in case Pee Wee went to the bowling alley when I was supposed to be there and wasn't. Ironically, he was the other reason I had chosen not to see Louis that Thursday night.

I had called the barbershop during my lunch hour to give Pee Wee a message from his daughter and was told that he'd left for the day. As usual, I didn't identify myself as his wife, and this time I didn't even attempt to find out where he'd gone. My dear, sweet Rhoda supplied that information herself a half hour later. She could not have called me up at a better time. I had just concluded a particularly disturbing call. A debtor had threatened to come to my office and blow my brains out if I "harassed" him again about a bill he claimed he was unable to pay. The threat had come right after I told him that when I'd called his number a few days before, his roommate had informed me that he was "still on his Mediterranean cruise." I had received numerous threats from debtors over the years. So far, none had carried out their threats, so I didn't let this one scare me much, either. Besides, I had other more serious situations to be concerned about.

"Is Pee Wee feelin' any better?" Rhoda wanted to know. "Did he make it home all right?"

"Better than what? What are you talking about?" I asked.

"I went to finalize the cake details at Joset's Bakery a little while ago, and I saw him comin' out of Dryer's Drugstore next door. He told me that he'd left work because he was sick," she said. "He had just picked up a prescription."

I was immediately concerned, but I didn't want to jump the gun. I decided to make light of the news Rhoda had just shared with me. "I bet it was some more Viagra," I replied.

"Some more Viagra? Is he really usin' that shit to perform?"

"He must be!" I exclaimed, my head throbbing and my ears ringing.

I still had no proof that my husband was seeing another woman, but trying to convince myself that he was made it easier for me to continue my behavior with Louis.

"Well, if he is seein' another woman, she must be fuckin' the livin' hell out of his ass. He looked like Rasputin with lead poisonin'."

"You should have seen him the day he came back from his alleged overnight fishing trip. He looked like roadkill."

"Anyway, Jade changed her mind about the cake again. Now she wants angel food."

"That was her first choice," I said, my voice rising. I wanted it to sound like I was a lot more concerned about Jade's wedding cake than I was about my husband.

The truth of the matter was, I was truly concerned about him leaving work to go home because he didn't feel well. I could not remember the last time he'd done that. I almost wished that Rhoda had not told me about him picking up a prescription. I wanted to believe that it was for Viagra and not something that I had to be worried about. I was concerned, but I was also curious. I wanted to know what was going on with my husband, but I knew that he was the only person who could tell me that. Well, I was now at a point where I was tired of guessing. I wanted to know what I was up against. What Pee Wee had to tell me would help me decide just how far I wanted to go with Louis.

He didn't answer the telephone when I called our house five minutes after my conversation with Rhoda. I tried every fifteen minutes for the next two hours. Finally, I left the office and rushed home, praying I wouldn't walk up on his corpse in my living room. Or something much worse. Like him fucking another woman in my bed.

I drove like a bat out of hell, narrowly missing a tree. A few blocks after that, I made such a sharp turn at a corner, I almost hit a mailbox sitting on the curb. A few blocks later I almost hit a pedestrian who was taking his good old time crossing the street. I almost hit several other vehicles along the way. I wasn't concerned about getting a few tickets, but I was concerned about causing a serious accident. Halfway to my house, I slowed down considerably. Turning on the radio helped; by the time I reached my street, I was fairly calm.

Our house was in the middle of our block. As soon as I turned onto Reed Street, I could see Pee Wee's car parked in front of the house. And from the looks of things, he had parked it in one hell of a hurry. One of the front tires was on the sidewalk. Right behind his Firebird was Rhoda's husband's Jeep. Otis had become so set in his ways and predictable, I could read him like a script. He visited only when he and Pee Wee wanted to sit around and drink beer and look stupid. And since Otis was the lead foreman at the Patterson Street Steel Mill, he could come and go as he pleased.

The last thing I expected to see in my own living room was a strange man stretched out on my sofa, with a can of beer in one hand and the telephone in the other.

"Who the hell are you?" I asked, walking toward him, with my hands on my hips.

"Me? Who de hell are *you*?" he had the nerve to ask. He gave me an annoyed look as he whispered into the telephone before he hung up.

"I happen to be the owner of this house!" I hollered, looking toward the kitchen.

Rhoda's husband, Otis, suddenly appeared in the living-room doorway. He shuffled into the room, with his shirt unbuttoned and his belly hanging over the top of his pants like a short apron. Like Pee Wee, Otis had let himself go to the dogs. His shoulder-length dreadlocks were almost completely gray and so matted, I couldn't tell where one ended and another began. His once handsome face was now hard, with hollowed-out cheeks and sunken eyes. It was hard to believe that forty-six years could do that much damage to a man who had once been so handsome. Now he looked bad enough to haunt a house. With a gremlin like him for a husband, it was easy to understand why Rhoda maintained a lover! He was the man on my sofa that I had not recognized, Ian "Bully" Bullard of London, England, by way of Montego Bay, Jamaica.

"Oh, ho! You are Annette! How cheeky of me not to realize it was you!" he shouted. At forty-nine, Bully was more handsome than ever and still had the body of a prizefighter. He and Otis were originally from Jamaica, but Bully had lived in England so long, his accent had become a combination of Jamaican and English. He had been Otis's best friend for decades and Rhoda's lover for almost as long.

"Bully, I'm sorry," I said, grinning. I reached out to shake his hand, but he gave me a bear hug instead. His embrace was powerful and comforting. This was what a woman liked. Not those little pats on the shoulder or the jaw that I got from my husband.

Bully had been an off-and-on houseguest at Rhoda's residence for most of this year and the year before, but I hadn't seen much of him during the last few months. And he wore a mustache now, which was why I had not recognized him immediately.

"You've become quite dry since de last time I saw you," Bully said, leaning back to look me over. He thumped both of my cheeks with his fingers, like he was inspecting a cantaloupe. For the first time in my life, my face was lean enough so that my cheekbones stood out prominently. Bully shrieked and jumped back like I'd bitten him. "Are you all right? What was it?" he asked, with a look of pity on his face.

I never could figure out why the first thing people thought when somebody they knew had lost a lot of weight was that there was something physically wrong with that person. Because I had eliminated so many pounds, I was in better shape now than I'd ever been in my life. Two doctors had told me that. I had more energy than I'd had since I was a teenager, and my blood pressure and cholesterol were finally at normal levels.

"Jesus surely must have wept for you," Bully said, shaking his head. He turned to Pee Wee, who had moved to the middle of the living-room floor.

The way Pee Wee was clutching his can of beer with both hands, you would have thought it was his dick. "Ain't nothin' wrong with her. She just stopped gobblin' up so much food. That's all," he had the nerve to say. "Baby, what are you doin' home so early?" He looked at his watch and snorted like a bull.

"I came home because I was worried about you," I said, glaring at him. "I kept calling and calling, and you didn't answer."

"Oh, was that you? I thought it was that fool boy Bobby at the shop, so I didn't pick up," said Pee Wee. He gave me a look that was so smug, it made my stomach turn. "I turned off the answerin' machine, too. I didn't want to be bothered."

"Apparently!" I hollered. "I just hope none of the calls you ignored were from your daughter."

"How could she call? I thought you told Rhoda that your mum and dad and de little one was out on a boat for a while," Otis interjected. "Which is a shame, because they can't be reached to hear about Jade's wedding in time to come, eh?"

"Uh, that's right," I muttered. One of the biggest problems I had with telling lies was that if I didn't keep them straight, I had to tell even more lies to keep the first one on track. "My folks can't be reached. . . ."

"Baby, you want a beer?" Pee Wee asked me, shaking his can in my direction.

"No, I don't want a beer. I want to know what's going on. Rhoda told me she saw you at the drugstore, getting a prescription filled." I saw no reason to tell him that I had called his work and been informed that he'd gone home sick.

"Well, if she had asked me, I would have told her that I was pickin' up some more of that salve to send to Charlotte for that rash she keeps gettin' on her legs and arms from them eels she can't seem to stay away from. Your mama called the other day and told me to pick it up and send it down there by FedEx."

"Oh. I didn't know," I replied. His explanation made sense, but it didn't explain why he had lied to his workers about going home sick. I knew that Otis was his close friend and drinking buddy. So he didn't have to lie because he wanted to spend some time with him. And besides, Pee Wee was self-employed and could do as he pleased. "Well, I have plans for this evening. I'll let you enjoy your company in peace."

Pee Wee was quite indifferent about me leaving the house again so soon. Not that he could have stopped me, anyway. I excused myself and got back into my car and slammed the door shut so hard, the windows rattled.

I drove past Rhoda's house, hoping she'd see me and come outside. I didn't want to take a chance and call her house again and risk having to suffer through another unpleasant encounter if Jade answered the telephone.

I didn't see Rhoda, and her SUV was not in the driveway, like it usually was. But her future son-in-law was sitting on the front porch steps, alone.

Not only did Marcelo look like a man who didn't have a friend in the world, but he looked like a man who was awaiting his own execution.

CHAPTER 41

I drove around for about an hour before I pulled into the parking lot of the Grab and Go convenience store on Liberty Street, near Rhoda's house. I needed to purchase a few things, and I couldn't think of anywhere else to go at the spur of the moment.

As I was collecting my items, I thought about paying a visit to Miss Rachel's, the beauty shop where I got my hair done, so I could catch up on my gossip. That idea didn't appeal to me for too long. The more I thought about it, the more I realized I really wasn't in the mood to sit around with a bunch of women, listening to them verbally crucify almost everybody I knew. By now they'd have all heard about Jade's upcoming wedding. It would no doubt be the main course on their shit list. I certainly didn't want to hear any more news about Jade anytime soon.

Just as I was about to leave the store, with the sugarless gum, deodorant, eyedrops, grape Slurpee, and some condoms—Louis forgot to bring some the last time—that I'd purchased, somebody tapped me on the shoulder. I whirled around to see one of the last faces I wanted to see.

"Hi, Wyrita," I muttered. I struggled to hide my irritation as I attempted to ease toward the exit.

Wyrita had on a pair of flip-flops, but that didn't stop her from goose-stepping up to my side, blocking the door so I couldn't escape. I suddenly felt like I was a hostage. "Girl, what do you think about Jade getting married, with her lazy self? She won't wash a dish, vacuum a floor, or do nothing else that a good wife is supposed to do. What kind of wife is she going to make?" Wyrita had a basket in her hand that contained a bottle of wine, several cans of sardines, and a large bag of Fritos. She lived just a block away, so I wasn't surprised to see her in a housecoat, with rollers in her hair. "And to a Mexican at that. Them hot-blooded Spanish dudes is mucho macho. He ain't going to put up with her shit. He'll be whupping her happy ass left and right in no time."

"Well, I just hope she'll be happy," I replied, and I truly meant that. As bleak as my opinion was of Jade, I still believed that she had at least one good bone in her body.

"Me, I'm going to make some man a damn good wife. I'm going to show you and everybody else. Especially the folks that laugh at me when I tell them that I'm going to be a perfect wife, like you."

I had to blink to hold back my tears. What Wyrita had just said was one of the nicest things anybody had ever said about me. I was truly touched. "You think that I'm the perfect wife?"

"Think? Uh-uh, honey chile. I *know* you are the kind of wife I want to be like. You got it all figured out. I've heard other folks say the same thing about you."

I had to blink some more. I knew that if I didn't leave that store soon, I was going to have to go back and buy some Kleenex tissue. I was just that close to tears. "Wyrita, it was so nice to see you again, and thank you for saying such nice things about me. I really appreciate hearing that." Wyrita had moved from in front of the exit, so I started to move toward it again. "I'll see you at the wedding."

"I hope Jade likes the salad bowl I got for her. I got it at Kmart for two dollars, but I stuck a forty-dollar Macy's tag on it. Then I put it in a Macy's gift box. Lizel got her a gift certificate to go to a spa after her honeymoon."

Wyrita followed me to my car, still talking. "And Marcelo is such a nice, easygoing man. I'm going to Mexico on my cruise for sure this Christmas. I'm going to bring me a Mexican back home with me, if it's the last thing I do. If Jade can get one, I know I can."

"I hope you will," I said, climbing into my car. Wyrita was still talking, so I had to roll down my window after I started my motor.

"And guess what? Lizel's been trying to play matchmaker for me and Louis Baines, that fine-ass catering brother!" she yelled.

No, she didn't say *that*! Yes, she did. Lizel was trying to hook Wyrita up with Louis. I wasted no time turning off my motor. "Oh? And are you interested in Louis Baines?" The last thing I wanted to deal with was competing with an attractive younger woman for Louis's attention. My heart began to beat about a mile a minute as I awaited her response.

"He is cute, but I keep telling Lizel that he ain't my type. I heard he was gay, anyway. Ain't nobody never seen him with no woman, so he must be." Wyrita was clearly disgusted by the thought of Louis being a candidate for the husband she so desperately wanted.

"I heard that same thing myself," I said, trying to sound as disgusted as Wyrita. "Maybe he is." I started my motor again. I couldn't get out of that parking lot fast enough.

I was glad to see that there were no cars parked in the vicinity of my residence when I reached my street. But I entered my living room with caution, anyway. Pee Wee had left the lights on in the living room and the kitchen. I was disappointed to see that the answering machine did not display any messages. My disappointment turned to anger when I saw that he had not turned the machine back on. There was no telling who had called. I could have missed all kinds of important calls! There was only one way to find out, and that was to call up some of the people I thought might have tried to reach me. . . .

"Did you call me?" I asked Louis as soon as he picked up his telephone.

"No, but I wanted to. I hope you are calling to tell me you want to be with me tonight," he said hopefully.

"I can't do that, but I will make up for it," I said, slowly sitting on my sofa. Something was poking me in the butt, so I had to wiggle around until I could retrieve it. I was annoyed to find an empty beer can in my living room, between the pillows on my sofa at that. "I just wanted to hear your voice. Is this a bad time?" I added, setting the beer can on the floor.

"There is never a bad time for you to call me," Louis told me. One thing I had to give this man credit for was the fact that he always knew what to say and when to say it. "I've got all the time in the world for you, baby." That was what I was talking about! The man truly had a way with words.

"I have to tell you right now that if you were not going to be at Jade's wedding, I wouldn't go," I confessed. "You know how I feel about that girl, and you know why."

"Sweetie, I know you are angry, and you have every right to be. But at some point, you have to let it go. The important thing is for you not to ever let yourself get in the position for shit like that to happen again."

"That's easy for you to say. She didn't hurt you," I protested.

"But she's still hurting you, and as long as you carry that anger, she will."

"Look, Louis, I do know what you are trying to say, and someday I will let go of my anger toward Jade. But what she did to me is still too fresh in my mind. Now that she is back in town and has already pissed me off, it's going to be that much harder to get over my anger."

"Don't let her win, Annette. Don't let her destroy you. That's what she wants. I know just how you feel. Trust me. I know what I'm talking about." Louis paused and let out some air. "You see, I've been betrayed, too," he continued, his voice cracking. "Like you, somebody I once loved hurt me clean to the bone."

"You? What happened?" The more Louis revealed about himself, the more comfortable I felt about him.

"Hold on, baby. Let me get a glass of water. Just thinking about this shit gives me a bad taste in my mouth. It feels like I've been chewing on an old sock."

He left me on hold for five minutes. I could hear soft music playing in the background. And I could hear Sadie, his cross-eyed cat, mewing up a storm.

"Baby, are you still there? I'm sorry I took so long. I had to feed Sadie. She's the only feline I know who would rather eat chicken wings than cat food." We both laughed.

"I'm still here."

"The girl I was going to marry ran off with my cousin. We called him Sticky because everything he touched stuck to him. Especially females. They've been married for five years."

"Oh. Now that's a pretty low-down thing for your girl and your cousin to do to you. Do you still talk to him, or her?"

"Naw. They moved to Atlanta right after they got married."

"Oh, Louis, I'm so sorry to hear that."

"That's not the half of it. The son that she had a year before, who I thought was mine, belongs to Sticky. A few months ago they came back to Greensboro for our family reunion. I had to leave the premises to keep from killing him. That's how I ended up here. That and the fact that I came up here to be with my uncle."

"I'm sorry about what happened to you, but I'm glad you ended up in Richland."

"After I moved here, every time I called home, Granny was on my case about finding myself a church home. I joined New Hope Baptist, and even though I don't go that often, all my spiritual needs are taken care of."

"I'm glad you're in the church, Louis," I said with a proud sniff. "Most of the men I know would rather go fishing or to a bar than come to church. Do you have a lot of friends?"

"A few. I play cards with the white dudes in the apartment below me. We get together and drink a few beers and talk shit. I keep myself busy."

"What about lady friends?" I held my breath.

"What about them?"

"Do you have any?" I was still holding my breath.

"Oh, sure I have lady friends. But if you mean serious relationships, there was just one before I met you."

I exhaled.

"Her name was Barbara Cundiff. She's a nurse at Richland General. We dated for a few weeks, until she decided she'd rather be with somebody else."

"You don't seem to have much luck with women, do you?"

"I do now," he said, speaking in a very seductive tone of voice.

"Thank you for saying that," I mumbled. "I hope you don't hold anything against women because of what the girl back home did to you, and the one you met here." I laughed when I realized how stupid that sounded. "I mean, there must have been other women between them and me that didn't hurt you."

"Not really. I have very high standards. I wouldn't feed my dragon to just any woman," he said quickly.

"Excuse me?"

"What I mean is, I am very particular about what I stick my dick in. I don't even fool around with jockstraps from discount stores."

"Now you're trying to be funny," I said, then chuckled.

"Seriously, I never had much time to do a lot of fooling around. My focus has always been my business. But that all changed as soon as I laid eyes on you."

"Louis, I really like you, and I couldn't have met you at a better time. But I still love my husband, and I plan to spend the rest of my life with him. I hope you understand that what we have is . . . uh, just an affair."

"I know you are not serious about me—"

"That's not what I meant! I love spending time with you!" I said defensively. "If a woman's going to cheat on her husband, it should always be with a man like you." I bit my tongue. It seemed like the more I talked, the more ridiculous I sounded. "I don't know what I'm saying!" I laughed so hard, my chest hurt. "But I think you know what I'm trying to say."

"You're a married woman, and you want to stay that way. I won't even try to change your marital status. But I want you to know, and I want you to know it now, if you ever do decide to leave your husband, I'd be glad to have you to myself. And to tell you the truth, from what you've told me, you and I have a lot more in common than you and *what's-his-name.*"

"What's-his-name is the father of my child. He will always be in my life. Listen, I think we should end this call now before one of us says something they will regret." I had to force myself to laugh this time.

"Baby, you have a blessed evening. If I don't talk to you any more this week, I will see you at this coming Monday's luncheon at your office, or at the Do Drop Inn on Thursday, if I'm lucky, or at that so-called wedding next Saturday. That is, if that crazy-ass Jade doesn't piss you off again enough for you to change your mind and not show up."

I sucked in a mouthful of air before I replied. "There is nothing else that Jade can do or say that she hasn't already done or said that would make me change my mind now. I will be at that wedding," I vowed.

CHAPTER 42

I hated what Jade had done to me in the past, but I did not hate Jade. And so, I had not become *that* bitter toward her, and I prayed that I never would. I had no use for her, and if she left town and never returned, I wouldn't care one way or the other. I didn't think that I was being too harsh. And despite her evil ways, I didn't sit around wishing something bad would happen to her, like some of the people I knew would have. That would have made me more like her than I cared to be. I had learned a long time ago that God don't like ugly, and that people like Jade eventually got what they deserved. I was confident that her downfall was already in the making.

I had not planned to buy a new outfit for the wedding. Nobody would care what I wore, anyway. For one thing, I didn't want to spend any money on something else I didn't need. I had plenty of clothes in my closet suitable to wear to a wedding. Jade was going to be the center of attention, anyway. She'd make sure of that.

The following Thursday I spent a few hours with Louis at the motel. It was the shot in the arm that I needed, because that damn wedding was scheduled to take place the following Saturday.

That Friday I ran into Scary Mary while I was on my lunch hour. I had just got my nails done and was coming out of the nail shop. She was going in, hobbling on her cane. Most of the elderly women

I knew had nails bitten down to the quick, but this old woman made weekly trips to the nail shop. Had she not seen me first, I would have ducked between two of the cars parked on the street and remained crouched until she'd passed.

It was a nice, warm, sunny day, but you never would have thought that by the way that old woman was dressed. She wore one of her quilt-looking, floor-length plaid skirts with a matching jacket, had a thick black wool shawl around her shoulders, and was slightly humpedbacked. She had on a pair of black suede boots with the most pointed toes I'd ever seen. She could have stabbed somebody with them.

"Annette, is that you?" she asked, shading her eyes with her hand to look at me. She gave the side of my leg a tap with her cane.

"Yes, ma'am," I said, with a muffled moan. Had Scary Mary not blocked my path like Wyrita had done in the convenience store, I would have kept walking.

"Where's Louis?" she asked, looking behind me.

"I have no idea where that man is," I replied, rolling my eyes. "Why do you ask?"

"Why do I ask? What's wrong with you, girl? You know I'm one nosy-ass bitch."

I nodded.

She glanced at my nails, smiled her approval, and then looked back at my face. She stared at me for so long, with a questioning look on her face, I got nervous.

"Uh, I guess I'll be on my way," I said, attempting to leave.

"You ain't gwine no place," she calmly told me, giving me a stern look.

"Oh, did you want something?"

"Jade told me she hope you don't upstage her on her big day by showin' up in one of them tentlike flowered muumuus of yours." Scary Mary was good about cutting to the chase, no matter what it was. "I told her I felt the same way," she added, patting my shoulder. We laughed at the same time. Despite her meddlesome ways, this old biddy had a sense of humor. And even though she was about as blunt as a sledgehammer, her comments were not meant to be malicious.

"Well, you can let her know that I haven't worn muumuus at all in a while." I tilted my head to the side and placed a hand on my hip, like I was about to prance down a catwalk. "And I'm the last person she should be worried about upstaging her."

"That little hussy! I'm gwine to fix her little red wagon. Just for her bein' so scandalous, I'm gwine to give her a *used* blender for her weddin' gift," Scary Mary chortled. "I bet you can't top that."

"I bet I can. She won't get a present from me, period."

For years I'd given presents to people I didn't like for one occasion or another. But the difference between them and Jade was, they had not betrayed me in as profound a way as Jade had. This girl was in a category by herself. And for that, I felt sorry for her. But I was not sorry enough to forgive her yet. I knew that my bitterness was probably causing me more pain than it was Jade, but I was working on reducing it and eventually eliminating it altogether. And, since Louis had brought so much joy into my life, I had made a little more progress.

"Oh? Now that don't sound like you. You ain't givin' Jade nothin'?"

"Nothing," I stated with a prim sniff.

"Well, now! She ain't gwine to like that!"

I simply shrugged.

"You sure enough done changed, Annette."

"Let's just say that I'm not the woman I used to be."

"You sure ain't. You was always the kind of gal that tried to make everybody you knew happy. Including that motherfucking, dead-ass Boatwright, who took advantage of your little pussy when you was a youngin'." Scary Mary paused long enough to catch her breath. "If I was you, I'd go pee on his grave on the anniversary of his death every year."

"I've thought about doing just that," I told her. After listening to a list of complaints about her business and health, I gave her a mighty hug, then went on my way.

I worked late that day, and when I got home around seven, Pee Wee was already sleeping like a dead man. He had not changed his mind about going to the wedding. In fact, he and I had not even discussed it again since I first told him.

I got up early that dreaded Saturday morning and made breakfast for Pee Wee. He had planned to spend the day hanging out with his friends. When I asked him which friends, he couldn't even look me in the eye or give me a straight answer. I left it at that.

Around ten I started to get ready for the wedding, even though it was scheduled for one in the afternoon. I had offered to help Louis set things up, but he had declined my offer. Around eleven Rhoda called me up.

"Annette, I would appreciate it if you'd come a little early. I just need you here for moral support," she told me.

Since she thought that Jade's wedding was a one-time event, I agreed. However, I had a feeling that Jade would go through several husbands in her lifetime. But I had already decided that I was going to limit myself to just one wedding in her honor.

I arrived at Rhoda's house a little later than I had planned, and I was surprised that the only vehicles parked in the vicinity belonged to Scary Mary and Louis. Both vans occupied the driveway, right behind Rhoda's SUV. Rhoda had hired several valets to take care of the parking, but I parked my car on the street myself.

The front door to Rhoda's beautiful one-story brick house was open, so I let myself in. A handsome, light-skinned man in a black tux smiled at me as I entered. He stood in front of the fireplace in the living room, with a saxophone in one hand and a half-empty wineglass in the other. I looked to his left and was surprised to see another man, also in a tux, sitting at Rhoda's white baby grand piano. The furniture had been rearranged throughout the house to allow the guests to move about more comfortably. The most delicate pieces had been covered in thick, clear plastic. The same type of plastic also covered Rhoda's wall-to-wall white shag carpet.

Bully and Otis were also in the living room, sprawled on the sofa, which had been pushed up against the wall facing the large-screen TV. They were drinking beer straight from the can. The way they were dressed, in jeans and dingy T-shirts, you would have thought that they were preparing to watch some ball game, not attend a wedding.

Lizel and Wyrita had sent out the invitations and run from one mall to another to purchase all the decorations. They had also helped Rhoda decorate her living room with pastel-colored balloons, streamers, and flowers. Those festive items went well with Rhoda's black leather sofa and love seats, gold and red brocade drapes, and glass-top tables.

Expensive oil paintings of Rhoda and her family covered almost every wall in the living room, which was a story within itself. The paintings made the O'Toole family look as normal and happy as Bill Cosby's TV family. Few people knew that that was not the case. Behind the toothy smiles and blissful scenes, Rhoda and her clan were as dysfunctional as a living family could be.

Even though she had not had time to do much planning, I could tell that this shindig was going to be as eventful as a coronation.

But I still couldn't wait for it to end.

CHAPTER 43

There were a lot of other people on the guest list that Jade had slighted on some level at one time or another. They included her so-called best friends, who did as much backstabbing as she did. It was no secret that a lot of people didn't like Jade and avoided her as much as they could. But I didn't know too many people in Richland who'd turn down an invitation to a wedding that would include a lavishly catered meal, a band, and a chance to show off a new outfit.

"De wife is in de bedroom," Otis told me, slurring his words. "You look d'licious, m'lady." He jabbed Bully in the side with his elbow. "Eh, mon? Irie?"

"Irie!" Bully yelled, smiling, nodding, and looking me up and down. "Irieeeeee . . ."

"Thank you," I mumbled. I didn't have a clue as to what *irie* meant. But from the way Bully and Otis were eyeballing me, it had to mean something good. "And irie to you both, too," I added, smiling and nodding back at them.

I had met a lot of Otis's Jamaican relatives and other island friends. I had to admit that the men from that part of the world held women in very high regard. Even women who didn't deserve to be held in any regard at all. I knew that because when I was a muu-muu-wearing plain Jane at my heaviest, Jamaican men still treated me like I was something good to eat.

I was glad to find Rhoda alone in the master bedroom. Like every other room in Rhoda's house, the bedroom looked like a showroom. Since Otis still slept in the same bed with her, I wondered how he felt about everything in the room being frilly and pink and white. It wouldn't have mattered what he thought. Everybody who knew Rhoda knew that she could crack the whip as well as Captain Hook.

I stopped in the middle of the room and admired her. "Girl, you look fantastic," I offered.

"So do you. Is that outfit new?"

"Something like that," I muttered.

She was dazzling in a light blue silk dress, with her hair in a French roll. But she looked completely flustered as she sat on the edge of her bed, sliding her feet into her panty hose. A pair of low-heeled blue pumps sat on the floor in front of her tiny, beautifully pedicured feet.

"Oh, I'm so glad you're here," she squealed, giving me a desperate look. "Girl, I had to send the tablecloths back to that fool of a dry cleaner twice to get them as white as they are supposed to be. And then that damn fool spilled some blue shit on the damn things—after he'd cleaned them! Holy moly! I swear to God, people just don't take any pride in doin' a good job anymore! He finally cleaned them right, though." Rhoda waved her hands above her head.

"Is there anything you want me to do?" I asked, hoping she'd say no. I folded my arms and shifted my weight from one foot to the other. My fear was that I'd have to deal with Jade more than I wanted to before everything was over. While I wanted to be at the wedding to support Rhoda and Otis, I had almost changed my mind at the last minute.

"Could you please do me a favor? Go to the dinin' room and check to make sure that everything is goin' well with Louis, uh, *our sexy caterer.*" She paused and gave me a conspiratorial wink. Then she let out a loud sigh, looked at her watch, and groaned. "He's been here for an hour, and I haven't had a chance to spend much time supervisin' him and his people. Oh! I just want to make sure we are all on the same page!"

"Rhoda, you need to calm down some. This is only a wedding," I whimpered.

"Yes, it is *only* a weddin', but it's for my *only* daughter," she reminded me, giving me a hot look. Then she got quiet, and a pensive look crossed her face. I bowed my head submissively as she continued. "Jade's my only chance to be a grandmother," she said, almost whispering. Rhoda's twenty-eight-year-old son, Julian, who lived in Alabama with his partner, was gay. And he had always made it clear that he wanted nothing to do with raising kids. Her other son, David, had died when he was a baby. I was the only person who knew that Bully had fathered that child. It was easy for me to understand why Jade's wedding was so important to her.

"Let's concentrate on today, Rhoda," I said in a gentle voice. "This is supposed to be a happy day."

Rhoda sniffed and blinked rapidly a few times. Then she glanced at me with a faraway look in her eyes. "You'll know what it's like in a few years with Charlotte." She shook her head like she was trying to shake something loose. "Oh shit!"

"What's wrong now?" I asked, rolling my eyes.

"You smell that?" She turned up her nose and sniffed the air.

"Whatever it is, it smells good," I told her. We both looked toward the door.

"Chicken wings! And *fried* chicken wings at that! Aarrgghh! I forgot to tell Louis to take those damn chicken wings off the list. I wish I had not let Bully talk me into includin' chicken wings on the menu! Jade almost had a cow when she found out. She said she didn't want anything too ethnic. And she's the one who told me to add tacos, chili peppers, refried beans, and Spanish rice so Marcelo would feel more at home. Now if that's not ethnic, I don't know what is. Can you believe that girl?" Rhoda paused long enough to catch her breath and shake her head some more. "And poor Louis. I've been ridin' his back all week over that damn menu! After this is all over, I'm goin' to apologize to him and give him a huge bonus. You can take care of the rest for me. . . ."

"The rest of what?" I asked, with a dumb look on my face.

"Makin' him feel good." Rhoda gave me a mischievous wink.

"You stop talking like that! Somebody might hear you," I warned, looking toward the door again.

Rhoda tilted her head to the side and shrugged. "Well, as long as everybody is happy with the food, that's all that really matters, I guess."

"Well, you don't have to worry about Louis. He always does a good job. I can vouch for him," I said with a few vigorous nods.

Rhoda jumped up from the bed, stumbled across the floor, and stood in front of the full-length mirror on the back of the door of one of the two large walk-in closets. She gave herself a critical look as she patted the side of her hair. "Did I tell you I found another gray hair the other day?" she said with a groan.

"Well, we are middle-aged women, Rhoda. Graying hair comes with the territory. But as long as they keep making hair dye, we don't have anything to worry about," I said, patting my own hair.

"Yeah, but we have to remember to keep our hair appointments, and I missed the last one. I forgot all about it."

"Well, memory loss is another thing we have to deal with. It's all downhill from here. . . ."

"Please stop remindin' me that we've tumbled over the hill. I can feel it in my bones every day."

I took it upon myself to lighten up the conversation. "How's the groom-to-be?" I had not seen the mysterious Mexican up close since that disastrous day at the mall. I still didn't know what to make of seeing him sitting on Rhoda's front porch the other day, looking like a lost boy.

"And that's another thing! Poor Marcelo is so nervous. Did you see him out there? He went to get a haircut three hours ago."

"I didn't see him," I answered, looking toward the window.

"Well, maybe he stopped off somewhere to have a drink alone. Poor thing. That boy is so nervous about all this. You'd think that a man who fights bulls for a livin' would have more balls. And that's another thing. I don't know what kind of money bullfighters make or how often they work, but he'd better brace himself. It's not goin' to be easy for him to keep Jade happy for the next forty or fifty years. That girl is more high maintenance than the Concorde. Do you know what she did last week?"

"There's just no telling," I replied, tuning my ears up to hear yet another horror story about Jade.

"She had maxed out her credit card, so Otis gave her a new one, with a ten-thousand-dollar line of credit. Twice the amount that we allowed her to have before. She maxed the new card out in one weekend. I just found out that she treated all her friends to extravagant dinners, bought a bag of weed and some new clothes for Marcelo, gave one of her friends a cash advance for a down payment on a new car, paid for one of her friend's upcomin' Caribbean cruise, and God knows what else! Remind me to get in her face after she returns from her honeymoon in Paris!"

I gasped so hard, I almost swallowed my teeth. "Honeymoon in Paris? She just decided to get married, but she had time to plan a honeymoon in Paris?"

"You know Jade. She's always bookin' ahead. I have a feelin' she and Marcelo started cookin' up this shit the day they met. By the way, what do you think about my future son-in-law?"

"I met him only briefly, but Marcelo seems pretty well grounded," I replied. "I don't think you have to worry about him."

"He's so quiet, though. I never know what he's thinkin'. And that worries me. My daddy used to say that still waters run deep, and it always scared me when he said that about somebody." Rhoda blinked and gave me a curious look. "Maybe Marcelo is just . . . you know . . . shy."

"Maybe he feels out of place. You told me that this is the first time he's been outside of Mexico," I reminded her. "This is a whole new cultural experience for him."

"Latin people are so complicated! They are as complicated as we are. Why can't black folks and Latinos be more like Asians or Jews? They've got it all figured out, and that's why they are so successful in just about everything they do! I swear to God. If I didn't know any better, I'd swear that God was havin' a bad day when he created blacks and Latinos. Half of the time, most of us don't know if we are comin' or goin'." Rhoda laughed. I was glad to see that she was in a jovial mood. That was going to make it that much easier for me to get through the day.

"Rhoda, you should be ashamed of yourself!" I scolded. "That's an insensitive, racist point of view—especially coming from a sister." I had to pause to catch my breath. "However, since it comes close to hitting the nail on the head, I won't argue with you about it." We both laughed. "Anyway, I am sure that Marcelo misses being around his own kind."

"Well, I introduced him to that Puerto Rican couple across the street. Unfortunately, that didn't help his mood much, because they think that with that blond hair on top of their dumb-ass heads—which is obviously dyed—that they are lily white. Remind me to introduce Marcelo to my banker. Javier is from Cuba. He hates blond hair so much, he won't even wear yellow clothin'. Poor Marcelo. None of his family could be here, and he's been bendin' over backwards to keep Jade from goin' off the deep end." Rhoda gave me another curious look. "All I want is for the child to be happy. I know she can be a bitter pill to swallow, but she's still my baby girl, and I love her to death. You know what I mean?"

"I know what you mean," I said, looking away. "I'll check on the caterers," I added, slowly moving toward the door.

"Did my boy Pee Wee change his mind about comin' to the weddin'?" Rhoda yelled.

I had my hand on the doorknob. At the mention of my husband's name, my entire body stiffened. "No. Uh, he wasn't feeling well," I said, shaking my head.

Rhoda gave me a blank look and shrugged her shoulders.

"Rhoda, I don't know how you do it, but I don't think that I could stand to be in a house with my husband and my lover at the same time. I'd be a nervous wreck!" I hollered. "Every time I see Bully and Otis together, they act like they are best friends."

Rhoda narrowed her eyes and gave me an incredulous look. "What's wrong with you, girl? They are best friends," she snapped, talking so fast her lips trembled. "You know they've been best friends forever. Otis is the one who introduced me to Bully." She stopped talking for a moment, but her lips were still moving. Her words couldn't keep up with her mouth. "How are things between you and Louis?" she asked in a much lower voice, with her hand cupped around her mouth. Then she continued in a whisper. "Is Louis feedin' that kitty cat like he's supposed to?"

"You mean Sadie? He's feeding that cross-eyed creature too well, if you ask me. He just bought her a collar that could fit around *my* neck."

"I was talkin' about the kitty cat between your legs," Rhoda told me, still whispering.

"Everything is fine," I whispered back, glancing toward the door again.

"Good, good! That's what I was hopin' you'd say. I can't say it to you enough. Enjoy it while you can." Rhoda chuckled and shook her head. "This may be your last time to get this loose."

CHAPTER 44

I had been in Rhoda's bedroom only for a few minutes, but by the time I got back to the living room, almost all the guests had arrived. I was glad to see that Otis and Bully had removed themselves from the living-room sofa, and I hoped that they were off somewhere getting dressed.

There was such a mob in the house now, I had to squeeze through bodies to get to the spacious dining room. Louis and two of his male employees, all three in tuxedos, were in the dining room, juggling large pans and bowls. They were scurrying around like bees, organizing things on a long table with a tablecloth that was such a bright shade of white, it hurt my eyes to look at it. I knew about the dreaded chicken wings, but I smelled all kinds of other wonderful things in those pans and bowls, too.

I walked toward Louis, taking slow, tentative steps. "You look so nice," I said as soon as I got close enough for him to hear me. I glanced around to make sure his employees were not listening or looking in my direction. I didn't want them to hear what I had to say or see me give Louis a playful tap on the chin with my fist.

"Hi, honey," he replied. "I'm glad you think so." He made a face like he was in pain. Then he rolled his eyes. "Wearing this monkey suit was not my idea. But since this is what the hostess wanted us to wear and she's paying such a pretty penny for it, what the hell?"

Louis smiled, and then he gave me a *dirty* look, his eyes bugged out, and he licked his lips. "Baby, you look so good to me. You just wait'll I get you alone again," he whispered.

"And I can't wait for you to get me alone again," I assured him, giving him another playful tap on his chin.

"I hope you like what's on the menu. In addition to deep-fried chicken wings, deviled eggs, several Mexican items, Yankee pot roast, smashed potatoes, quiche, crawfish, and every veggie in the book, I made some roasted duck."

"I'm standing in front of the best thing on the menu. Roasted *dick,*" I whispered. I slid my tongue across my bottom lip.

I was so glad that I had come to this wedding now. I just wished that I could spend my whole time behind the scenes, like in the kitchen with Louis, instead of in the living room, with the rest of the guests. I enjoyed watching him do his thing. He had prepared a mean feast, and he deserved all the glory.

I gave his cheek a hungry little kiss and his crotch a naughty little pat. He moaned and then froze in his tracks like a pillar of salt. I had witnessed this behavior before. This was how he looked when he was in ecstasy. Every time we made love, he moaned and froze just before he climaxed.

"That's payback for what you did to me with your fingers in Antonosanti's restaurant that day we went there for lunch," I quipped. I leaned close to his ear. "I just hope you don't leak out as much love juice as I did that day."

Louis had stopped moaning, but he still seemed frozen in place. It was the sudden frown on his face that startled me. He nodded toward the door. I was afraid to turn around to see who it was, but I did.

"Y'all need to get a room," Scary Mary laughed as she entered the dining room, waving her ubiquitous cane in the air. When she got to Louis, she stopped in front of him, grinning like a fool. "Louis, you look sweet enough to eat. If it wasn't for my arthritis, and if I was five years younger and wasn't still recovering from a severe case of grippe, I'd drop to my knees and blow that young tallywhacker between your legs to kingdom come. And don't think I couldn't do it! I done had seventy years of practice!" The old madam laughed some more. "And ain't I cute?" she asked, posing. She wore a multicolored, flowing robe with ruffles on the sleeves, and a matching turban. She looked like a cross between a piñata and the Dalai Lama.

"You do look cute today," I hesitantly agreed.

"I know I look good, girl. I always look good," she told me, looking me up and down. "You do, too. But the next time I hope you leave them earbobs at home. They look like clovers."

"They are clovers," I said, clearing my throat.

"Well, at least they match that green dress you got on." Scary Mary glanced around the room. "I came in here to let my mouth inspect a mess of them chicken wings. Them damn things is screamin' so loud, I can hear them all the way in the livin' room. Can smell them damn things all the way out in the livin' room, too. That means they *gots* to be good to eat!"

Without waiting for permission, she lifted the lid off one of the large pans and helped herself to two deep-fried chicken wings, clutching them between two fingers. She chewed and spoke at the same time, her eyes back on Louis. "Young man, you might want to wipe that lipstick off your jaw. This is gettin' to be a habit with y'all, ain't it?" She paused and swallowed hard. Then she looked at me. "Annette, you might want to drag your tail into the bathroom yonder and spread on some more lipstick. You look like you been mauled."

I excused myself and entered the bathroom near the empty kitchen, on the other side of the dining room. I took my time repairing my makeup. As I was walking through the kitchen on my way to the living room, the kitchen telephone rang. I ignored it at first, but when it didn't seem like anybody else was going to answer the call, I did.

"This is the O'Toole residence," I said, actually sounding cheerful. A few moments of silence followed. "Hello?"

"Who is this please?" The caller spoke with a Spanish accent. His voice was low and hollow. And, he sounded frightened.

"This is . . . Annette. Marcelo, is that you? Is everything all right? Did you get your hair cut?" My first thought was that the poor man had gotten lost on his way to or from the barbershop, and this was a call for help.

"Everything is not all right," he muttered.

"Marcelo, where are you? Hold on so I can call Rhoda or Otis to the phone."

"No!" he hollered quickly. "I don't want to speak with either one of them. *Ay caramba!*"

"Marcelo, are you all right? You sound like you're in pain! Are you in trouble? Have you been injured?"

"Oh God. Something like that," the poor man moaned.

This was a call that I was sorry I had answered.

"Then hold on while I go find Jade—"

"No! I *really* don't want to speak with *her*! *Ay caramba!*"

My heart started to beat like a bongo drum. I knew that whatever Marcelo had to say, it wasn't going to be pretty. I didn't know much Spanish, but something told me that *Ay caramba* was an expression of despair. Something also told me that the shit was about to hit the fan in a big way.

"Tell her for me, I will always love her. But I cannot marry her," Marcelo said, his voice trembling. "I must go now."

I had heard about brides, and a few grooms, getting jilted on their wedding day. And when I was younger and had zero confidence, I had thought that something like that would happen to me. Never in my wildest imagination had I thought it would happen to Jade. But that was exactly what was happening! If this was just the beginning of her downfall, she had a dark row to hoe ahead of her.

"You're what?" I shrieked. "Did I just hear you right?" More silence followed. "Marcelo, please tell me this is a joke. And if it is, it's not funny at all."

"You heard me right. I have to leave this country today!"

I didn't want to believe my ears, but I had to. I still felt some degree of compassion for Jade. She was about to get part of what she had coming. There was no doubt about that. But *this* was something that I would not have wished on my worst enemy.

"Boy, why did you wait until today to do this?" I asked. "Do you realize what you're doing and how many people you are going to hurt?"

"I realize I can't marry Jade! I never wanted to marry Jade! I've been trying to tell her that ever since she told me we was getting married! I never asked her to get married!" He paused and lowered his voice by a few decibels. "She just come to me one morning, hand me a coffee, and say, 'By the way, we're getting married soon.'"

"That was it?"

"That was it! At first I thought she was making a joke to me, so I said, 'Sure, no problem.' But she was for real! What do I know about being a husband? I don't know nothing, that's what. I only been shaving my face for one year, and I've only had two girlfriends so far. I'm not ready to give up my life to get married!"

"Marcelo, are you telling me that you shared all of this with Jade, and she still went through with her wedding plans?"

"*Sí, señora!* Even last night I tell her I am not happy about this."

"Well, what did she say?"

"Nothing! She cover my mouth with her hand and tell me to shaddup and do as she tell me because she is the boss! I must go now!"

CHAPTER 45

"Marcelo, don't hang up yet! Just tell me where you are. Let me come get you and bring you back here," I pleaded. "Don't do this. Don't cause this much pain! You'll regret it for the rest of your life!"

"Tell Señor Otis I will leave his car in the airport parking lot. Tell Señora Rhoda that I will pay her back the money, because I took some money from her purse this morning to use to pay for my way back to my home in Mexico, where I belong."

"Oh my God! Look, you're in enough trouble already for stealing Rhoda's money. We can fix that. But don't run away, Marcelo. Get back in that car, and get back here as soon as you can. It's not too late. If you leave now, you'll make it back in time for your wedding," I pleaded. "And I won't tell anybody about this phone conversation."

"No! I've been thinking and thinking about this for a long time. I never wanted to hurt Jade, and I thought I'd go through this marriage just for her. But it was just to make her stop crying all the time about how jealous you were of her and how bad *you hurt her* last year. She said you was such a mean lady to her because of a little joke she played on you that she tried to kill herself!"

When Marcelo paused, I could have jumped right in and defended myself. But I didn't even bother. I knew that Jade had done a pretty thorough job of demonizing me behind my back. And I knew that it was beyond repair. That was why I didn't even comment on what Marcelo had just shared with me. He was the one in pain now.

He sniffed a few times, and then he continued. "I told myself to marry her, anyway, and maybe things would work out. If nothing else, marrying her would have meant I could get American citizenship. I told myself that up until last night. But this morning . . . I don't know, señora. It all hit me like a bat! I don't want citizenship in heaven bad enough to go through with this! I—I—I can't do this! Jade is not the girl for me. I don't know what she needs, but whatever it is, I don't got it. She needs a king or a president or some man up high. Me, I'm just a little bullfighter—and not even that completely yet. I'm still in training! I have no money, no nothing!"

I was so taken aback, my head was spinning. I had a dozen more questions running through my head. "Marcelo, had you gone through with this marriage, how in the world were you and Jade going to support yourselves?"

"She told me not to worry, that as long as her mama and papa had money, they would take care of us! She told me she was going to make them buy us a house on Roseville Avenue, and it had to be on the same block as the mayor of this city so that we could rub it in his racist face, she said!"

I got sad and angry at the same time. Just the thought of Jade expecting her parents to continue supporting her and Marcelo, and to buy them a house in Mayor Stargen's neighborhood, was enough to make me sick. There was no end to this girl's nerve! "You're already at the airport, aren't you, Marcelo?" I asked. He didn't even have to answer that question. I had figured that out on my own when I heard a flight called over a loudspeaker in the background on his end.

"I have to go now!"

"Don't hang up that telephone, boy!" I yelled. But it was too late. Marcelo mumbled something in Spanish; then he hung up. I stood there staring at the telephone in slack-jawed amazement. "Oh my God," I mouthed. "Oh . . . my . . . God."

I closed my eyes for a moment, and when I opened them, Jade was standing in the doorway, with her hands on her hips. She had the nerve to have on a white wedding dress, with a train that must have been six feet long, the way she was holding it in her arms. She had on a gold tiara.

She looked me up and down as if I were less than nothing. From the horrified look on her face, I could tell that she was not impressed with the snug-fitting green dress I had on. I was so glad that I had not spent any money on something new and had not even bought her a wedding gift.

"Jade, I need to talk to you. I need to tell you something," I began.

"Shet up!" she hissed, wagging a finger like a dog's tail in my direction. "You listen to me, and you'd better listen good! You are lucky that I gave in and let you come to my wedding—especially after all you did to me! And if Mama hadn't threatened to cancel my Paris honeymoon, you wouldn't be here!"

"I can be out of here in five minutes," I managed to say in a level voice. I carried a purse with a long strap. It dangled off my shoulder like a snake with a big head. The telephone was still in my hand. I was itching to tell her who had called, but I decided to let her run her course.

"That's fine with me. But if you do stay, I would appreciate it if you would stop sneaking around in this house, tying up our telephone line! And when our phone bill arrives, I'd better not see that you just made an out-of-state call, or you're going to be sorry! My mama and daddy have enough bills to pay without you adding more." She let out a prolonged snort, and then she rubbed her nose with the back of her hand. Something made her sneeze. She seemed embarrassed by it, even though the only witness was me.

She quickly composed herself and resumed her attack. "You are not at home! Marcelo might be trying to get through, and here you are, with your tacky-looking self, tying up our phone line!" she wailed. "If you just *had* to come here today, the least you can do is get in that dining room and make sure that damn fag caterer is doing his job right."

Like the prized palomino pony that she thought she was, Jade pranced across the floor, toward me. Her eyes looked like they were on fire. She snatched the telephone out of my hand so fast and hard, she almost knocked me down. Her behavior made it easy for me to report what I'd just learned.

"That was Marcelo. He's on his way home," I said, struggling with my words.

"He'd better be! And he'd better not be late for my wedding, if he knows what's good for him. I've told that dumb-ass spic a thousand times not to mess with me. By the time I get through with him, he may be making arrangements for his own autopsy before this day is over. Where was he calling from?"

I cleared my throat. "He didn't say, but I'm pretty sure that he was calling from the airport. I heard flight information being announced over a loudspeaker. And, if I'm not mistaken, I heard airplane engines, too."

"Airport? What airport?"

I shrugged. "I'm not sure if it was Akron-Canton or Cleveland."

Jade gave me a puzzled look. "What? What do you mean? What the fuck is he doing at *any* goddamn airport? Who is he . . . Is he picking somebody up? He didn't tell me. . . ."

I shook my head so hard, it felt like everything in it rattled against my skull. Now I was truly sorry that I was the one who had taken Marcelo's call.

"He's not coming back, Jade," I told her.

Her jaw dropped, and the blood drained from her face so fast, she looked almost two shades lighter. Words could not describe the pain on her face. It was a look of absolute defeat. Goliath must have felt the same way when David brought him down. It occurred to me that Jade might have to arrange for her own autopsy, too, before the day was over.

I watched her meltdown in horror for a few seconds. I didn't know what to do or say. I held my own breath as she began to choke on hers. It was the most profound panic attack I'd ever witnessed.

I finally got my wits about me and did what was prudent and humane: I slapped Jade on her back until she was able to breathe normally again. She sighed like a baby for a moment. But a few seconds later, her eyes rolled back in her head, and she swayed from side to side like an old willow tree. With a loud hiss, she fainted and fell forward into my arms like a sack of dirt.

CHAPTER 46

Right after three burly paramedics strapped Jade to a gurney, her beautiful wedding gown soaked with her pee, tears, and snot, they hauled her away in an ambulance.

Since it was such a nice, sunny day, most of the neighbors on Rhoda's block were already outside or had their doors and windows ajar. A nosy mob quickly gathered in Rhoda's front yard, trampling her neatly manicured lawn and littering with everything from cigarette butts to empty beer cans.

Ever since Jade had regained consciousness in the kitchen, she had kicked and screamed like a hog about to be slaughtered. She was still kicking and screaming when the ambulance pulled away.

Rhoda, almost as hysterical and delirious as Jade, rode along in the ambulance, and Otis followed in his Jeep. I decided to stay at the house to help Bully, Scary Mary, Lizel, and Wyrita deal with the stunned wedding guests. Some of the older women were weeping and wailing, and needed to be hugged and assured that Jade was going to be all right. You would have thought that this was the aftermath of a funeral.

Even though Scary Mary complained about all the snot and teardrops that the women smeared on her outfit, I was glad she was there to help out. Despite her age and the mysterious condition of her health, she was a trouper and could always be counted on in a crisis. The same was true of the other women who had offered to stay behind and help maintain some control. However, some of the guests had less noble motives for remaining on the premises. I saw a couple of women scurry into Rhoda's bedroom and come out wearing some of her most expensive perfume. I saw another woman inspecting the contents of the refrigerator. Then there were a few who were so nosy, all they really cared about was hearing the whole story about "that Mexican and how he had clowned Jade on one of the most important days in her life." But most of the people chose to hang around because they wanted to take advantage of the feast that Rhoda had ordered.

"Don't y'all let me leave here without a plate," Wyrita said as we all stood in the living room, consoling each other. "And that bowl I got at Macy's that I was going to give to Jade for a wedding present. She won't be needing it now." Wyrita gave me a conspiratorial glance. I nodded to let her know that her secret was safe with me. Under the circumstances, I was fairly certain that nobody would have cared that she'd purchased her wedding gift from Kmart and stuck a Macy's price tag on it. I sure didn't.

Bully was beside himself. He was sobbing almost as loud and hard as some of the women. "Jade . . . is like a daughter to me, but she can be quite beastly. We must pray . . . for her," he stammered, with a look of extreme concern on his face.

"And I feel the same way!" Lizel added. "Had Rhoda and Otis whupped that child on a regular basis, we wouldn't be in this mess." Clarence, Lizel's long-suffering husband, stood behind her, behaving like a mute. It would not have surprised me if he had bolted and made a run for the border like Marcelo.

After the commotion had died down considerably, we fed the guests who wanted to stay. For the folks who wanted to leave, we fixed plates for them to take home. I thought it was pretty tacky that most of the guests took their gifts back, but there was nothing I could do to stop them. I didn't get a chance to talk much to Louis, but before he and his people packed up and left, he took me aside and told me to call him when I could.

I was exhausted, and not just from helping attend to the guests. My latest confrontation with Jade had drained me. I plopped down on the sofa in Rhoda's living room, and before I knew it, I dozed off. Scary Mary pinched my arm to wake me up. She ordered me to either get a blanket and pillow, and prepare myself to spend the night, or go home. I chose to go home. Lizel and Wyrita—even though they were both inconsolable—volunteered to stay with Bully, Scary Mary, and her five prostitutes to help them keep an eye on Rhoda's house until Rhoda and Otis returned from the hospital.

One of the many things that I didn't like about bad news was that it traveled fast and far. Especially when it originated in a small city like Richland. Less than *two* hours after I arrived home, I got a call from Daddy. I could hear loud laughter and calypso music in the background, and for a brief moment, I wished I was on that island, drinking rum and playing with an eel, like my hardheaded daughter was probably doing right now.

Daddy didn't even greet me. He jumped right in, feet first. "We heard about that Jade. We heard she cracked up like a walnut under a elephant's foot. I'm surprised it didn't happen sooner," he said in a gravelly voice. "Wretched as she was, I still feel sorry about it, though. Hold on! Let me get my cigar."

I was glad that Daddy had not called me up collect. Because I held on for ten minutes before he returned to the line.

"Is she gwine to be all right?" he asked. I could hear the ice clinking in his glass and him puffing on his cigar.

"I hope so, Daddy. She was devastated," I told him, rubbing the back of my neck. "I just talked to Rhoda and Otis. They're still at the hospital with Jade. This was a big blow to them."

"I bet it is. But the truth about it is, the girl had it comin'. She been makin' her bed all her life. Now it's time for her to stretch out in it." Daddy's voice was so loud and clear, it was hard to believe that he was over a thousand miles away. "And another thing. That's what she gets for hookin' up with somebody outside her race."

I gasped so hard, I had to rise from my seat at my kitchen table. "Daddy, you ought to be ashamed of yourself for saying something like that! This is not about race. This is about two immature people who should not even have been thinking about getting married in the first place. And speaking of race, you left Muh'Dear and me for a white woman, remember?"

"Huh? Who me? That was different! I was confused!"

"Jade was confused, too, I guess."

"My situation was way different. I thought if I could get close enough to the white folks, I'd be able to figure out what made them treat us so bad."

I shook my head. "Daddy, that's the most original excuse I have ever heard from a black man as to why he married a white woman. Did you get close enough to the white folks to figure out why some of them treated us like crap? Was she worth deserting your family for?"

"Hell naw! And I learned my lesson! I'm a changed man!" he protested. After I mentioned his relationship with a person outside of his race, he couldn't get off the telephone fast enough now. I was glad for that because I was so tired, all I wanted to do was rest. But I had a feeling this was going to be a long night.

Pee Wee wandered in about ten minutes after Daddy's telephone call. He came into the kitchen immediately, where I was still sitting at the table, nursing a bottle of beer. I had changed out of the outfit I'd worn to the wedding and slid into my nightgown. Even though it was still fairly early and wasn't even dark outside, I was ready for bed.

"I heard about Jade gettin' jilted. A bunch of women that had been there when it happened were yip-yappin' about it at the Red Rose a little while ago," he said, standing in the doorway. "That's a damn shame. I feel so bad for the girl." He looked and sounded truly sincere. I knew I was sorry about everything that had happened. However, most of my sympathy was for Rhoda and Otis. "But . . ." He paused to give me a confused look. "She had it comin', and it's goin' to keep comin' at her if she don't change her nasty ways."

"I am not going to argue with that, but I still feel sorry for her," I admitted. What he did next surprised me. He walked over to me, leaned down, and gave me a hug. And then he squeezed my hand. "What's wrong with you?" I asked, rearing back in my seat.

"There ain't nothin' wrong with me. Can't a man show his woman some affection without somethin' bein' wrong with him?"

I didn't have a quick answer to that. All I could do was stare into his eyes.

"Well, it's been so long since you did . . ." I muttered after a moment, still staring into his eyes. Since I had not looked at him this way in such a long time, I had not noticed how much his eyes had changed. There was an eerie and total hollowness in his eyes, like there was nothing to them except what I could see.

"I know, I know." He stopped and squeezed my hand again. "But I had a reason." He looked away, then stood up straight, keeping his back to me as he leaned against the sink. "I had a real good reason."

I couldn't wait to hear what his reason was. And it had to be a damn good reason to satisfy me. But my main concern was the effect it was going to have on our marriage—and my relationship with Louis.

"Annette, I got somethin' to tell you," he said. His voice faltered, and he looked all tensed up, like he was afraid I was going to bite him.

I held up my hand. "Let me help you out. I already know about your visits to . . . that woman," I snarled.

He whirled around. "Who told you?" he hollered, with his eyes open so wide, they looked like bull's eyes.

"Never mind who told me. I know, and I've known about it for some time now." Despite my accusation, I prayed he didn't know anything about my intimate relationship with Louis. It was the only leverage I had, and for the time being, I wanted to keep it intact.

"Shit, baby. This is somethin' I wanted you to hear from me," he mouthed. "I can't stand these bigmouthed motherfuckers in this town. You can't do a damn thing without them blabbin' it!"

We were silent for a minute, which seemed like an hour. He kept his eyes on the floor the whole time. I kept my eyes on him. My mind was doing flip-flops. I didn't know when and if I should offer my own confession. It all depended on Pee Wee and what he planned to do next. I didn't know how I'd react if he planned to leave or divorce me. But unlike Jade and other women who thought their shit didn't stink, I had already prepared myself for the worst: the end of my marriage.

"All right. You can stop beating around the bush," I said, giving him a guarded look. "But I don't want to hear any shit about your feelings, or what I didn't do to keep you happy! I don't want to hear any of that shit!" I yelled. Then, in a much lower voice, I said, "It's too late now."

He looked at me, with his mouth hanging open.

"Did I make myself clear? You low-down, funky black dog!" I shrieked.

His mouth dropped open even wider. "My God, Annette! You . . . you ain't makin' no sense," he said, with an incredulous look on his face.

"And neither are you!" I boomed. I rose from my seat so fast, it fell to the floor. Even though I'd lost a pile of weight, I still weighed more than my husband. And even though we'd never had a physical confrontation and he was stronger, I knew that if we ever had a smack-down, I'd give him a run for his money. And he knew it, too. That's why he started backing out of the room as I moved toward him, with my fists balled.

"Annette, calm down," he managed, holding up both hands.

"Calm down? Calm down my ass," I shouted. "All I want to know is, who is the bitch, and what does she mean to you?"

CHAPTER 47

Pee Wee carried more weight on his frame than he needed. So by no means was he a puny weakling that a strong wind could blow over. But from the look on his face now, I was convinced that a ball of cotton could have knocked him to the ground. His shame had to be of the highest magnitude. I decided that that was the case by the way he kept looking away from me. Every damn time he turned his head, I turned mine. Whatever he had to say to me, he was going to say it to my face.

"I'm waiting. Are you going to answer my question or not? I want to know who the bitch is," I hollered.

He looked me in the eyes and shook his head.

"No, you won't tell me who she is? No, you are not fucking another woman? Which one is it?"

He shook his head again. His face was blank, emotionless, like he didn't give a damn about my feelings, and that angered me even more.

"The thing is, I've had a few problems down there." Pee Wee nodded and pointed at his genital area.

"Tell me about it," I snapped, my anger rising like a pan of biscuits in progress.

He was still looking down. When he lifted his head, he didn't look directly at my face. Instead, his eyes shifted from side to side.

"You just hold on now!" he roared, holding up his hand and waving it in my face. "You got it wrong, baby! You got it all wrong if you think I been foolin' around with another woman! That's somethin' I couldn't do if I wanted to." I was getting more and more confused by the second. He paused and took a deep breath.

"Why did you stop? Need more time to get your lies straight?" I hissed.

He took another deep breath and then lifted a glass off the counter. He filled it with water from the tap, drank it all, and then turned back around. "Like I just said, I've had a few problems . . . *down there.*" I gave him a confused look until he pointed to his crotch area again, this time tapping his crotch with his finger. "Discharge, blood, burnin'."

I could not believe my ears! Things were much worse than I'd thought. I'd never suspected that on top of everything else, I had to be concerned about having a damn venereal disease!

"You caught something!" I screamed, with a lump in my throat that felt like it was the size of a golf ball. "Somebody gave you something, and you gave it to me?" It hurt for me to swallow, but I had to. The lump in my throat was choking me.

"Not exactly," he muttered.

"Not exactly what? Please get to the point, Pee Wee," I ordered, my blood rising like floodwaters.

"Will you be still and just listen?" he said calmly. Next, his eyes rolled up, and he stared at the ceiling for a few seconds. Then he sucked in a mouthful of air and let it out like it was his last breath. "I went to two different doctors. One said that what I had was untreatable. He advised me to 'get my house in order,' 'cause six months was about all the time I had left." He paused at this point and looked at me. This time I was the one who sucked in a mouthful of air and let it out like it was my last breath. I opened my mouth to speak, but he stopped me by holding up his hand. "Well, if somebody is goin' to tell me somethin' like that, I want to make sure it's true. I went to Dr. Epstein over in Canton."

There were not enough words in the English language to describe how I felt at that moment. I felt like I had shrunk and shriveled up like a prune that had been in the sun too long. I didn't know what to think now. The next thought that entered my mind was, Could I have been wrong about him having an affair all this time?

"What did Dr. Epstein tell you?" I asked, my voice so low I could barely hear myself. "The same thing?"

Pee Wee shook his head. "His diagnosis was even worse. He said he was surprised that I was still alive. That sucker said my white blood cells were gobblin' up my red blood cells like Pac-Man. He was so cold and casual about it, I wanted to sock him in the mouth. But I didn't, because I've always felt that that coldness was so typical of doctors. That's why I always hated them suckers. That and the fact that some quacks misdiagnosed both my grandfathers and treated 'em for somethin' they never had. Both died within two months of each other." This was the first time Pee Wee had ever offered me a reason as to why he had so much contempt for doctors.

My head suddenly felt like somebody had bounced a tire iron off it. My eyes were so full of tears, it was almost impossible for me to see clearly. I blinked hard several times, until Pee Wee came into focus again. I tried to be compassionate, but denial was lurking around me like the devil's advocate. For one thing, he certainly didn't look like a dying man! What if the fantastic story that he had just told me was just another one of his lies?

"You look like you don't believe me," he said.

"I'm trying to," I muttered. "Go on. Get to the end of this story, because it's making me sick myself." I stood in front of him, wringing my hands.

"I didn't stop there. I went to that lady doctor out on State Street." He stopped again and gave me a sheepish look. "She's that other woman I've been seein'."

Now my head felt like it wanted to explode. "Are you telling me the truth? Is that all just a cover-up so I won't know what you've really been up to?" Pee Wee was not the kind of man to joke about something as serious as his health. The more he talked, the more I felt like he was telling me the truth. But there was something on the side of my brain that was *still* trying to convince me that him having an affair was *all* I had to deal with. Him dying was something I *knew* I couldn't deal with.

"I'll be back in a minute," he said, leaving the room before I could say anything else. He strolled over to the refrigerator and opened the door next to it that led to our basement. He rushed downstairs, with the soles of his shoes clip-clopping on the wooden steps like the hooves on an overweight horse. He returned a couple of minutes later with some papers in his hand.

"This is just part of the insurance paperwork. I left some at the shop," he told me, handing the papers to me. "I know how you like to snoop, so I kept them hid in a box in the basement, in that corner behind the furnace. I thought that'd be the safest place in the house because of all them spiders' webs you've always been so afraid to go near."

As soon as I glanced at the first sentence on the first document, I saw one of the most feared words in the English language: *cancer.* I stopped reading and looked at the wall, trying to digest what I'd just read. The tears returned to my eyes, and this time I had to blink twice as much to get rid of them.

"If you flip to the next-to-last page, you will see Dr. Emmogene Stone's detailed diagnosis," said Pee Wee.

I had seen all I wanted to see for the time being. I handed the documents back to him. My hands were shaking, but his were shaking even harder than mine. He dropped the papers twice before he could grip them more securely.

"How long did she say you're going to . . . be . . . alive?" I never thought that I would have to ask my husband, or anybody else I loved, an ominous question like that. I was in a hellish position. But the position he was in had to be a million times worse.

Pee Wee gave me a mysterious look before he filled the same glass he'd just drunk from with more water. He took a sip, then handed it to me. I drank it, even though I knew it was not going to do me any good. I needed something a lot stronger than water.

"Stoney—that's what she tells her patients to call her—is the kind of individual that goes against the grain. She studied in Sweden and Germany for a while before she set herself up here. Stoney leaves no stone unturned. As soon as she told me about my cancer, which is a rare form of a prostate condition, she also told me about some experimental treatments she'd heard about. It was a long shot, but I had nothin' to lose."

"So you *have* been going to see a doctor every Friday?"

Pee Wee gave me a relieved look. "You knew about that? Who in the world told you? I bet it was that loose-lipped Bobby Jones!"

I nodded. "Bobby didn't know it was me when I called, though. I've known since June."

"How come you never asked me about it? You don't have no trouble askin' me about anything else."

"I didn't want to start up a lot of mess until I got all the facts," I explained.

"All what facts?"

"I just needed more evidence. It was hard and painful, but I wanted to make sure I knew what I was talking about when I confronted you." My excuse was weak, and I knew it, and from the slack-jawed look on Pee Wee's face, he thought so, too.

"So you chose to walk around thinkin' I was fuckin' another woman? Look, Annette, when I married you, I told you I was through with other women, and I meant that. I don't know why you ever let that notion enter your mind in the first place. I've been as faithful to you as you've been to me."

I looked at the telephone on the wall. And the next thing I knew, I burst into tears and cried like a baby for the next twenty minutes.

CHAPTER 48

"Annette, please stop cryin' and finish drinkin' that water." Pee Wee held the glass up to my lips, but my lips were so numb, I could barely feel them. He parted them with his fingers and managed to get the lip of the glass in between them. I managed to take a few sips, but that didn't make me feel any better. I dried my tears with the back of my sleeve and wiped my nose with a paper towel that he'd snatched off the towel rack and handed to me.

I looked at him long and hard before I spoke again. "Your health is more important to me than anything else involved," I rasped. "But I need to know everything there is to know." I took the glass from his hand and drank the rest of the water and then set the glass on the table with a thud. "If I'm going to be a widow, I want to know as soon as possible," I said firmly, wiping drops of water from my lips.

"Anyway, Stoney has a relationship with a doctor in Toledo," he continued. "That doctor had already dealt with another man who had the same ailment I had. Or one similar to mine, I should say. That dude's case was so serious, he was peein' through a tube. The good doctor had treated the dude with some kind of shots. Don't ask me what kind of shots. Shots is shots to me. Anyway, the man responded for a while, but then the shots stopped workin', and his condition got even worse. The doctor talked with some other doctors, and one hooked him up with some sort of cocktail. That cocktail concoction, combined with the shots, had some success. It took several months, but that patient got better. That was five years ago, and that man is still walkin' around."

"You didn't answer my question. I want to know how much time that Stoney woman gave you," I said, my voice cracking.

"Well, I'm forty-six. I should be around for at least another thirty or forty years. If you don't kill me first because of somethin' you think I'm doin'." He gave me a dry look. I just blinked and bit my bottom lip.

"Go on," I advised, with a sharp nod and a guarded look.

"As of three months ago, there is no trace of the cancer in me at all. But Stoney wants me to continue with the shots and the cocktail for at least another six months."

"If all this is true, why didn't you just tell me? I am your wife, and I had a right to know. When was I supposed to find out? When the coroner called me to come identify your body?"

"I didn't want to worry you if I didn't have to. I know how hysterical you get when you hear bad news," he replied, his hand in my face. "I couldn't tell anybody. I was scared to death." I could see the fear in his eyes. He looked like he wanted to cry. "All I could think about was that. I was angry about it, and I took out a lot of my frustration on you. Makin' love to you—or any other woman—was the last thing on my mind. Besides, I couldn't get a hard-on even if I had put a ton of starch in my dick."

He dipped his head and pursed his lips. "Ever since Stoney gave me a somewhat clean bill of health yesterday, I've been as hard as Chinese arithmetic. I was just waitin' until after that weddin' today to approach you, when you'd be more relaxed. . . ." He took my hand and placed it on his crotch. It felt like there was a brick inside his pants. I didn't respond. I didn't know how. He stood back. "Baby, I know you got a lot on your mind now. What I just told you needs to sink in so you can adjust to it. But when you're *ready* for me, just let me know." There was a naughty look in his eyes now.

I looked at the telephone again, wishing it would ring so that I could have a brief respite. I needed time to absorb everything my husband had just told me. When the telephone rang, I was so happy I could have kissed it.

"I'd better answer that. It's probably Rhoda calling to give me an update on . . . Jade," I said. I couldn't even feel my legs as I wobbled over to the phone. It was my mother.

"So Jade had a nervous breakdown, huh?" she asked.

"Something like that. I'm sure she's going to be fine, though. She's young. She'll bounce back," I said hopefully.

"Well, you reap what you sow," Muh'Dear said with a casual sigh. "Listen, if you get a chance in the next couple of days, go by the beauty shop and pick me out a wig hat and send it down here by the FedEx folks. This humidity is wreakin' havoc on my hair. That perm Claudette gave me before I left was bogus. As soon as you see her, complain."

"Yes, ma'am."

"Don't send me no wig hat that'll make me look like Tina Turner. It's too dangerous to be lookin' too sexy down here with all these frisky island mens. They already lookin' at me like I'm somethin' good to eat. I'd feel safer with a do more like the kind Aretha Franklin is wearin' these days. Do you hear me?"

"Yes, ma'am."

I was glad when Muh'Dear hung up. I returned to my seat at the table. Pee Wee had pulled out a chair and was seated directly across from me.

"I am real sorry about everything," he said, tapping the side of my arm.

"You have nothing to be sorry about," I assured him. "If you were worried about your health, you had a right to focus on that." I blew my nose into the same paper towel that he had handed to me earlier.

We looked at each other for a long, uncomfortable time. Had he not spoken when he did, I would have fled the scene. "Remember that bed-and-breakfast place we went to last year with Otis and Rhoda? You want to go up there for a weekend?" he asked.

"A bed-and-breakfast? You and me?"

He nodded. "I think it would do us both a world of good. Besides, we got a whole lot of hoochie-coochie homework to catch up on." He gave me a weak smile as he tapped my arm again. Then he grabbed my hand and squeezed it. "I'll even bring some of my island CDs, some tacky flowered T-shirts, and some baggy shorts so we can pretend we are down there in them islands, too. Don't you think that sounds like fun?"

"I . . . I guess so. That does sound nice," I muttered, rising. "But if you don't mind, I'd like to stay close to home for a while. Rhoda might need me for emotional support."

"Aw shit. Jade is goin' to be all right. Devils like her always land on their feet," he said with a dismissive wave. I knew that he was concerned about Jade, but I was glad that he was not overreacting.

"I know. But I'm doing this for Rhoda and Otis. I am sure they would do it for us if Charlotte was the one having a problem, Pee Wee."

"I guess you're right," he agreed with a shrug. "Listen, if it'll make you feel better, I'll swing by Rhoda's house tonight just to pay my respects."

"She's probably still at the hospital with Jade, so just wait until we hear from her or Otis. In the meantime, do you mind going out to get us some takeout?" I needed to be alone in the worst way.

Pee Wee gave me a surprised look. "You didn't bring home none of that good stuff you told me was goin' to be served at the weddin'? Knowin' how that caterer dude likes to show off his kitchen tricks, I know he put both his feet in whatever he cooked up."

"Uh-huh," I mumbled. "I'm sure he did, but I didn't bring any of it home with me." He was still looking at me with that surprised expression on his face. "There was nothing left that I liked after everybody had taken what they wanted."

"Oh. Well, that's *us*. We descend on free food like locusts. If black folks could eat while they were gettin' embalmed, they would." He laughed at his stupid comment. I did, too, even though I didn't think it was funny at all.

"I don't mind if you just swing by Al's for some ribs, or McDonalds or Burger King."

"Oh, hell no. I know better, and you know I know better. I will go by your smiley face caterin' dude's place because I know that's what you really want, and it's what I want, too. I just hope he's still open."

"They stay open until ten every night," I reported. "Except Friday and Saturday. They stay open until eleven on those nights."

"Did you get a chance to talk to your caterin' boy at all today?"

"Huh? About what?"

"Well, I thought he might have said somethin' to you about his restaurant hours for today. With him caterin' that weddin' and all, I thought he might close up early."

"I didn't talk to him at all this afternoon. He had everything under control, so I didn't need to. I think he knows how to handle his business," I mumbled.

"Sure enough! Brother Louis Baines can do no wrong in the kitchen," Pee Wee told me, with a sly grin.

Or in the bedroom, I thought.

"You know, he is a nice dude. I don't mean no harm when I make fun of him," said Pee Wee. "We ought to throw a cookout and invite him. I'm sure either me or Otis could hook him up with a lady friend, if he ain't already got one. We'll wait until Jade gets better so we can include her, too."

I stared at Pee Wee in stunned disbelief.

"Hospitality and forgiveness are a big part of our culture. What do you think about that?" he asked.

Hosting a cookout in my backyard, with Louis and Jade among the guests, was a fate worse than death as far as I was concerned. My face was so stiff, all I could do was blink. I tried to talk, but my lips wouldn't even move.

"Annette, what's wrong with you? You look like you just seen a ghost," Pee Wee said with a concerned tone of voice.

"I . . . I'm fine," I croaked. "Uh, let's hold off on having a cookout until Muh'Dear, Daddy, and Charlotte get back from the Bahamas. We can celebrate everything at the same time."

He gave me a thoughtful look and then a broad smile. "You're right, baby. We'll do it then. All right?"

When pigs fly, I thought to myself.

CHAPTER 49

This had been one of the most eventful Saturdays in my life. I didn't think that anything else could happen that would top Jade's wedding mess and Pee Wee's news about his health. I was wrong. My husband made love to me that night.

It felt like the first time, in more ways than one. It seemed like he had forgotten where certain things went and what they did once they got there. He was so clumsy, he accidentally bopped the side of my head with his elbow so hard, we had to stop so I could go take some Advil and press a warm, wet bath cloth to the spot where he'd hit me.

When I returned to bed, he jumped on me so fast, we both rolled to the floor. After we returned to bed, he ejaculated twice before he even got his dick in me.

"Baby, please be patient with me. I've been hibernatin' for so long, it's goin' to take a lot of practice for me to get back up to speed," he said with an apologetic look. "Besides that, there is another reason why I can't get my shit together like I used to."

"And what is that?" I asked, rubbing my throbbing neck where his teeth had clamped down on me like a pit bull.

"There was a whole lot more to you the last time we made love. Now I got to get used to all these shrunk-up parts on your body."

He played with my titties so long, they got sore and then so numb,

I couldn't feel them at all. Just when I thought he was making progress, he ejaculated again before it was time. Since his dick wasn't even all the way in me when it happened, semen splashed all over the inside of my thigh. After that he petered out like a deflated balloon and stayed that way for about ten minutes.

The longer and harder we tried, the worse it got. By the time it was over, I was ready to climb up one side of the wall and down the other. We tried again an hour later, and it was so much better. I actually enjoyed it. Afterwards, he fell asleep in my arms, and that was where he was when Sunday morning rolled around.

He was still snoozing when I untangled myself from his embrace and leaped out of bed. I grabbed my housecoat from the chair by my nightstand. After I had put it on, I stood by his side of the bed for a couple of minutes, just watching him sleep. Then I padded downstairs to use the phone in the kitchen. When Rhoda answered my call, she was glad to hear from me.

"I meant to call you last night when we got home from the hospital," she told me. "But I was so exhausted and upset. And bein' around all those doctors and nurses didn't help, because that brought back some painful memories."

Like Pee Wee, Rhoda hated doctors, hospitals, and anything else related to the medical profession. She had felt that way since she'd lost her breasts to cancer shortly after Jade's birth. And if she had not had a stroke ten years ago, she probably would not have gone near a hospital if you paid her. I was glad that she still managed to visit her doctors for regular checkups.

"Rhoda, you don't need to explain anything to me," I told her. "Your daughter comes first."

She let out a great sigh. "God is so good. Jade's goin' to be all right. Dr. Long wants to keep her for a few days for observation. And . . . and I overheard a couple of nurses talkin' about how they had a suicide watch on her. Annette, if I lose that girl, I don't want to live myself." For the next few moments, she cried like a baby.

I listened as Rhoda sobbed. "Rhoda, stop talking crazy, and you stop that crying. You are not going to lose your daughter," I insisted. Well, one thing was for sure, I couldn't dump my latest tale of woe on Rhoda. At least not yet. She already had enough on her plate, so she didn't need to hear what Pee Wee had finally told me.

She blew her nose, cleared her throat, and coughed a few times. When she spoke again, her voice sounded dry and scratchy. "Did you get a chance to spend some time with Louis yesterday? He looked so handsome in his tux."

"Uh, no, I didn't."

"Well, you should. You've got to keep him happy if you want to keep him. If you need me as an alibi before our next bowlin' date, just let me know. I know you still care about Jade, so I know all this mess is botherin' you, too. So you might want to chill out for a while, too. How's Pee Wee?"

"He's fine, Rhoda. He's still in bed, and he wants to take me to a bed-and-breakfast soon."

"Excuse me?"

"My husband wants to take me to a bed-and-breakfast. The same one that you and Otis and Pee Wee and I went to that time."

"For what?"

"Rhoda, the man is still my husband. He still likes to do nice things for me."

"Except make love to you."

"Well, that changed last night."

Rhoda remained quiet for a few seconds. "What voodoo potion did you use to make that happen?"

"Nothing."

"Horsefeathers! Somethin' had to happen. Was he drunk?"

"The man was as sober as an embryo," I replied. "Listen, I know this is not the time to go into great detail, but we had a very serious conversation yesterday after I got home from your house. He shared some information with me that I'd like to share with you when the time is right."

"What's wrong with sharin' it with me now? I've got time."

"And you've got your own problems right now, too. Besides that, I need to make sure it's all right with Pee Wee for me to tell you what he told me."

"I see." Rhoda cleared her throat. "Whatever it is, I'd like to hear it ASAP, and I don't care if you tell me, or Pee Wee. Now what about Louis?"

"What about him?"

"Is he still on your agenda now that things between you and Pee Wee have changed?"

I hesitated before I responded. "Uh, for now he is. But I need to give that situation a lot of thought in the next few days."

"I see. Tell me this. Do you still want to be with him?"

This time I was the one who got quiet for a few seconds. I was so uncomfortable that those seconds seemed more like minutes. "Uh-huh." My bedroom was directly above the kitchen. I heard Pee Wee stumbling around upstairs. I glanced at the doorway before I continued. "When I let Louis down, I want to let him down gently. He's been good to me, and I feel I owe it to him. It's the . . . it's the right thing to do."

"Girl, please! Can't you hear how melodramatic you sound? This is Rhoda you are talkin' to, not Father Flannigan. Don't lay any of that 'it's the right thing to do' shit on me. If you were so concerned about doin' the right thing, you wouldn't have jumped into bed with Louis in the first place."

"You can say what you want, Rhoda. Louis has been good to me. There were times when he treated me better than I treated myself. Men like him are rare. I'd feel better about ending the affair with some dignity."

"Shit! I wish I had a violin so I could play some of that sad violin music you hear in the movies when somebody says the kind of stupid shit you're sayin' right now."

"Rhoda, you can make fun of me and yip-yap all the gibberish you want about how I should handle my relationship with Louis. But I still think that I owe it to him to let him down gently."

"Unless he lets you down first," Rhoda quipped.

"If he does, he does. I won't lose much sleep over it," I said firmly, annoyed that Rhoda would make such a comment. And that it made so much good sense. I was glad when she hung up.

Louis called me up the next morning at my office. After a few sympathetic comments about Jade, he went straight to the point. "Can I see you later in the week? I really miss you." I couldn't believe how weak I was. I agreed to leave work immediately and meet him at his apartment.

"Gloria, I have a family emergency I need to take care of. Can you keep an eye on things until I return?" I said, stopping in the doorway to Gloria Watson's cubicle on my way out. I had bolted out of my office like a bronco in a rodeo.

"Don't worry about nothing here," Gloria told me. Out of the corner of my eye, I could see some of my rubbernecked workers trying to find out what was going on.

I lowered my voice to almost a whisper. "My husband is worse than a child. . . ."

"Girl, I know what you mean. That fool of mine would set the house on fire if I didn't keep an eye on him. I can see how frazzled you are. You all right to drive? I can drive you in my car, and Cindy Pang can hold down the fort."

"I'm fine," I insisted, wondering why Gloria had such a puzzled look on her face.

"You got your sweater on inside out," she informed me.

"Thanks, Gloria," I said, embarrassed. I removed my sweater and draped it across my arm. "I don't know when I'll be back," I called over my shoulder as I sprinted out to my car.

Five minutes after I arrived at Louis's apartment, we were naked and wallowing on a quilt that he had placed in the middle of the floor and surrounded with candles.

CHAPTER 50

I had lunch with Rhoda on Tuesday in my office. Over fried rice and egg rolls, I gave her an abbreviated report on Pee Wee's condition. All I told her was that he'd had a slightly serious, mildly cancer-related prostate situation. It had worried him, which was the reason he had neglected me, but it had not been as serious as he'd first thought. He had responded well to treatment, and according to his doctor, he had nothing else to worry about.

"Hmm. Well, anything remotely connected to cancer, whether it's serious or not, can surely wreak havoc on a person's sex drive. I know from experience. The important thing is that things are back to normal between you and him, right?"

"I guess," I muttered. "Uh, I'd appreciate you not mentioning what I just told you to him. Wait until he brings it up."

Rhoda gasped. "I can offer him some comfort, too, you know. After all, the man is my boy," she told me with a stern look on her face and a firm nod.

"Well, the man is my husband," I reminded her. "It took him almost a year to tell me."

"What if he had never told you about it?" There was an unbearably sad look on Rhoda's face.

"Rhoda, he took his time telling me because he didn't want me to worry. He was doing enough for both of us. If he wants you to know, he'll tell you. Now can we bury this subject and move on?"

Rhoda gave me a reluctant nod, but the sad look was still on her face and remained there until we finished our lunch.

Jade was released from the hospital the following Wednesday. I had not visited her in the psych ward, but I had sent flowers and a get-well card from me and Pee Wee. Bully was the one who told me that Jade never even opened it, because she saw my name on the return address. That did not surprise me, and frankly, I didn't care.

For the life of me, I could not figure out why that child still had such a hostile attitude toward me. Especially when she was the one who had tormented me, not the other way around. But I was not going to waste any more of my time trying to figure that girl out. I knew that some people were just bad to the bone. Apparently, Jade was one of those people. And if she didn't change her ways, bad karma would always be a part of her life. I didn't want to think about what all could have happened to Rhoda had she not changed when she did.

I knew that Rhoda was going to be busy for the next few days attending to Jade's needs, so I didn't even attempt to call her to tell her that I had decided to continue my relationship with Louis.

Even though my marriage was back on the right track, Pee Wee and I still had a long way to go. He had made love to me several times since he'd revealed his medical condition to me. It was still not as good as it used to be, but I was thankful that it was getting there. Therefore, Louis's services were still necessary. Besides, the way he fawned all over me every single time I saw him still did wonders for my morale and recovering ego. With Pee Wee back on the right track, I felt like I had the best of both worlds. What woman who had been neglected by her husband wouldn't want to be in my position?

I knew that my affair was not going to be as ongoing as Rhoda's with Bully; it had to end eventually. I told myself that as soon as I regained my comfort level with my husband, I'd start weaning myself off Louis. In the meantime, I would see him every chance I could.

* * *

What I said and what I did were two different things. Before I realized it, my affair with Louis was out of control. It felt like I was trapped on a runaway train and I couldn't get off. But the thing that scared me the most was the fact that I wasn't ready to get off, anyway. I was enjoying the ride on Louis's train. And speaking of trains, that was one of several words he used when he referred to his penis. It sounded a lot better than poker. Now that was a word that I had never heard anybody else use in a sexual way, not down South or anywhere else.

Since Rhoda was not that available for the bowling date ruse until further notice, I had to get more creative. I spent time with Louis during the day, when my coworkers thought I was attending staff meetings at the main office. But that was an excuse I couldn't run into the ground, for obvious reasons. I didn't want some busybody like Gloria to get too suspicious of my actions and call up the main office to check up on me, so I claimed I had doctor's appointments, too. That was the only excuse I didn't like to use. Not because somebody could check up on it, but because it was the excuse that Pee Wee had used—which turned out not to be an excuse after all. I used it only a few times. In addition to that, I started saying I had to leave the office for a couple of hours to go meet with my lawyer, then my banker, and once even a fictitious old friend from school.

One night when I got an overwhelming urge to see Louis, I told Pee Wee that I needed to go out to pick up something from the Grab and Go convenience store. He insisted on going for me until I told him that I needed to purchase tampons, douche powder, and butt spray.

"Eeyow! I ain't about to go up in that store to buy all them gruesome female doodads," he said with a grimace and a shudder. "You know how I feel about all that mess."

"All right. Are you sure you don't want to think about it some more?" I asked, knowing damn well he didn't want to go. But I had to make it look good, for his sake as well as mine. I had my car keys in my hand. I did have to pick up everything I had mentioned, but the main reason I had to visit the convenience store was to pick up some more condoms for Louis to use with me.

Pee Wee didn't even bother to answer my last question. He just gave me an exasperated look and waved me toward the door before he plopped down in his La-Z-Boy.

I knew that Louis was still struggling to make his business succeed, so his finances were not as stable as mine. Before I knew it, I was the one paying for motel visits when we didn't want to go to his apartment. I was also paying for gas for his van and for dinner in out-of-the-way places. I didn't mind, because it was worth it to me. As a matter of fact, Louis never asked me to pay for anything; I always did it on my own. Mainly because had I not, I would not have been able to see him as often as I wanted to.

Despite my eagerness to be so generous, there was one situation that made me curious about Louis. The oven in his restaurant had stopped working all of a sudden. For every hour that it didn't work, his business lost a hell of a lot of money. He adamantly "refused" the three-thousand-dollar loan I offered him to get the oven repaired or replaced. I didn't know anything about the price of a restaurant oven, but three thousand dollars to get it fixed or replaced seemed like a lot to me, but it was an amount I could manage. "I wasn't raised to take handouts," he'd claimed, slapping my hand when I pulled my checkbook out of my purse. "Besides that, I wouldn't want to put you in a financial bind." The man was as noble as King James. I admired him for that.

I couldn't stand to look at his long puppy-dog face during the days he was scrambling around, trying to get loans from various banks. That was why I approached the situation from a different angle. Since he wouldn't let me help with the oven, because he thought it would be a financial hardship for me, I proposed an offer that he could not refuse. I decided to dummy up a bogus invoice to make it look like he had catered another event at my office, in addition to our regular Monday luncheons. I decided that a "performance recognition" event that included myself and some process servers—who didn't exist—sounded good in the comments section on the invoice. Since I had been so hands-on in setting up my original deal with Louis, he and I were the only ones who kept copies of his invoices. Under these circumstances, he accepted my offer to help him replace his oven without hesitation. And he was more concerned about me getting caught than I was.

"Baby, I'd die if you got in trouble with your boss for something you did for me," he told me. I assured him that there was nothing to worry about. When I handed him the check for the bogus service, his hand was shaking, and he was so hesitant to accept it, I had to slap the damn check into his hand and close his fingers around it.

CHAPTER 51

"You stupid bitch!" That was what Rhoda screamed at me when I told her about all the money that I'd invested in my relationship with Louis.

"What do you mean?" I asked stupidly.

"Girl, what's wrong with you? Have you lost your fuckin' mind?" she hollered. It was a Thursday, and we were having lunch at a pizza parlor not far from my office. "What good is a lover if you've got to pay him for his time? I have nothin' against gigolos, but if a paid lover was the best I could do, I'd service myself. Lord have mercy." Rhoda had to fan her face with her napkin.

"Gigolo? If Louis Baines is a gigolo, I'm the happy hooker. It's nothing like that," I wailed. "Louis wants to be with me. He's the one who initiated this affair. He has *never* asked me for any financial assistance. As a matter of fact, I practically had to make him take the check to get his oven taken care of."

"And that's another thing! Don't you think that three thousand dollars sounds like a lot to replace an oven?"

"I did think that that was a lot for an oven," I replied, giving Rhoda a thoughtful look. "But there must be some that cost that much."

"Well, maybe that's what an oven would cost in the White House or Buckingham Palace. But we're talkin' about an oven in a pooh-butt restaurant in Richland, Ohio, that serves baked chicken gizzards!"

"Look, Rhoda, the man said it cost three thousand, and I didn't question him."

"You should have! You should have asked him to show you where he was gettin' an oven from that cost that much."

"Why, Rhoda? Like I said, he didn't ask me for the money, and I practically had to make him take it," I said, knowing that my defense was weak.

"Why? His problems are not your problems. Listen to me. Havin' an affair is one thing. It could cause a lot of trouble, and a lot of people could get hurt. That's why it's so important to keep it in perspective."

"I don't want a little thing like a busted oven to keep us apart. When that damn thing fizzled out, he was too distraught to see me, even though he wanted to. I went to his apartment one night, and he couldn't even get a hard-on. I just went through that impotence shit with my husband. I'll be damn if I go through it with my lover, too."

For a moment, I forgot where I was. I glanced around to make sure that none of the other patrons in the pizza parlor were listening to my conversation with Rhoda. The slice of pizza on my plate had gotten cold. I had only nibbled on it since we sat down. I still had not completely regained my passion for pizza, thanks to Jade.

It had been three weeks since Jade had come home from the hospital. This was the first time that Rhoda had been able to leave the house. Even though Lizel and Wyrita had everything under control. Not only were they running Rhoda's child-care facility, but they were tending to Jade's numerous needs, too.

"Well, it's your life. I can't tell you how to live it," Rhoda said with a thoroughly disgusted look. "I'm just glad you're happy." She pressed her lips together and looked at me for a long time.

"Rhoda, I've never been like this before in my life," I said evenly.

"Like what?" she asked, giving me a look that I could not interpret.

"Doing all this crazy shit with and for Louis. It must be my midlife crisis, huh?"

"Midlife crisis, my ass. You're just a damn fool. That's all this is."

"As my best friend, I expect a little more compassion from you," I said, pouting. "You don't have to sound so coarse with me, Rhoda. This is a very confusing time for me. My marriage is on the rocks and a hard place. My parents both have one foot in the grave. And, my damn menopause must have kicked in, because I've been experiencing hot flashes all week, not to mention periods that are no longer regular."

"Please don't go there. I'm goin' through the same thing."

"It explains a few things. I've been doing a lot of stupid shit lately."

"Tell me about it. And that's just my point. You've been doin' a whole lot of stupid shit lately. I just don't want you to get yourself into somethin' you'll regret," Rhoda told me. "And since you brought up the subject of a midlife crisis, that's an excuse we can both use, I guess. I mean, why else would upstandin', well-respected women in the community like us risk our marriages?"

I didn't bother to remind Rhoda that she'd been with her lover for most of her married life. "Since when did *you* need an excuse to justify your actions?" I asked with a sneer. "Especially one like menopause."

Rhoda wet her lips with her tongue and rolled her eyes at me. Then she gave me a dismissive wave. "Did Pee Wee take you to that bed-and-breakfast yet?"

I shook my head and chuckled. "No, he has not even mentioned it again. Why?"

"Lord knows, I need a break after all I've been through." Rhoda pushed her plate away and took a drink from her Diet Pepsi. She cleared her throat and sat up straighter in her chair. "Bully has to go back to London again next week to wrap up the sale of another one of his buildings. He'll be gone for a whole week. We're goin' to spend this weekend together before he goes, though."

"And?"

"Bully really likes you. And I was thinkin' how nice it would be if we all spent the weekend together—at a different bed-and-breakfast, of course. I know a place in Cleveland."

I gave Rhoda one of the most incredulous looks I could manage. "What about your husband? What are you going to tell him?"

"The same thing you're goin' to tell yours. We'll tell them that we're goin' to a spa in Cleveland."

I gasped. "You want me to bring Louis?"

Rhoda gasped back at me. "I know damn well you didn't think I was talkin' about a romantic weekend getaway with our *husbands.*" Rhoda laughed.

I tried not to laugh myself, but I did, anyway. Because under the circumstances, spending a romantic weekend with our husbands was ludicrous. We both wanted to have some fun, and we knew that that would not be the case with our husbands. Otis hadn't made love to Rhoda in years. And Pee Wee, well, he still had to get back up to speed for me to enjoy having sex with him again. Why waste a weekend at a bed-and-breakfast with two duds like our husbands? I prayed that it really was menopause that was making me act like such a fool. And I prayed that it would end soon. I really didn't like the woman that I had become. . . .

I looked around the restaurant and lowered my voice before I spoke again. "Rhoda, you told Bully about me and Louis?"

"So?"

"So what if he gets drunk and blabs to Otis? Otis is one of Pee Wee's closest friends."

"Get a grip, woman. Do you think Bully and I would still be hittin' it after all these years if he was the kind of man to shoot off his mouth?"

I shrugged. "I don't know if Louis can get away on such short notice. He's going to be very busy trying to get caught up now that he has a new oven to work with. I'll call him up when I get back to the office," I declared.

"Well, I need to know by noon tomorrow. We have to confirm our reservations by then. And, by the way, it's nine hundred a night per couple. Plus gratuities."

"Nine hundred a night?"

"You get what you pay for. Donald Trump spends money like that for things like this all the time."

"Well, he's Donald Trump. We're not. And you had the nerve to question a three-thousand-dollar oven."

Rhoda released an impatient sigh and gave me a look that let me know that she was annoyed with me. "Look, if you can't afford it, it'll be my treat!"

"You don't need to pay for me to be with Louis," I protested.

"I'm just tryin' to help," she said, softening before my eyes. "It's just that we haven't done anything like that together in a while."

I held my hand up to her face. "Shut up. I'll go. I can use my American Express. The one Pee Wee doesn't know I have. The money is no problem for me," I said, knowing damn well that if Louis and I went, the money would come from my pocketbook. Since I'd only agree to do this once, it didn't seem so bad. I eased my guilt by reminding myself that I knew a lot of women who had done things much worse than what I was doing now. And, it helped for me to convince myself that as long as my husband didn't know, it wouldn't hurt him.

I didn't know why, but for some reason, that bogus invoice entered my mind a few seconds later. It was the first time I wished I had not done something for Louis. And I didn't feel too comfortable doling out another large sum of money on his account so soon—even though he knew nothing about the bed-and-breakfast weekend yet.

I promised myself that if Louis agreed to spend a weekend at a bed-and-breakfast in Cleveland, it would be the *only* time that I would finance such a venture. I was happy spending time with him at that cheap-ass Do Drop Inn motel or his apartment, and he had told me time and time again that that was good enough for him, too.

CHAPTER 52

Louis was not at his place of business when I called him an hour after I returned to my office after my lunch with Rhoda. His assistant day cook told me that he had left work for the day and was probably at his apartment.

I went out on the floor to see if there were any issues I needed to address. I was glad when Gloria assured me that everything was under control. After I signed some documents that she had shoved into my hand, authorizing one of our process servers to pay a visit to one of our most defiant debtors, I returned to my office and closed the door.

I called Louis's apartment every half hour for the next two and a half hours, and all I got was a busy signal. I looked at the clock on my wall and realized that three forty-five was close enough to quitting time that I could just leave for the day. Since I had not been able to reach Louis by phone, I decided to try and catch him at home.

Since Louis had given me a key to his apartment, I didn't think it would matter if he knew I was coming or not. Nevertheless, I didn't like to make surprise visits to people, because I never knew what I would stumble into. One time I let myself into my parents' house unannounced and walked in on my mother and father making love on the kitchen table. It was not a pretty sight. I prayed that I would never again see a man and a woman in their seventies having sex as long as I lived.

Before I left my office, I called Pee Wee at his barbershop just to hear his voice. I knew that I had to do my part to help restore our marriage, and every little thing helped as long as it was something positive. He was glad to hear from me.

"Baby, I can't wait to get home so I can get my hands on you again," he told me, whispering like an obscene caller. Then he did something he had not done in years: he made kissing noises. That brought tears to my eyes. "I've said it before, but I will say it again. God was showin' off when he made you. And if He made a woman better than you, he kept her for Himself." This was the man that I had known and loved most of my life. I was glad to have him back. And, I was tired of deceiving him. . . .

During the ride to Louis's apartment, something attacked me that I had been denying, dodging, and fending off for a long time: regret. I could not ignore it, because it hit me like a sledgehammer. I truly regretted getting involved with Louis Baines. I knew right then and there that I had to end my affair soon.

By the time I got to Louis's street, I had decided that immediately after the weekend at the bed-and-breakfast, I would sever our relationship. I had to. There was no excuse for it now. It was going to hurt me as much as it hurt him, but it was time for me to do the right thing. Besides, I was tired of all the sneaking around and all the lying. How Rhoda and other women managed to have affairs for years and years was a mystery to me. I'd only been at it for a couple of months, and it had almost driven me crazy.

Now, I had to admit that it had been fun, but everything I believed in had convinced me that all good things had to end at some point. I was glad that I chose to end the relationship while it was still exciting. I would never forget Louis, and I knew that he'd never forget me. I'd walked on the wild side, gobbled up some forbidden fruit, and nobody had gotten hurt. A weekend rendezvous at a bed-and-breakfast would be bittersweet. But it would be the perfect way to end a whirlwind romance. It was all good. Life was good. I was a happy woman. Yankee pot roast, his specialty, would never be the same in my eyes again.

When I didn't see Louis's van in the parking stall in front of his apartment building, I decided to go home and attempt to reach him by phone again later. But before I drove back out to the street, I changed my mind and decided to let myself in and leave him a note. I didn't think he'd have a problem with me being in his residence in his absence, or he wouldn't have given me a key in the first place. And he had told me that I was welcome to visit anytime I wanted to.

My pulse started to race as I approached his apartment. I could hear him inside, laughing, before I even knocked on the door, and that made me smile. He sounded so cute. I was glad he was in a good mood. Had things worked out differently between Pee Wee and me and had we parted company, I sincerely believed that Louis and I could have had a serious chance for a real future together—in spite of the differences in our ages and backgrounds. We enjoyed each other's company, and we were both ambitious. However, I didn't know any woman, especially a woman in my position, who would marry a man who was broke as often as Louis was. It was a struggle for him to pay for our motel rooms and the expensive meals that we enjoyed at Antonosanti's.

When he couldn't afford to take me to that fancy restaurant, he relied on coupons that he cut out of the newspaper for "buy one, get one free" meals at other restaurants. One night, when the motel declined his credit card, we made love in the back of his van. I couldn't bring myself to do it in my car or on that sofa in his apartment. I had sunk pretty low, but I didn't see things that way. All I could see was that I was having fun. Because of Louis's ambition, and the fact that the young brother could "burn" any meal as well as my mother, if not better, I knew that one day his business would be much more successful. And that I would reap the benefits—if we were still together.

I knocked gently on the door at first, but there was no response. I looked around and waved to one of the white boys who lived in the apartment next door. Even though I knew Louis was home, I started to leave. I stopped when the boy spoke from his opened window.

"Yo," he said with a sly grin. He was so blond and fair skinned, he almost looked like an albino.

"Yo," I said back, giving him a casual wave.

"You looking for L. B?"

"Excuse me?"

"You looking for Louis Baines?"

I nodded.

"Well, his van broke down on Liberty Street today, and he's depressed about it. He could probably use some cheering up."

"Thanks," I muttered, then headed back toward Louis's apartment.

I didn't knock this time. Instead, I took a deep breath and let myself in. I saw right away that Louis was talking to somebody on the telephone, and he was still laughing. He was kicked back in a low-back, metal folding chair in front of the larger of his two rear windows. His bare back, still displaying some scratches that I had given him, was to me. He stopped laughing and listened, nodding, to whatever the party on the other end was saying to him. His bare feet were propped up on a hassock.

I gently closed the door and stood a few feet in front of it. Sadie let out a meow and rolled her crossed eyes at me as she padded across the floor to a bowl near the door with some fried chicken wings. I was glad to see that Louis had removed some of the meat from the bones before filling Sadie's bowl. I had advised him to do that so that Sadie would have less trouble eating her meals.

Since I didn't want Louis to turn around and think that I was trying to eavesdrop on him, I thought that it would be smart for me to make my presence known. I was just about to cough or clear my throat to get his attention. But I didn't get a chance to do either one.

He suddenly laughed some more and then resumed his conversation, spitting out the words "that funky, old, fat woman." I widened my eyes, shuddered, and forced myself not to laugh. I felt sorry for the target of his roast. But what he had just said, and the shrill, concise way in which he had said it, was downright comical. However, since I'd often been somebody's target myself, I was not one to make fun of people. I didn't approve of it when other people did, either.

My desire to laugh disappeared as soon as I heard him mention *my* name. "Annette is the one you should be thanking for making our dreams come true. God bless her! I never would have thought that a *bill collector* would be the one to save my ass after all the ones I had to dodge back home. That's what makes this so sweet!" He placed so much emphasis on his words, they seemed to hang in the air. He paused and guffawed so long and hard, he started to choke on some air.

As soon as Louis composed himself, he continued. "Sweetheart, this is turning out way better than we planned! I . . . huh? Did I . . . Uh-huh, I did. Well, baby, I can't lie to you. There was just that *one* time that I slept with her. You know how women like her are!" He paused for a few moments, and for a split second, I thought he had felt my presence and would turn around and explain himself. But he didn't.

He resumed his conversation with vigor. "That heifer! She wouldn't take no for an answer. I . . . What did you say? Did I enjoy it? Hell no, I didn't enjoy touching that woman! Fucking her was like sticking my dick in a piano! A nasty-ass piano that smelled like catfish stew at that! I had to soak my poker in Epsom salts and warm water after I got rid of her that night." He paused for about a minute and a half. Whatever the party on the other end was saying must have bothered him, because he let out several loud sighs, gasps, and gulps, and he waved his fist in the air a few times before he spoke again.

"Sweetheart, I know I promised you that I wouldn't, but she practically raped me, and I had been drinking a lot. I have a feeling that she even slipped something into my drink to reduce me to such a weakened condition! You know how big-boned women like that can be, and this one came after me with a bag full of tricks. She didn't stop until she had put me in that trick bag! I didn't want to piss her off. I knew that a hefty woman like that could stomp my place into the ground like Godzilla did Tokyo if I made her mad enough." He paused and laughed some more, slapping his knee and stomping his foot on the hassock so hard, he almost fell off his chair.

When he continued, the rest of his words burned through my ears like acid. *"Baby, if my plan works, I can be up out of this hick town and back in Greensboro by Labor Day. We can get married on Thanksgiving weekend, like we planned. No, baby, not a single bank in this town will come through for me with a loan. But that greasy black bitch Annette is much better. God is so good to me! He led her to me in the nick of time! After I finalize the sale for that pooh-butt restaurant, I'll put the bite on her for another three thousand. Then I'll be on my merry way, with that three grand and the money she thought she was giving me to replace my oven, which there is nothing wrong with.*

"I don't have to worry about paying her back like I would have with the bank! I don't want to be greedy, like I was with that suspicious sow that I hooked up with before the Lord sent Annette into my place that evening, so I'll stop with the six thousand. I'd feel real bad if I put her into too big of a financial hole, like I used to do when some hag forced herself on me. See, baby, I'm slowly but surely becoming righteous.

"After we get married, I won't even sniff in another woman's direction when I need financial assistance. I will work for it! That's the least I can do. If you can get out of that escorting business with those old dudes, I can get out of this. We've socked away more than enough money to get a toehold on the future we deserve. We'll get back into the church and get saved and baptized before we get married. Yippee-ki-yay! Stop laughing, honey! Baby, I better get off this phone in case Annette's trying to get through. I will call you again tomorrow. I love you, too, sweetie. . . ."

CHAPTER 53

To this day I didn't know how I was able to stand in the middle of Louis's floor as silent and stiff as a statue. Of all the betrayals that I had experienced, this had to be the absolute worst. I wanted to shoot across that floor and beat the dog shit out of him. No, I wanted to do a lot more than that. I wanted to kill him dead. But I was so paralyzed that I couldn't move or make a sound. For a split second, I thought that maybe I had died from the shock of what I'd just heard, and that that was the reason I couldn't move or speak.

After Louis hung the telephone up, he continued to sit in front of his window, with his back still to me. Sadie trotted over to him and jumped into his lap. He started to stroke Sadie's back, whistling like a man who not only had the world in the palm of his hand, but one who didn't have a care in the world. He was a happy man. Well, he wouldn't be for long!

Finally, I managed to clear my throat, loud enough for him to hear me. As soon as I did that, his body stiffened. But it was several seconds before he turned around. From the way his jaw dropped when he saw me standing there, you would have thought that he'd seen the angel of death. Sadie sensed something was wrong, so she leaped off his lap and ran into the bathroom.

"Annette? What . . . when . . . how long have you . . . been standing there?" he said in a high-pitched voice. I could see his hands shaking as he gripped the back of his chair. He rose and stood ramrod straight, looking like the condemned man he was.

My jaws were clenched together so tightly, I didn't know how I managed to open them wide enough to speak, but I did. "I've been standing here long enough to hear enough. You low-down, funky, double-crossing, lying, meat loaf–and chicken wing–cooking bastard!"

"Now, you hold on there, dammit!" he ordered, raising both hands in the air like I'd just aimed a gun at him. Then he started shaking his finger at me. "Let's get one thing straight right now. You do not come up into my home unannounced and start bad-mouthing me like that," he told me, one hand still in the air. "I can explain everything." He went from looking like a condemned man to looking like a deer caught in somebody's headlights.

"And you want to know something, I'd like to hear your explanation," I responded. "Who were you just talking to?" I moved toward him, with my hands on my hips. His key was still in my hand. I knew that I would no longer need it, so I let it fall to the floor.

"Huh? Just a friend! I . . . I was just talking to a friend. And . . . and . . . and that was a private conversation, so it's really none of your business who I was just talking to!"

"Is that what you think? Brother, I've got news for you. Since I was the subject of your conversation, it is my business! I hope that that bitch is not as stupid and gullible as I was. You really had me fooled! But I'm glad I got your number before you made an even bigger fool out of me. Our business relationship is over as of this minute. I'd rather treat my employees to wolf manure for lunch than allow your Yankee-pot-roasting ass to serve them another one of your meals! Thank God I wasn't stupid enough to let you lock me into some long-term agreement! And as far as our personal relationship is concerned, I never want to see your slimy dick—or duck—again as long as I live!" I turned to leave, but he trotted across the floor and jumped in front of the door.

"You are not going no place, bitch. Our business relationship is not over yet. On Monday, my people and I will be there to deliver and serve. And for the record, it'll be Yankee pot roast, like you requested."

"Let me tell you what you can do with that shit and every damn thing else you cook up. Stick it up your ass and rotate on it! I am through with you! Now get the hell out of my way!" I screeched, attempting to walk around him. He refused to move.

"Like I said, we are still doing business, and we will be until I decide to end our arrangement," he said, glaring at me as if I was the culprit and he was the injured party.

"Ha! Do you think for one minute that I'd let you continue to cater my affairs? Do you think I'd ever eat anything else you prepared? So you can spit in it, then laugh at me even more behind my back? Hell no! Now if you know what's good for you, you will get out of my way."

"This relationship is not over until I get paid," he told me in a frighteningly calm voice.

It already felt like the wind had been knocked out of me. Now I also felt like I'd been dragged and stomped on. "Get paid? Get paid for what? I don't owe you a damn dime at the moment. I personally made sure that all your bills got paid on time. My account with you is up to date to the very minute! The only way you will ever get another cent from me is if you rob me at gunpoint. Now move out of my way! Move on!"

He grabbed my arm when I raised it to try and make him move. His grip was so tight, I didn't have a chance. Cursing under his breath, he forced me to the sofa and pushed me down so hard that my neck almost snapped, and the sofa's front legs rocked up off the floor and back down, with a violent thud. Then he stood over me, with his hands on his hips.

"I will move on, but, like I just said, not until I get paid."

"What the fuck are you talking about?" I could not believe that this was the same man that I had wallowed around in bed with so many times and risked losing my husband over. I could not believe how smug and evil he looked. Had I not seen this side of him with my own eyes, I wouldn't have believed that he was capable of such unspeakable behavior. What was this world coming to?

"I'm sorry you had to find out this way. Honest to God, I am. You've been real nice to me, and I appreciate that. But, no offense, you and I are from two different planets." His words felt like bricks going upside my head.

Despite all of the rock-hard evidence in front of me, I still had the nerve to ask him one of the stupidest questions that I had ever asked anybody. "You never cared about me?"

For a moment, he looked like he wanted to laugh. I was glad he didn't, because I would have *really* lost my composure, and there was just no telling what I might have done to him. "Look, lady, I care about everybody that's nice to me. There is no use in me lying about that. I cared about you, but not the way you think."

"Well, that's news to me. Then tell me the way it was. I know I am not the smartest person in the world, but what was all that wooing about? Why did you come on to me in the first place?" I asked, shaking my head in stunned disbelief.

"Look, I cared about you because you struck me as a nice woman from day one. That's all there was to that. If you had been hostile and loud like some of the other sisters that come into my place, you would not have appealed to me the way you did. I like women with some class. It's just that, well, that was not enough in your case. You're fun, in bed and out, but I need more than that in a woman. I've got real high standards." His last comment hurt me so much that I could not even address it.

"So I was nice? Is that all it took for you to pursue me the way you did? What about the other women that you so graciously referred to in your telephone conversation? Did you hook up with them, too, because they were nice? Do you try and con money and pussy from all the nice women you meet?"

"Look, you horny bitch, I . . . I don't have to stand here and explain—"

"You sure as hell don't! No matter what you say now, it would not change what I just heard. Can I leave now?" I sprang up from the sofa like a weed.

"I am sorry if I hurt you. But I . . . um . . . still need one last favor from you. I know you might not want to do it, but for your own good, I hope you will. For old time's sake and the good times we did have."

"Oh, you are sicker than I thought! You are one sick-ass puppy!" I hollered. He pushed me back down on the sofa.

"You are not leaving here until we get our negotiations in order.

I need another three grand, and I need it by next weekend. Any questions?"

"Don't count on it! You can kiss my ass and then bark at my hole!"

"I already did, remember?" He leered at me. "I did all of that and more. . . ." Louis paused and wiggled his nose like a rabbit. I didn't know if he was stalling for time, or what. I couldn't imagine what else he had to say. "Let me tell you something. Let me offer a little inducement that might help you get busy." He reared back and looked down at me. The sneer on his face made him look like the devil. "What if I tell your husband about how you've been playing footsie with me all summer?"

"You don't have to. As soon as I get home, I will tell him myself." I wobbled up from the sofa again. I was so angry and hurt, I suddenly felt superhuman. I didn't bother to ask Louis to remove himself from my path again. I gave him such a mighty shove that he had no choice.

He stumbled around until he fell against the wall and then to the floor. With a bloodcurdling yelp, he landed on his back like a turtle. He got up and strode back over to me, seething with anger. His eyes looked so evil. The rest of his face was so twisted, it looked like he had had a stroke. "Let me ask you something. How long do you think you'll have that job when I tell your boss how you dummied up an invoice to pay me for some services I didn't deliver?"

I had my hand on the door and was about to open it. I whirled around and looked at him, with my mouth hanging open. "After all I've done for you, you'd do that to me, Louis?" I roared, giving him my most horrified look. The volume of my voice dropped to a whimper. "You played me like a fiddle, and now you want to make me lose my job, too?"

He nodded and gave me a weak shrug. "Not if you help me out one more time."

I saw red. I saw stars. I saw the face of every single person who had ever done me wrong or hurt me in some way. Louis represented them all. Like that possessed man in the Bible, he represented a legion of demons. Well, I slapped as much of the devil out of him as I could when I went upside his face with my purse. He fell to the floor again. I gave him a mighty kick in his side before I stepped over his vile body, flung open that door, and ran. I didn't stop running until I got to my car.

I drove like a bat out of hell all the way to my house. Then I tumbled out of my car and staggered into my house like I was drunk. I paced back and forth in my living room for so long, I was surprised I didn't wear a hole in my beautiful carpet.

It was almost impossible for me to absorb what had happened at Louis's apartment. And I knew that if I didn't talk to somebody about it soon, I was going to lose my mind. And like every other time I got myself into a mess, there was only one person I could turn to.

Rhoda answered her telephone, with a dry, anxious voice. "Annette, I'm so glad you called. I've been wantin' to talk to you again." She was talking so fast, I couldn't get a word in edgewise. In a way I was glad. It gave me a little more time to organize my thoughts. "Jade's decided that a change of scenery would do her good. I agree, and so do her daddy and Dr. Long."

"Oh? Is she going back to Louisiana?" I asked, trying to keep my voice under control. I had eased down into a chair at my kitchen table. I had to cross my legs to keep them from shaking.

"I wish. I had wanted to send her to Jamaica to let the folks on her daddy's side deal with her foolishness for a change." Rhoda paused and muttered under her breath. "They screamed. Anyway, Aunt Lola, Uncle Johnny, and my son Julian told me to send her down South to them, and they'll all keep an eye on her. She'll have her own place in Julian's buildin', and he and Uncle Johnny and Aunt Lola will pay her livin' expenses until she gets a job and can fend for herself."

"That's nice, Rhoda. I'm so glad to hear that," I managed. I was happy to hear that things were working out well for somebody on such a bleak day in my life. Especially Jade. She was in a much worse place than I was in, but that didn't make me feel any better.

"She's leavin' tonight. By the way, did you talk to Louis about you and him joinin' Bully and me for a weekend at the bed-and-breakfast?"

My face froze like a sheet of dry ice. It took me a few seconds to thaw myself out enough to respond. "No," I mumbled with a sniff.

"Annette, you don't sound too good. Is everything all right?"

I took my time answering. "No, Rhoda. Everything is not all right. As a matter of fact, everything is all wrong." I lost it right then and there. The next thing I knew, I was howling like a big dog.

CHAPTER 54

"Annette, stop cryin', and tell me what is goin' on now. Please tell me what . . . omigod! Did Pee Wee find out about you and Louis?"

Somehow I managed to stop crying. "No, but he's going to. I'm going to tell him everything as soon as he gets home this evening. The whole story." I sniffled and blew my nose into a napkin.

"Look, I do not want to sit here and play games. You tell me the whole story," Rhoda ordered. "And you tell me right now."

I had to take several deep breaths first. Then I started talking in a low, detached tone of voice. "I left work a little early and went to Louis's apartment to talk to him about us going away for the weekend with you and Bully. I let myself into his apartment and . . . I overheard a telephone conversation he was having with . . . his fiancée."

"His what?"

"His fiancée."

"I didn't know he had a fiancée."

"Neither did I. But he does, and he's probably had her from the get-go. Rhoda, he never cared about me. All that sweet talk and over-the-top attention were just an act. He had a long-range plan to get some sucker to help get him out of the financial hole that he had dug himself into by taking over his late uncle's business. And that sucker turned out to be me." I had to stop for a few seconds to catch my breath. "He even lied to his bitch and made it sound like I was some horny, desperate older woman who had seduced him, and like his interest in me was about finance, not romance."

"Hold on. Let me go into the bedroom so I can have more privacy. I don't want anybody else in this house to hear what I'm talkin' about." Rhoda picked up the phone in her bedroom about a minute later. "I'm back," she said, speaking in a low voice. "Go on."

I suddenly got so light-headed, I dropped the telephone. It landed on my toe, but if it hurt, I didn't even feel it. I leaned down to pick it up, almost toppling over on my face. I was moaning as I returned the telephone to my ear. "When he finished his call, he turned around and saw me standing there."

"Oh shit!"

"Oh shit is right."

"Are you all right? Do you want me to come over?"

"I'm going to be fine, Rhoda. You know, for a woman who's been through some of the shit I've been through, you would think that I'd have stopped letting my guard down. How could I still be stupid enough to trust people the way I do? What's wrong with me, Rhoda?"

"What do you mean by that?"

"Why can't I stop making so many damn stupid-ass mistakes?"

"There is nothin' wrong with you. You're human, and you will be makin' stupid mistakes until the day you die. Don't beat yourself up over this. It could have happened to any other woman. Shit, that nigger was so slick, he could have pulled the wool over my eyes just as quick as he did yours. What was his reaction when he saw you standin' there?"

"He was so busted, he couldn't stand it. We had a showdown, and he made it clear that if I didn't give him three thousand more dollars, he'd go to Pee Wee and tell him about us, and he'd go to my boss and tell him about the phony invoice I used so I could issue him a check for an event that never took place. Uh, that was the money I gave him to get his oven replaced—which was another one of his lies!"

"Oh, hell no! No, he didn't! Girl, I hope you kicked his ass to kingdom come!"

"I gave him a mild coldcocking. If I hadn't left his place when I did, I probably would have killed him," I admitted. My big toe was still throbbing from the kick I'd given Louis as he lay on the floor.

"Are you at home now? Do you want me to be there when you tell Pee Wee?"

"No, that's all right. You need to concentrate on getting Jade on her way to Alabama," I said. "Besides, things might get real ugly up in this house this evening. I'll call you as soon as I can to let you know how he took it."

"Do you want me to pay Louis a visit? I could be dressed and out of here in five minutes."

"Oh, God no! There's no telling what he might do to you!"

Rhoda took her time responding. "Do you think for one minute that I'm worried about what he might do to *me*? If anything, you should be worried about what I might do to his punk ass. I know a way to straighten him out . . . for good."

This time I took my time responding. "I know all that, Rhoda. You've . . . *we've* been lucky all these years that nobody ever found out about some of the things you've done to people. But I think this can be settled without any bloodshed . . . or something worse."

"That bastard! All this time . . . all this time, he was plannin' to bushwhack you."

"I guess so. It sure enough looks that way. He was just using me, and I was too stupid to see that—*all this time*! But, Rhoda, he didn't do anything to make me think he wasn't for real! Look how long he was overly affectionate and puppy-dog eager to be with me every chance he could. He *never* asked me for any type of financial help. How could he have been with me for that long without me seeing that side of him? And . . . and what if I had not caught him talking about me? I wonder how long he would have kept stringing me along, performing a role."

"You don't need to know now. Just be glad you got his number before it was too late."

"Too late? Rhoda, the minute he threatened to tell Pee Wee about us, and my boss about me misappropriating company funds, it was too late."

"This is some crazy shit, girl," Rhoda snarled. "Since you won't let me straighten out this mess, what do you plan to do?"

"Well, he won't get another fucking dime from me. I'd rather lose my husband and my job than let him win."

"Annette, if you lose your husband or your job, Louis wins. He might not walk away with any of your money, but you'll be the one losin' the most. Don't you want to give this a little more thought?"

"More thought for what? Are you suggesting I pay him off? If I do, how do I know he won't come back for more?"

"You don't. But we could turn the tables on him and tell his customers what he's tryin' to do to you. Scary Mary is practically payin' his rent. So are a couple of other regular clients I know of. And don't forget about me."

"What about you?" I asked in a raspy tone.

"I've been linin' his pockets quite nicely—which I won't be doin' anymore after today! Even if he got three thousand more from you, he'd be losin' a hell of a lot more if we put a major dent in his business."

"It won't matter. From what I heard him say on the telephone, he's planning to go back to his hometown, anyway. He claims he's already got a deal to sell his business." I wiped tears off my face with the back of my hand. "When Pee Wee told me about his medical situation and assured me that everything is going to be all right, I was so happy. I thought that things couldn't get any better for me. Now this!" I slammed the top of my kitchen table with my fist. "If only I had not been stupid enough to get involved with this man!"

"Don't beat yourself up any more than you already have. You're human, so you are goin' to make mistakes. I want—"

"Oh shit!" I hollered, cutting Rhoda off. "I have to go! I just heard Pee Wee come in the front door."

Before she could respond, I hung up and rose from my chair. Pee Wee entered the kitchen, holding the largest bouquet of red roses that I'd ever seen before in my life. I looked at him and burst into tears again.

"Aw, now, don't go gettin' all emotional on me. I know I should have been bringin' you roses more often," he told me in the sweetest, most caring voice that he had ever used with me. He laid the flowers on the counter and rushed over to me. His strong embrace kept me from falling to the floor. "Everything is goin' to be all right now. I promise you that. There won't be no more secrets between us. No matter what the issue is, we can work through it as long as we do it together."

Right after his last comment, I stopped crying and looked up to face him. "I hope you mean that," I said, sniffling so hard that the insides of my nostrils felt like somebody had lined them with lye soap.

"I mean it," he said, patting me on my back.

"Because . . . because I've done the worst thing a woman can do," I began. I stopped talking because as soon as I said that, his body stiffened, and I heard him groan under his breath.

"Annette, what have you done?" he asked, the tenderness gone from his voice. "It can't be that bad, can it?"

"I've been sleeping with another man all summer. . . ."

CHAPTER 55

I held my breath and was about to get into a defensive mode, by covering my head with my arms. I had known my husband since we were thirteen, and I had never known him to hit another person. Not even during the times in junior high school when he was getting his brains beaten out by the vicious bullies that we'd shared.

Last year, when I thought he was fooling around with another woman, I had tried to beat his brains out. He didn't even hit me then. But after what I'd just told him, I honestly expected to get slapped, at the very least. I had it coming, and I would not have hit him back. I deserved the harshest punishment that he could administer, like a good old down-home whupping. But I didn't get that from him. He just released me and said, "Oh, is that right?" I had never in my life seen such a hurt look on his face, or on any other face, for that matter. It was painful to me to know that I had caused this much anguish. After he blinked at me a few times, he shook his head, waved his hands in frustration, and walked to the kitchen door.

He went out onto the back porch and sat on the banister, with his head in his hands. He didn't even look up at me when I sat down next to him and attempted to rub his shoulder. He gently pushed my hand away as if it was a serpent, so I stood back up.

"I know just how you must be feeling," I told him.

"I . . . I doubt that," he stammered, his head still in his hands.

"We need to talk about this," I told him. "You need to hear everything."

He looked up and glared at me, with an expression on his face that could have scorched a rock. "Just tell me one thing. Is it somebody I know?" he asked. I bobbed my head like a cork, and that made him look even more upset. "Who is he?"

"Louis," I mumbled, sucking in my stomach and tightening every muscle that I could. I did that because I didn't know what else to do with my body.

Pee Wee gave me a puzzled look. "Louis? Louis who? The only Louis I know is that—*that caterer*!"

I bobbed my head again. By now my head felt like it was hanging from a thread.

There was such an extreme look of surprise on his face, for a moment I thought that he was going to burst into laughter. "I know damn well you didn't cheat on me with that sissified motherfucker!" he roared. "Do you mean to look me in the eye and tell me to my face that you sank that low?"

"Yeah," I mumbled.

"Annette, I know I ain't no Casanova. But do you know what it does to my ego to hear that you chose a punk like Louis over me?" He gave me another disgusted look. "I'm through." He started to walk off the porch, but I grabbed his arm.

"There's more," I told him, holding on to his arm so tight, he couldn't move. "There's a lot more that I need to tell you."

"Oh, he wasn't the only one?"

"He was the only one. Look, it was a setup all along. He was using me." I let go of Pee Wee's arm and moved back a few steps.

"Did he force himself on you?" he asked.

I shook my head. "Pee Wee, I was with Louis only because I thought you were having an affair, and I wanted to get back at you."

"I see," he said, his voice cracking. "He was usin' you, but you were usin' him, too!" He started to walk off the porch again. This time I grabbed him by both arms.

"You need to come back into the house so we can finish this conversation."

"I just told you that I was through! Turn me loose!" He rapidly slapped my hands and pinched my fingers, but I still didn't release him.

"I'm not through. This is a lot more serious than you think."

"You want a divorce so you can be with Louis? Is that it? Well, you won't get one. If you think for one minute that I will step aside so you can move that bastard up in here to be around my daughter, you got another thing coming! Now get the fuck out of my way!" he shrieked, again trying to pry my hands from his arms, this time with his teeth. That didn't work, either.

"Pee Wee, will you please let me finish!"

"Finish? You want me to let you finish? Well, I got news for you. You are finished. We are finished!" He gave me such a mighty shove, I fell back against the porch wall, and then I tumbled to the ground. Before I could get up, he had disappeared around the side of the house. I brushed myself off and went back into the kitchen. As soon as I sat down, he came back in, too. He shot me such a hot look as he crossed the floor, I almost fainted.

"He threatened me. I thought you should know that," I yelled as he was about to leave the kitchen and enter the living room. "He said if I didn't pay him off, he'd get me fired."

Pee Wee stopped and whirled back around. "This story gets stranger and stranger. What the hell kind of shit did you get yourself mixed up in, woman?"

I licked my lips and pressed them together. It seemed like my mouth didn't want to continue this walk of shame with me. "I overheard him talking to another woman, and when he saw that I'd heard what he said, he told me that if I didn't pay him off, he'd tell you about us, and then he'd go to my boss."

"What's your boss got to do with this shit? You fuckin' him, too?"

"I told you that Louis was the only one. He needed some money to get the oven in his restaurant fixed. I didn't want to take it from our bank account, so I used some of my company's money. There was nothing wrong with his oven." The words tumbled out of my mouth so fast and so close together, it sounded like one very long word.

"So in addition to committing adultery, you stole money from your job?"

"Well, not exactly. I plan to pay the money back. But now Louis wants another three thousand so he can haul ass back to North Carolina to . . . to be with that other woman."

Pee Wee looked at me with an expression on his face that was way more than just plain contempt. I had never seen such a look on another human's face. "I can't believe my ears. I can't believe that you of all people could be so fuckin' ignorant! You dumb-ass hoochie whore bitch!"

I gasped and almost lost my breath. "That's the most ghetto-sounding bullshit you ever said to me!"

"Ghetto? Who are you callin' ghetto? I ain't nowhere near bein' ghetto!"

"Look, you've made your point. I've fucked up in a big way." I sniffed, blinked, and groped for more words. I started talking out of the side of my mouth. "Pee Wee, I'm going to start going to church more often," I mumbled.

"Church?" He threw his head back and laughed long and loud. When he returned his attention to me, he had tears in his eyes. "Do you think that goin' back to church is goin' to get you off this hook? Huh?"

I tried to answer, but I couldn't get a word in edgewise.

"Sister, I got news for you. It ain't goin' to be that easy. Do you mean to stand here and tell me that you think you can do all the shit you want to do and run back to the church, and that will make everything right again? You know your Bible, so you know that Jezebel didn't get off that easy, either!"

"I just thought—"

"You thought shit! You done made a fool out of me and our marriage, not to mention yourself. But you can't make no fool out of God. Shit, God ain't blind. Every time you crawled your nappy-headed ass into bed with that punk, God had his eye on you, woman."

"You didn't have to go there! This is not Judgment Day," I had the nerve to say. "What . . . what do you want me to do, Pee Wee?"

He let out a great sigh, and then he gave me a pitiful look. I hadn't known he was capable of making so many different faces in such a short period of time. "Annette, why can't you be more like Rhoda?"

Those words almost made me laugh. "What did you just say?"

"If you was more like Rhoda, we wouldn't be standin' here havin' this conversation."

"Brother, if I was more like Rhoda, you probably would have been dead a long time ago."

He gave me such an incredulous look that I knew he had no idea what I was talking about. Years ago I had told him about the people Rhoda had murdered. He didn't believe me then, and I was sure he still didn't.

"Rhoda is the most straight-up sister I know. She was a virgin when she met Otis, and he's the only man she's ever been with. She told me that to my face, out of her own mouth."

"Is that right?"

"Damn straight! And, for the record, I know about that little fling Otis had with that woman some years ago. Rhoda told me, but he came to his senses. Bein' faithful is the one thing that me and Rhoda have in common."

"I . . . don't know what to say, Pee Wee." My mouth was so dry; I didn't think it would ever feel normal again. What he'd just said about Rhoda was still ringing in my ears. "This is not about Rhoda, so let's stay on track. This thing with Louis just happened."

"Sister, a one-night stand just happens. A drawn-out affair don't just happen. It takes plannin', and it involves lies on top of lies. You wanted to do it."

"But I told you why I did it!" I wailed.

"That ain't a good enough reason!" he roared.

"It is as far as I am concerned!"

"Where can I find that punk? Where does he live?"

"Why?"

"'Cause I want to know!"

"He lives in that apartment building on the corner of Pike and Bleecker streets. Why do you need to know that?"

"Either you sleep someplace else tonight, or I will." Pee Wee turned on his heels and literally ran out the kitchen door. I remained in my seat until I heard him drive away.

I was still sitting in the same spot when he returned about an hour later. There was a cut above his eye, his shirt was torn, and there was a bruise on his cheek.

"What happened to you?" I asked, slowly rising from my chair. I stumbled up to him and tried to put my arms around him, but he jumped out of my reach.

"You don't have to worry about Louis no more," he told me, breathing through his mouth. I looked down and saw that the knuckles on both his hands were bruised and bleeding.

"Pee Wee, what did you do to that man?"

"You got his address! Why don't you go over there and see?" He stomped out of the kitchen, with me close behind. I stopped when we made it to the living room. He gave me a dirty look, and then he ran upstairs, taking the steps two at a time.

I plopped down on the sofa and started to twiddle my thumbs. I wanted to run upstairs and try and talk to him. But I didn't know what else I could say to make things better.

Fifteen minutes later, he ran back downstairs, with a suitcase. I didn't say anything or try to stop him from leaving. Had I been in his shoes, I would have done the same thing.

As curious as I was about what Pee Wee had done to Louis, I was not brave enough to go back to Louis's apartment. But I was brave enough to call him.

He answered immediately. "Yeah." His voice sounded so weak and raspy, I pictured him stretched out on the floor again.

"It's Annette."

"What the fuck do you want!" he hollered.

"In case you still want to drag this on, I just wanted to let you know that I plan to tell my boss everything tomorrow." I didn't intend to tell my boss anything if I didn't have to. "My husband is probably going to divorce me, so nothing else you can do to me matters, anyhow. . . ."

"Look, bitch, I don't want to see or hear from your skanky ass ever again. You, that jackass you married, that Jew you work for, y'all can all kiss my ass! I don't need you. I don't need your money. But let me tell you one thing. If that black-ass nigger of yours ever comes near me again, I won't be responsible for my actions!" Louis slammed the phone down so hard, my ears rang for two whole minutes.

CHAPTER 56

I got about three hours' sleep that night. I was such a wreck, I couldn't even drag myself out of bed the next morning, let alone go to work. I called in sick.

I had no idea where my husband had spent the night, and when I had not heard from him by noon, I called his barbershop. I hung up when he answered. A few seconds later, he called me back.

"You forget I have caller ID now?" he asked in a gruff voice.

"I just wanted to make sure you were all right," I muttered. "Uh, when do you want to talk?"

"About what?"

"Pee Wee, we need to discuss what we plan to do. I know I was wrong for what I did, and I am more than ready to accept the consequences. I just need to know what they are."

"Was Rhoda in on this?"

"Huh?"

"You heard me, woman. I want to know if Rhoda knew about you and that sucker."

"Uh, what difference would it make? I'm your wife, not Rhoda."

"Did Rhoda know about this?"

"Why don't you ask her?"

"I'm askin' you!"

"Pee Wee, you and Rhoda were best friends when I met you and her. I love you both, and I don't want to be the one responsible for ruining your relationship with her, too. Let's leave her out of this. I am the only one responsible for this."

"All right then. If you want to be a bitch about this to the bitter end, you go right ahead. I just want you to do me a favor. *If* Rhoda was in on this, I don't ever want to know. I've known her a lot longer than I've known you. She's always had my back, but if that's no longer true . . . well, I don't want to know."

I remained silent for a few awkward moments. "Is it over between us?"

"What we once had is over. You made sure of that."

"Look, I'm not going to beg you to forgive me. If you want to try and work this out, I am more than ready to do so. If you don't, well, what the hell. You can go your way, and I will go mine. But I want you to know that I'm really glad you're going to be all right—health-wise, I mean. And, just so you'll know, I told Rhoda only the basics about your condition. If you want her to know everything, you can tell her. After all, you were her boy before you were mine."

I heard him sniff a few times and then clear his throat with a deep cough. But he didn't say anything.

"Pee Wee, are you still on the line?"

"I'm still on the line," he said flatly.

"Did you hear what I just said about you telling Rhoda about your condition?"

"You let me worry about Rhoda," he said, his voice sounding like it was coming from beyond the grave. "I have to go. I will see you when I see you." He hung up.

I didn't see Pee Wee for a whole week. And when he did come home, it was only to pack more of his clothes. He didn't acknowledge the fact that it was also my birthday. He floated through the house like a ghost, totally ignoring me. Muh'Dear, Daddy, and Charlotte called right after he left to wish me a happy birthday, but even that didn't do much to help lift my spirits.

Muh'Dear called again on the Saturday before Labor Day to assure me that they'd be home in time for Charlotte to attend the first day of school, which fell in the first week of September. I had several telephone conversations with Rhoda during the time Pee Wee was away. It was always good to hear from her. Especially now that Jade was in Alabama, recovering from her so-called breakdown.

"Jade's got a new boyfriend already," Rhoda told me, laughing, during one of those conversations. "I just hope this relationship works out for her."

"I'm glad to hear that somebody is doing well," I said.

"And what about you? How are you doin'?"

"I'm fine, Rhoda." I wasn't. My marriage was a shambles, and now that I no longer sponsored Monday lunches at work, my workers were back to their old tricks. But I had another plan up my sleeve. I'd let my mother cater our lunches when she returned. Had I used her in the first place, that devil Louis would have never entered my life. And I believed that my marriage would still be somewhat intact.

Pee Wee moved back into the house a day after my last conversation with Rhoda. He slept in the living room that night and told me that if it was all right with me, that was where he'd be sleeping until further notice.

"This is still your home," I told him as we passed each other going in opposite directions on the stairs leading to the second floor. I was in my nightgown and on my way to my bedroom. He was in his pajamas, and I knew he was on his way to that damn La-Z-Boy in the living room. "And I'm still your wife."

"A wife that cheated."

"A wife that cheated because she's not perfect," I pointed out.

He gave me a weak nod. Then he looked me up and down, like he was inspecting me. "I hope you don't mind me sayin' so, but you've gained back a little weight." It didn't sound like a malicious comment. It just sounded like a general observation. And since it was true, I didn't get upset.

"I know," I muttered shyly. "Those neck-bone casseroles will sneak up on a woman's hips like a mugger."

"It looks good on you," he told me, stopping at the bottom of the steps.

I stopped at the top of the steps. "As long as I don't get to be as big as I was, I'm all right with gaining some of that weight back. I don't think I could ever be happy with the way I used to be."

He shuffled his bare feet and gave me a thoughtful look. "You know something. I think I could be happy with you the way you used to be. Not the weight, I mean. Well, some, but not all of it. I was proud to have you as my wife."

"I'm still the same woman, Pee Wee. Just a little frayed, that's all. Like everybody else." I started to walk toward my bedroom, but I stopped when I realized he had started to walk back up the steps.

"Annette, it'd be nice if we could sit down at the kitchen table and have a few drinks, like we used to. I guess it's time for us to talk things through. We need to decide where we're goin' from here."

"Oh? Oh," I said dumbly, stumbling back down the steps. "Should my lawyer be present?"

He shook his head. "Well . . . not this time." He pinched my arm and gave me a gentle sock on the cheek with his fist. "But the next time for sure. Next time . . . next time . . . aw shit. You still got a long-ass way to go to get yourself out of this mess, woman. And don't think I am ever goin' to let you forget it."

"I know you won't forget it. And I won't, either," I assured him as I escorted him to the kitchen.

I attempted to put my arm around his shoulder, but he prevented that by ducking. I didn't like that, but I didn't complain. I was just glad that we had made some progress on the rocky road that our marriage had ended up on.

"Are you home to stay?" I asked when we made it to the kitchen.

"I might stay, and I might not," he responded with a shrug. He removed the large bottle of tequila that we kept in the cabinet above the stove and poured himself a shot glass full first. He wasted no time putting that glass up to his lips.

I chose the largest glass I had in the house and poured tequila in it to the brim. But I stopped drinking after just a couple of sips.

"What's wrong now?" he asked. He had already finished his drink.

"I think this is one time that I really need to be sober, so I'll know what I'm saying," I answered. "I've said enough stupid shit for a while." I poured the tequila in my glass back into the bottle. And then I pulled out a seat at the kitchen table and sat down. For a minute I thought he was going to pour himself another drink, but he didn't. Instead, he gave me a dry look, and then he sat down across from me. "Let me tell you what I think I should do," I began.

"Let's get one thing straight right now," he said, shaking a finger in my face. "It ain't up to you to decide what we should do. If I can't offer some input, too, we can stop this conversation right now."

"That's not what I meant," I protested. "*We* need to work on things together if we want to repair this marriage."

"That's better. Now, woman, what the hell were you thinkin'? This wasn't like you. Was this little ditty with Louis because of your midlife crisis, were you crazy, or were you just a horny bitch?"

"Maybe it was all three," I mumbled. "I know now that I was wrong, and I swear to God, it will never happen again. I am going to do everything I can think of to make this up to you." I cupped his hand with both of mine and squeezed. I was disappointed when he slapped my hands until I released his.

"You do that, Annette. You make this up to me. That'll be a start." He got up, with a groan, and walked slowly into the living room.

I drank a glass of water and turned off the kitchen light before I joined him. He had already plopped down in that La-Z-Boy and had a blanket covering him up to his neck. He didn't even look at me as I walked past him to turn out the living-room light.

There was just enough light coming from the hallway upstairs for me to see my way up the steps. I took my time going to my bedroom, where I expected to sleep alone for a while.

Things had not changed much by Thanksgiving, but I had a lot to be thankful for, anyway. For one thing, Louis had left town. When Rhoda and I went snooping around his apartment building, one of his neighbors told us that he'd purchased Louis's van and adopted Sadie. The neighbor also told us that Louis had left Richland a few weeks earlier with a pretty woman in a black station wagon with North Carolina license plates.

Some Asians were now running Off the Hook. And since Mr. Mizelle never said anything to me about the company money that I had misused, I decided that Louis had not spilled the beans on me, after all. There was no way I could return that money to the company's account without making somebody suspicious. Instead, I used it to treat my staff to a weekend retreat at a resort in Cleveland. My parents and my daughter had returned from the Bahamas in one piece and were planning to go again for Christmas.

Pee Wee approached me in the kitchen, where I was putting away the leftovers from our sad Thanksgiving dinner. We had not made love since the day before my confession. It was still difficult for us to look at each other, but we did when we had to. His eyes were positively indifferent as he looked at me now.

"Annette, your mama called a few minutes ago and wanted to know if we want to spend Christmas with them at that white woman's beach house in the Bahamas."

"Oh? Well, I'll have to think about that," I said. "Do you want to go?"

He nodded. "It might be good to get away for a few days," he said with a heavy sigh. "But it'll be hard for us to behave like everything is all right in front of your folks."

My parents were the last people on the planet who needed to know about what I'd done. And Pee Wee and I had agreed that they didn't even need to know about the medical condition he had endured.

"I know," I admitted. "But if we go, we'll have to act like everything is all right. Even though it's not, and probably never will be again."

"I thought you wanted to work on that," he said, giving me a puzzled look.

"I did. I mean, I do. But like you said, this is not something that I can fix on my own. We both need to work on this."

He let out a heavy breath and rubbed the side of his neck. "Let's go with them. If we can't mend things on a beach in the Bahamas, we can't mend things nowhere." He dipped his head and looked at me, with his eyebrows raised. "I just hope I can trust you down there around all them handsome young men. . . ."

I was not surprised to hear Pee Wee say such a tacky thing, and it ruffled my feathers, to say the least. But these days he wasn't making half as many crude references to my affair as he used to. "You don't have to worry about that," I insisted. "Not in the Bahamas, or anywhere else."

I finished putting the leftover food away. We went upstairs at the same time to decide now what to pack to take to the Bahamas next month. It was going to be hard for us to act lovey-dovey while sharing the same beach house with my parents. But if he was willing to try, I was, too.

READING GROUP DISCUSSION QUESTIONS

1. Annette had an affair because she thought her husband was no longer attracted to her. Do you think if Pee Wee had told her up front about his medical condition and its affect on his sex drive, that she would not have had the affair?

2. Annette's dramatic weight loss and extreme makeover made her much more attractive and appealing. However, she did not encourage other men to pay more attention to her. Do you think that if Louis Baines had not pursued her so vigorously, she would have remained faithful to her husband?

3. Most con men don't care what a woman looks like as long as she's a cash cow that he can milk. But since Louis didn't know that Annette had money until he got to know her, do you think that he had some feelings for her in the beginning?

4. Do you think that Louis would have initiated the affair a year earlier when Annette was still grossly overweight and plain?

5. Annette was reluctant to have an affair with Louis. Rhoda badgered her to do it until she did. Do you think Rhoda should have shared the blame for the mess that Annette got herself into?

6. When Jade returned home after flunking out of college were you surprised that she had not changed for the better? Were you surprised that she still had so much contempt for Annette?

7. Pee Wee was still angry with Jade for harassing Annette the year before and refused to have anything to do with her. After the way Jade taunted Annette at the mall, do you think that Annette was a fool for agreeing to attend Jade's wedding?

8. Jade was the daughter from hell. But Rhoda still doted on her and bent over backwards to plan Jade's unexpected wedding.

It was important to Rhoda for Annette to be on the guest list. As soon as Jade saw that Annette was among the wedding guests, she greeted her with a few more insults. Do you think that it gave Annette some pleasure to be the one to drop the bombshell and inform Jade that her Mexican fiancé had run for the border an hour before the wedding?

9. Jade was so stunned to hear that she'd been jilted; she urinated on her beautiful wedding gown. Her meltdown was so severe she had to be hauled out of the house on a gurney and rushed to the hospital mental ward. Annette felt sorry for her. However, she also felt that Jade got what she had coming. Did you feel sorry for Jade?

10. Annette was devastated when she found out why Pee Wee had stopped being affectionate with her. But Pee Wee was more devastated when she told him that she was having an affair with Louis. If Louis had not tried to blackmail Annette when she severed their relationship, do you think that she still should have told Pee Wee about the affair?

11. Annette was furious when she overheard Louis talking about her like a dog on the telephone to his real girlfriend. If you were in a similar situation, would you leave quietly and with some dignity, or would you get loud and violent like Annette did?

12. Not only did Annette jeopardize her marriage, she risked losing her job. Embezzling money from her employer to give to Louis was way out of character for her. Did Annette's behavior surprise you?

13. Do you think that Annette's marriage can be restored? Do you think that she no longer deserves a good man like Pee Wee? Since Annette had accused Pee Wee of having an affair so many times before she got involved with Louis, would you blame him if he had an affair now?